Addicted for Now

Addicted Series

RECOMMENDED READING ORDER

Addicted for Now

KRISTA RITCHIE
and
BECCA RITCHIE

BERKLEY ROMANCE
NEW YORK

BERKLEY ROMANCE
Published by Berkley
An imprint of Penguin Random House LLC
penguinrandomhouse.com

Library of Congress Cataloging-in-Publication Data

Names: Ritchie, Krista, author. | Ritchie, Becca, author.
Title: Addicted for now / Krista and Becca Ritchie.
Description: First Berkley Romance edition. | New York:
Berkley Romance, 2023. | Series: Addicted series | Addicted for
Now was originally self-published, in different form, in 2013.
Identifiers: LCCN 2022051578 | ISBN 9780593639597 (trade paperback)
Subjects: LCGFT: Romance fiction. | Novels.
Classification: LCC PS3618.I7675 A645 2023 | DDC 813/.6—dc23/eng/20221104
LC record available at https://lccn.loc.gov/2022051578

Addicted for Now was originally self-published, in different form, in 2013.

First Berkley Romance Edition: March 2023

Printed in the United States of America
5th Printing

Book design by Kristin del Rosario
Interior art: Broken heart on wall © Valentina Shikina / Shutterstock.com

To you, the reader:

When we originally wrote the Addicted series, we were in college with big, lofty dreams and hopes of Lily and Lo's story finding some people. It became so much more than just one romance between childhood friends, thanks to readers who wanted to see more.

It was about sisters, written by two sisters. It was about friendship, and the family you have and also make along the way. Rose's and Daisy's stories—the Calloway Sisters spin-off series—are woven so intrinsically into Lily's novels because we believe that one life does not stop while another goes on a journey. Every novel impacts every character. So the best way to read Lily's story and not miss a thing is by combining her series with the Calloway Sisters series in a ten-book reading order. It's the order we wrote the novels—all three sisters intertwined together.

This is the Addicted series. Ten books. Six friends. Three couples. One epic saga.

We hope these characters bring you as much happiness as they've brought us throughout the years.

As Lily would say, thankyouthankyouthankyou for choosing them and us. Happy reading!

All the love in every universe,
Krista and Becca

Part One

People talk about you like you're Jesus, but you're not. You only pull out the miracles to save yourself. Which kind of makes you the opposite of Jesus, doesn't it?

—Hellion (Julian Keller) *X-Men: Legacy* Vol 1, 242

One

Lily Calloway

Of all the days in the month, I have to be stuck in traffic on the one that means the most to me. I try not to badger Nola, my family's driver, on our ETA to the house I share with Rose. Instead, I anxiously shift on the leather seat and rapidly text my sister.

Is he already there? Please say no, please tell me I haven't missed his homecoming. I'm supposed to wait on the white wraparound porch of our secluded house in Princeton, New Jersey: many acres of lush land, a crystal-blue pool, black shutters. The only thing it's missing is the picket fence. I'm supposed to give him a tour of the cozy living room and the granite kitchen, leading him upstairs to the bedrooms where I sleep. He won't be in one of the two guest rooms. Nope, he'll be making residence in mine for the first time ever.

And maybe awkwardness will linger at the idea of sharing a bed and a bathroom day and night, at the idea of cohabitating beyond a kitchen. Our relationship will be one-hundred percent real, and there'll be no nightcaps of bourbon or whiskey. I'll be able to say *don't do that*. And he'll be able to grip my wrists, keeping me from compulsively climaxing until I pass out.

We're supposed to help each other.

For the past three months, that's what we've planned. And if I'm not there to greet him—then I've already messed up in some way.

After three whole months of being physically apart, I thought I'd be able to get this right—the celebration of his return from rehab. On top of desperately wanting to touch him, for him to hold me in his arms, I feel a sudden wave of guilt. *Please be late like me* is all I think.

The text pings, and I open the message, a knot tightening my stomach.

He's unpacking—Rose

My face falls, and a lump rises to my throat. I can just picture his expression as he opened the car door, expecting me to fling my arms around him and start sobbing into his shoulder at his arrival. And I'm not there.

Was he upset? I text back. I bite my nails, my pinkie starting to bleed a little. The habit has made my fingers look ghastly these past ninety days.

He seemed okay. How much longer will you be?—Rose

She must hate being alone with him. They've never been good friends since I chose to spend time with Lo more than I do with her. But she's been kind enough to allow him to stay with us.

Maybe ten minutes. After I text her, I scroll through my contacts and land on Lo. I hesitate before I type another quick message. I'm so sorry. I'll be there soon.

Five slow minutes pass with no response, and I've squirmed so much on the seat that Nola asks if she needs to stop somewhere so I can use the bathroom. I decline. I'm so nervous that my bladder probably won't function properly anyway.

My phone buzzes in my hand, popping my heart from my ribcage. How was the doctor?—Lo

Rose must have clued him in on the reason for my absence. I scheduled my gynecologist appointment four months ago because she's crazily booked, and I would have canceled if I thought I'd be able to nab an appointment sometime soon. But that's doubtful. And it didn't help that my gynecologist is near the University of

Pennsylvania in Philly, not even close to Princeton where I now live. Having to drive back has eaten up all of my time.

I had to wait for about an hour. She was running behind, I text.

After a long moment, a new message flashes. Everything's okay though?—Lo

Oh, that's what he was asking. I'm so hung up on missing his homecoming that I didn't think about him being worried. I type back. Yep, looks good. I cringe, wondering if that was a weird reply. I basically just said my vagina looks good—which is kinda strange.

See you soon—Lo

He has always been a brief texter, and right now, I'm cursing him for it. My paranoia grows and the pressure on my chest does not subside. I grip the door handle, about ready to stick my head out of the moving vehicle to puke. Dramatic, I realize, but with our situation—recovering alcoholic and a struggling sex addict—we're anything but mundane.

Ninety whole days passed and I stayed faithful to Lo. I saw a therapist. But sex still has a way of making me feel better, masking other emotions and filling a deep hollowness. I'm trying to find the healthy kind and not the compulsive "I have to fuck every day" type of sex. I'm still uncomfortable talking about it, but at least I made progress the same way Lo did in rehab.

My mind whirls right up until Nola pulls into my driveway. All thoughts vacuum out into another dimension, and I dazedly say thanks and drift from the car. Purple hydrangeas frame the three-story house, rocking chairs lined in a row on the porch, and an American flag clings against a metal pole near a weeping willow.

I try to inhale the peacefulness and bury my anxiety, but I end up choking on springtime pollen, coughing into my arm. Why does the prettiest season also have to be the most foul?

I shouldn't hesitate in the front yard. I should rush right inside and finally touch the man that plagues my fantasies. But I wonder how different he will seem up close in person. I worry about the awkwardness from being apart for so long. Will we fit the same way we used to? Will I feel the same in his arms? Or will everything be irreparably different?

I muster a bit of courage to walk forward. And by the time I climb the porch, the door swings open. I freeze on the highest stair and watch the screen door clatter into the side of the house. Then he emerges, wearing a pair of dark jeans, a black tee, and an arrowhead necklace I gave him for his twenty-first birthday.

I open my mouth to say something, but I can't stop my eyes from grazing every inch of him. The way his light brown hair is styled, full on top, shorter on the sides. The way his cheekbones sharpen to make him look deadly and gorgeous. The way he reaches up and rubs his lips, as though hoping they'll touch mine. He rakes my body with the same impatience, and then his head tilts to the side, our eyes finally meeting.

"Hi," he says, breaking into a breathtaking smile. His chest falls heavily, nearly in sync with my uneven rhythm.

"Hi," I whisper. A large distance separates us, reminding me of when he first left for rehab. Picking up a foot and closing the gap feels like crawling up a ninety-degree angle. I need him to help me reach the top.

He takes a step near me, snapping the tension. All these sensations burst in my belly. I love him so much. I missed him so much. For three months, I felt the pain of being separated from my best friend while trying to fight my sexual compulsions. I needed him to tell me that everything was going to be okay.

I needed him by my side, but I would never take him away from rehab for my benefit, not when it would be detrimental to his recovery. And I want Lo to be healthy more than anything. And I want him to be happy.

"I'm back," he murmurs.

I try to restrain my tears, but they flow unwillingly, sliding from the creases of my eyes. I should be emerging from the doorway to greet him, and he should be the one lingering on the porch stairs. Why are we so backward all the time?

"I'm sorry," I tell him, wiping my eyes slowly. "I should have been here an hour ago . . ."

He shakes his head and his brows pinch together like *don't worry about that*.

I stare at the length of him again with a more confident nod. "You look good." I can't tell that he's sober exactly. He hasn't lost that look in his eye—the one that seems to kiss my soul and trap me altogether. But he's not beaten or withered or gaunt. In fact, he has more muscle to his name, his biceps supremely cut. And after a Skype session some time ago, I know his whole body matches those arms.

I wait for him to say *so do you*, but his eyes trail me once more, and I watch the way his chest collapses and his face twists in pain.

I blink. "What is it?" I glance down at my body. I wear jeans and a loose-fitting V-neck, nothing out of the ordinary. I wonder if I spilled coffee on my jeans or something, but I don't see what he does.

Instead of telling me what worries him, he inches forward, the deep hurt in his eyes frightening me. What did I do wrong? I shuffle back—a reaction I hardly would have predicted for today. I nearly stumble down the stairs, but his arm swoops around my waist, drawing me to his chest, saving me from a plummet into the grass below.

His warmness snares me, and I clutch his arms, afraid to let go. He stares intensely before his gaze drifts to my arms . . . my hands. He peels one off his bicep, his fingers skimming over mine, stealing the breath right from my lungs. He raises my hand in between us and then lifts my elbow, giving me a good view of my arm.

My chest sinks, realizing the source of his confusion and hurt.

"What the hell, Lil?" he says.

I scratched my arm raw during the last therapy session yesterday, and an ugly red welt will most likely scab tomorrow. Even with gross, bitten fingernails, I managed to irritate my skin.

Lo inspects my nails, his nose flaring to hold back even more emotion.

"I'm fine. I was just . . . anxious yesterday. Therapy was harder. You were coming home . . ." I don't want to talk about this now. I want him to hold me. I want our reunion to be epic—*The Notebook* worthy. And my stupid anxiety and bad habit has ruined the perfect outcome I imagined. I reclaim my hand and touch his jaw, forcing him to stop focusing on my problems. "I'm okay."

The words feel a little false. I am not one-hundred percent okay. These past three months were a test I could have easily failed. At times, I thought giving up was better than fighting. But I made it. I'm here.

Lo's here.

That's all that matters.

His arms suddenly slide around my back, and he melds my body to his. His lips brush the top of my ear, sending shivers spiraling across my neck. He whispers, "Please don't lie to me."

My mouth falls. "I didn't . . ." But I can't finish because tears begin to pool, burning on their way down. I grip his shoulders, holding him tighter, afraid he plans to pull away and leave me broken on the porch. "I'm sorry," I choke. "Don't go . . ."

He edges back, and I cling harder, desperate and afraid. He's a lifeline I cannot quantify or articulate. I depend on him more than any girl should depend on a boy, but he's been the backbone of my life. Without him, I will fall.

"Hey." He gathers my face in his hands. His glassy eyes bring me back to reality. To the fact that he feels my pain just as I feel his. That's the problem. We hurt so much for each other that it's hard to say no. It's hard to take away the vice that will numb the agony of the day. "I'm here," he says, a silent tear dripping down his cheek. "We're going to beat this together."

Yes. "Can you kiss me?" I ask, wondering if that's allowed. My therapist handed me a white envelope filled with my sexual limitations—what I should and should not do. She advised me not to read it and to give it to Lo instead. Since I'm supposed to strive for intimacy, not celibacy, I need to relinquish my control in bed to him. He'll set the guidelines and tell me when to stop.

I handed the envelope to Rose yesterday and told her to deliver it to Lo just in case I chickened out. As concerned as Rose has been for my recovery process, I'm sure that was the first thing she did when Lo walked through the door.

I have no idea how many times I can kiss him. How much I can climax or if I'm allowed to have sex anywhere other than a bedroom. I'm so compulsive about intercourse and foreplay that *limits* have to be set, but following them will be the hardest part of my journey.

His thumb wipes away my tears, and I brush his. I wait for his answer, my eyes glued to his lips that I want to kiss until they sting and swell. His forehead lowers, dipped down toward mine, and I become so aware of how his fingers press into my hips, of the hardness of his body. I need him to close that gap between us. I need him to fill me whole.

Hastily, I meet my lips to his, expecting him to lift me up around his waist, to plunge his tongue in my mouth and slam my back into the siding.

But he doesn't give in to my desires.

He leans back and breaks the kiss in a matter of seconds. My stomach drops. Lo rarely tells me no when it comes to sex. He'll play into my cravings until I'm wet and wanting. Things, I realize, are about to really change. "My terms," he whispers, his voice husky and deep.

My whole body already pulses from his nearness. "Please," I beg. "I haven't touched you in so long." I want to run my hands over him. I want him to thrust into me until I cry. I imagine it over and over, torturing myself with these carnal thoughts. But I also want to be strong and not throw myself at him like he's only a body I missed. He means so much more to me. Maybe he's hurt by my persistence to kiss him? Maybe he sees it as a bad sign? "I'm sorry," I apologize again. "It's not that I want you for sex . . . I mean, I do want sex, but I want you because I miss you . . . and I love you, and I need . . ." I shake my head. My words sound stupid and desperate.

"Lil," he says slowly. "Relax, okay?" He tucks a piece of hair behind my ear. "You don't think I know this is hard for you? I knew we were going to run into this moment." His eyes fall to my lips. "I knew you were going to want to kiss me and for me to take you quick and hard. But that's not going to happen today."

I nod rapidly, hating those words but trying to soak them in and accept them. Uncontrollable tears begin to flow because I'm afraid I may not be able to restrain my compulsions. I thought being away from Lo would be the difficult part, but learning how to have a healthy, intimate relationship with him suddenly seems impossible. He's a man that I want to take advantage of every minute of the day. If I'm not doing it, then I fantasize about it. How can I stop?

His breathing shallows, as though my tears are driving knots into his stomach. Mine has already collapsed. I feel utterly destroyed by guilt and shame and desperation.

His fingers dig harder in my sides, as though reminding me that he's here, touching me. "What's going to happen," he breathes, "is that I'm going to carry you through this door. I'm going to draw out every single moment until you're exhausted. And I'm going to move so slow that three months ago will feel like yesterday. And tomorrow will feel like today, and no one in this fucking universe will be able to say your name without saying mine."

And then he kisses me, so urgently, so passionately that my lungs suffocate. His tongue gently slips into my mouth, and I savor each and every movement. He kneads the back of my head, gripping my hair, yanking and sending my nerves on overdrive.

His hands fall to my ass, and he effortlessly lifts me up. I wrap my legs around his waist, squeezing tightly into a front-style piggyback. He guides me inside, just as he promised. I hook my arms underneath his and press my cheek to his hard chest, listening to the unsteady beat of his heart. We're so close, but I still ache to be closer. My breath shallows for it.

He kisses the top of my head and carries me into my bedroom on the second floor. Well—*our* bedroom. My net canopy is pulled back, the comforter black and white with red sheets. Lo rests my back against the mattress, and I reach up to grab a fistful of his shirt and yank him on top of me. But he steps back and shakes his head.

Slow, I remember. Right.

My legs dangle off the edge, and I prop myself on my elbows as he stands in front of me.

"I'm yours," he tells me. "I will always be yours, Lily. But now it's time for you to say it."

I sit up and my eyes flit over all of him. In all our life, he has never once said to me, *you are mine*. He has never taken me the way I've taken him. He has *given* himself to me. And I realize, it's my time to make this right and give myself to him.

"I'm yours," I whisper.

The muscles in his jaw twitch, almost smiling. "I'll believe you when I see it."

I squint. "Then why'd you tell me to say it?"

He leans forward, his lips so close to mine. His palms set on either side of my body, forcing me to fall back a little. I hesitate to kiss him. He's testing me, I think. "Because I love those words."

My lips part. *Kiss me*, I plead. "I'm yours," I breathe.

His eyes drop to mine, watching me, drawing out the moment.

The spot between my legs aches for him. I want the pressure of his body—to rock against me, to fill me, to say my name over and over.

Kiss me. "I'm yours," I choke, wide-eyed in utter suspense.

And then he sucks on the bottom of my lip. He teasingly bites it and then sinks his pelvis into mine. I buck my hips to meet him and he lets me.

Lo grips the hem of his shirt and tugs it off his head, tossing it aside. Before I run my palms over his taut chest and newly sharpened abs, he laces his fingers with mine. Simultaneously, he puts his knee on the mattress and pulls me higher onto the bed, my head finding the pillow.

He climbs on and keeps my hands trapped in his. Then he stretches my arms high above me, our knuckles knocking into the headboard.

His body hovers over me, no longer melded together. I squirm beneath the space I dearly hate, my heart thudding and raging to be even closer. "Lo . . ." I can't take it anymore. My back arches a little as I try to meet his body again, and he tilts his head, disapproving.

So I stay still. I try to let him take control since I need to go slow. His lips lower but linger from touching mine. He keeps that distance as he unbuttons my jeans, relinquishing the hold on my hand. He uses his other to guide my palm to his zipper.

Yes.

It takes only seconds before I have him unzipped and unbuttoned, tugging his jeans off with familiarity. I wiggle out of mine and he lifts the shirt off my head, in nothing but a black lacy bra and panty set. I did know he was coming home today, after all.

He soaks in the curvature of my body with headiness, and he begins to remove his last article of clothing. "Eyes on me," he says huskily.

They are permanently fixed to the bulge in his boxer briefs. "They are," I mumble. Technically this is *a part* of him.

"My eyes, love, not my cock," he says, a smile behind the words.

I raise my gaze as he slips off his boxer briefs. Watching the way he looks at me nearly sends me into a tailspin. I swallow and can't help but catch a glimpse. Oh God, I need him now. He's hard and as wanting as I am, but yet, he has restraint.

I do not.

He could easily take advantage of my eagerness—most guys would. But in order to help me, he has to control my impatience and my compulsion to go again. And again. Because my addiction isn't entirely a one-way street the way his is. I need his body in order to satisfy these unhealthy desires.

So he must say no at some point. I just don't want it to be soon.

He leans forward again, and his lips begin their descent from my neck to my belly button, sucking, nibbling—teasing. My hands grip his back while I hold a moan deep in my throat.

He kisses my hip bone and gently slips off my panties, the cold air nipping the most sensitive places. I expect his lips to warm the spot, but he eases off me and unclips my bra, sliding the straps off my shoulders so, so slowly. The light touch taunts my nerves and my sanity. His tongue runs between my breasts and then dips back into my mouth. And that's when his arms scoop around me and lift me up in a tight embrace, my breasts melding into his muscles, my limbs nearly tangled in his. My legs wrap around his waist, and I ache to lower onto his cock. But he keeps his arms locked around my chest, forcing me above his lap.

"Sit on your legs," he tells me.

"But . . ."

He lightly kisses me and tears away while I try to go in for another stronger one. "Sit on your legs, Lil. Or I'll do it for you."

That sounds better. He sees the glimmer in my eyes, and he picks up my right leg and bends my knee so my heel is underneath my butt. As he goes for the left, his hand skims up my thigh and to the crease of my ass. Holy . . .

Okay, I'm sitting on my heels now, trying not to come before he enters me. What if my therapist wrote that I can only climax *once*? Besides that sounding like torture, I hope to have sex with Lo today. I will not ruin that by going crazy with foreplay.

I'm still sitting straight up, and his body has not drifted from mine. His heart pounds against my chest, and he cups my face in his hand.

"Breathe," he tells me. "Just remember to breathe."

And then with measured unhurriedness, he gradually rests my back onto my comforter and slowly begins to slip inside of me. The position allows for such deep entry that I cry out and grab onto his shoulder for support.

His forehead rests near mine, and he raises my chin, kissing me forcefully, just how I like it, before he begins to rock agonizingly slow. Each movement mimics our heavy breaths. My parted lips brush his as he digs deeper. I whimper, my toes already curling, my head already flying off my body.

His hand massages my breast, but his eyes never once leave mine. Hot tears seep from the creases, the intensity and emotion driving me to a peak so high that every time I breathe in, he breathes out, as though keeping me alive for this moment. I melt into his slow movement, the way he disappears inside of me, and the pace that causes my body to light on fire.

"Don't stop . . ." I cry. ". . . Lo . . ." I tremble, and his arms slip around my back again, holding me tighter.

He speeds up a little, and I feel the top of the hill. I see us climbing together.

And then he thrusts and holds inside of me. I buck and cry and claw at his back. My whole body pulsing, my heart thrumming—I am his.

I collapse back onto the bed, too exhausted to lift an arm or a leg. He takes care of me, bending my knees and stretching my legs out from the last position. He rests his hands on my kneecaps, and leans forward to kiss me again. I taste the salt from our sweat, and I raise my hand to grab the back of his hair, my eagerness suddenly replacing the tiredness from our emotional sex. But he laces his fingers into mine, stopping me.

I frown. "No?" *Only once?*

He shakes his head and then kisses my temple. "I love you," he whispers, his breath tickling my ear.

"I love you too," I tell him. But I do want to wrap my legs tightly around him, giving him no choice but to harden and take me again. He scrutinizes me closely, and he must see my impatience for round two.

His eyes narrow. "Not now."

I bite my lip. "Are you going to tell me what's in the envelope?" What did my therapist restrict? The answer is killing me right now.

"Nope," he says. "You'll just want it even more if you know it's forbidden."

I squint at him. "You're getting too smart."

He grins. "When it comes to you, I am." He kisses the outside of my lips. I love and hate when he does that. "Just so you know," he whispers, "I'd love nothing more than to fill you again. I'd do it a million times a day if I could."

"I know," I murmur.

He brushes my sweaty hair off my face.

And I inhale a deep breath. "I'm just glad you're home." I have Lo back. That's all that should matter right now. Not a round two or a three, but just him present, on the road to being healthy, and in love with me. That's all I should need.

I can't wait to reach that place. I just hope it's attainable.

He relaxes next to me, and I rest my head on his chest, listening to his heartbeat while he runs his hand through my hair. This is nice.

I almost drift to sleep, but the chime of a cell phone snaps my eyes open. "Whose is it?"

He reaches over onto my nightstand. "Mine." He flips the cell in his palm, and I crane my neck over his shoulder and see a text box.

I know your girlfriend's secret.—Unknown

I shoot up, fear snapping me cold. Did I read that wrong? I snatch the phone out of his hand, and he grabs it back.

"Lil, calm down," he says, trying to shield the screen from me as he types a reply.

"Who is that?" I've been so careful. I've never told anyone I had a sex addiction other than Lo, and now Rose, Connor, and Ryke. Did they let my secret slip to someone else?

I bite my fingernail, and Lo clasps my hand while texting with the other. His eyes flicker to me, narrowing in disapproval.

When the *ping* sounds again, I basically climb on top of Lo so he can't hide the message. I read quickly.

Who the fuck are you?—Lo

Someone you hate.—Unknown. Okay, that does not narrow anything down. Lo's enemies from prep school and college are numerous and vast. It happened when he retaliated against all the people who thought they could bully him into submission.

Lo tries to push me off, but I have my arm wrapped around his neck, close to choking him, so he lets me be. We're still naked, but I'm too frantic to be aroused.

Fuck off—Lo

"That's your response?" I say, wide-eyed. "You're egging the person on."

"If you don't like it, then you shouldn't be reading my personal texts or spidering me like a koala bear."

True.

And lose out on all the money the tabloids will pay me when I tell them that Lily Calloway is a sex addict? . . . Never—Unknown

I blink. Reread the text. And gawk. No.

"Lil," Lo says, shutting off his phone. "It's okay. That's not going to happen. Look at me." He holds my face in his hands, forcing my eyes to his. "That's not going to happen. I won't let it. I'll hire someone to go find this asshole. I'll pay him off more than he'll get from the tabloids."

He's forgetting something. "You're broke," I say. His father took away his trust fund because he dropped out of college. Lo hasn't spoken to him since he left for rehab. He's alone and poor and all my money is tied up with my family. And they don't know about my addiction either. I'd rather not tell them. Ever.

His features darken, remembering. "I'll think of something else then."

The shame that my family will feel if they find out—the hurt and disappointment—I can't bear to even *think* about it. A female sex addict? A slut. A male sex addict? A hero. How much will I tarnish my father's company with the news? Sure, not a lot of people outside of our social circle know my name or who I am, but could this make tabloid headlines? Why wouldn't it? *Lily Calloway: Daughter of the Founder of Fizzle, a Sex Addict and a Whore.*

It's juicy enough to satiate gossip columnists everywhere.

"Lo," I say as tears threaten to fall. "I'm scared."

He hugs me, drawing me close. "Everything is going to be okay. I'm not going anywhere."

I hold on to his words and repeat them over and over, hoping that will truly be enough.

Two

Loren Hale

I fist a bottle of cheap vodka by the neck. I can't think straight. My emotions are black. My heart is about there. My lengthy stride is filled with deplorable hate. I don't run. I walk quickly up the steep driveway, the alcohol clenched in my hand, a million-dollar home staring right back at me.

The door. All I see is that black door and the bronze knocker.

I slam my fist against it, pounding. No one answers. I don't even hear footsteps. "Open up!" I yell. I pound again and again. *Fuck this.*

I take the bottle and swing. The glass smashes. The contents shatter, the liquid dripping down the bronze knocker, trailing the black wood and running beneath my soles.

"Fucking hell," Ryke curses behind me. "Was that necessary?"

The door blows open.

"Yes."

I told Ryke to wait in the car and I mentioned how the only way Aaron Wells would creep out of his parents' home (like the rat that he is) is if I started fucking with his things. Starting with that door. I was prepared to move onto his BMW—a shard of glass to decorate the hood. Now I don't have to go that far.

But I'm not surprised Ryke parked on the curb and followed me up the hill. He likes to do that—tag along and make sure I'm not about to self-destruct. That's usually Lily's job, and I'd choose her over him any day of the week. But not right now.

Not when an old prep school prick stands five feet in front of me.

He has dirty blond hair (practically brown), blue eyes, and that smug Dalton Academy smile that I remember so well. He's the first guy that came to mind when we received the texts. What I did to him back in prep school was fucked up, but our rivalry should have never included Lily. And he shouldn't be tormenting her now.

Aaron appraises the shattered glass. "I shouldn't be surprised. The stench smells exactly like you."

Ryke is about to take a step forward, and I grab his arm to stop him. We're not punching Wells, as much as I'd like to. This is not that type of fight.

"I've met you before," Aaron says, scanning Ryke from his dark hair to his lean muscles that nearly match mine. "Where was that?" He feigns confusion.

Ryke glares. "I should have smashed your fucking face in."

When I heard what happened while I was gone, I really wish Ryke had.

Lily's mother paired her with Aaron at a company party, and he threatened Lily the entire time, basically telling her that he'd screw with her to get to me. (Why? Because he hates me. There's no other reason for that.) And I just had to hear the news in rehab without doing a goddamn thing. Now that he's moved to Level 2—somehow learning about her sex addiction and wanting money—I'm here, ready to fuck with him the same way he fucked with her.

"Oh right," Aaron says without missing a beat, "I was Lily's *date* to a Fizzle event, and you showed up like her white knight while this one was in rehab." He cocks his head at me. And I internally grimace at the reminder that Ryke was there for Lily these past three months. I wasn't.

But this right here is why I know Aaron sent those texts. He's recently made it clear that he wants to toy with me by going through Lily, stirring up our old rivalry.

Two can play this game.

"Thanks for escorting her," I tell him. "She said it was painful staring at your ugly face all night, but I think we all know you weren't there to please her." My double-edged words even make me cringe. I don't like to think about any other guy *pleasing* Lily. Not before we became a real couple. And definitely not after.

My heart beats so fucking fast. I take a step toward him, the glass crunching.

He stiffens, and I wait to see if he has the balls to shove me back.

Nope. I take my chances and squeeze between the doorframe and his immobilized body. He stares right at me. Eye for eye. And I invite myself inside.

"Wow, this place hasn't changed," I say, walking farther in. I stare at the high-vaulted ceilings and the marble floors. Ryke follows me, and Aaron closes the door behind us, his lip curled. I point at the cellar door by the kitchen. "Should we crack open a bottle of wine?"

His eyes flash murderously.

"Maybe not then."

Ryke hangs back, but if Aaron even raises a fist, he'd be right by my side. That kind of support feels good. I've never once had that. Growing up, I always took the beating or found an escape. Fights were always me against a million. No one was in my corner. I wouldn't let Lily be involved, and if she was, it was guys like Aaron that deviously pulled her in, knowing she was my best friend.

They'd fuck with her just to reach me.

And that's not happening.

Aaron watches me closely.

"Who's home?" I ask him.

"No one," he says, his face blank.

I don't believe him. "Your parents are in Barbados for the weekend." Thank you, Connor Cobalt, for your great tech-savvy skills.

Aaron lets out a dry laugh. "Did your father find that out for you?"

Oh yeah, Ryke wasn't the one to deter Aaron at the Fizzle event. While Lily was trying to dodge Aaron all night, she told me that my father came in and saved her. Leave it to my dad to inject debilitating fear into someone. Lily said Aaron fled the event after that. Never made a peep again. "My father didn't help me figure out who's at your house," I say, "but I should call him up, thank him for molesting you with his words."

"You're a sick fucking guy," Aaron says, "you know that?"

I'm just getting started. "Julie!" I shout. "Julie, come out, come out!"

Ryke wavers behind me. He's seen me like this. I used to attack him. I still do. Plenty of times. But this is different. I am fueled by hate so deep that I can barely breathe.

Aaron glances hesitantly at the balcony above the double staircase. His house was used for debutante balls just for that entrance.

"JULIE!" I yell.

Aaron steps toward me, his hand leveled out as though he comes in peace. "Hey, I told your father I'd lay off Lily, okay? We made a deal. I stuck to it. I haven't done shit to her since the event."

"JULIE!"

The door clatters upstairs.

Aaron talks faster, "I was *pissed* that night. I applied for a job, and they denied my application. I didn't even get an interview because of you."

"You're going to blame me?" I glare. He should. With my father's help, I called up his dream college and had the dean take a second look at Wells. Next thing you know, he's going to his safety school, not even waitlisted to the place he thought he had in the bag. We rerouted his future.

"I can't compete with Ivy grads. Now I have to work for my father."

A pair of feet pads across the second story.

"Don't do this," Aaron sneers, but he's pleading. "I only scared Lily a little. I wasn't going to force her or anything. I promise you." He's never had sex with her, thank God. If I ran into one of her old hookups, I don't know what my reaction would be.

"That's what you always do, isn't it?" I say. "You scare her. Well, grab a membership card, Aaron. You're about to be fucking terrified."

Right on cue, a girl with the same dirty blonde hair grips the balcony railing, leaning over to stare at me from below. "Loren Hale."

"Julie, go back to your room," Aaron tells her, fear spiking his voice.

"What am I, four?" she snaps. She wears dark lipstick and a shit ton of eyeliner. She's his fraternal twin. And a girl I may have fucked once or twice when I was sixteen, depending on the day. The difference between Lily and me is that I actually dated Julie (for two whole weeks) at a time when I wasn't in a fake relationship with my best friend.

Lily, however, fucks once and then moves on.

And after a long, long struggle, I have finally become her only exception.

"Hi, Julie," I say. "Can you come here for a second?"

"What's this about?" She looks between Aaron and me, taking in Aaron's stiff posture. "Aaron, it's been years since I was with Lo. Seriously, get over it." But she's wrong. Our fight didn't start because I dated her. She was just a bullet in my gun. One of the things I used to hurt him. Fucking his sister—that's the easiest trick in the book. Something my father would have done. Something that I hate I did. I can barely even stomach the memory.

I just thank God that Julie is as deplorable as her brother and me. She used me just as much as I used her—wanting to get back at her ex-boyfriend. He didn't care as much as she wished he did.

"Julie," I snap. "Come here. Now." I'm not fucking around. *Well, I kind of am.* But you should see Aaron's face. He's about to shit his pants. He has no idea what I'm going to do. Hell, I have no idea what I plan to do either. I just know that his family is his weak spot the same way Lily is mine.

She descends the stairs barefoot. Her curious gaze lingers on Ryke. "You're hot."

"Julie," Aaron cringes.

"Can I see your phone?" I ask Aaron. Now that Julie is here, he'll be more willing to hand it over. She's a distraction and a warning.

His brows furrow. "What for?"

"Just give it to me."

Julie sighs heavily like this is boring her. "Just give him the phone, Aaron."

Aaron slips his phone out of his pocket and hands it to me. I scroll through his previous texts, trying to find my number stored somewhere. But the entire thing is blank.

"Why'd you delete all of your texts?"

"I always do," Aaron says. "My mother likes to check my phone."

"You're twenty-two." He's not a teenager needing approval to sleep over a friend's house. He's an adult.

"Yeah? That hasn't changed her from being nosy."

I still don't believe him. I can't.

"What's your name?" Julie asks Ryke, biting her lip as though that'll drop him to his knees.

"Ryke," he says.

"Ryke, how do you know Loren?"

"He's my brother."

Her brows shoot up. "Wow, I didn't know he had a brother."

"Neither did I," I say, shoving the phone back in Aaron's palm. "Did you use a fake phone? A disposable?"

"What the fuck are you talking about?" Aaron says, his eyes wide. "I didn't do shit to you or Lily. I told you, your father—"

"I don't believe you," I say, not really sure what I believe. He could be lying. Out of everyone I know, he's the most likely to threaten Lily. If I can end it all right here, right now, that's what I'll do.

"You're out of your fucking mind!" Aaron screams.

Ryke steps forward to my defense. "Says the guy who spent two hours chasing a girl around a ballroom, terrifying her beyond fucking words."

"Wow," Julie says, "you're sexy when you're mad."

"Julie!" Aaron shouts. "Leave, now. Get the fuck out of here."

Julie rolls her eyes and drops off the tips of her feet like Aaron popped her entertainment. She nods to me. "It's nice to see you again, Loren. I'm sorry my brother can't get over our relationship."

"Yeah, he has trouble letting things go." If I was him, I would still be full of resentment. I don't blame him at all. I just hate that I drove him to this place—to a point where he could attack Lily while I was at rehab. I was such a stupid fucking kid. I still am sometimes.

I could be going about this the wrong way right now. But it's the only thing I know how to do. And it works. I use my words. Threaten the guy who's threatening me.

Julie walks off to the kitchen, in plain view. Mostly so Ryke can see her bend low as she grabs a pan from the cupboard. She looks back to make sure he caught sight of her ass. He didn't. His eyes haven't left Aaron. But as I watch her, Aaron is seconds from imploding, dropping on his knees, and giving me what I want. I can't take credit for that. I think, partly, my father's previous threats have already sunk in.

"Where's your disposable phone?" I ask again.

Ryke puts his hand on my arm, and he whispers, "I don't think he did it."

I don't want to believe that. Because then I'll be clueless.

I'll have no idea who else it could be.

Aaron holds up his hands in defense. "I don't know what happened, but I'm not the only guy who hates you, Loren. So whatever is going on, maybe you should think about who else you pissed off all these years. I can't imagine college was that pleasant for you."

Yeah . . . I may be fucked.

I nod to myself. But if he is the guy who sent me those texts, I'm not just going to leave here without insurance that he won't do something again. I have to have the last word. So I lean in and I say, "If you scare my girlfriend again, you'll wish all you had to worry about was working for your fucking dad." My eyes flicker to Julie once. "And you should start eating your sister's makeup. Your insides are fucking ugly."

He could easily say *as are yours*. But nothing comes from his mouth. He's solidified in a mixture of hate and fear—emotions that are floating all around his house right now.

I don't wait for him to reanimate.

I leave.

And on the way to the car, Ryke says, "You didn't tell me that you'd be fucking with his sister."

"Does it matter?"

He stares straight ahead, his eyes dark.

"She was objectifying you, Ryke," I tell him. "She was two seconds from pulling down your pants and climbing on your dick."

"Like Lily?" he snaps back.

"Fuck. *You*." I swing open the car door. It's not the same thing. Lily—she's my best friend. I'm not a conquest of hers. If that were true, she wouldn't still be with me. I wouldn't be able to satisfy her for so long.

"Sorry," Ryke barely apologizes, his harsh tone never softening.

"I just don't want to see another girl get caught in the fucking crossfires of your feuds."

"I'm not going to hurt her. He just has to think I am."

Ryke stares at me for a long moment. "Did our father teach you that?"

"Yeah," I say. "He also taught me how to get in a car and drive the fuck away."

Ryke nods. "Glad to know you're still an asshole, even without the booze."

"Must be genetic."

Ryke smiles at this, and we both climb into his Infinity. I don't feel better after this. Because I don't even remember some of the people I pissed off.

I drowned most of them in a haze of whiskey and bourbon.

They're gone from my mind for good.

Three

Lily Calloway

s this an interrogation or a meeting?" Ryke asks roughly. He slouches on our navy Queen Anne chair with a deep scowl, sweat stains seeping through a Penn track shirt.

There are only *three* people who could have possibly spilled my secret. And the guy at the top of my suspect list has yet to crumble. Although, very little ruffles Ryke Meadows.

And here he sits—edged, all hard lines, his eyes perpetually narrowed and his demeanor cocky and self-assured. He managed to become a part of Lo's life. He infiltrated our group, and he has never made a move to leave. He either cares about his brother so much that he's willing to endure almost anything or he's scheming for something greater—something that could overturn my whole world.

So it's true that I've been hammering Ryke with questions, and I'm about one step away from shining a blinding light in his face to get real serious. But I have a right to freak out. My life is seconds from crumbling.

Lo passes Ryke a bottle of water.

I shoot Lo a wide-eyed look. He shouldn't be giving him sustenance until we have answers. That could have been our only bargaining chip.

"Who says he gets water?" I blurt out.

Their brows crinkle as though I've lost some brain cells. Okay, so I'm being irrational. What else is new?

Ryke raises a hand. "I'm sorry, but is anyone else concerned for my safety here?"

Lo ignores his brother and clasps my hand, pulling me to the sofa. My leg touches his, but the closeness doesn't calm me. Since I read the text, panic has overpowered my chance at being composed and sane.

I don't want to act like this, but my only other way of coping with high-stress situations involves grinding and climaxing and everything I'm *not* allowed to do.

Rose's heels clap down the hallway. "Connor should be here any minute now." She sits on the pale yellow loveseat adjacent to the couch, crossing her ankles. In a black pleated skirt and a high-collared silk blouse, she looks far classier than anyone else in the room.

"Great, so you can direct this interrogation on someone else," Ryke says, eyeing me with a tad bit of scorn. But in Ryke Meadows's case, there's probably a little pinch of love in there. At least I hope we made some progress while Lo was in rehab. Sure, we had a rocky three months, but Lo was always our common ground.

But if he's behind some larger plot to ruin Lo's life—and consequently mine—I'll never forgive him.

Lo runs a hand on my bouncing leg, trying to settle my nerves. "I'm going to take care of it, Lil," he says softly.

Ryke gives him a dark, furtive look. I've seen it before. It's the kind you share with someone when you have a secret.

I gasp. "Have you done something without me?"

Lo shakes his head. "No." He won't meet my eyes.

I smack his chest. "You're a lying liar, and we're supposed to be truthful."

"Well," he draws out the word, "if the guy keeps texting us, we may or may not be able to cross Aaron Wells off our suspect list."

"May or may not?" Rose says. "That sounds like no progress."

"I did what I did. I'm not going to take it back." His voice is sharp.

All I hear is *Aaron Wells*, and I go cold. "What did you do?" Aaron is not someone I ever want to see again.

Rose mutters something under her breath that sounds like *vandalize*.

"I just talked to him," Lo says.

I look to Ryke for verification. Clearly he was a part of this plot, which only makes me more nervous.

"Yeah, we just talked," Ryke says. "All of Aaron's texts were deleted, which was suspect."

Lo nods in agreement, and then he leans closer and kisses my cheek. "Okay?" he whispers to me.

I don't think that's the right word. I stare at the rug with a faraway gaze.

"What about Ryke?" Rose asks. She holds a small teacup between her tight fingers. She offered me a glass earlier, but I declined. I'm not sure my body can handle ingesting anything else today. I'm already bloated with fear.

Ryke groans. "Not this *again*."

"You know about Lily's sex addiction. You could have told someone."

He glares. "So do you."

"Be real. She's my *sister*. I'm not going to backstab her."

"And she's my brother's girlfriend," he snaps back. "Why don't you focus your attention on the guy who could easily spill this information for a fucking price?"

"Don't you dare." Rose points a warning finger at him.

"Why? Connor came into the picture around the same time I did. He learned about her sex addiction at the same exact time as us, and he has more to gain than we do. And he has less to lose."

"He would lose me," Rose retorts.

I never wanted to believe that Connor could turn on me like that. I still won't entertain the thought for longer than a second. He's too nice (in his own way). But Ryke . . .

Lo scrutinizes his brother for a long moment. "Maybe Rose has a point."

"What?" Ryke leans forward. "You can't be serious."

"You may be my half brother, but you're also a liar. I think we established that the moment we met."

"Oh come on."

"Let's go back a few months. You came into my life, told me you're some student wanting to do a fake project on heirs to billion-dollar companies—"

"Lily made that lie up," Ryke interjects.

I gape. Way to throw me under! But I already came clean to Lo about that, so there is only a morsel of shame.

Lo rolls his eyes. "Whatever, you knew the whole time that I was your brother, and yet, you never said a word to *any* of us."

"You've got to be shitting me," Ryke says. They must have had this argument multiple times while Lo was in rehab. I wasn't allowed to visit him, but under some strange guidelines, Ryke was. I'm a little confused how their relationship has developed since I've been away from Lo—but clearly bitterness has festered.

Lo lets out an unhinged laugh. "I'm the *bastard*. I tore apart your parents' marriage when I was born. You should hate me. *I* would hate me." He takes a small breath. "And then I would build an elaborate scheme to tear me down. Piece by piece. Starting with Lily. So forgive me if I'm having a hard time trusting you one-hundred-and-ten percent."

I can't tell if Ryke is angry or upset by Lo's declaration, but I know this goes beyond my silly accusation. Deep hurt fills Lo's words.

"Really? Even after everything I've done while you've been in rehab?" Ryke asks.

"You mean keeping your cock away from my girlfriend. Yeah, thanks."

My eyes bug. I would jerk away from Lo if his hand wasn't pressed so tightly to my hip. Something's wrong. I can sense it. We handle stress differently. I fuck and he drinks. Now that we can't do either, we're both trying to learn how to deal with it in a healthy manner. *Trying* is the key word here.

"You know that's not it," Ryke refutes.

"Sure."

This one word makes Ryke look more livid than the past twenty, and I think *this is it*. Ryke is about to throw up his hands and leave. Lo tenses beside me, probably expecting the same thing. We alienate people. It's what we're good at.

"If I wanted to hurt you by creating some elaborate plot, I would have already screwed Lily. And I sure as hell wouldn't bother spending time with you."

I want to trust Ryke, mainly because he's the only family Lo has for support, but he's a good liar like Lo said. He even fooled me.

Lo flashes his usual bitter smile, normally accompanied with the raise of his bourbon. I can't make sense of where his thoughts lie.

Before I can whisper in his ear to ask, the front door opens, and the silence settles like a weight. Connor's loafers hit the hardwood, the noise heightening the tension.

He appears from the foyer, his thick wavy brown hair styled perfectly, as though he's ready for a congressional speech at any moment. He slips his cell phone in his black slacks, his white button-down tucked in the waistband. From afar, he inspects Ryke's stiff posture on the Queen Anne chair and Lo's death clutch on the couch's armrest.

"I missed something," Connor states. "Was it good?" He looks to Rose.

"Only if you enjoy the unintelligible mumblings of Neanderthals." Her tone is pure ice.

"Good one, Rose," Lo says flatly.

But Connor rubs his lips to keep from smiling farther. And when Connor smiles at my sister, I instantly straighten up and lean forward like two orbiting stars are about to touch and kiss. I want to be present when they do.

Lo pinches my hip as Connor takes a seat next to Rose, sliding his arm along the back of the cushion behind her.

"You're my girlfriend," Lo whispers huskily in my ear, teasing me to take his side of things. But in a game of wits, I should choose the smart option and go with my sister. Or Connor. Lo is a losing battle.

"You're my boyfriend," I say the obvious. He edges closer, and my heart pounds, his lips *right there. Kiss me. Kiss me. Kiss me.*

He eases back.

Damn. I wish I had Professor Xavier's power, but then again, I wouldn't want to force Lo to kiss me. I'd want him to *want* it as much as I do.

Connor gestures a hand between Ryke and Lo. "I'm sensing tension here."

"Lo was just thanking me for not fucking Lily," Ryke says.

"Exactly," Lo replies, his voice equally as dry.

Connor doesn't even blink. "Must be a brother thing." He casually turns to Rose, whispers something in her ear and presses a light kiss on her cheek. I cannot believe I'm envious of a kiss right now. But I really am. I want that kiss. Not from Connor! Just to be clear. From Lo. I want the kiss from *Lo.* My cheeks redden just accidentally thinking the wrong thing. Jeez.

"You okay?" Lo whispers.

I nod, squirm a little, and rest my cheek on the crook of his arm, safe in his embrace. His muscular body dwarfs my overly skinny frame. I'm working on being healthier too. All skin and bones is not a good look.

Rose puts her hands up to Connor's chest, blocking him from scooting closer. "A brother thing? What's going on here is not normal between *brothers*. You don't see Greg Brady thanking Peter for not having sex with Marsha."

"No because that would be incest," Connor says.

She shoots him a look. "It's not *incestuous* because Marsha is only the stepsister."

"True." His eyes flit to her lips and back to her sharp gaze. "And I'm surprised you used the word *normal*. I thought we agreed last week that it's arbitrary and too subjective to have any real merit."

She gives me a look like *why am I with him again?*

I smile and really want to say: *Because you're two nerd stars, orbiting and meant to kiss.* But that won't make sense to anyone but me.

Rose and Connor have had an odd three months together, constantly breaking up over intellectual disputes like this and reuniting only a week later. Their relationship is something I can't quantify or really understand. I think maybe you have to have a higher IQ or something. But I love watching them like Lo and I do Japanese cartoons. We can't comprehend what they're saying, but it's still fun to tune in every week.

Rose points a manicured finger at his chest. "You can't discount an entire word just because you don't think it has merit, Richard." Ooh, she used his real first name. "You're basically saying Foucault's entire sociological studies were worthless."

My head hurts trying to listen to them, but I'm strangely enthralled.

"Hey," Lo cuts in, clapping his hands. They both look at us like we've just appeared in the room. "You two can discuss normal people and Faulkner later."

"Foucault," Rose corrects him.

"What?"

"It's *Foucault*. Not Faulkner."

"Whatever, they both start with an *F*," Lo snaps. "You know what else starts with an F?"

"Fuck you," Connor beats him to it. He also says it so casually—like he's trying to answer an Academic Bowl question. I can't help but break out into a grin.

Lo catches me smiling and gives me a look. I press my lips together to try to contain it, but it's too hard and I probably seem goofy instead. The corner of his mouth quirks. My heart flutters because for the first time in three months, I can see these reactions.

He draws forward and places a light kiss on my nose. I didn't even have to chant *kiss me* for him to do it. I bite my bottom lip, giddiness replaced by dangerous thoughts. Of yanking Lo into the bedroom, easing him onto the mattress, straddling his waist and skimming my fingers over each ridge in his abs. And then his half smile will extend to his whole face, the grin enough to light up my body.

I could mumble some lame excuse to leave the meeting, but my throat tightens and guilt festers, even though I haven't taken a step toward my bedroom yet. Planning out the events makes me feel like a failure. Why is that?

"You look good, by the way," Connor tells Lo.

"Thanks."

I forgot they haven't seen each other since Lo's stint in rehab. I squint at Connor and put him on my pedestal of suspects. Maybe Ryke is right. In return for the info about my sex addiction, Connor could bribe his way into Wharton—the prestigious graduate school at Penn where he plans to go for an MBA.

Connor meets my gaze, and his brow arches like he knows I'm unlawfully incriminating him.

He can see straight through me.

My cheeks redden, and I immediately overturn my hasty judgments. There's no way Connor would sell me out. He finds cheating too easy, and he's more moral than 99 percent of our family's social circle. So that leaves Ryke. And Rose. But Rose would be more likely to burn her entire fashion line—Calloway Couture—than throw me to the cannibalistic media. And she loves her collection like a mother does a baby.

Lo isn't so quick to let Connor go free. "Did you tell anyone?" he asks.

"No one," he says calmly.

Lo scratches the back of his neck. "We spent *years* without anyone knowing Lily's secret. Then she tells you guys, and a few months later, she's being threatened about it. I may have dropped out of college, but I can fucking add those pieces together."

Connor looks him over once. "You were expelled from college, but it's nice to hear that you're taking accountability."

Somehow that insult didn't seem so bad. It's all true.

Penn kicked Lo out after he stopped showing up to class, and he could have attended another college, but he decided to go to rehab and work on getting sober instead.

Lo sighs heavily, frustrated. He just wants answers. I think we all do.

"You're missing a piece," Connor tells him.

Lo tenses, and a little bit of hope surges through me. If anyone can uncover this mystery, it'll be Connor Cobalt. And most likely Rose too.

"Lily just started seeing a sex therapist who specializes in addiction."

"You think someone saw her go into the office?" Lo asks.

"It's probable. Why don't you try tracing the number?"

"It's unknown."

"So?"

"I'm sorry. Hacking into phone numbers just isn't in my repertoire. Lily, you?" He looks to me, and I shake my head. "Didn't think so."

"Oh, no," Connor says quickly, "I know you can't do something that difficult. I just thought maybe you knew someone who could."

Ryke cuts in, "You're actually admitting you can't do something, Cobalt?" He looks about ready to jump off the Queen Anne and call the press. Oh wait, he is the press. Maybe he'll write an article about it tomorrow in *The Philadelphia Chronicle* and title it: "Connor Cobalt Doesn't Know Everything!"

"Don't be ridiculous," Connor says, poker-faced. "I *know* how to do it. But I won't. It's illegal."

Ryke rolls his eyes and grips his water bottle tighter. I guess that article won't be happening.

Rose takes a dainty sip from her tea and says, "It's still illegal if you pay someone to do it for you."

"And if you're smart about it, you won't be caught."

That thing I said about Connor being moral? Scratch that. He masks his emotions so much that I didn't see his cunning ways. Still, I don't think he would risk losing Rose for a seat at Wharton. At least, I hope not.

"Lo and I already discussed tracing the number," I speak up. "All my contacts know my family. My parents would start asking questions if I hired a private investigator." And the whole goal is to keep them in the dark as long as possible. I'm thinking *forever* is a good amount of time.

Lo nods. "We also don't want to involve any unreliable third parties. I don't want to be screwed over by them."

I perk up as I think of an example. "Like a hacker that lives in his parents' basement."

"Yeah," Lo says. "I don't see that going very well."

"I have a trustworthy PI that I can hire," Connor says. "That's not a problem."

Rose smiles into her last sip of tea.

"I'll pay you back," I tell Connor.

"I prefer favors."

Okay, that sounds sexual. When I think of favors, I picture blow jobs.

My face immediately heats, and I try looking away but everyone is already staring at me. I'm doomed.

"Lily!" I hear three voices in varying pitches chastise me. Lo puts an arm over my shoulder and I restrain myself from hiding in his bicep. I will not cower.

I point to Connor accusingly. "He said it, not me!"

"I wasn't talking about *sexual* favors," Connor refutes calmly.

I point to my chest now. "Sex addict here. My brain has an automatic setting. I'm not going to be thinking *party* favors."

Bringing up the words *sex addict* was a bad idea, and I regret it as soon as Ryke says, "Speaking of being a sex addict." I could punch him. "How's your recovery going to work now that Lo's back? Are you two allowed to have sex together?"

"It's complicated," I mutter. "And I don't think I should be discussing it with *you*."

"She can have some sex," Lo clarifies, apparently uncomplicating it.

I want to disintegrate just a little.

"What is *some* sex?" Ryke asks.

Okay, a lot—I want to disintegrate a lot, a lot.

"I can't talk about it," Lo says evasively. But really he means: *I can't talk about it in front of Lily.* Because I have no idea what "some" entails either. It's going to drive me bonkers.

I also don't like that Lo is so quick to share intimate details of our private lives, but I guess he's trying to be better about opening up. And it must be easier to focus on my addiction than his own.

"What happens if you start enabling her?" Rose asks, setting her teacup on the table.

"I won't," Lo says with an added glare.

I wish I could conquer my addiction by myself, but my therapist already explained that abstinence isn't the answer since sex is a natural part of life, unlike alcohol. A person can go forever without tasting liquor, but almost everyone has sex when they reach a certain age. And sex involves two people.

So I have to learn how to have a healthy sex life with Lo instead of the one where he feeds into my compulsions. And I can work on being more self-reliant without turning to self-love.

I sigh. It's all so complicated. It all feels so hard.

"This isn't the same as Lily giving you a glass of whiskey, Loren," Rose says. "We'll all be able to tell if you drink, but none of us will have a clue if you're enabling her." Because that means he'll let me fuck him exactly how I want, when I want. I'll be so high and so full of Loren Hale that I won't ever want to leave the bedroom and meet real life.

It sounds so much better than it should.

"You didn't know I was an alcoholic for years," Lo refutes. "Believe me, you won't know if I fall off the wagon one time. It's the same."

"I'll be able to tell," Ryke says.

"And me," Connor adds. "I had no clue Lily was addicted to sex, but it didn't take more than a day for me to figure out that you had an alcohol problem."

Ryke scratches his hard jaw, cut like stone. "You knew he was addicted, and you drank beer with him? In fact, I saw you buying him Fat Tire at a bar."

"He's a true friend," Lo says with a bitter smile. He says things just to agitate people, I swear.

Ryke looks like he wants to stand up and smack the back of his head.

Rose spins on Connor, but he doesn't cower beneath her penetrating gaze. "You knew and you drank *beer* with him?"

"I just met him. I wasn't planning to revolutionize his life."

"You mean you saw what made him happy, and you gladly enticed him with it to become his friend."

Lo cuts in, "You're acting like he shot me up with heroine."

"He may as well have," Ryke retorts.

Okay, when did this meeting become a platform to gang up on Connor?

"Just drop it," Lo snaps.

Connor stays quiet, and Rose doesn't look like she's ready to forgive him so easily. I'm sure they'll have a whole philosophical discussion about it later.

And unfortunately, she remembers the source of our argument.

"Your addiction, Lo, is not the same as Lily's," she says. "When you weren't here, supporting Lily was simple. Now that you're back, I feel like you're the only person allowed to be involved in her recovery process. And how healthy is that? You just got out of rehab."

Should I even be here for this conversation? It feels beyond me, even though they're talking *about* me.

His voice softens considerably, losing the usual edge. "I don't know what you want me to do. I'm her boyfriend. She's a sex addict. Of course I'm going to be the most involved in getting her healthy. I know what you're saying. I know what you're *all* saying." He looks to Ryke and Connor. "I can't tell you to just trust me, not when I have twenty-one years of being a shitty person on my record. But this situation is weird and unconventional and really, really fucked up. And we're going to have to figure out how to do it."

I stare at my hands, a little uncomfortable but also a little grateful they're not talking behind my back.

"All I want," Rose tells him, "is for you to not close us all out. If you think you're doing something wrong or you can't handle it, don't just ignore it. You have to tell someone, and it doesn't have to be me. If you feel more comfortable talking to Ryke or Connor or even the therapist, whoever. I just don't want Lily to suffer because you can't reach out."

I understand her fears. We've isolated ourselves for so long that closing everyone off would be a natural regression. I just never really thought about it outright.

"I promise."

She looks a little taken aback by how easily he relented.

"We both want the same thing," Lo reminds her.

For the first time Lo and Rose seem to agree on something, but it only puts an insane amount of pressure on me. They may think Lo will enable me. But I fear I'll screw everything up all on my own.

Four

Lily Calloway

Ryke and Connor leave after we establish a plan to track down the texter. Connor will call his private investigator and then the rest of us will start making a list of Lo's enemies. I just hope I don't see my face on the cover of *People* tomorrow.

Lo is already in bed when I shut the bathroom door. The lamp bathes him in a warm light, and he looks content as he scribbles in a journal. The nightstand seems so bare without his glass of whiskey. We're both going through a monumental change, and we haven't even discussed our futures or anything serious since he's been back. The texts kind of sent us into an immediate tailspin.

His gaze rises from his journal, and he studies me as I stand in the middle of the room, unsure about what to do.

I've lasted three months without sex, but I also didn't have him here, in bed with me. The equivalent for Lo would be snuggling with a bottle of Jack Daniel's. Cuddling with my own vice seems dangerous, but I can't be abstinent forever. I have to figure how to do this the right way.

"What's wrong?" he asks and closes his journal, the pen sticking from the pages.

"We're not going to have sex tonight?" I ask for the third time today.

"No, love, not tonight."

I try to let the words sink in again, but they hurt and my chest tightens in return. It feels like rejection even though it shouldn't. "Maybe I should sleep on the couch," I say softly. "Until I get used to you being back." *Until I can stop thinking about you inside of me.*

"I can handle you, Lil. I won't let you break your vows."

My vows. The four personal rules I set for myself, unlike the blacklist that my therapist set for me.

No porn.

No masturbation.

Less compulsivity during sex.

And never, ever cheat on Loren Hale.

How can four simple tasks feel so out of my control? Especially the third one. I hear what he's saying, I do. But somewhere between his lips and my ears, everything distorts and my insecurities win out.

"I can be very persuasive," I mutter.

His lips rise. "I think I'll survive."

"You're a guy," I remind him—as if this changes *everything*.

He full-on grins. "That, I'm aware of."

My anxiety peaks, unable to even relish in his sexy smile. "But if I'm on the couch, I won't be tempted. And . . . and when I'm in bed with you, I know I'll try to have sex with you, even when I know I shouldn't."

"Lily—"

"And I don't want to be weak and begging, but it's inevitable, right? You're like my crack."

"Lil—"

"That's me: the pathetic, horny girl who jumps her boyfriend and keeps on doing it when he says *no*." I gasp. "Oh my God. I'm like a rapist. I'll try to rape you every night."

He touches my cheeks and I flinch back instantly.

"Whoa! When did you get over here?" My heart pounds so hard that it beats like a drum in my ears.

He doesn't move away, his hands cup my face tenderly, his eyes full of raw concern.

"Did you get a superpower in rehab?" I ask in a small voice, already knowing the truth. I freaked out to a new degree, not even noticing him climb off the bed.

"Yeah," he whispers, so close to me now. "Just not the one you think." He brushes off an escaped tear with his thumb. "You're sick."

I inhale a strained breath. The words from his lips are soul-crushing, even though they're true. I try to jerk away but his hand slides down the back of my neck. The other one on my shoulder keeps me rooted here.

"I'm sick too," he says, "and there will be times where we're weak. Where we beg for the things we can't have. But you can't be scared of that, Lil. You can't live your life sleeping on a couch because of it. You just have to believe that you'll be strong enough in the end. Even if the middle is all fucked up."

No distortion of his words this time. I understand him. I close the distance between us and bury my head into his chest.

He holds on to me and kisses the top of my head. "And you're not a rapist." I can sense him smiling. "You're my girlfriend who can't control her compulsions."

"I like that better," I mumble. We stay still for a little while, and I let him rub the back of my head until my pulse eases to a temperate rhythm. Why does something so small, like sleeping in a bed, have to be such a challenge?

I detach from his warm body and climb into bed, slipping beneath the soft sheets.

He watches me as I build a pillow barricade between my side and his. I'm sure I'll destroy it later. I look up when I finish. "Stop smiling," I tell him.

"No cuddling?"

"Not tonight."

"That's my line."

I sit halfway up as he stores his journal in the nightstand drawer. "You learned a lot in rehab, huh?" A part of me thinks I missed out on a secret to beating addiction. Lo seems to know more than me or at least his confidence level towers over mine. But I couldn't go to rehab. Not without outing my secret to my family, and anyway, group therapy doesn't sound like the right avenue for me.

Now that we're home, Lo decided not to attend AA meetings. Even Ryke said he shouldn't go to them. I don't understand why that is. And Lo doesn't share much about his recovery, but he did say that he's still going to see his therapist regularly—one that lives in New York. Some days I have to pinch myself to believe that he went to rehab only an hour from Princeton. I'm glad I didn't know. I probably would have found a way to see him when I wasn't sup-posed to.

"I learned enough there," he tells me, sliding his legs under the covers. "And I plan to teach you everything I know."

I smile. That sounds nice. I lie back down as he leans over and yanks the cord to the lamp, blanketing the room in darkness.

There's something invigorating about the dead of night. How, right before you go to sleep, your mind springs awake. My thoughts flood all at once. Between the threatening texts and my barely passing grades in Princeton, I'm overflowing with anxiety. Not to mention that with Lo back, his problems seem to become mine. He's broke, jobless, and has quit college. His relationship with his fa-ther was already complicated, and now I don't even know if he'll have one at all.

I have more problems than I can solve in one night. I shut my eyes, willing on sleep. But it stays locked away. Great, I've con-quered getting *into* bed but now I can't even sleep.

I roll onto my side and pull down the top pillow in my pillow barricade. It's enough to see Lo's face. He turns a fraction, and with my eyes adjusted to the dark, I can see him pretty clearly. "Did you learn a trick to fall asleep?" I whisper.

"Don't think about anything."

"That's impossible."

"Then try picturing a fuzzy television."

"Do you not remember *The Ring*? If I try that then a girl is going to crawl out of the imaginary TV and slaughter my subconscious."

I expect him to laugh but his voice turns serious. "How did you fall asleep when I wasn't here?"

I go quiet. It varied nightly. Some were spent crying myself to sleep, others I masturbated until I passed out. When I gave up self-love, it took me hours to doze off the proper way, and in the end I resigned to fantasies to distract me into a light slumber.

"Normally," I end up saying, even if the word reminds me of Connor and Rose's argument earlier. "It just takes me awhile. I'll try the fuzzy television trick. Maybe it won't be so scary."

We roll away from each other again, and I close my eyes. I can't picture the TV long enough to stop my thoughts. I remember how easily it is to fall asleep after some self-love. It's the best natural sleeping pill in the world.

My hand rests on my stomach, and I lower my fingers until I touch the hem of my pajama shorts. The impulse bites me and writhes in my belly. I hear that little voice telling me it'll be okay. That I can do it this once and Lo won't even know. I'll stealthily slip my fingers into my panties and just rub my clit until everything feels better. I'll climax and then fall asleep.

The steps prepared for me are just so easy to follow. My fingers slide beneath my cotton shorts and onto the top of my underwear. I flick my fingers up and down outside of them, trying to gain the courage to go farther . . . or stop. But I somehow always remain in purgatory, fighting for one side or the other.

This is wrong. I know this is wrong.

"Lo," I say very softly, thinking maybe he'll still be asleep. Maybe it's fate.

"Lil, you say something?" he whispers back.

I don't move my hand. Hell, I don't even blink. Words tumble in my head like a Bingo machine and I can't seem to connect them together to form sentences.

I must hesitate too long because he flips on the lights, and my eyes shut quickly. I freeze, hoping he won't notice anything under the covers. He can't see my hand in my shorts after all. As soon as he goes back to sleep, I'll stop myself from going farther.

I'll make this right.

I just don't want him to think that I didn't conquer anything while he was away. I was strong, dammit. I stopped looking at porn. I stopped with the self-love, and I never once cheated on him. But he'll only see *this*. And I can't fix the immediate assumptions. That I'm no better than I was when he left.

Silence bleeds into my head, and I almost think I've succeeded. And then cold air prickles my skin, the blanket leaving my body. Oh shit.

My eyes shoot open. Lo has invaded my territory, knocking over the pillow barricade and gripping my covers. His eyes target my lower half, where my hand disappears into my shorts. This is so not good.

Five

Loren Hale

Here's the thing about Lily Calloway. She's obsessed with masturbating. Not the I-love-to-get-off-before-I-sleep or jerk-one-out-in-the-shower kind of self-pleasure. She fucks to come, and if that means fucking herself every minute of the day, then she gets it done.

Regrettably, I even facilitated her habit. I thought that every video I bought her was one less dick she would ride. One less risk of disease and guilt. I was so fucking stupid.

I grip her wrist tightly. When she told me that she stopped masturbating for a full month, it was difficult to believe. I've watched her hide in a bedroom for hours on end just to please herself. Quitting seems like the biggest accomplishment she's ever had. Now, I'm not sure it's true, even if Rose vouched for her progress.

I slowly shift the hem of her pajama shorts. My shoulders drop in relief. Her palm rests *above* her panties. Maybe Rose was right. Maybe she did stop masturbating, but obviously it's harder for Lily when I'm here.

I'm her drug, her means to a high. But I see the life she'll lead if I'm gone—really gone and never coming back. She'll return to strangers, to sex with random men. She may even venture into the dangerous side of her addiction—chat rooms and anonymous sex. I can't let her go down that road.

I retrieve her hand and lace her fingers with mine, not gently. My hand squeezes hers like she's dangling off a cliff. She might as well be.

"I didn't do anything," she defends.

"You were going to, Lil." I don't know if this is true, but it's a fear that rattles my heart as much as hers.

She sucks in a breath. "This is too hard," she says. "I feel like I can't escape my addiction. If I'm with you, I want to have sex with you. If I'm alone, I want to fuck me. Nowhere is safe."

Christ.

My hands slide to her wrists, and I pull her into my arms. Our embrace isn't soft. I'm not a teddy bear that girls can clutch. I'm sharp and hard, the thing that braces a girl to the bed, the one who grips her strongly and whispers with a husky, edged voice. I'm as rough on the outside as I am black on the inside.

Holding Lily usually solves our problems, but she fights me this time. Ramming her tiny fists into my hard chest, trying to push me away. "Are you not hearing me?" she says, shoving my bicep. "I can't sleep next to you."

I keep her in my arms easily, my muscles flexing as I wrap them around her. "Lil, shh," I say, my lips finding her ear.

"I can't!" she shouts, tears beginning to pool.

"Lil, you can," I whisper deeply. "Shh." I lock her arms together for a minute, her body wedged between my legs. Tonight will be the most difficult, I remind myself. It's confusing for her. She wants to be with me, but my mere presence tempts her. I don't ever want her to believe that being alone, being apart, is the solution.

It's not.

She needs me as much as I need her. We just have to find our footing in this relationship. And that takes time.

She grows restless, so I roll on top of her, pinning her legs down with mine, trapping her small frame. She seems to settle, but her chest rises and falls heavily, fear swimming in her eyes.

"Who do you trust more, me or you?" I ask.

"You." She doesn't even hesitate.

"Then this is how we're going to sleep."

She frowns. "I'm not sure I can hold your weight."

I smile. This is why I love her—why I relish in the fact that I'm going to wake up next to her, my arms wrapped around her delicate body. She's fucking adorable. "No, like this . . ."

I slide off Lily and easily readjust. I tug her closer, and my arm holds her small waist against me. We're spooning, her back to my chest. Now, where is that fucking hand?

I find her right hand curled up underneath her breast, and I take it in mine. Then I intertwine my fingers with hers, securing them with determined force. *No more masturbating, Lil.*

I'm about to officially instate our new sleeping position, but her ass presses harder into my cock. She's scooting back, either on purpose or subconsciously, I have no clue. It's still kind of cute, but it doesn't help.

I lean back and grab a small pillow, and then I wedge it between my dick and her ass. "Better?"

"Depends who you're asking—Horny Lily or Good Lily?"

I love them both. I press my lips to her ear. "I love you."

". . . I don't have much love for myself at the moment," she mutters in a small voice. I can see her shrinking internally, her self-worth dropping lower and lower from the guilt.

"Hey, I'd be passed out already if I had to sleep in the same bed with a bottle of booze. You're doing all right. And this is new for both of us, Lil. It's going to be lots of trial and error. Now we know that we have to sleep like *this*. Okay?"

"Are we going to have sex in the morning?"

The question doesn't annoy me. Still, I'm not used to telling her no. I'm usually the one teasing her until she's hot and bothered. But I can't do a goddamn thing. Because that would be *enabling*.

So I say, "We'll see."

She sinks back into me—and that damn pillow—as I watch her drift to sleep. When I know she's safely in slumber's hold, I allow myself the same luxury.

Six

Loren Hale

My heart beats wildly, my muscles burn and my legs pump. I run. Around and around. There is no end.

If I stop soon, I'll start screaming. The tendons in my calves strain with each foot on the cement track. And I focus on my breathing. In and out. Inhale, exhale. One, two, three . . .

I've always been good at running. Even when I screwed up every fucking thing, I did a decent job at sprinting right away from the cops, from prep school guys wanting to smash my face in, from my father and my problems.

Running has kept me alive.

And if I learned anything from rehab, it's ways to stay busy. But my warring thoughts only make me want to drink. Even bringing up my father, college, the text messages that threaten Lily—any fucking thing, my chest collapses, and I know just the solution that'll fix everything. Whiskey, bourbon—an amber glass will melt all the pain away.

Yesterday, I almost walked into a bar.

I lose my steady pace on the track, my breath staggering. One . . . two . . .

Each foot feels heavier than before. I want to be light as a freakin' feather. I want to float right on out of here. But I keep *thinking* about it.

A smoky bar was directly across the busy intersection as I waited for Ryke to pick me up from therapy. Traffic, honking cabs, and bike messengers never stopped me before. Why should they then? The Jack Daniel's poster in the front window called out to me like a siren singing her deathly serenade on the edge of a dock.

And I nearly drowned in that sea of bourbon.

Stupid little fuck.

I exhale deeply, which only screws with my pace again. Ryke runs by my side, and his eyes flicker briefly to me. He purposefully slows his quick stride. Right now, he could sprint laps around me. But he chooses to be here. I should be glad that he wants to work out with me, but I hate that he won't run as far as he can. I hate that I'm holding him back.

I want to scream.

So I push harder, and I race ahead of him.

Not long after, Ryke catches up to my side again, and then he taps my shoulder and veers off the collegiate track toward the bleachers. I follow him, trying to avoid the other athletes in Penn shirts as they sprint down the lanes.

I probably shouldn't have driven all the way to Penn to run around a fucking circle with Ryke, seeing as how I was expelled and he's not my favorite person at the moment. I don't believe that he's the guy threatening to reveal Lily's secret to the tabloids. There's mistrust in our relationship, sure, but he spends too much time driving me to therapy and hanging out with me to have some ulterior motive. He could let me ride alone to New York and give me just enough slack to hang myself with.

He could be uncaring.

But Ryke Meadows is many things—uncaring is definitely not one of them.

I gave him a hard time about the text messages because I'm an asshole, and a huge part of me resents him for things that I can barely process. Each time I try to understand his childhood where he knew about me and had contact with my father, my hands shake for a sip of something strong.

I unscrew my water bottle, and two girls approach us, one brunette, the other blonde. Both wear cross-country shirts. I'm surrounded by athletes right now—Ryke being one of them.

"Hey, Ryke," the blonde says. "Who's your friend?" She looks me over from head to toe.

I try to wear disinterest, drinking my water, shuffling through my gym bag, anything.

"My brother," Ryke says so easily. I can barely admit that he's half of my brother to Lily. Saying that we're related is so easy for him. But I have to remind myself that he knew about me for years. He just never voiced the truth until three months ago.

"Oh yeah, I see the resemblance," she says, her blue eyes flickering between us.

"Yeah, we both have brown hair," I say. "Shocking, isn't it? She could even be our sister for all I know." I gesture to the brunette hanging by the blonde's side. My tone is not even close to friendly. And I can't help it. This is how I normally say hi to people. My manners died somewhere around my eleventh birthday.

The blonde lets out a small laugh, trying to blow over my rudeness.

Ryke sets a hand on my shoulder, and he whispers, "Do me a favor and don't talk."

If he wants to hook up with one of them, by all means. Have at them. I'm not going to be his wingman on this one. I have a girl waiting for me at home. I check my watch. Yeah, she should be back from class right about now. I'd rather be there than here. I'd rather be holding her in my arms, even if I have to tell her *no* by the end of it.

She's the only good thing in my life.

"This is Laura," the blonde says, bringing her friend toward Ryke. "She's a freshman. I thought I'd introduce her to the captain of the track team."

Ryke checks her out with a slow once-over. The girl is almost as thin as Lily, but muscles pad her legs and arms—they're just lean like most runners. "How have you liked Penn so far?" Ryke asks.

The girl shrugs, shifting her weight off one leg and to another. "Oh . . . you know."

Ryke does that to women, I've noticed. He either stupefies them with his dominance or they start spitting out lame lines that make no sense.

I've yet to really see a girl that can keep up with him.

"That good, huh?" Ryke says, trying to be nice, but this only causes her face to redden.

"It's been good." Laura nods.

This is just awkward and slightly painful. I can't watch the girl be debilitated by embarrassment and nerves anymore. Ryke is slowly peeling off a Band-Aid. I'm going to rip the damn thing for her.

"Hey, Laura," I say. "You and your friend are on the cross-country team, right?"

Laura nods again.

"I'm Maggie," the blonde says, perking now that I've shown a tad bit of interest.

"Oh great," I say. "So you and Laura will have no problem running *that* way." I point to the other side of the track.

Maggie's face falls.

I flash a smile. "Bye."

"Asshole," she curses. "Come on, Laura." She grabs her hand and shoots Ryke a look, guilty by association. When they disappear, Ryke turns to me with a glare.

"Sorry," I tell him dryly. "I couldn't remember how long you told me to keep my mouth shut. It snapped back open, couldn't stop it."

Ryke throws his sweaty towel at my face.

I grab it and fling it back. "Hey, that brunette was two seconds from fainting. I did both of you a favor."

Ryke shakes his head. "You did yourself a favor. Don't pretend that insulting them was for me. I know your motives by now."

"Yeah, and what's that?"

"Isolate as many people as you can. Drive everyone away." He zips his gym bag. "Not going to happen with me, not even if you run off every girl I come into contact with."

I touch my chest. "You would abstain from sex just to be my brother? Wow. That's generous, Ryke." My dry humor barely darkens his eyes. I'm looking for a different reaction, one that comes with a fist to the face, but Ryke never goes there, even if he wants to.

"I'm your older brother no matter what," he refutes. "Get that through your fucking head and maybe I wouldn't have to repeat it all the damn time."

"Can you say that again? I couldn't hear you," I quip.

He rolls his eyes, and then we both actually share a smile.

I check my watch subconsciously.

"She's fine," Ryke assures me.

"Look, you can pretend to know everything about me, but you can't understand Lily the way I do." I've watched her cry and shake in a bathroom because she craved sex—because she couldn't have it. And she wouldn't turn to me for help back then. Now that we're together, I should have the power to take her pain away. But I don't. Because she's trying to control these impulses. And so I'm back where I started, watching her shake, watching her eyes grow big and wide, pleading for something *more*. And I have to deny her that pleasure. Over and over.

"You forget that I was here while you were in rehab," Ryke says. "I've seen her at a low."

No, I never forget that. "Great."

"You'd rather be there with her, I know that. But didn't Rose tell you—"

"I get it," I snap. Our relationship needs room to breathe— Rose so very *pointedly* put it the other day. I'm trying to give Lily more space. I'm making a conscious effort to change our co-dependent relationship.

That doesn't mean it doesn't fucking suck.

But I have nowhere else to be but right here. No other invitations from friends (I have none) or family (my father practically disowned me). No job. No school. I am a worthless piece of shit. I grimace and turn that into a half smile, shaking my head. I chug half of my water to drown these stupid thoughts.

"Have you started taking Antabuse yet?" Ryke asks.

The doctors at rehab prescribed me a drug for my recovery, and I forgot I told Ryke about it. If I drink on the meds, I'll have stomach pains and severe nausea. It's supposed to deter alcoholics from falling off the wagon. And even though I decided not to attend AA meetings, I still need to follow the right steps to get healthy.

I didn't tell Lily why I'm not going to AA. The reason will make her think I'm even more fucked up. I'm a hard person to be around, and when I was in rehab, I pushed two recovering addicts to drink and break their short sobriety.

I always say the wrong things.

And the facility administration forbade me from going to group meetings because I was "adversely affecting my peers." They also highly advised I *not* attend AA meetings in fear that I would be the same asshole there.

Ryke agreed with them.

So here I am.

"I haven't taken it yet," I tell Ryke. "I think I'm going to start tomorrow." I've heard horror stories about people becoming violently ill just from a sip of beer. I wanted to have a couple days without that suffocating fear before I started.

"You should take it now. Do you have it on you?" Ryke asks. He's such a fucking pusher.

"No," I snap. He doesn't listen to me, already unzipping my bag and rummaging through it. "What is this, TSA? Leave my shit alone, Ryke." He finds the inside zipper easily and holds up an orange bottle. His eyebrows rise accusingly.

My teeth ache as I bite down. "Wow, you found my pill bottle. Congratulations. Now put it back."

I wait for him to yell at me for lying. I prepare for the verbal onslaught with narrowed eyes, ready to combat or storm away.

But he never mentions it. Instead, he uncaps the bottle and doles out a pill on his palm. "Take it," he says roughly. "If you're waiting for yourself to fuck up, then you might as well fuck up while you're on it. I'm sure puking all night after a shot of whiskey will do you some good."

He's right.

I hate that he's right.

I take the pill from him and toss it back with some water. It feels official. Like this is it. No alcohol. Forever.

Forever.

God.

I have a sudden impulse to run to the bathroom and stick my finger down my throat. Somehow my Nikes weigh me down on the trimmed grass, and I clench my water bottle as I take another large swig.

Ryke starts to stretch, pulling his arm across his chest. "Have you spoken to Dad?"

"No." I leave it at that, not wanting to be probed about our father. No one really understands my relationship with him. Not Lily. Definitely not Ryke.

And it's more complicated than just *hate* and *dislike*. It's what drives my mind wild. It's what makes me seriously want to kick that fucking bleacher and grab a beer.

But I remember Lily, and I immediately tell myself *no*. No alcohol. Ever. One memory has kept me grounded for a while, deaf to any compelling arguments from the devil on my shoulder. It's what stopped me from heading into that bar yesterday.

In my foggy memory, I wake up, glazed and half delirious to the people in my kitchen. Rose, Connor, and Ryke camped out in my living room like the Scooby Gang. And the three of them told me the night's events—as though I wasn't even there. My body was, but my head was floating in another dimension.

And Ryke was the only one who could stomach the words. "You fucking passed out while a guy attacked Lily."

And "attack" was an understatement. Something could have happened that night. But it didn't. Ryke and Connor stopped the guy when that should have been me. My whole life, I had one fucking job. Protect Lily. Make sure her addiction doesn't get the better of her. Make sure she doesn't get hurt. She did the same for me. And I failed her. Somewhere down the line, I fucked up.

Never again.

Ryke holds out his arms like *what the hell*, and I remember what he asked me. *Have you spoken to Dad?*

"I said no," I tell him again, like the answer isn't registering in his head.

"*No*, that's it?" Ryke wants more. Everyone wants more.

But I feel like I'm giving everything I have.

"I thought it was a yes or no question. What else is there?" *Lots*. But nothing I can bear to say out loud. My father left me a few messages on my phone the past week.

I want to have lunch, Loren.

We need to talk.

Don't push me out of your life over something this fucking stupid.

Call me back.

I've ignored him so far, but I can't forever. There'll be a point where I'll have to face my father. It won't be for money, but the allure of a handout will always be there. Because it's so fucking easy. Drinking, that's easy. Taking his money, that's easier.

The hard things are the right things, I've learned. But I'm not Connor Cobalt—built with the infallible ability to go the extra mile, to do the extra work. I'm the kinda guy that always stops short.

But I do have a plan for some cash. The only problem—it involves a conversation with Rose Calloway.

"He's going to try to buy you back," Ryke tells me. "That's what he fucking does, and you're going to have to say no. He's your fucking trigger, Lo. You shouldn't be around him while you're recovering."

"I'll keep that in mind," I say, lugging my bag over my shoulder. Most days, I regret asking Ryke to be my sponsor. Even if he's pretty good at it. Trigger or not, Jonathan Hale is *my* father. Ryke doesn't understand him the way I do.

He's not all bad.

Seven

Lily Calloway

My second test score came back last week, and it was a big fat F. I knew transferring from an Ivy League to another Ivy League wasn't the cure for my poor grades, but I hoped that Princeton would kick my lazy butt into gear.

With Rose running around the same campus as me, I should be more motivated. Plus, my hours are no longer wasted away on porn and self-love. But I didn't predict that my time would be consumed by therapy in New York and trying to rebuild my relationships with my sisters. Getting healthy and making amends is almost as big a time bandit as wallowing in my addiction.

A tutor sits beside me, though he's not doing much tutoring.

For the past thirty minutes, I watched him browse Rich Kids of Instagram, a site that I boycott and find generally revolting. I nudge him to help me twice, and he points to my book. "Do another problem," he says without peeling his eyes from his phone.

I miss the days where Connor Cobalt gave me a hundred-and-ten percent of his tutoring attention, even going as far as making me flashcards.

Sebastian Ross may just be the worst tutor alive.

He invades my personal space for a second, and I think he may actually be showing me how to do a Statistics problem.

He sticks his phone beneath my nose. "Whose watch do you like better?" He extends his wrist and holds it by the screen, the band gold and the gadgetry so complex that my eyes hurt. The one in the picture is no simpler. A teenager stands outside his gray-bricked mansion, wrists displayed like he's preparing to box.

"Neither."

"Amuse me."

Amuse *him*? How about amuse *me*! I'm the one who should be entertained by numbers and words. Connor would know how to make studying fun.

I try not to glare. "I like my watch."

Sebastian's *one* eyebrow arches, so smarmy and elitist that I have to give him props for mastering the technique. He snatches my wrist to inspect the device. He huffs. "You're wearing a toy." He flicks the plastic cap, nearly causing the hands of the clock to stop.

"Hey," I say, retracting my arm and clutching my wrist to my chest. "That's Wolverine, you know." The yellow-and-blue band buckles on my bony wrist, and the X-Men hero is printed inside the watch face.

He looks mildly interested now. "Is it a collectible?"

". . . maybe."

He restrains the urge to roll his eyes. "Where'd you get it?" he asks. "The kid's section in Target?"

My cheeks redden even though they shouldn't. "No," I retort. "Lo won it from a vending machine. You know, the ones where you put a quarter in and it drops out the little egg thing." We had a seventy-five percent chance of getting either Superman or Batman, so when Wolverine popped out, it seemed like fate. We were easily entertained.

Sebastian grimaces. He has a pretty good stink face too. "You touched those things?" He returns to his phone, scrolling. "Sometimes I wonder how you're related to your sister."

Sometimes I wonder why she's friends with you.

I would exchange Sebastian for a better model, but not when Rose asked him, her *best* friend, to tutor me. Before Connor came into the picture, Sebastian escorted Rose to every social function, her go-to arm candy.

He leans back on the couch, wearing khaki slacks, a blazer, and glasses with wide frames and thin rims. I have a suspicion that he's someone who only wears glasses for show, not function. And his honey-blond hair is slicked neatly and parted on the side, groomed and styled.

Even if he didn't take the time to look good, Sebastian is the kind of person who was born to be pretty.

Normally I'd be tempted. But I have Loren Hale.

And Sebastian is gay. So there's that.

When he snorts out loud, I catch a glimpse of his cell. There's a picture of a guy sitting in a hot tub on a million-dollar yacht, surrounded by expensive bottles of champagne.

Now I roll my eyes. I really want to grab the phone from his hand and chuck it across the room. "Have you even taken Stat?" I ask.

"Stats."

"What?"

"It's called Stastic*sssss*," he says, hissing the S for further emphasis. "Not Statistic." His gaze stays fixated on that stupid phone.

"Have you taken Stat*sssss*," I hiss back.

"Yes, it's an under level requirement for business majors at Princeton," he says sharply. "Obviously Penn has different standards."

Being insulted by my tutor isn't a new thing for me, but I'm not taking *his* jabs easily. Maybe because he seems more interested in pictures of rich kids showing off their Ferraris and guzzling liquor.

"You know, Rose claimed that you're some kind of hotshot tutor on campus—that you even have a waiting list," I snap.

"I am. And I do."

"People actually pay you to ignore them?" I shut my book. I've known Sebastian since I was ten, but I spent more time at the Hale residence than my own, so *know* is really up for debate. He has always been into appearances, especially clothes (which, as a fashion designer, Rose values in a friend), and his ostentatiousness is nothing new.

But I didn't know he was such a raging dick.

He's actually *looking* at me this time. "They pay me for other things."

Like *sexual* things? I frown. No, that can't be right.

Can it?

He sees my brows scrunch in confusion.

"I do have a waiting list," he says, "but not for tutoring."

That clarifies nothing. A naked Sebastian pops in my head, getting propositioned for sex. I withhold the urge to ask if he's a sex worker. Although it's there, threatening to be blurted out.

"Then . . . what?" I mumble. Wow, that took a lot of self-control.

His leg drops from his knee and he leans forward to grab his leather briefcase. What if he sells sex toys? Okay, doubtful, but he would jump up ten points in likability for me.

He pulls something heavy out and sets it on my textbook before zipping his briefcase closed.

These aren't dildos or vibrators or Ben Wa balls.

It's paper. Stacks of stapled *paper* with red markings along the margin.

They're old exams.

This is one of those moments where someone hands you a joint and you have to make a choice to either pass it on or take a puff.

"Isn't this cheating?" I ask, not touching the papers on my lap. Fingering one may just corrupt me.

Sebastian slides a pack of cigarettes from his pocket and slaps the carton on his palm. "Don't scribble the answers on your hand," he says. "Memorize them. That can't be too difficult for you, can it?"

He twirls a cigarette between two fingers.

"Rose won't like it if you smoke in here."

Sebastian arches that one brow again and gives me a look like *I know Rose better than you.* He lights the cigarette.

Fine. Rose will do a better job reprimanding him anyway. I flip through the old exams, most of them marked up with A's. "What if the questions are different?"

"You have Dr. Harris," Sebastian says. "He always recycles questions from tests. Just be sure to memorize all of them."

I thumb through the stack. "There must be fifty exams in here." How can I memorize *all* of them?

"They date back ten years. So yeah, there's a lot."

I hesitate to use them as a study tool, even though it's not outright cheating. "And you can't actually tutor me?"

He blows a line of smoke toward the ceiling. "You didn't just sort of fail your first two exams, Lily. You *bombed.* Most students would be crying in a corner, and if they had me as a resource, they'd be riding my—"

"Okay," I cut him off. And then realize that sounds like I actually want to ride his . . . "I mean, never mind." I shake my head, roasting from the forehead down.

He wears a crooked smile as he puts the cig to his lips. "To pass the class, you have to make A's on the last two tests and the final. I'm not a miracle worker."

"Connor Cobalt is," I mutter under my breath.

He must hear because he says, "Connor thinks he pisses rainbows, but he's not that good. And he's definitely not better than me." He leans forward and taps ash in my plastic cup—full with Fizz Life, Fizzle's new soda, zero calories and no aspartame. I stare at the soiled drink for a long while, trying to process what he just did.

But when I turn, I see him tapping more ash into the porcelain vase on the end table that a friend of Rose's gifted her from Prague. "Rose is going to skin you alive."

He smiles that smarmy smile again. "She's all growl."

I'm not so sure about that. When we were kids at a beach resort, she saw a freckle-faced boy picking on a girl near a water slide. He called the young girl fat and pointed at her one-piece. Rose intervened and used some choice language that would make eight-year-olds blush. When the pudgy boy didn't respond how she hoped, she grabbed his swim trunks and yanked them to his ankles.

After that, I was glad to have my sister on my side. I *never* wanted to cross her. And even as I think about that story, I realize she would kill *me* if she knew I was even sort of cheating.

But what's worse, hearing her wrath after I use the tests or seeing her disappointment by failing out of Princeton? Disappointment can cripple me. So the former is definitely more appealing.

"Look, Lily," Sebastian says. "College is all about beating the system, and the smartest people are the ones who figure that out. You want to be smart, don't you?"

For the first time in a while, I have a fighting chance to do well. "Okay."

"So you keep those and you memorize hard. I have copies of them, of course." He rises and buttons his navy blazer. He wanders around the living room, bored. "And don't mention this to Rose. I love her, but she's moral to a fault. It's kind of annoying actually."

I ignore his last slight. I can't believe I have to lie to Rose, but this seems like the right path. I can't fail more classes. I'll be in college until I'm forty.

I set the old exams next to a tall stack of tabloid magazines on the coffee table. I went out this morning and bought every gossip mag in the gas station. I checked for my picture, any article, any brief mention of my addiction. Rose even searched through the newspaper and online posts, but we both came up blank. Either the blackmailer is stalling or he's waiting for another opportune moment to strike.

We don't even know what he wants yet. He just keeps *threatening*.

"So . . ." I trail off as I watch Sebastian pick up a porcelain ballerina on the fireplace mantel, checking the underside for the designer or the authenticity. "If Rose believes you're actually tutoring me, what do I tell her when you're not here on Thursday?"

"I'll be here, pretending. I can even bring more old exams for your other classes." He sets the figurine down. "You copy them, though, and I'll make your life a living hell." His blasé voice makes the warning worse, somehow.

My phone pings, and I pick it up to check the message. The sound interests Sebastian enough to saunter over and plop by my side again.

Is Rose home?—Connor

Not yet. I text back.

Sebastian catches the conversation over my shoulder. He puts his cigarette to his lips, waiting for the response, but there is none. I'm about to slip my phone in my pocket, but Sebastian says, "Give that here." And he steals the cell from my hands.

I should protest and put up a fight, but his *I'll make your life a living hell* line is ringing in my head. He's kind of scary.

Sebastian types quickly and sends, Why do you want to know? He's too curious, nosy, and bored.

I left her something at the gate. I wanted to know if she's seen it yet.—Connor

Sebastian snorts. "This is just sad."

I frown. "Why? He bought her something." Presents are *sweet*, not sad.

"He's trying to win her back," Sebastian says. "They had a fight, and he wants to see if his gift has cheered her up."

"Whatever they're fighting about, she'll forgive him over time," I say with a nod.

Sebastian tosses my phone back. "No she won't."

"You can't know that," I say, defensive of a couple that I find destined and beautiful. They belong together the way books fit in a library. When I needed help, they both dedicated hours to researching sex addiction. Connor even escorted Rose to therapists, and they pretended to be Lo and me to find a perfect one. Who would do that, other than people who love me and people who love each other?

He stands. "She's listened to my advice since we were children. She'll realize that I'm right about Connor, and she'll toss him aside like she has every short-term fling."

I glare. "That's her *boyfriend*." Connor isn't some *fling*. This is Rose's first real relationship. Sebastian should want her to be happy.

"And I don't like him," he says simply. Sebastian is egocentric, self-centered, and self-absorbed. I suppose Connor has taken his place in Rose's life. Sebastian no longer gets to attend all the lavish parties hosted by the Calloways and peers. She brings Connor instead.

"Their relationship isn't about what you want," I say.

Sebastian snubs his cigarette on a magazine. "Rose is my best friend. I'm just saving her from the heartbreak." He lights another. But his words sound incredibly fake. I don't believe him one bit.

"Why are you telling me this?" I ask, crossing my arms. I want to warn Connor about Sebastian's determination to break them up. Hell, I'm going to tell Rose what a horrible friend she has. And she would believe me. I'm her sister.

"You can't say a word," he says matter-of-factly.

"Yeah, I can."

He shakes his head, taps some ash right on the carpet. "No you can't." He nods to the stack of papers on my textbook. "Rose will not condone your new studying tactics. And Connor Cobalt would be even more displeased." He sucks on the cigarette.

Oh . . . shit.

He's trapped me so quickly. I slump back, winded as though he spun me through a washing machine.

I can't tell my sister that her friend is planning on ruining her life. I should do the right thing and come clean, not be an awful human being.

But I *need* those tests.

And Rose can take care of herself. She's the strongest girl I know.

But as Sebastian tosses that ballerina figurine in his hand, I wonder how she's been blinded by someone like him for all these years. It can happen again.

My only hope lies in Connor.

He'll have to foil Sebastian's plans. He'll have to prove to Rose that he's the best man for her. I can't warn him, but if I had to put money on a match between these two, I'd always bet on Connor Cobalt.

Eight

Loren Hale

After spending lunch with my brother, I end up in Rose Calloway's Escalade. She conveniently showed up at the café. They acted all surprised about it—like she just happened to spot us, driving past Rocco's Deli on her way home.

But I figured out quickly that Ryke called her to cart me to our house while he went back to Philly for college. Like I have to be equipped with a twenty-four-seven babysitter, like I can't be trusted in a cab or for a brief stroll down the sidewalk alone.

I am the equivalent of a ninety-year-old lady needing a person as a crutch to cross the street.

It's ridiculous.

And even if I do want to talk to Rose about my plan to earn some cash—I would never volunteer to be alone with the girl.

She hates me.

And Lily may not see it like that, but Rose and I have an understanding that we're never going to be best friends. We withstand each other for Lily, and that has to be enough. Growing up, Lily would choose me—a boy—over Rose, her sister, and that type of jealousy accumulates over the years into something deep and raw.

No apology will matter.

And I get it.

I would be resentful too. I've never wanted Rose to cut me slack, which must be why I poke the coals, stirring the flames and provoking her temper. I deserve every cold look, every biting comment. I deserve that fucking pain.

I get it.

"You look loads of fun today, Rose," I say as she clenches the steering wheel, spine straight and eyes focused on the street. I should be a good person and ask what's bothering her, but I can't form the words. Caring—that's Ryke's thing.

"Look in the mirror," she says icily.

I do. Just to humor her. And what stares back at me is a scowl that could shatter the reflection. Sharpened jaw and dark circles beneath my amber eyes, showing everyone how fucking tired I actually am.

There's no sleep for the wicked.

"I grow more beautiful with age," I deadpan. "Must be the alcohol."

"That's not even a little amusing."

"Maybe because you lost your funny bone in your Gucci handbag."

She glares and then drives up to our gate.

My phone buzzes, and I check the text with a palm over the screen so Rose doesn't catch a glimpse.

Your girlfriend is a whore.—Unknown

I clench my teeth, my insides broiling. I want to find this bastard more than anything, but I'm running out of options. I can't knock on the door of every enemy that I remember. There are too many. And I've already poked one burning coal that may have been simmering down. Since I threatened him, Aaron Wells could be reinvigorated to come after me even more—or he could be ready to bury his head in a hole. That's the chance I took by visiting his house and assuming he was the texter. (He still could be for all I know.)

But I'm not sure it's wise to do the same thing to guys who haven't spoken to me in years.

Tracking the texts—that's the best shot I have, but I hate that it's out of my hands.

I'm about to slip the phone back in my pocket, but another text chimes.

How many guys have fucked your girlfriend? Do you think the news will tell us the number?—Unknown

"Everything okay?" Rose asks as the car slows down by the gate.

"Yeah," I lie, typing quickly.

What do you want? I text back.

If it's money, I'll find a way to pay him off. I can ask my father for a loan. I'll double the amount that the tabloids are offering him. I just don't want Lily's secret to reach her family's ears. Once her parents learn that she's a sex addict—I'm not sure Lily will be able to handle that shame. I don't think she's ready for it.

Satisfaction—Unknown.

What the fuck does that mean? Of what? I text.

My leg jostles as I wait for the reply. I realize that Rose has put her Escalade in park, waiting by the gate's keypad. She rolls down the window but watches me closely before she types in the code.

"Don't," I snap at her. I really don't want to hear her ideas or thoughts on the matter. She probably has tons of opinions about how I should be responding to this guy, and I'm positive that she would handle this differently.

"You shouldn't provoke him."

"I wouldn't." *Yeah, I kind of would*. That's what I do, even unintentionally.

Her lips purse. "Please. I know you."

My phone vibrates on my leg.

I want the satisfaction of hurting you the way you've hurt me. —Unknown

The bottom of my stomach drops. This isn't about money. This is payback for whatever I did. I'm not a saint, and I wouldn't begin to defend myself. I just never wanted to believe that Lily would be the one destroyed because of me. So I text, Don't go after her. You can do whatever the hell you want to me. Just leave her out of this. And I hesitate before I press send.

I'm sniveling. I'm giving this guy exactly what he needs. Ammunition to use against me. My father would never show him weakness like this. And what is the guy going to say in reply? *Oh, I'm so sorry, Lo. I didn't know she meant so much to you.* No, he's going to tell me to eat shit and watch my girlfriend burn.

This is not the way to win a fight.

So I delete that text and rewrite: I'll find you, you motherfucker. Don't ever doubt that. Send.

I pocket my phone and meet Rose's moody gaze.

"What?" I say.

"You did exactly what I told you not to do, didn't you?"

"Yep."

She mutters under her breath, shaking her head. And as she leans out of the window to type in the key code, her eyes fall to something down below. I'm glad for the distraction. The phone feels less heavy in my jeans. I begin to shelve the texts in the back of my mind. On a normal day, I'd just go grab a bottle of Macallan and call it a night.

"Drop a bracelet?" I ask.

Her lips tighten.

"Worse than a bracelet? Damn, we're at a DEFCON 1 then. Better prepare for nuclear war."

She actually looks impressed. "You know what DEFCON means?"

"Yeah. I also know how to spell 'duh' and 'hurry the fuck up.'" I don't add that *X-Men* uses a version of the term for an imminent mutant crisis. How I learned the facts shouldn't matter anyway.

She shoots me the signature Rose Calloway glare—the one that looks like she's two seconds from eating your soul. I glower back, but internally, I want to run the fuck away. I don't know how Connor *smiles* when she looks at him like that. She's not bluffing. I bet she eats the hearts of every womanizer for the hell of it.

She flings her door open. "Wait here."

Yeah, where else am I going to go?

She rummages out of sight for a minute, and curiosity gets the better of me. I unbuckle and stretch over the driver's seat, peering down through the window.

Rose squats on the ground next to purple hydrangeas, ivy spindling up the iron gate beside the robust flowers. White petals flutter by her side, but her back blocks whatever's in front of her.

"What are you doing?" I ask like she's gone insane. I think there may be a screw loose in all of the Calloway girls. Well, maybe except Daisy. She seems pretty normal.

"He can't just send me things and expect to be forgiven," she says in a huff. "It doesn't work like that." She grunts a little, and more petals burst.

And then she stands and turns. She clutches the stems to what *was* a bouquet of white roses, but they look pathetic in her tight fist. Every petal has been ripped apart and fallen to the grass below.

"You just mauled a plant," I say flatly. There's something disturbing about this, and yet, I can't help but laugh.

She glares harder. "Hold this." She shoves a glass vase through the window.

"You're not going to shatter it?" I ask. "All in the name of love? For your broken heart?"

"My heart isn't broken."

"I forgot, you're made of steel. The bionic, unfeeling woman. Connor must love cuddling with your nuts and bolts." I slip back to my seat.

She slams the car door, not even wasting another glare on me. She has yet to go for the worst look—the "I'm going to castrate you" one. I think she must be saving it for Connor. I am so glad I'm not him.

"What'd he do?" I ask. "Misspell your favorite word? Beat you in a game of Scrabble?"

She doesn't say anything. She just retypes the code and puts the car in gear as the gate groans open. When the car rolls along the driveway toward the colonial house, it hits me.

"You can't be serious," I say. "You're still angry at him because he gave me some beer months ago, when I wasn't even planning on being sober?" I don't want to ruin anyone else's relationship. It's why Lily and I closed off to people—so no one else had to get hurt because of our mistakes.

She pulls into the garage and turns off the ignition. "You wouldn't understand." She's about to climb out of the car, but I lean over her and flick the lock, trapping her in the confines of the Escalade.

Connor told me not to defend him. Right after they had that fight in our living room, he took me aside and said to stay out of it. But I can't let him be attacked for this. He was just being a friend in a time when I wouldn't let anyone in my life.

"Give the guy a break," I say. "He bends over backward for you."

Rose stares at me for a long moment, biting her gums, it seems. And then she tries to unlock the car again, but I beat her to the button, flicking it faster than she does.

"Loren," she warns.

"Just say it," I retort. "Say what you mean." She doesn't think I can handle it, but I can.

"You don't understand," she snaps. "Connor knew you were addicted, and he handed you beer. And you think that's okay. You're sitting there, telling me that it's okay when it's not. Do you see how wrong that is?"

"Rose, he didn't do anything wrong." I grimace as soon as I hear myself. And I understand immediately why Connor told me not to say a word in his defense. Because I am making a great case why he shouldn't have given me an ounce of liquor. I'm the alcoholic—the one who believed I could live a life drinking every minute of every fucking day. Vouching for Connor makes him look guilty. And maybe he is to some extent.

"What he did was awful," she says, "and I don't care if it was just a means to be your friend."

I run a shaky hand through my hair, and when I glance back at her, she pales a little. "No, I'm fine," I say. "Honestly, I'm not going to go race to a liquor store after this conversation, okay?"

She nods, stiff and unmoving.

"Rose," I say. "I'm not trying to defend the guy, but . . ." This is hard for me to say. I even clear my throat, the words lodging for a second. ". . . I don't know if I would be right here if he didn't find a way to enter my life and Lily's. He was the first nonjudgmental person that I could stand to be around. He never looked at me like I was fucked up, even if he was probably thinking it. I liked having him as a friend. I still do."

I hand her the vase, and she no longer looks willing to chuck it at the wall.

"He's human," I remind her. "He's not perfect. No one is."

Her lips twitch. "Wise words from Loren Hale. You must have plagiarized a fortune cookie."

I let out a weak laugh, actually smiling at that one. She's good.

Nine

Loren Hale

I unlock the car. From the back garage door, we enter the house, walking into the granite kitchen.

Lily must have heard the garage because she breezes through the archway with a zipped backpack. She sets it on a chair and waits patiently for me to approach her by the barstool. She's doing well, and then I notice the way she fiddles with her fingers, the way she presses her thighs tightly together.

I slide my arms around her shoulders. She rests her cheek to my chest, but her body doesn't sag in relief. No, it tightens in eagerness. Lily doesn't do hugs. She fucks until she passes out.

And I so badly want to fix her, but I can only help. The real mending—that has to be her job, her fight, her battle. I can't win this one for her—just like she can't defeat my demons.

Shoes tap along the hardwood, and I expect to see Connor Cobalt cresting the archway. Instead, I'm met with Sebastian Ross.

He's still here after tutoring Lil?

I internally groan.

His self-confident swagger rubs me wrong. Always has. He wears a smug grin ninety-nine percent of the time, and he makes certain he knows what's going on in everyone's life. Sebastian and I have never seen eye to eye. Maybe because I say more mean comments to Rose than nice ones. He thinks I'm an asshole.

I am.

And he has full right to dislike me. I'll give him that.

I guide Lily over to a small breakfast table and sit on the chair, bringing her on my lap. She opens her mouth, probably about to ask when we're going to have sex, but she shuts her lips and blushes.

Before rehab, this is when I'd tease her. Run my hand down her thigh and watch her breath catch. It takes every ounce of strength to shake my head. Her eyes widen in slight horror, but I press a kiss to her temple.

I want to distract her from sex, so I ask, "Anything good on TV?"

"I taped *Earth's Mightiest Heroes* while you were in rehab," she says softly. "It's pretty good, but they make Captain America look kinda weak."

I smile. "Spoiler alert?"

"No, he wimps out early on." She seems to relax, which makes *me* relax.

"How was the meeting?" Sebastian asks Rose, a lit cigarette burning between two fingers.

"The meeting was fine," she says. "The menswear collection just shipped, so everyone was excited." When she turns to him, she spots the cigarette between his fingers, her eyes narrowing. With Connor's vase still clenched in her hand, she plucks the cigarette from Sebastian. "Outside only." She snuffs it in the sink and makes no other comment about it.

He gets away with more shit than any other guy in Rose's life.

Lily resituates herself on my lap, straddling me on the chair all of a sudden. Fuck.

It's the middle of the day. We shouldn't have sex. It's not considered the norm. I remind myself of all the reasons why this can't happen. Not to mention Rose and Sebastian are halfway across the kitchen from us.

"How's tutoring going?" Rose turns to Lily at this. She's trying to delay what I think is the inevitable—my cock in Lily, her body and mind appeased, coming with a blissful high.

Lily points to her chest, flushed. "Oh, me?"

Rose gives her a look—one that tells her to relocate her common sense. Lily tucks her hair behind her ear and sits up a little from my chest. Progress, yes. But I can't move my hands from her thighs. I'm afraid she'll freak out by the lack of touch.

"I know why people call the class Stats and not Stat now." She flashes a strained smile, hoping that's enough for Rose.

"She's doing fairly well," Sebastian says nonchalantly. But his gaze descends to the vase between Rose's fingers. He grabs the clear glass. "Is this crystal?"

"Yes," Rose says tiredly. She pulls her glossy brown hair into a sleek pony.

Sebastian pauses for a second, and I realize Lily is entrapped with the scene, watching with more interest than she normally would have.

I squeeze her leg and lean forward to whisper in her ear, "What's going on?"

But Sebastian speaks, cutting off any chance for Lily to reply. "Where are the flowers?"

"Dead."

Sebastian opens a cupboard and slides out the trash.

"What are you doing?" Rose asks, her pitch spiking.

"He really expects to win you back with *flowers*. Come on, Rose." Huh, I'm surprised Rose felt comfortable enough to share intimate details of her fight with *Sebastian*. I just didn't think she opened up her frigid gates to anyone.

Rose stares questioningly at the vase in Sebastian's hand, considering trashing Connor's present.

Oh fuck that. "It's crystal," I remind her.

"Yeah," Lily adds.

Sebastian looks unperturbed by the voices of dissent and rests an elbow on the counter. He passes the vase to Rose, but she hesitates by the trash bin.

"It's Lalique," she says under her breath, her fingers running over the smooth face. The vase is cut like a square, and the bottom has an intricate knot design.

"What does that mean?" Lily asks.

"He has good taste," Rose says.

Sebastian makes a show of rolling his eyes.

Rose clutches the vase to her chest. "It's my favorite brand."

Only Rose would have a favorite kind of crystal at twenty-two. But more than that, Connor *knew* exactly what she liked. That detail has to count for something. I'm not even that perceptive.

Sebastian taps the counter, watching Rose closely. "You can keep it," he says, "but what kind of message does that really send? Every fight, he'll try to buy you back. Personally I'd be fine with that type of relationship. I have a pair of crocodile leather shoes from Max in my closet, but I know you, Rose. After the fifth piece of jewelry, you're going to be sick of him."

Rose looks conflicted.

"Connor is trying to say he's sorry," Lily pipes in.

Sebastian looks bothered by Lily's interjection. He tilts his head, his eyes flickering to her backpack. I'm missing something important. It doesn't take a genius like Connor to figure that one out.

Lily hesitates, and she recoils into my chest. I wrap my arms around her and assault Sebastian with my glower. That's what life in the first-class world is—a series of glares, half smiles and scowls. Each one is lethal, each one like a fucking razor. And I've learned all of them from the best. Not Rose Calloway. My father could destroy her with his sharp "go-the-fuck-to-hell" stare.

He's even almost destroyed me with it.

Rose sets the vase on the counter by the coffeepot, uncertain. "I have a box I need to grab from the car. I'll be right back." Partly, I think she's leaving to hide how flustered she's become. When she exits out the back door, Sebastian straightens up and grabs the vase off the counter.

Lily's spine goes erect like a surprised cat. "What are you doing?"

"What Rose can't. She'll thank me later." He chucks the vase in the trash bin.

"No!" Lily springs from my lap. I follow her, only because I don't like that look in Sebastian's eye. It's the kind that I've seen from too many rich kids—the one where they think they're invincible. That no one can touch them.

I've probably worn it on occasion.

Sebastian kicks the cupboard closed and extends his arms across the counter behind him, blocking Lily from the bin. She squats to go through his legs to reach it, but Sebastian holds his foot out. "Remember what's at stake, Little Calloway," he says casually, a voice so smooth that I want to tear it to shreds. Mine is nothing like that. I'm all edged, all something harsh and severe.

Lily freezes and slowly rises. I place my hands on her shoulders, confused as ever.

"Are you blackmailing her?" I ask.

Lily shakes her head first. "It's okay," she says to me. She places her palms on my chest and begins to push me away from the counters and toward the breakfast table again. It's not okay. What the fuck is going on?!

The door opens. Rose enters with a paisley box labeled *Spring/Summer Men's Collection*.

"So you're really doing menswear?" Lily asks, her hand slipping in mine. She squeezes once, a sign that she'll explain the Sebastian stuff later. I have to trust her.

Rose nods and pulls out a blue men's sports coat and passes it to Sebastian.

"I like the pocket," he says and inspects the lining. "I'm glad you went with this print."

"Me too. The mini checkers were too much." She turns to Lily. "Sebastian's been helping me with the collection."

Lily told me Rose has been nervous about branching out since Calloway Couture has been strictly for women only.

"I know this is probably a busy time," Rose says to Lily, taking the coat from Sebastian and folding it precisely, "but I could use your help at the office. Would you mind working more hours?"

Since my stay at rehab, Lily has occupied her time as Rose's assistant, even if two other girls work at Calloway Couture for social media, online sales, and whatever the hell Rose needs them for. Lily told me that she's Rose's numero uno bitch—and she said it all with a flourish of pride, which I found pretty adorable.

"Sure," Lily agrees with a solid nod. But she grips my hand tighter, and then she blurts out, "But what about the male models?" And then her eyes dart to Sebastian and she pales, forgetting his presence.

"Oh yes," Sebastian says, "they're gorgeous. Maybe Rose can find you someone better to date than that one over there." He points at me.

"And maybe she'll find someone to replace you." I mockingly pause. "Oh wait, she already has." Where's Connor Cobalt when you fucking need him?

The corner of Sebastian's mouth tics. Good.

Rose sets the sports coat back in the box. "Sebastian, I think it's time for you to go. I'll call you tomorrow."

"Sure." He kisses her cheek, and then he waves to Lily. "Study hard."

"I will," she says tensely.

With this, he departs, and when the door slams, Rose sets her hands on her hips and faces Lily. "I won't ever schedule the male models for fittings when you're in the office, I promise."

"I'm just scared," Lily admits. She can't even look at me.

I try to hold back a cringe. I should have more faith in her—that she won't cheat on me, but I spent years hearing her fuck other guys through the walls. Being monogamous isn't natural for her, and I'm honestly shocked she's made it this long with just me. I wait for the day when I'm not enough, especially now that I can't feed into her desires. I can't give her what she can so easily receive from some other douchebag.

"I'm not going to put you in that position," Rose tells her. "I promise."

And if my plan works, then Lily shouldn't be worried at all. But right as I muster the courage to ask Rose, the door opens and we all stiffen.

Sebastian is back.

But the shoes on the hardwood sound different, more confident, faster and determined.

Connor strolls through the archway with a stack of French bread pizzas. He slides them on the counter just as the tension eases. Well, technically only Lily and I relax. Rose's shoulders lock like she's preparing to crush someone underneath her heel. "Who did you think I was?" he asks us. He must notice the shift in the room.

"Sebastian," Lily says.

"We were talking about sex," I clarify.

He nods, understanding now. "How'd the tutoring go?" he asks, about to approach Rose and kiss her, but she stares at the wall, not at him. *Come on, Rose, let the guy in.*

Connor only studies her, more determined to win her affections. He leans against the counter and then gives Lily his full attention.

"It was fine. I think Sebastian is going to help a lot."

Really? I always claimed I'd switch from whiskey to bleach if I had to talk to him for longer than ten minutes. Obviously, there's something going on between Sebastian and Lily, but I don't want to bring it up now.

"That's good," Connor says. "I'm sorry I can't tutor you. If I had more time this semester, you know I would."

"It's fine, really." She keeps saying that, and I think we all know it's not fine.

Connor flips open one of the boxes, and Rose peers over his shoulder, risking the touch of his arm.

"Artichoke and mushrooms?" she asks.

He pulls out the second box and faces her. But he holds on to the pizza. "And feta."

Lily mouths to me, *Her favorite*.

He's smooth. And Lily is grinning so hard, watching her sister and Connor reunite. Her whole face glows. Fuck it. I slide my arms around her waist, and I draw her to my chest, her warm body making my cock throb. She lets out an audible sigh, but Connor and Rose are lost in their own intellectual world.

Rose waits for Connor to pass the box, but he's not going to let her have the pizza so easily. I sometimes forget that he's willing to test her as much as she does him.

"You broke the vase, didn't you?" He must have seen the crumpled white roses by the gate. If he's hurt by the fact, I can't tell. Rose and other genius-types must be the only ones able to read him.

"What? No, I . . ." She glances over her shoulder by the sink—where she had previously set the vase. But it's no longer there thanks to her "best" friend. Her gaze drifts to the cupboard with the sliding trash bin.

Connor follows her eyes, and he opens the cupboard and lifts out the expensive crystal, a fissure running through the side. Cracked, broken. He sets it by the sink and then passes her the pizza.

"I didn't do that," Rose immediately says. Her eyes light with fire. "I'm going to kill him." I've heard her say that about Sebastian too many times to take the threat seriously.

"Sebastian?" Connor wonders.

Rose nods tersely. She puts the pizza down, no longer interested in eating, and she inspects the vase with delicate hands. Her shoulders drop. He comes behind her and whispers in her ear. When his voice grows, I catch the syllables, but I don't understand the words.

He's speaking to her in French.

She answers back in the foreign language, fluent. He kisses her head, and then she spins around and kisses his lips, standing on the tips of her toes.

Lily turns to face me at this, and her eyes grow wide and eager. *I want to, Lil. God, do I want to.* Now's the best time to talk to Rose. Even if it'll break her moment with her boyfriend, it'll save me from rejecting Lily again.

"Rose," I say.

She drops to her feet, but Connor keeps his hand tangled in her hair, intoxicated by Rose's commanding movements. She possesses him, but he's equally as possessive of her, which I still find strange. I thought for sure Rose would devour any man she touched, but they have this symbiotic relationship instead of the parasitic one I share with Lily.

"Yes?" she asks.

My throat swells at the thought of asking her for help. Even as the words rest on my tongue, saying them is so fucking hard. So I turn to Connor. "Have you heard anything from the private investigator?"

"He's working on tracing the messages. We'll see if we can find any leads." After the wave of texts in the car, that's not exactly the news I wanted to hear.

"Lo," Rose snaps. Her hand flies back to her hip. She could tell I was dodging. "Spill."

I inhale. "As you know . . ." I rub the back of my neck, heat flushing my body all of a sudden. I'm not used to that. ". . . I don't have a college degree, so getting a job that pays better than minimum wage is going to be a challenge."

The silence lingers, waiting for me to continue, three sets of eyes boring into me in curiosity and hesitation. They think I'm on the verge of giving up, of throwing my hands in the air and saying I can't do hard, physical labor. I can't flip burgers. I can't fucking be a normal lower-class guy who has to work for his money. I've *never* had to do that, but that doesn't mean I wouldn't try. They think less of me, and I haven't given them reason to believe otherwise.

"I'd have no problem flipping burgers," I explain, "but I owe Ryke forty grand for rehab that I'd like to pay him in a reasonable amount of time . . . plus, you know, rent." I pause again, half expecting Rose to bail me out and say, *you don't have to pay rent, Lo, you're practically family.* But I forget who she is for a brief second. Maybe her little meltdown over a vase tricked me, but she stands resolute, strong, unwilling to let me take the easy road.

Good.

Still, I glare. Habit. "You're going to make me ask, aren't you?" I say.

She smiles icily. "Last year in the Cayman Islands, you said that not even the abominable snowman would want to fuck me."

Lily gasps, "You did not."

"I did."

She punches my arm. I mock wince. Yeah, I deserved that.

Connor stays completely impassive. But he holds Rose closer, as though silently saying I'm wrong. Clearly guys with insanely high IQs want to fuck her.

I let out a deep breath. Here it goes. "I've already been scouted by modeling agencies before," I explain. "You'd be an idiot not to use me in your menswear campaign." *Way to go, Loren. Call her an idiot. That's definitely the way to land a job. Jesus Christ, no wonder you've never had one.*

"I remember that," Rose says stiffly.

"How come you've never modeled if you were scouted?" Connor asks.

"I may have walked into the interview drinking straight from a bottle of Jack Daniel's." I was fucking with the agency, wasting people's time and mine. I didn't really want to model. I still don't, but it'll be quick money. And this is a chance for me to redo my past mistakes. I can make things right.

Connor lets out a long whistle. "Impressive."

"I think so too."

Rose looks ready to reignite their old argument, but Connor leans in and whispers into her ear again. French. Can't understand a fucking word. She eases considerably.

"I need a translator," Lily whispers to me.

"Or an interpreter." Preferably not a *male* interpreter. I can just picture Lily getting aroused and flushed from some French guy. Even that proposed fantasy makes me cringe. Jealousy is the one thing I don't ever want to tear us apart. But it's there. Festering.

Rose finally pins her eyes back on me. "Modeling is difficult," she says, her voice much softer. "It's not just about having a good body or a pretty face. Ask Daisy."

"I know," I say. "But Rose, this isn't going to be a career for me. I just need to make enough money to pay back my debts and get on my own two feet. That's it." I glance at Lily for a second. "And you won't have to mess up your schedule for Lil. I'll be there while the other models are. It'll be better."

Lily holds on to the waistband of my jeans, and she says, "And what are you going to do after modeling?"

I have no idea. The fog of my future is too thick to clear. "One step at a time," I say. She nods, understanding.

Rose mulls over my proposition for a minute. And then she says, "Fine."

I break into a full grin.

And she adds, "But just so we have things clear, I'm doing this out of pity."

My smile vanishes. "You could have stopped at fine."

It's her turn to grin. "I know."

Ten

Lily Calloway

Two days pass and I still haven't had sex. And on top of that, I whiffed on telling Lo about the old tests. But I plan to. I just need to . . . phrase it correctly so he joins my immoral side of things. And Connor has yet to find any evidence about the so-called blackmailer (or whatever he is—considering he still hasn't asked for anything in return).

"What about Patrick Bomer?" I sit with my legs crossed on the bed, an old navy-blue Dalton Academy yearbook on my lap. Big black circles outline certain faces and on others I've drawn X's . . . and mustaches.

I raise my head and catch Lo's frown through the circular mirror mounted above our dresser. He spent a solid twenty minutes dressing this morning and another ten minutes on his hair. It's his first job at Calloway Couture. Hell, it's his first job *ever*, and he's freaking out about it.

"Why would Patrick hate me?" he asks, disheveling the thicker pieces of his hair on purpose.

"You won first place in our art class's end-of-the-year projects."

Lo took a five-minute video of a plastic bag blowing in the wind, which was beyond boring and beyond unoriginal, seeing as how *American Beauty* did it first.

He turns to look at me. "What? That's not my fault. My project was damn good."

"The entire class fell asleep," I remind him. And Patrick made a bronze sculpture of Apollo, but it was hardly appreciated by Mr. Adams.

"So he should be pissed at the teacher, not me."

I don't refute because he's right. Teachers gave Lo special treatment, even so much as awarding his crappy video the highest prize because he's a Hale. Because his father is a multibillionaire with connections so intricate that a spider would be jealous of the web Jonathan Hale weaves.

I glance at my computer screen on the bed. "Maybe he's not angry anymore," I add. "He's at Carnegie Mellon for art now."

"How do you know that?"

"Facebook."

Lo groans. "Please tell me you didn't sign up." We've had an anti–social media rule since high school. We like privacy too much to waste it away on cyberspace.

"I didn't. I signed you up."

His eyes darken.

"The way I see it," I say quickly, "is that if someone hates you, they'll probably start slandering you on here." I point to the screen. "It's like a flytrap for suspects."

Surprisingly, he risks his wrinkle-free, steam-pressed khakis to sit down on the bed beside me. Our canopy net tangles in his leg, and he curses under his breath, swatting the fabric away. "I swear I'm going to cut this stupid thing down."

"I like it." Even if I got caught in the net like a praying mantis last night. I roll sometimes when I sleep. It happens.

"We're not in a jungle trying to ward away bugs."

"Rose designed the room," I remind him. She decorated it while Lo was away at rehab. "She'll be hurt if I change it because of you."

"Even better," he says. I doubt he believes that.

"I'm going to forget what you just said," I mutter and swivel the computer screen to him.

Lo gapes. "You had to use that photo as my profile picture?"

I break into a wide smile, and I can't stop staring at the photo. He's shirtless except for a pair of Spider-Man pajama pants. He looks sexy *and* cool.

The website consumes his attention, and he scrolls through the profiles of old students. "Married, married, pregnant, dead, engaged, pregnant, married," he lists. "Did anyone stay in their twenties after high school or did everyone just pass GO to collect a 401k and diapers?"

"Maybe they're in love," I defend.

"We're in love. You don't see us getting married or having babies."

I frown, not sure why this hurts me a little. Marriage isn't really a plan of mine, at least not until I'm older and move past this awkward, confusing stage of life. But the way Lo said those words— well, he makes marriage seem nonexistent. Like instead of a *maybe*, he's saying *never*.

"You don't want to get married?" I ask softly. I can barely meet his gaze. I'm twenty, just stepping out of my teens. I shouldn't worry about marriage and babies, especially not when we're struggling being healthy ourselves.

He hesitates. "I don't know. I'm not closing that door. I just can't think about it." He pauses. "Do you . . . think about it?" He frowns deeply, worried that we're not on the same track. We usually are, and it's kind of terrifying to see him veer off without me.

"Not a lot," I say. "Before I was with you, I never thought I'd be married." I slept with random guys. I thought monogamy wasn't a lifestyle I could ever conform to. Now that I'm starting to find a good groove, I'm beginning to fantasize about normality.

"But now you do?" he asks.

I shrug. "I guess but definitely not anytime soon. I want to get through the terrible twenties first." I wave my hand. "Let's not talk about marriage or having babies. It's stupid anyway. We have more important things to deal with."

I didn't think it was possible, but his face contorts more, even graver than before. "You want kids?"

Oh . . . I can tell just by the way he says it that he doesn't want them. A lump rises to my throat, and I feel like this is going to be a trick question. I look over my shoulder for the right answer but it's not concealed there. "Umm . . ." I mumble. "I don't know."

He blinks, watching me as I watch him. The answers seem to spill out of our silence.

"Maybe," I blurt out, not able to hold back any longer. "When I'm older but not too old, I guess. My eggs are on a clock." I nod and then grimace. "I mean, you know . . ." I am two seconds from burrowing underneath the comforter and never coming out. *Hide, Lily, hide!* My face flames. I really wish my feelings weren't so visible.

"Lil," Lo breathes, his eyes softening considerably. I am one of those sea vessels wobbling in the ocean before they're hit by a wave. "You . . . and me . . ." Here it is. "We probably shouldn't have children."

I stare blankly at the black-and-white comforter, gathering my thoughts. I never allowed myself to dream that far ahead, to construct a reality where Lo and I start a family together. Maybe because deep in my heart, I knew it doesn't exist.

His words paint the blackness of my future into a clearer picture. And it's an image I want to return to the store. A life where we don't have kids. Where our family consists of me and him. And that's it.

I understand where he's coming from. We're both addicts, and even if we could raise a kid, alcoholism is still hereditary. Lo wouldn't wish his troubles on anyone, especially his own child.

"I know," I say with a sadder nod. "I just don't want to think about it."

He distracts my sullen mood by pointing at a picture in the yearbook. "You gave Jacqueline Kinney a mustache. That's just mean."

My lips slowly rise, and I glance at his head. His hair sticks up in different directions. And I'm sure he thinks that's what super-model hair looks like, but Rose will not be pleased.

I scoot over, pushing the laptop away, and I run my fingers through his locks, combing his thick brown hair on top. He jerks back almost instantly.

"I spent valuable time on this." He clutches my wrist.

"I think all that time was spent ogling yourself," I refute. "Let me fix it." But my gaze drifts from his hair, landing on his pink lips that hover so very close to mine. I imagine how they'll feel on my soft ones. And I ache to press up against them.

His lips begin to move, but I don't hear the words from them. I'm transfixed, and when they go still, a magnetic hold propels me to his mouth.

I touch his lips with mine, and he kisses back at first, soft and sweet. A raspy moan tickles my throat, and I crawl on his waist, straddling him, ready for something more. I just need him . . . I knead my fingers through his hair, and I squeeze my thighs.

He pulls back.

No. I breathe heavily like I'm currently running a half-marathon. I'm just starting to race up that steep incline, and he stopped me midway.

"Lily . . ."

My hands dip below his shirt, and I trace the ridges in his abs, gliding each finger along his bare chest. I unconsciously dig my pelvis, rocking a little, needing him more and more.

A groan escapes *his* lips this time, and he has to grab my wrists.

I don't want to stop. It feels like I haven't touched him in so long. It feels so unbearable. I remember the exhilaration and burst of coming. I want that sensation to ripple through me. I want my body to vibrate until I can't see straight. I miss that so very much.

But when I meet his hard eyes, I see the answer. *No. No. No.* But I want to hear *yes* just once. I want to sigh in relief with the word.

"I haven't had sex in days," I say like it's an accomplishment. "I thought I get rewarded for good behavior."

His mouth curves into a genuine smile. I've won, I think. This is it. I tighten my legs around his waist again, his hardness driving me to new levels of eagerness.

"Whoa," he protests, lifting me up underneath my arms. He sets me on his knees. No fun. "How about I make a deal with you?"

"I like deals," I say, my gaze drifting to his cock.

"Eyes on me, Lil."

I try. I'm trying. I am. "But aren't deals against the rules?"

"Not this one."

Now I'm curious. He rubs my leg, semi-splayed on his lap. I guess this is better than being chucked off him entirely. The movement grabs my attention, and I desperately wish his fingers would rise higher, to the spot that throbs so desperately for his touch.

"You can choose one thing to do right now. I can kiss you until you're breathless." He leans forward and places a small, fleeting kiss on my lips before his breath tickles my ear. "Or I can put my fingers inside of you and make you feel full." *Yes.* "Or . . ." There's another option? Oh jeez. I scoot forward, even against his wishes, and I grip his T-shirt between my fingers. I can practically feel him pulsing beneath me. Or maybe that's just my need growing out of control. ". . . I can run my hand over your pants and make you come." *Double yes.* "But . . ."

My shoulders drop at the realization that there's a stipulation. I guess that's why it's called a deal and not a free-for-all . . . or a free-for-Lily. "I don't like buts . . ." I trail off because I realize I do like butts, only the round kind.

"You're turning red," Lo notes. "Are you thinking about my ass?"

I drink in his rich amber eyes. "More like *my* ass and your—"

He covers my mouth with his hand and whispers in my ear again, "My cock isn't going anywhere near your ass, Lily Calloway, but I'd be glad to put it somewhere else." He whispers a couple places, and I realize that I've latched onto his lap like a monkey, clinging so hard that I'm already wet and ready.

"*But?*" I say, reminding him that there was a big fat roadblock that he constructed.

"You can only pick one option. Or you can forgo all of them and choose to wait until tonight, and we'll have sex. It's up to you." All I hear is *we'll have sex*. But I have to wait for it. And right now, waiting eight minutes is torture that I don't want to endure. How can I wait eight *hours?*

"I don't like this deal."

"Neither do I, but we have to practice self-control. Both of us." Oh.

I mull the options and realize that if I choose something right now, he won't be receiving any sort of pleasure. "I choose head. To give *you* head, I mean," I say one of the most unladylike phrases I've ever used, but the last thing I care about right now is sophistication. And for a brief moment, I wonder how Connor and Rose are in bed—do they spout off anatomical parts or speak in beautiful prose? I'd ask Rose, but she's private about that stuff. And I'm pretty sure her sex life is nonexistent since she has intimacy issues. And I hope she would tell me if she lost her virginity.

"Leave my dick out of this," Lo says, equally classy.

"Why?" I frown and then my eyes widen. "Are blow jobs on the blacklist?" We still haven't attended therapy together, but I imagine

I'll be begging my therapist for the details of that list next time I see her.

He covers my mouth again. "Stop . . . talking," he says sternly. He shifts a little underneath me, and I'm about to glance down, but he lifts my chin before I catch a glimpse of his hardness.

Obviously I'm not the only one with raging hormones. I could smile, but I also feel guilty that he has to suffer because of my addiction.

My eyes flicker to his lips, and there's a part of me that wants to give in and choose kissing. But kissing always leads to more with me, and being denied that will be harder than not having Lo at all.

I grab his wrist and pull his hand from my mouth. He gives me a warning look to not bring up his body parts. But that's precisely the reason why I'm choosing tonight, the only option that offers him any sort of pleasure too.

"We can wait," I say softly and slowly. Begrudgingly, I slide off his lap and the bed. I flip my laptop closed and go to straighten out my shirt in front of the mirror. The worst part—I won't be able to release my pent-up frustration right now. The pulsing between my legs will have to stay. Because I've committed to no self-love. Once I start down that road, there's no stopping. I'll turn back into a compulsive beast, and I don't want Lo to see me like that.

"Are you sure?" Lo calls from the bed.

He's as surprised as me. Normally I'd take one of the immediate gratifications, even if it was fleeting. I'll regret my decision in a couple of hours, but at least I'm making the smarter choice now.

I meet his eyes, and I swear they lighten, like he's proud of me. "Positive."

Eleven

Lily Calloway

n retrospect, I should have gone for the fondling over the clothes bit. I would have come and all would be well. Even after a shower, I sit behind my desk at the Calloway Couture offices with tension so crazy that I reflexively rub my lower half against my chair. My face flames when I catch myself, and I look up, wondering if Trish and Katie notice.

But both blondes type away behind their white desks, the workplace more like a loft, no cubicles. Racks of clothes shield the walls. Rose has a glass office that overlooks the rest of us, and right now, I miss her constant peeks across the room, her reprimanding gaze darting from her computer screen to my desk.

Her chair is empty, and I keep eyeing her office, wanting her to remind me why I shouldn't sneak into the bathroom and do something naughty and just plain wrong.

But it will feel so good.

I'm two seconds from smacking my forehead on the desk. But I focus on my computer and the Excel spreadsheet. I try not to picture a naked Lo, which has already popped in my head three times. I fantasize about him too much, but I am thankful that no other guys infiltrate my thoughts. Missing him for three months has temporarily cured me. It was like my brain could only process one image: Loren Hale. All day, every day.

But by being alone, I can't stop the sinful images from seeping right on in.

They begin with Lo walking toward me, still in the office. He shoves everything off my white desk and lifts me up roughly, none of his movements soft and slow. And in this particular fantasy, I'm wearing a dress.

And all he needs to do is shift my panties a little, and then he yanks my legs so they wrap tight around him, my back cool against the desk. And everything thrums so much. He tears down the top of my dress, his lips finding my breast, sucking, and then he thrusts . . .

Okay, I need to stop.

I squirm in my seat, the spot between my legs now pulsing, for real. There's no doubt about it.

Maybe I can just log on to a porn site and once I stare at the pictures, all will be good. I'll scroll through Tumblr's naughty photos, and no one will know. I'll hit that high I crave, and it will be okay again.

It's an itch, a subconscious pulse. This time, I do slam my forehead down onto the keyboard, pounding my frustration until my computer lets out a screech. Shit.

I roll back a little, exhale deeply. And then a doorbell buzzes. Trish stands, her suede gray booties making the short trek to the door.

Rose is probably here. My anxiety starts to lessen. Her presence will surely keep me in line. I zone in on the Excel spreadsheet that details the collection's current inventory. We have to ship a few more pieces to H&M because I messed up the order. I accidentally put a maxi dress in the spring collection, and Rose has been trimming most of her clothes because they're more flattering on the everyday girl.

My phone pings just as Trish opens the door. I check the text.

Whore—Unknown.

My heart explodes.

He has my number. He's no longer going through Lo. What if it's not the same person who texted him? I never thought it was possible that there could be *multiple* people involved in the text threats.

I quickly log into the search engine and type my name, wondering if my secret has already been spilled. My fingers tremble as I scroll through a list of Lily Calloways. Most articles about me discuss my involvement with Fizzle. Some even call me a "soda heiress," which is a cooler title than I think I deserve. No trashy headlines pop up. Nothing about sex addiction.

I let out a short breath of relief, even if the word *whore* is still on my cell phone. Replying back may just fuel him to do something drastic—like call the tabloids—so I abandon the pursuit.

"Come on in," Trish says. "Just stand along the back wall by the window. It's tinted, so you don't need to worry. I'm going to bring out the men's clothes from our backroom. Help yourself to coffee and water on the table."

What? I thought the male models were coming later today. Like in two hours. I check my clock on my phone. Oh . . . time really does fly when you're stuck inside your head.

The guys file in. One by one. Each of them as striking as the next. It's hard not to stare since that's what they're here for. I try to remember Daisy. I wouldn't want anyone to gawk at my sister like I'm doing to these guys, but yet, I can't stop.

I count off the models in my head. One, two, three . . . and when I reach nine, the door closes. Wait. Where's Lo? And Rose? Rose and Lo. I need both of them here. And Lo *should* be the tenth model. Rose was going to drive him to the office since she had to run a few errands and would be here during the fitting. But yet, she's not here.

Trish departs to the backroom, and Katie stands, ushering the guys toward my desk where they'll linger. I sit by the window with a view of the city, and to the right of me is a table with freshly baked muffins, coffee, and bottles of Evian.

I freak out.

I don't know what else to call it. Just as Katie begins to look in my direction, I act as though I dropped a pen, and I squat to pick it up. Then I scuttle underneath my desk, hiding, and I quickly dial Lo's number. Thankfully no one can see me, but I am sure they're all wondering where the loony assistant disappeared to.

Maybe they'll think I just teleported. I try to convince myself of the ridiculous, impossible notion. But at least I can't see them. Their deep voices and low laughter make me more paranoid than aroused. I just don't want to stare at them for too long and begin to fantasize. Because sometimes I'll try to turn those fantasies into realities. And I will not cheat on Loren Hale.

Not for anything.

I press my phone to my ear, the ringing incessant. "Pick up, pick up," I mutter under my breath. I hug my knees to my chest, practically in a scared, little ball.

"Hey, it's Lo."

"Lo—"

"Leave a message, and I *may* get around to calling you back. But really, you should just call me again. And if it's not important, then don't bother calling at all." *BEEP.*

"I hate that you haven't changed your stupid answering machine," I whisper angrily. "It tricks me every single time. And it's not nice."

A pair of jeans land near my desk. I jump, my eyes wide. They're undressed. One of them is without pants. Oh. My. God . . .

I shut off the phone and redial. Answering machine. I swallow hard and say under my breath, "Um, Lo, where are you? Bye." I hang up quickly, and I dial my sensible sister. The line rings twice before she answers.

"Are you okay?" Rose asks.

"Why is Lo not answering?" I wonder, biting my nails.

"He left his phone at the house." Her voice muffles as she pulls the receiver from her lips. "Okay, okay, Lo, I understand. Calm down." She huffs and then says louder, "Are the models already there?"

"Yep," I say, catching a glimpse of a pair of bare ankles and legs—which means that he can see me curled up here. But I don't dare move. "All nine Captain Americas have reported for duty. Where are you?" It's not like Rose to be late.

"Stuck in traffic," Rose tells me. "I told Connor I would pick up his dry cleaning, and there was a long line."

"You could have told Harold to do it," I say softly. The bare ankles are moving closer! I shut my eyes. *Go away. Go away.*

"I'd rather not use our mother's butler, thank you." Yes, I suppose that comes with some sort of stipulation. Like spending an extra couple of dinners in Villanova, and Rose already commits to Sunday get-togethers.

"Mmm-hmm." The legs pause, too close now.

"Lily . . ." Rose trails. "If you're uncomfortable, you can go wait in my office, okay? You don't have to be around those models."

I think it's too late for that.

The male model squats, and I am met with beautiful brown eyes, tan skin, and full dark hair, swept in a perfect way. He has charm in his blinding smile. He tilts his head. "What are you doing under there?"

"I work down here," I blurt out. I am roasting from head to toe.

He laughs a husky laugh.

"Lily." I flinch at the sound of Lo's voice, and I look over my shoulder, met with the back of the white desk. Right, I have the phone pressed to my ear.

"I'm Julian," the model says, extending his hand.

My palm is too sweaty. He'll think I'm weird if he shakes a slippery hand, so I point to my phone and give him a nervous smile. "Work stuff," I say.

"What's going on?" Lo asks through the receiver. "You okay, Lil?" His worried tone drives knots in my stomach. I don't want him to be concerned that I'll cheat. I know it's a valid fear, but I wish he could trust me one-hundred percent. But he can only do that when I begin to trust myself.

Julian says, "When you're finished, you should come out from under there. Your office has a great view."

I know he's just trying to be nice since I'm the antisocial monster hiding beneath her desk. He's not hitting on me, but I can't stop looking at his pretty eyelashes.

He stands, and I try to focus my thoughts on the phone call. "Lo?" I question whether he's hung up.

"Lil," he says slowly, "you're freaking me the fuck out."

"Sorry, I'm fine."

"Where are you?"

"At my desk." That's not a lie, right? Technically I am right here. "I just . . . thought you were going to be in the room too." I don't want to cheat on him. I don't want to even give my mind the ability to contemplate the thought—to wander and fantasize. That will kill me. Keeping them out of sight is best, even though it's not healthy to avoid the opposite sex when Lo's not around.

Once I have a handle on controlling the things that tempt me, it'll be better. Today's just not a good day. I am overly aroused.

"You don't have to talk to them," he reminds me.

Too late.

"I thought you said you were at your desk."

"I am."

"Then how come I don't see you?"

He's here? I can't even crawl out from underneath my desk anymore, not even to greet Lo and Rose. Because everyone by the muffins will laugh and look at me funny for being down here. I just want to stay hidden until they all leave.

"Maybe," I say, "because your superpower is to turn me invisible."

He pauses. "That's a horrible power. Take it back."

"Okay fine. I may be here. But I'm not *here* on my chair," I whisper.

And then I see a pair of ratted Vans. He bends in front of me the same way Julian did, but his face isn't full of kind amusement. His eyes darken, and his brows harden in concern.

"Go model or try on clothes or, you know, do what you do," I tell him. "Don't worry about me. I'm working on something down here."

"Like what?"

Uhhh . . . "A report . . . thing."

"Okay," he says, and I relax, glad that he's letting me off the hook. "Can I have a hug before I go?"

I crawl forward a little, still blocked by the desk sides, and I wrap my arms around him. He smells good. Like mint soap and a hint of citrusy cologne. Just before I let go, Lo's arms tighten around my waist, and he begins tugging me out of my sanctuary.

"Lo," I whisper fiercely. I shove his chest, trying to escape and crawl back to my den.

But he brings me into the light, and I bury my face in the crook of his arm, unwilling to meet the mocking gazes of the other models. I don't want people to look at me like I'm a weird, abnormal girl.

Lo strokes the back of my head, and his lips brush my ear. "Hey, you're okay. Lil, no one cares."

"I care," I mumble.

And then he clasps my face and before I can lose it, his lips touch mine. He kisses deeply, his tongue slipping into my mouth. My thoughts, my insecurities—they whoosh out of my head and all my built-up tension starts to tighten again.

The distraction works too well. Because when he draws back, a few of the models clap and whistle in jest. Lo shakes his head at me as my elbows blush.

"Don't listen to them." He rolls out my chair and guides me until I'm sitting behind my desk once more. And he hangs onto the back, his head dipping low as he meets my ear. "Just think of finishing that kiss tonight."

I turn my head a fraction to see his sharp features, all ice. "And what if I can't wait?"

"You can," he assures me, but his muscles flex, worried by my sudden claim.

"You're right," I say. "I can." I nod, knowing I have to. I have to wait in this chair, with my back to ten male models, and I have to finish double-checking my spreadsheet. I nod again, trying to build confidence.

He kisses my temple one last time, leaving me completely aching. And every so often, my arousal turns to embarrassment and shame. I wonder if any of those models can read my sinful thoughts—or if they just think I'm a bizarre girl. I shouldn't care about the latter, but being reminded that I'm not normal makes me feel . . . wrong and dirty.

After Rose assigns the models outfits, she stops by my desk. "You look flushed."

I shrug sheepishly. What else is there to say to that?

"You don't have to be here, Lily," she says. "You can go home early."

"I need to finish this." I tap my screen. "And I want to ride home with Lo."

"You're uncomfortable," she says.

I am, but I'm desperately trying to do the right thing here. I'm trying to be better. "It's okay."

She pats my shoulder. "If you change your mind, let me know. I won't be upset by it." She returns to the models, and she flocks Katie and Trish, making sure they're doing their jobs well.

After ten minutes, I regret drinking two mochas this morning. I have the worst urge to pee, and that means spending time alone in the bathroom. And hello, I'm aroused too, and the allure of self-love is overpowering like a drug.

I cannot squirm any longer in my seat. I don't want to attract more unnecessary attention to myself. So I stand and walk tentatively to the bathroom past both Trish's and Katie's workstations. I look over my shoulder just once, and I spot all the models pulling on sports coats, button-downs, collared shirts, and golf shorts, all of the clothes tailored and chic.

Lo meets my gaze. He's full of questioning. I mouth, *bathroom.* He nods, but he must see the need creeping over me like a cancer because his worry never disappears. But I can wait to have sex. I'll be fine, I try to convince myself.

I shut the door behind me, and after I finish on the toilet, I touch my panties, about to raise them around my thighs. But I hesitate for one strong second. Because the place between my legs throbs so badly, and I remember the blissful feeling if I just touch once. I'll be floating. I want that.

I shut my eyes and spend a great deal of time in a mental battle. I end up pulling on my panties, but my jeans stay around my ankles. I close the toilet lid and sit on the maroon suede covering. The bathroom smells like pine and cranberries, a glass vase of potpourri emitting the aroma.

It makes leaving ten times harder.

And then the door opens. *I forgot to lock it!* I internally shriek. I struggle with my jeans. "Someone's in here!" I shout, but the body slips inside anyway.

With his back to me, Lo locks the door and then turns around, catching me frozen—with my jeans midway up my legs, with the toilet seat closed.

"I didn't . . ." I start. Does he believe me?

I wouldn't. I've been caught with my pants down.

It looks like I didn't even try to wait. It looks like I gave up.

Twelve

Loren Hale

rub my lips, not sure what to make of Lily sitting on the toilet lid with her jeans halfway up her ankles. I worry about her heavy breath and the shakiness of her hands. She's an addict who needs her next fix.

"Lo, I didn't," she says again.

And I believe her this time. Tears threaten to spill down her cheeks, and I rush to her before she has a major breakdown. I squat to match her height, and I place my hands on her knees. "Hey, shh." I cup her face and rub a fallen tear with my thumb. "You're okay."

She shakes her head.

"Can you wait?" I ask her. "You have five more hours."

She shudders.

I can't watch her crumble like this. My lungs constrict, my whole chest clenching.

"You should go back," she says. "You're working."

I've changed out of the Calloway Couture clothes, and I wear my regular black shirt and jeans. "They're writing down the alterations for the other models. I have time." I'm supposed to be putting on my second outfit, but Rose is preoccupied with measurements and test shots. She won't miss me for long.

Lily stares at her hands in her lap, barely meeting my eyes. "I can wait," she says under her breath, so meek that I don't believe her for a second.

"Can you?" I ask.

She nods and wipes her nose with the back of her hand. I tuck her hair behind her ear, wanting so badly to pull her into my arms and to make it all better. But that's not how this new chapter of our lives is supposed to go, is it?

"I didn't have sex for three whole months," she says softly. "What's five hours?"

"This is different."

"Why?" she asks, her chin quivering. She so badly wants to grab me. I can see it in the way her eyes flit over my body for a brief moment. She catches herself and stares back at the floor.

"Because I wasn't there," I tell her. "You didn't have the opportunity to touch me. It was easier." I imagine three months without me was like being locked in a house without booze. If there's nothing to drink, then you're not going to get drunk. But there are always liquor stores. The same way there are always other guys to fuck. She also had the option to touch herself, but she's eliminated that completely. She stuck to her vows.

And I know that if I leave her like this, she'll break one by masturbating. She can't last five hours, and she won't ask me to have sex with her. So she'll be drawn to the next best thing, thinking that self-love is the right solution. She won't cheat on me. She'll just cheat on herself.

So while she sniffs and wipes her tears, I rack my mind for that damn blacklist with the therapist's rules. My head is fuzzy, distracted by Lily's constant trembling and the way her knees begin to turn inward.

"Lo," she cries. "I think you should leave."

My chest falls. "I'm not going anywhere."

And before she can refute, I kiss her. I part her lips with my tongue, and she clenches my shirt, her soft moans like *thank yous*.

Each one drives me harder, and my movements become as hungry as hers. I lift her in my arms, her legs instinctively wrapping around my waist. And I knock her back into the wall. Her voice is lost in the base of my neck, her forehead pressing to my shoulder.

"I need you," she whispers, panicked. "Please . . ." The fear in her voice cuts a new scar.

"Shh, love." I rub my hand through the back of her hair, and I nip her ear with my teeth. She shudders against me. I want her to release, but I feel like there's no winning with this one. If I let her go, she'll masturbate. If I fuck her, she'll hate herself. If I make her come, she'll still be filled with shame and guilt for not lasting five hours.

There is no right answer, no fucking break. And so each stroke against her flesh is seared with tension and a strong ache, my heart pounding like a jackhammer to cement.

And I kiss her again, my lips swelling beneath her eagerness, her insistency to push deeper, to go further. She runs her bitten nails across my back, not sharp enough to draw blood, not even long enough to truly scratch, but she digs her fingers into my skin. She grips so fiercely, as though I am two seconds from dropping her. From saying no.

My brain clicks, and the blacklist isn't hazy anymore. *We can't do this.* I retract my lips from her, and I don't meet her eyes.

I fucked up.

I want to punch the wall. I want to scream. More than anything, I want to go sit at a bar and forget the road I was about to pull Lily down. What the fuck is wrong with me?

"Lo . . ."

I bring her to her feet, and she wobbles unsteadily. I keep a hand on her waist, but there's considerable amount of distance between us.

"What did I do . . . ?" Her high-pitched voice lurches my stomach.

"Nothing," I say, tucking another piece of hair behind her ear.

"Then we can do something . . ." She grips my shirt again, clenching the fabric between two panicked fists.

I pry her fingers from me. "We can't have sex here, and I can't touch you here either." But she can't wait until tonight.

She nods rapidly. And as the news settles with her, she pulls her shoulders back like I've seen Rose often do. She raises her chin, trying to be strong. Christ, I want to kiss her for it and to apologize for tempting her even more. I should have taken her to our house where we can have sex. In fact, that's what we're going to do now.

"Grab your stuff," I tell her. "We're going home, and I'll make you come there." My tone isn't sexy. It's clinical. I just want her to be able to wait until we reach our bedroom.

I find her jeans on the ground, and I help put her legs in each pant hole.

"Wait," she says.

I don't want to give her the chance to convince me to have sex with her in the bathroom. It's not happening. I already screwed up by arousing her more—I don't need to break anything on that blacklist.

Public sex—yeah, that's not fucking allowed.

I zip up her jeans and fish the button through, towering over her with dominance that makes her squirm. I want to kiss her. God, I just want to hold her. But instead of drawing toward Lily, I have to draw back.

"Wait," she says again, more forceful this time. She grabs my wrist to stop me. "You're not going home."

"I'm not leaving you," I say. I don't add that I don't trust her. Her fingers may slip into her panties; she may give herself what I've denied.

"You're *working*," she reminds me, tears building again. "I'm not ruining your first job." She inhales a strong breath and adds, "I'll stay at my desk, and when you're done working, we can go."

I hesitate.

"You should only be one more hour. I can wait that long."

"Plus the ride home," I remind her.

She nods quickly. "Yes, yes."

I like this option. Mostly because Lily came up with the idea, and it'll lessen whatever guilt she'll feel for not being able to wait tonight.

"Okay." I kiss her cheek. And she sighs, but as she walks to the door, the tension becomes apparent in the way her thighs press together.

I lead her out of the bathroom, and we enter the loft space where Trish and Katie fling clothes at each other, fixing the garments on the models quickly. I look around for Rose, but she's nowhere in sight.

Lily keeps her eyes pinned to the desk and nowhere else. "I'll be okay," she says, more to herself than me.

"I know you will."

I watch her make the short journey to her desk. She slides into her chair and studies her computer screen, focused and concentrated. Maybe it's all a facade. But I know she's trying damn hard.

Thirteen

Loren Hale

I need to find Rose to tell her that I'm leaving right after I finish with the fitting. There aren't many places she could be. Besides her glass office, there's only the backroom. I saunter down the short hallway, my shoulders stiff. I stuff my fists in my pockets so they'll stop shaking. I feel high on fear and concern, my adrenaline spiked badly. I just need a drink.

Her icy voice echoes from an open door. I rest my arm on the frame, my eyes darting around the dimly lit area that's filled with marked boxes, racks of clothes, and clear plastic tubs. Rose has her back to me, a phone pressed to her ear.

"I don't want to have this conversation with you right now. We have a photo shoot next week and a runway show in two months—"

"Which is precisely why I called." I'd recognize Samantha Calloway's biting voice from the fucking moon. I'm not surprised that she called her daughter. She's been involved with Rose's company from its birth.

"Don't start," Rose warns her. "This isn't going to end well, Mother."

"You're right. It's not going to end well for you. I have helped your father market Fizzle for twenty years. What you're doing is going to *ruin* Calloway Couture."

"He's just a model!" Rose shouts. "He's not the face of the company."

I freeze.

"He's an alcoholic," Samantha retorts. "And his face will be plastered in magazines and billboards next to your brand. Your company will suffer for it."

It suddenly feels hot in here. I tug at the collar to my shirt. *Why is it so fucking hot?*

"And who sees Loren Hale and immediately thinks *alcoholic*? Your friends? Because I sure as hell don't know anyone else in this fucking country who would give a shit." Venom laces Rose's words.

"Don't speak to me that way. I'm your mother, and it's my job to give you advice."

"I hear it," Rose says. "Your advice, while I know you mean well, is judgmental and cold. Loren will be a model in the campaign. He'll be in photos, runway shows, and commercials, so if you have a problem with that, then turn off the television, divert your eyes, but don't scold me."

Samantha Calloway sighs. "Is there anything that can change your mind, Rose? You're making a very big mistake."

"Nothing," she says.

"Well then, I'll see you Sunday." She pauses. "I'm sorry I yelled."

Rose sighs just as heavily. "Me too." They both hang up, and when Rose spins around, she jumps back, her hand to her chest in surprise. "Lo, I . . ."

"Don't," I say with a bitter smile that turns into a grimace. "Look, I didn't know that my role in your company would impact you nega—"

"It doesn't," she interjects. "She's just overdramatic."

All these feelings scorch my insides, and if I don't speak my mind now, I'm going to be driven down the street to a place I shouldn't go. "Your mother is right," I tell her, the words sinking low. "And I won't screw with your career just because I need some cash. I'll find another way."

"Don't," Rose tells me now. She holds a manicured finger directly at my face. "You're *staying*."

"I'm not." I can't stay. I can't fuck up another Calloway's life with my problems. Lily is so much a part of me that there's no disentangling from her now, but Rose—I'm not going to trap her inside my vice. I'm not going to lead her down this dark path that I walk on.

I turn to leave, and Rose grabs my arm. "You need this job."

I jerk out of her grip. "I appreciate your help, I do, but you have to let me go."

"I can't," she says with such determination. "I promised you this job, and you'd still be here if it wasn't for that phone call."

I shrug. "Yeah? Shit happens, Rose. One day, I was an only child, and the next, I have a brother and an empty bank account. I've learned to deal." I'm about to cross through the door, but she slides in front of me, blocking my exit.

"I won't beg you to stay," she tells me.

"Good," I snap. "Then we have an understanding." I go to pass her, but she extends her arm, trapping me. "Rose."

"You haven't even tried, Loren. You're giving up."

Veins pulse in my neck, and I lean in low. "Rose," I sneer, "for a girl who cannot stomach a crying baby, who wouldn't be able to empathize with a child if she tugged on your goddamn sleeve, you *really* should stop trying to understand the human race." My words cut deep. Rose has been incredibly open-minded since she learned about Lily's addiction. She's been there for her every single minute of the day, and I know she would drop her whole schedule if I asked her to.

But I just need her to let me go—to realize that she's lost this battle. For a girl who always wins, that's a tough one to swallow.

Rose purses her lips and then she relents by edging out of the doorway. "If you change your mind—"

"I won't." I can't even tell her thank you. I realize I am back to square one. Jobless and without a real plan.

"I'll write you a check for your time today."

I nod. "Just don't overpay. I'll be able to tell." If anyone is going to *accidentally* hand out more money, it's going to be Rose and Connor. But I don't want to accept their charity. Not because I'm too prideful. I just want to prove to myself that I can do this on my own.

Her eyes darken, so I know that's exactly what she planned on doing. I pat her arched shoulder, and I head back into the main room. Lily's forehead is almost pressed to the computer. I walk up to her, noticing that her nose touches the screen.

I smile. God, I can't believe I'm *smiling* after all that has happened. The fact that this girl can upturn my lips after such a bad day makes me never want to let her go. "Are you planning on eating your spreadsheet?" I ask her. "Or are you trying to disappear into cyberspace?"

Her cheeks rose, and she leans back. "I was making sure my numbers were right." Her eyes trail my body. "Shouldn't you be in a collared shirt?"

"Nah," I say. "It's not my style." I reach out and hold her hand. "Come on, let's go."

She frowns. "But, you're not done with work yet."

"I quit," I tell her.

Her face twists in so many emotions. "Not . . . not for me, right? Lo, you can't." She points to the muffins. "Go back."

"Lil," I say softly, bringing her to her feet, my hands at her waist. "I'll explain everything in the car. But you have to trust me that none of this is because of you, okay? It's my choice."

"Did Rose . . . ?" She looks over my shoulder, ready to dart toward her sister and convince her that I should stay. But she has it backward.

"Rose wants me here. I don't want to be."

Lily processes the words. "Okay . . . okay, so we're going?"

I nod.

"You promise you'll tell me why? And you won't lie to me?"

"No lying," I assure her. We have to be honest. It's the one thing we need to be good at.

She leans over her keyboard, closes out Excel, and shuts down her computer.

As Lily steps forward, she whips her head from side to side, paranoid that someone can see straight through her—that they can tell just how aroused she is. They can't. But I sure as hell can.

I swoop in behind her, my hands planted on her waist, and my lips brush her ear. "Want a ride?"

She brightens almost immediately. I don't wait for her to say yes. I crouch a little in front of her, and I lift her up on my back. She holds tight around my neck, and I keep my arms underneath her legs, willing to carry her as far as she needs to go—just like when we were kids.

Some things never change.

Fourteen

Loren Hale

I finish telling Lily about the phone call between Rose and their mother about the same time that we reach the parking deck. Lil still clings to my back like a koala bear to a tree, and I wish I didn't have to set her down. But I drop her onto her feet while I search my pockets for the keys to her car.

"I'm glad you told me," she says, no judgment in her eyes, just complete understanding. I'm about to kiss her, but I remember that she's aroused, her eyes glazed for something more than just a peck on the cheek.

She holds on to my belt loop with two fingers, silently tugging me toward her body. I don't even think she realizes that she's doing it.

Right as I fish out the keys and unlock the doors, she lets out a sharp breath and scuttles behind my back.

"Hide me," she whispers, gripping the hem of my shirt and using my body as a shield.

"What?" I frown and scan the dark parking deck.

"Is that Lily Calloway?" a guy says, not even twenty feet from us. He just opened his Jeep door and climbed out, a couple spaces to the right of Lily's vehicle. He walks toward us, and I spot a Penn soccer sticker on his gas cap.

The guy looks vaguely familiar. He has tan skin, and his trim build matches soccer players. But I can't place him. Not yet. He's swimming in a fog.

Lily reveals herself now that she's been sighted. "Hi . . ."

"Do you remember me?" he asks, his eyes briefly flickering to me and then back to Lil. I know, just by the way that he's looking at her, that they've had sex.

If I was tense before, I'm wired now, my muscles tightening into taut strands. I'm used to being the one who knocks on Lily's door in the morning and escorts her one-night stand out of our apartment. I'd even grab the poor guy a cup of coffee. But he's not a face that I remember being charitable to. I don't think he ever stepped foot in our old apartment.

"Yeah," Lily says, reaching for my hand. She holds it tightly, and I do her one better. I wrap my arm around her shoulders. She relaxes only a little, and the guy—well, he acts oblivious to my claim over her. Do I really need to wave a giant flag that says BOY-FRIEND in his fucking face?

He nods. "I was just thinking about you the other day." His eyes rake her body. Is he serious? I'm standing right *here*. I glare so hard that my eyes start to burn.

"Lo," Lily says, "this is Mason Nix. Remember that frat party we went to our freshman year?" We went to a lot of parties when we were eighteen. I feel like I've shelved this memory so far back that it's going to take an hour to find.

"Right," I say vaguely, still drilling holes into Mason. He meets my gaze but looks completely unaffected by my warning. What's this guy's deal?

"Anyway, it's funny that I'm running into you, Lily. I was going to call you yesterday—"

"You have her number?" I question.

"Yeah," he says, his lips rising. "And I have yours. Loren Hale, right? She gave me your number too, said something about how she always loses track of her phone."

She must have been drunk. Lil doesn't usually give out her number or mine. She said it "promotes stalking"—which clearly seems to be the case.

My blood ices over, and my hand on Lily's shoulder suddenly feels like a weight. So he has her number, and mine. He has the ability to text us, but he hardly seems vindictive toward me, definitely not enough to threaten Lily.

He licks his lips and nods to her. "So, I was thinking you'd want to hook up later." *What?* "Maybe tomorrow, around eight. Same frat house, same place. If you want to be fucked hard, I'm your guy."

Lily balks. "I . . ."

"No," I sneer. "She's my girlfriend, you asshole."

Mason lets out a short laugh. "That's funny." He looks back at Lily, waiting for her response.

Am I invisible? Am I not speaking clearly? I don't fucking get it! I step in front of Lily, letting go of her hand. "She's my *girlfriend*. You're *never* going to fuck her."

"I *already* did," he retorts.

My jaw locks, and I clench my fingers into a fist.

"So what do you say, Lily? If I'm not enough for you, I can call up some of my buddies. I know you like that."

The memory hits me all at once—the one I tried to suppress. And I have the sudden urge to vomit until I pass out. I can't even talk about it. I can't mention what happened or else I think I may explode. I may beat him until he can't stand on two legs. And it's not his fault for what happened. Not really. It's mine for not stopping Lily.

For not holding her in my arms and telling her that I truly loved her. That I would be enough, and I'd quit drinking so she'd quit fucking other guys. That's all I had to do. Choose her before alcohol. And I picked wrong for so many years.

He tries to step toward her, and I put a hand on his chest, pushing him back. Things have changed. "She's with me. She's not going to fuck you. If you can't understand that, then go read a damn book to understand the English language."

"And she was your girlfriend two years ago. That didn't stop her before. In fact, you waved her toward me."

I want to strangle my past drunken neck. Our fake relationship is coming back to haunt me. "That was different. She's not seeing anyone else but me now. So fuck off."

Mason lets out another laugh. "There's no way that girl is only with you." He knows. He knows she has a problem. And I wonder if he sent those texts. He was thinking about her recently, didn't he say that?

"Were you really thinking about Lily the other day, or were you just blowing smoke?"

He smiles as though I've given him permission to pursue her. Over my dead fucking corpse. "I mentioned her to my friends a couple weeks ago. We were talking about the girls at Penn who give the best head. Everyone agreed she was the best cocksucker on campus."

And I can't help it.

I deck him. Right in the face.

It didn't feel good. My knuckles are on fire, and Mason touches his split lip, shocked.

Lily comes up behind me and starts tugging my arm, trying to lead me to our car.

I follow her, walking backward so he doesn't break my sharp gaze.

And then he says, "I knew it."

I stop. My face falls because the look he wears—it's full of detest, but it's the kind of hate that's been there for a while, cumulated throughout the years. He should be pissed about that punch to the jaw, not something so deep-seated.

"You were the one who slashed our tires because we fucked your girlfriend." *We*. I cringe, never ever wanting to hear that again. *We*. Not *I*. Not *me*. Multiple guys.

And I may have popped a tire or two. I was drunk. I was eighteen. And I was pissed and resentful, more at myself than at anyone else. But I took it out on this guy. And I buried the memory.

"Have you been texting me?" I glare.

Mason grits his teeth.

Lily tries to drag me off again, but I stay my course.

"Have you?!" I shout. What I did—that was two years ago. But there are some things that no guy can let go. This is probably one of them.

"Bye, Lily," Mason says, his eyes only planted on me. "We'll hook up soon, yeah? And maybe I won't tell anyone else what a good little slut you are."

I shake off Lily, and I go crazy. I grab him by the face, pinching his cheeks together with one furious hand, and I shove his back over the hood of Lil's car.

He struggles to stand up from my hold, but I pin him down, my kneecap pressing into his dick.

"You touch her, you even *think* about her, and I'll have you in the ground before you can say *thank you, Loren Hale*. You go to the media, the press, and I will ruin you, starting with your soccer career. You don't even know who I am, you motherfucker."

He spits in my face, and I throw him off the car and onto the cement.

I think he's about to come back and tackle me, but he staggers to his feet.

I don't give him the last word. Lily physically pushes me into the passenger seat, knowing that I'm too crazed to drive right now. And she rolls up the window while Mason begins yelling again.

We can't hear him in the car, but he smacks our hood with two fists as we pull out.

And then we drive off, his middle finger in the rearview mirror.

My hands shake, and my heart pumps a mile a minute.

Lily says nothing. She stares far away at the road, the silence blanketing the car. I need a drink. I need a goddamn drink right now. I run my hand through my hair, and then I glance back at her, checking her state of mind . . . and body.

Her eyes glass, but her knees are locked together, and her leg bounces. Fuck. I forgot. We're on our way home to have sex. I lean back, hitting the headrest with an exasperated sigh. Everything is just so far out of my control.

When we're stuck in traffic, bumper to bumper, Lily finally breaks the quiet. "You slashed their tires?"

I rub my mouth. "I may have . . ." It was a long time ago. We just entered college. There were more guys for her to fuck. She was gone almost every night, and I worried about whether or not she'd wake up crying. Whether I'd find her bruised and disposed of. It was horrible.

She nods to herself, letting this sink in. "What if he wasn't the guy texting us?" she asks. "You just made him angrier."

"Yeah . . . I see that." I didn't think running into her one-night stands would be this hard. I also didn't think they'd ask to sleep with her while I was present. That sucked.

Lily breathes heavily.

"Hey," I say, leaning toward her. I slide my hand on her leg. "It's okay. We're going to be fine."

She nods, trying to believe it as much as me. If I don't find this guy soon, I'll lose my mind. I think I'm about there.

She turns on the radio, and we listen to music all the way home, our breath slowing together. Sometime later, we finally reach the house and pull into the garage. Lily snaps off her belt and turns to me.

"I don't need to have sex anymore. I'm okay now." Her words sound practiced, like she's been reciting them in her head for the past hour.

"I don't believe you," I tell her.

Her face pales. "No, really, Lo, I'm fine."

My eyes fall to her legs, her thighs pressed tightly together. "So if we're not having sex anymore, what are you going to go do?"

She shrugs, her shoulders tense and locked. She's so fucking aroused. *Just admit it, Lily.* "Maybe . . . take a shower."

"And masturbate?"

Her eyes widen. "No-no," she stammers. "No, just shower."

I lean forward and finger the button on her jeans.

"What . . . what are you doing?" she asks. Her chest collapses with a heady breath, something that has my need building.

"I'm checking."

"For what?" she asks in a small voice.

I unzip her, and I watch her eyes plant on my hand as it descends down her pants and underneath her panties. She grabs my wrist as I slip my fingers inside of her. And she contracts around them, wet and eager and so ready.

"You're not aroused?" I ask again.

Her head tilts back, her eyes closed, her hand gripping my wrist so I don't move. "No," she breathes.

"You're a little liar."

"I'm not." She gasps as I push deeper, in and out. "Lo," she cries. Her back begins to arch, trying to drive my fingers farther inside.

We need to move this upstairs. I disentangle from her tight clutch and slip my fingers out. "Go upstairs," I tell her. "Take off all your clothes, lie still on the bed, and I'll make you feel better."

She nods wildly, wanting nothing more than for me to take her mind off of what just happened. She opens the door and then hesitates. "Are you not coming with me?"

"I'll be there in a second."

"Lo—"

"I just need a minute."

She glances at the raw skin on my knuckles, and then she nods again and heads into the house. When the door closes behind her, I grab my phone and dial a number.

The line clicks after the third ring. "Hey. How was the first day on the job?"

I can't speak. I shouldn't have called him. I'm about to hang up.

"Lo?" Ryke's voice turns serious. "Hey, talk to me."

I let out a breath. "Tell me why I shouldn't." I pinch my eyes. I want this to end. This torment. These feelings. I want to help Lily without needing something to drown my own thoughts.

"Because one drink isn't worth what you'll feel in the morning."

"That's not good enough."

"You'll puke," he reminds me. That's right, I'm on Antabuse. One sip of alcohol and I'll be sick.

I pause, wondering if I still could test it out. Maybe I could. I grimace. Maybe I couldn't.

"Because you love Lily more than *that*."

And it hits me. I'm here. In the fucking car. Debating about a stupid glass of alcohol when Lily is waiting for me upstairs, fighting her compulsions, probably seconds from touching herself. And I'm supposed to be there to help her say no. To stop her. I'm the guy looking out for her the way Ryke is there for me.

Rose trusted that I would be able to stay sober and help Lily. And this is the one thing I want to do right.

"I have to go," I say.

"Wait." His voice pitches. "Do I need to come over? Are you okay?"

"Yeah, don't come over."

"Are you sure?"

"Ryke, unless you want to walk in on me fucking my girlfriend, you need to stay at home."

There's a long pause, and then, "See you tomorrow?"

"Yep." We both hang up.

And I step out of the car.

Ready to help Lily. Ready to be there.

Ready to change.

Fifteen

Lily Calloway

pace back and forth in the kitchen. I'm a ball of string that needs to be unwound, an anxious mess and a compulsive freak. I didn't follow Lo's orders to retreat upstairs to our room and shed my clothes.

I stay right beside the back door, pressing my ear occasionally to the wood, waiting for him, hoping and praying that he's not doing something bad and dangerous. I bite my nails, listening carefully at the sound of shuffled footsteps.

In the car, he looked like he wanted to sink and drown to the bottom of a dark, cold ocean. And I can't let him do that. I can't let him go.

The car door slams.

I peel my ear away and scuttle backward, not quick enough. The door swings open and Lo catches me right here in the kitchen, disobeying his orders. A horrible, insane part of me wonders if he'll hate that I care about him, if he'll reprimand me for it.

I blurt out, "I'm sorry. I was just worried, and you looked upset . . ." I trail off while he stays stationary near the wall, his cheekbones sharpening. And I imagine what could have happened if he drank, if he did something worse in that garage. If he left me.

For real this time.

The truest deepest part of me suddenly speaks.

"I don't know how to live without you." And I shake my head quickly as tears pool. "And I don't want to know how. I don't want to find out."

He is my breath. My soul. My life force. I have spent forever with him. Being apart is the most unnatural feeling in the world. Three months—I could handle that like a bad itch. Forever *without* him? *Just kill me now.*

He slowly walks to me, and his hand skims my cheek, his eyes never softening, his sharp demeanor never changing. He's Loren Hale. Ice and whiskey. Powerful and intoxicating.

He's my very best friend.

His forehead presses to mine, his lips so near. In a low whisper, he says, "You'll never have to find out, Lil."

I ache to kiss him, to solidify those words as truth.

His lips nearly brush mine, but he teases, a sliver of space tempting me and causing tension to build between us. His amber eyes flicker to me. "I will never learn how to live without you. I couldn't fucking bear it."

I grip his arms, keeping him close. This feels imagined, like a part of my fantasies. But I'm touching him, cut muscles, his legs against my legs. I let out a breath. "And what if everyone says we shouldn't be together—that it's not right?" Every person has to learn to live alone at some point in their life. *Why do we?* I always wonder. *Because it's right*, my conscience says. *But I love him.* But you're codependent. *But I love him.* But it's not okay.

I want our love to be right.

Why can't it be right?

"No," he immediately says, holding my face in two large hands. "If the whole world says living without each other is what we should do, then this will be the last wrong I make."

Yes.

We connect to each other fully, his lips touching mine in passionate desperation, as though two people are literally trying to pull us apart, as though we're giving them the middle finger, telling them to fuck off.

Fuck off. I love Loren Hale. I can't live without him. However silly that may be, it is the undying truth. Even if he was with another girl. Even if we never could touch. I could not live without Lo. He is as much a part of me as the sun is a part of the sky, as the Earth is to the universe.

I need him in order to wake up in the morning.

I need him to feel whole.

He clutches my hair, the long kiss stealing my breath. And without warning, he picks me up and throws me over his shoulder. Oh God. His hand grips my ass as he carries me out of the kitchen and up the stairs.

My heart has traveled to my throat.

On the second level, he opens the bedroom door and tosses me roughly on the mattress.

I struggle to catch the air that escapes my lungs, and when I do, I prop my body on my elbows and watch him watch me.

He unzips his jeans, never breaking my gaze. His shirt comes off next, uncovering his defined muscles that beckon me to touch. I undress with the same mastered efficiency, breathing so heavily that my ribs jut out and in with quick succession.

In this moment, I have no desire to touch myself. I want him on me. In me. I can wait for his hands, for his body, for his breath.

So I watch him as he walks to the nightstand, only in black boxer briefs while I stay completely bare. He opens the drawer.

I sit on my knees, my eyes widening in delighted anticipation.

When he shuts it, my mouth drops a little. "I thought . . ." *you were just getting a condom.* "Are those . . . ?" I'm imagining them. This has to be a fantasy. "Where'd you find those?" I would have seen silver handcuffs in our room! I would have jumped for joy and paraded them around like they were a bag of galleons.

He climbs onto the bed, on his knees in front of me, towering over my small frame. His lips lift in a devious smile. "A little black box," he tells me.

"I need to start opening more boxes," I say in a breathless whisper. "Are you going to cuff me to you?"

His grin lights up his whole face. "No, love." And then he lifts me by the waist and sets me closer to our pillows. He clips one cuff around my wrist and then the other to a rung in the headboard.

Ohhh . . . my . . .

"Don't move," he instructs as he slips off his boxer briefs. When he lowers his body against mine, I instinctively run my free hand across his shoulder, his bicep, sliding my fingers along his abs toward his cock.

He grabs my hand before I reach the best place. He shakes his head at me once in disapproval, but his lips betray him, rising as he soaks in my eager gaze.

"No touching," he says, his voice forceful. He climbs *off* the bed, leaving me cold and alone on the mattress.

"Wait, I won't—I promise." *Come back.*

He disappears into the closet, and I wonder if this is a test that my therapist concocted. Is he supposed to leave me wanting and craving? Am I supposed to overpower this compulsive demon while I am in desperate *need*?

I'm going to fail.

I already know it.

I bite my lip, weight crashing into me. I stay entirely still, expecting Lo to walk out fully dressed, to wave goodbye and go meet Ryke somewhere. This was all a game to get me to this point, imprisoned on my bed with only one hand for use.

And then he exits.

But he's naked, like before.

He holds a scarf, and I can barely process what this means. My head floats away as the bed rocks, as he edges near me, lifts my other hand, and ties my free wrist to the headboard.

I am not as excited as before, mainly because I just freaked out.

When Lo looks back down at me, his smile fades into dark concern. "Hey, Lil . . ." His thumb skims my cheek. "You're okay." He must recognize the fear in my eyes. "I won't ever desert you, love. Not for a goddamn moment. You're mine to take care of, you understand?"

His words instantly fill my heart. I nod quickly. "Yes."

"I'm going to take care of you now. I'm going to fill you so deep that you're going to wish you could touch me, but you can't." *Yes.* "You're going to come each time I slip in." *Yes.* "You're going to ask me to stop to catch your breath." *Yes.* "I won't."

Please.

His hand descends to the spot between my legs, wet and ready. He spreads my legs open with his knees, and his fingers pulse inside of me. I writhe and buck up to try to meet him. But he contains me on the mattress; he softens my jagged, impatient movements with a hand to my hip.

I try to reach forward and run my fingers through his hair, but the silky scarf stops me, and the hard cuff digs into my other wrist. He dictates the position, the speed, the tempo of our love.

He replaces his fingers with his long, thick cock, so big for me, and I cry out, jerking against the restraint. He keeps my legs spread open and bends my knees. When he leans forward to kiss me, his whole cock slowly dives into me, no space to breathe.

I let out a staggered moan that turns sharp and needy. His lips hover right over my parted ones, and he rubs the sweaty hair out of my face.

In a low, husky voice, he whispers, "Every inch of me is inside of you."

"Lo," I cry. I want to touch him. I want to wrap my arms around his shoulders and never let go.

He doesn't pull out or rock just yet. He stays deep, my need building fiercely. He breathes just as heavily as me, nearly kissing, nearly shifting, but he remains in this single, taunting position that has my nerves singing.

"Tell me the first thing that comes to your head," he says.

In an aching whisper, I say, "I love you."

His eyes graze me with sheer want. "How much do you love me?"

"So much."

"How badly do you want me?"

"So badly," I say with a short gasp. "Please."

"How do I feel inside of you?"

I struggle to form words, my toes beginning to curl, my muscles spindling.

"Lily?" he says forcefully.

". . . Good." I manage to sputter.

"How good?"

I shake my head. I can't describe. "You're unlike anyone . . ." He's my best friend. My best friend is all the way inside of me. If I think back years ago, when I wouldn't allow myself to even fantasize about this moment, I would have died and come right there.

He slowly slips back and then slowly slips in. I shudder as soon as he fills me again. "How was that?" he asks with a growing smile. He knows *exactly* how that was.

"I can't . . ."

"You can't what?"

"Breathe." I can breathe, of course—I'm talking. But it feels like my lungs are about to explode.

"I'm not stopping," he reminds me. *Please don't ever.* He slips out the same way for the second time, and when he eases himself completely inside of me, my cries must breach the walls of our bedroom.

"Lo, Lo, Lo!" I repeat in hurried succession. I constrict around him once and then twice.

He lets out a deep groan, his mouth parting like mine, unable to tease me with a lingering kiss any longer. "Lil," he says, sitting up off my body to see the way he disappears between my legs. I want to see that too, but Lo shifts even farther forward, and I constrict again. Holy . . .

My back arches, and I tug against the cuff and the scarf, the metal digging into my skin, the sharpness reminding me of Lo, igniting something intense within me.

Even as I come, I prepare for him to pull out and say *enough is enough*. One peak is all you get, Lily.

But he continues that mocking routine. Slipping out so very slowly. Slipping in so very slowly. Stopping, waiting, watching me.

And I come again.

He's bursting every nerve in my body. He's causing my world to spin.

And I can see how much he's waiting for his release, how his own peak closes in, and how he restrains himself from coming, from ending this. Each time I tighten around his cock, he groans and finds a way to stay sane, to stay back in order to help me. In order to allow me to reach this place many, many times.

He's filling my every single need.

He's taking care of me.

Only Lo can satisfy every part of my all-consuming soul.

He is truly my everything.

Sixteen

Loren Hale

The therapist's office rests in the heart of New York City, and on the ride here, Lily can't keep her legs from bouncing. I've spent three months spilling my guts to doctors and psychologists; one sex therapist isn't going to scare me off. I just wish I could take away Lily's nerves.

I told her it won't be weird—that this lady has probably heard some wild things—but it wasn't enough to stop her head from whipping toward the door like she was ready to fling herself out.

I take her hand, intertwining her fingers with mine. Her shoulders slacken and she turns to look at me, releasing a giant breath at the same time. I can't help but smile. She's cute, even when she doesn't mean to be.

After paying the cab, a tense elevator ride, and a short walk down the hall, we wait in a small area that looks more like a modern living room: glass bookshelves and light streaming through long windows. The office door swings open, and the therapist motions us inside. A leather couch sits along the coffee-colored wall, and a robust black leather chair lies directly across.

As she takes a seat with a little notebook in hand, I embed her looks in my mind. I'm not sure how I pictured Lily's sex therapist, but she definitely wasn't middle-aged with a short black bob. The woman is even tinier than Lily, probably no taller than five feet.

"You must be Loren." She extends her hand before I sit on the couch. "I've heard so much about you."

I shake hers and then settle beside Lily, my arm curving around her waist. And I watch the therapist, seeing if she notices the touch and if she's going to criticize me for it. She doesn't say a word, but her eyes do catch our embrace.

"It's actually Lo," I correct her. "Obviously Lily didn't tell you everything." My words taste nasty in my mouth, and they sound even worse.

And yet, the therapist smiles good-naturedly.

I don't know why this irritates me. I wish she'd snap at me like Rose does for being rude and insolent.

I glance out the window. Her vast view of the city probably costs a shit ton—especially with a park directly in sight.

Of course Rose picked out the most expensive therapist in a hundred-mile radius. Not that money means anything to Lily. But I wouldn't be able to afford having a cracker with . . . I read her name on the plaque of the oak desk. *Dr. Allison Banning.*

Lily never mentions her by first name, always referring to her as "Dr. Banning," but if I have to expose my personal feelings to someone, I don't want to act like she's a complete stranger.

"So Allison . . ." I watch her cross her ankles and focus her whole attention on me. No wonder Rose liked her. "Do you get many sex addict, alcoholic couples?"

"You're my first."

"Shocking."

Lily elbows me in the side, and I can't tell if it's because of my sarcasm or because I called her Allison. The therapist stays unblinking, already mastering that complacent face and cool exterior. She could give Connor Cobalt a run for his money.

"Why don't you tell me how it's been since you moved home?" Allison asks me.

"About sex or in general?"

Lily turns a bright shade of red and slumps in her seat. I'm more comfortable talking about fucking, not because I have a dick or because she's shy—even though she kind of is—but because I'm not the sex addict. I don't feel ashamed about sex. She does.

I raise my arm to her shoulders, and she eases into my body a little, relaxing more.

"Either one," Allison tells me. Her eyes flicker between Lily and me with rapt attention now. She's definitely going to pick apart every single movement we make. "You decide."

Lily opens her mouth, but I cut her off on purpose. I don't want her to dodge the subject. "We had sex a few days ago," I confess. Explaining my inability to be with Lily without arousing her— well, it feels like walking through quicksand. And so I purposefully keep it short, direct, to the point. She doesn't need to know the messy details.

Like how she couldn't wait until the night. How, after an hour, I had to pry myself off her to stop. She was satisfied, but with Lily, it's a momentary fulfillment. It leaves the second she wishes to feel a climax again. I wanted to fuck her as much as she wanted to be fucked, but I had to watch her face crumble as she realized that was it.

For the first time, I'm looking at the bigger picture—the future—but Christ, no one ever mentioned how I'd have to endure preliminary pain to get there.

"You had sex a few days ago," Allison repeats. "What exactly happened?"

"I put my penis in her vagina." Embarrassment and remorse swim with the black tar in my chest. My filter—it's permanently on the fritz. I think my father must have busted it one night. But not with his fists. He's too civilized for that.

Lily lets out a laugh, which makes me feel a little better.

"Not anatomically," Allison clarifies. "Did you only have missionary? How long did it last? What time of day? And how did it end? What were your feelings afterward?"

So many fucking questions, but I take them one at a time. "Only missionary. It was about seven o'clock."

Lily immediately reddens at the time of day.

My eyes narrow, knowing full well that I just got caught by Lil's ability to turn into a cherry.

"It's best if you don't lie," Allison tells me.

"It was around three," I say with a shrug. "She couldn't wait until later, but she did hold out until we got home."

Allison nods. "That's really good, Lily."

She brightens a little at the compliment, and I squeeze her shoulder, realizing that my words don't hold the same power as her therapist. To hear a professional say *You're doing good* must be a relief.

I wouldn't know, really. Even though I learned a lot, most of the people at rehab wanted me out of there. And my therapist stares at me like I'm a world-class fuck up. And Ryke—well, compliments from him aren't worth much. He's trying to make amends for being absent in my life, for leaving me alone with a father that he knew ranked low on the World's Best Dad chart.

"And what happened afterward?" Allison asks.

"I pulled away from her," I say, "but she tried to keep going. I ended up just holding her in my arms until she fell asleep."

The brief happiness in Lily's eyes begins to flicker out, replaced by silent humiliation once more.

"You didn't fall asleep with her?"

I frown. "What does it matter if I did or didn't?" I don't understand how this pertains to Lily. I shift on my seat, and Lily turns her attention to me. I don't like that at all.

"You have a problem too," Allison says, "and your addiction will affect her. It already has."

I cut her off. "I get it. I should stay away from her. I should say goodbye and let her have a fighting chance."

Lily's eyes widen, and she clenches my shirt between pallid fingers.

Even thinking about letting her go puts a pain so deep in my gut. No one knows me like Lily Calloway. She's my best friend, and without her—God, what's the point?

"No," Allison says flatly. "I was going to say that I'm here for you too, Lo. Your recovery is congruent with Lily's. In order for her to be healthy, you need to be as well." She pauses, glancing only once at her notebook. "I don't think separation is the right action here. Without a monogamous relationship, Lily may fall back into her old routine, and it's best to strengthen the one that's already in place, not destroy it."

I nod, her words slowly sinking in. I wait for the relief, but it barely hits me. I think all my happiness is buried beneath the torment of what's to come.

"So," she begins again, "why didn't you fall asleep with her?"

I lick my lips, more willing to clear my thoughts now that I know she's on our side. "Sleep has been really difficult for me lately. It takes me longer than Lily." My leg jostles a little, and Lily is the one to press her hand to my knee, to give me much-needed comfort, even though I'd rather be her rock right now. "Every night for years," I say, "I'd drink until I passed out. Alcohol—that was my sleeping pill." It was the very thing that stopped my restless thoughts and tucked me into bed. Without it, I'm constantly exhausted.

Allison asks me why that is, and I explain my alcohol dependency. Though I give her brief details, not wanting to focus the whole session on me. So I'm glad when Allison directs her next question to Lil.

"How did it make you feel when he told you to stop?"

A long pause strains the air.

Lily is weighing the truth with a lie. It's what we do. We construct a pleasant story to mask the pain, to soften the hurt. We're both so good at it that sometimes we even begin to believe the lies ourselves. I am terrified to travel down that road again, but it's an easy one to take.

She opens her mouth and then closes it, unsure.

"It's okay," I prod. Even if the truth is ugly and cold, I want to hear it. I'm ready for us to lay everything out until we're completely bare and exposed. I don't know how else to make this work.

Allison rewords the question, softening its existence. "It won't be the first or last time he's going to tell you to stop. Now is a good time to talk about your reaction to the situation. So how did it make you feel, Lily?"

She only hesitates a second. "Not good." Her eyes land on her knees, and her shoulders curve forward. She looks small and sad and very, very heartbroken.

A wave of emotions slams into me, and I have trouble picking each one apart.

"And I just . . ." she stammers. ". . . I don't want to be *that* girl. The one who begs for something she knows she can't get. It's like I'm asking a boy I like on a date and he says no, but I don't listen, and I just keep asking and asking like the answer will be different. I feel . . . pathetic."

I don't ever want to make her feel like that.

"You're not pathetic, Lil," I manage to say, my throat swollen. I pull her into my arms and kiss the top of her head. I want to take her pain away, but the irony is that I've caused it.

"I think, Lily," Allison says, "you're going to have to start understanding that when Lo tells you to stop, it's not rejection. It's a form of love. I know that's hard to grasp, especially since you both have done things completely opposite."

Lily lets out a short nod. It won't be easy for her to just believe Dr. Banning's advice. I have the same problem. Our brains are wired a little differently than everyone else. But I'm willing to ride out this roller coaster with her—until we're both free from misery.

"Now let's talk about your restrictions and the letter I sent home with you," Allison says.

"We call it the blacklist," Lily tells her. "But I didn't read it. I gave it to my sister to give to Lo, and we agreed that it's better if I don't know. Now . . . I'm kind of starting to regret that." She turns to me. "Do you think I should read it?"

Allison beats me to it. "Actually, Lily, I think it's a great idea that you haven't read it. It shows support on Lo's end and trust on yours. It also gives you a chance to relax about limitations."

"How am I supposed to relax when all I can think about is what's been blacklisted?"

"If you do read it, wouldn't you still be thinking about what sexual activities have been banned?"

Lily's face falls. "I guess."

"Why don't you try this way for a while then," Allison suggests. She looks to her clock. "The last thing I want to discuss are fears. This relationship is new for the both of you, and I think it would be helpful if you told each other one of your fears by it."

Lily's lips snap closed, so I take the opportunity to go first. For her.

"Well . . ." I say and quickly realize I haven't thought this through. My fears? I have plenty. Lily cheating. Me drinking. Both of us fucking up until we can't see straight. "I'm scared that . . ."

Lily turns to face me, and I am lost for a minute in her eyes. I suddenly realize that I'm scared of everything. Of losing the only girl I've ever loved. Of having her secret voiced to the whole world and watching her disintegrate from the repercussions. She's already so small and fragile, something like that would kill her, I think.

But Lily and I made a decision not to tell Allison about the threatening texts. It's too dangerous when we don't know who's sending them. And partly, the situation feels new and raw, and talking about it is like pressing on an infected wound.

"Lo," Allison urges at my silence.

"I'm scared," I start again, "that there's going to be a point where you become angry and bitter and resentful every time I tell you to stop, that you realize someone else can give you what you want."

Lily's head whips from side to side, like I'm so wrong. That kind of reaction feels good.

"No one else could ever give me what I want," she breathes. "I only want you."

I hold on to the words, even if we both know they're not completely true. She wants to fuck. She wants the high of a climax the same way I want to drown in a bottle of bourbon. I want the rush, the flush and the ride to purgatory and back. We are not each other's first wants and needs. I am second to her. And she is second to me.

I want that to change.

I take her hand and kiss her knuckles, but she doesn't smile because she knows it's her turn.

"Lily?" Allison asks.

Lil keeps her eyes on me, and I give her an encouraging smile. "I'm scared," she says, "that you're going to hate being on some sort of sex schedule and hate being barred from your own pleasure. It's not fair to you, and you'll find someone who will make you feel better than I can."

My mouth opens in surprise. I didn't ever think she was worried about that. I didn't even believe it could be an option. I love her beyond the great sex. "Lil—"

She interjects quickly, throwing up her hands. "What if I can't ever give you a blow job?" she asks, a little hysterical now. "I mean, what if that's on the blacklist? That's not right, Lo! You have needs too!"

I'm grinning and trying so hard not to laugh. It's probably shitty that my smile has spread to new proportions, but I can't help it. Not when she's freaking out over *this*.

"This isn't funny!" she shouts, but her lips start to rise, mimicking mine. "*Stop.* I'm being serious."

"I'm sorry." I can't even pretend to sound apologetic, nor can I stop smiling. "It's just cute." She blushes, and it only makes me want to gather her in my arms and cage her against the couch. To take her right there. She would love that.

"Okay, well . . . I'm giving you a blow job after this then," she demands.

That *almost* gets me hard. I have to think about something else. Like the fact that Allison is sitting right here. "How about I let you know when I want one," I rephrase. I've read the blacklist, and while it doesn't exclude blow jobs, it does have certain stipulations. In fact, I think Lily would be genuinely surprised by what it actually says.

Lil narrows her eyes. "You're just going to keep telling me *later* until later becomes a year."

"Within the week," I say, my eyes lighting up. Only with my girlfriend do I have to basically negotiate her out of giving me head.

Her forehead wrinkles, like it does when she's thinking hard. After a moment, she looks to me and nods. "Deal."

Allison pipes in. "That's good, really good. You two are communicating very well with each other and letting your voices be heard. What I want you both to work on is getting your sex lives to a point where they don't interfere with relationships, school, jobs, or even daily activities. I know in the past you two had a very active sexual routine."

Active doesn't describe what we were doing. When we both were in the lowest of the low, we rarely even left the bedroom. It was an all-consuming affair. Waking up. Drinking. Fucking. Sleeping. Occasionally eating. It was both the best and worst time of my life.

"I think you're each ready to make a change," Allison continues. "And that begins now."

Seventeen

Lily Calloway

After my Stats exam, I get another inflammatory text. This time Unknown has become a bit more creative and called me a tramp *and* a cocksucker. It's a little ironic that I just begged Lo in therapy to let me give him head. But other than that, these texts are starting to unravel me. Whoever said that sticks and stones will break bones but words never hurt have obviously never been teased or insulted.

We're meeting Connor today to talk about the private investigator's discoveries. I planned to bring up the new messages with Lo and Connor, but after the Mason incident in the parking deck, I don't think revealing my texts will do anything other than enrage Lo. And I don't want him to Hulk Smash anything or drive him to drink. Hopefully Connor has a better lead on the guy and we can figure out what he wants.

I throw my backpack onto my bed and rush to the bathroom, needing to at least fix my hair before we leave. When I swing the door open, I find Lo by the sink, twisting the cap onto a pill bottle. It must be Antabuse. He told me he was taking meds that will make him sick if he drinks alcohol. I'm more proud of him than he knows.

"You ready?" I ask, trying not to make the pills a big deal. I look into the mirror and nearly die at my hair. I pulled an all-nighter to memorize those old exam questions. Taking a shower dropped on my priority list. My hair is greasy and flat and looks kind of gross.

"Just about." Lo opens the medicine cabinet and grabs a stick of deodorant. I make a bold decision and turn on the sink faucet. Then I lean over the marble edge, trying my best to stick my head in the basin and underneath the surge of water.

"What the hell are you doing?" Lo asks as he simultaneously rolls the stick under his armpits. He's shirtless, and I really can't stare too long.

"Washing my hair," I tell him. I pull some wet strands through my fingers, and I'm about to squirt some hand soap into my palm.

"That's not shampoo," Lo says quickly.

"What are you, the soap police? It'll work." I reach for the bottle again.

"Wait," he says. I lift my head up a bit and move some sopping strands out of my face. He fumbles around in the shower and then closes the glass door on his way out, a bottle of Herbal Essences in his clutch. I hold out my hand while twisting my neck to avoid dripping all over the counter.

"You're going to create a tsunami in here," he says, pushing me back to the sink. My stomach hits the edge of the counter, and I bend again, losing sight to my wall of hair. Then I feel his hands on my head, rubbing the shampoo into my scalp. Oh.

This feels nice.

His fingers knead in and out, running up and down, and even pressing against the back of my neck. I never thought that a head massage could feel so damn good.

I stifle a moan, but the pleasured noise escapes as soon as he closes the space between us. His body melds right up against my ass. We haven't done anything except missionary since he returned from rehab, and I'm starting to become paranoid that anal is on that blacklist. I want it. Right now, I think. I'm probably in the minority of girls who enjoy that position. But I like the tightness. It's a different kind of climax, and I can't deny how much I want it to happen.

"Lo." My voice comes out hoarse and wanting.

He scoots back from me, air replacing his body. The rejection hurts, but I try to remember what we talked about in therapy. I have to get a grip.

"How was your exam?" Lo asks, probably trying to distract me.

"Not bad." I have yet to come clean about Sebastian supplying me with old exams. I don't think Lo would care that I'm semi-cheating, but I don't think he'd approve that Sebastian is embedding me in his scheming ways either. It's better to avoid that conversation.

"So Sebastian is actually helping?" he asks in disbelief. He returns his body right behind me again, and the pressure on my ass ignites wild thoughts.

"Yeah," I mumble. I can't ask him for sex. He'll say no. I have to try to relax so he doesn't move away, so I can revel in the fact that this—him behind me—feels too good for words. I have to believe that this is enough . . . that I don't need more.

"So you think you passed?"

"Ummm . . ." *Focus.* "I think I made an A."

He stops massaging my head, but he doesn't move his body off mine. "Did you cheat?"

"What?" I squeak. I'm about to lift my head, but he puts a hand on my back and pushes me down so I don't drip water all over the floor.

"You did. You cheated." His shock outweighs all other sentiments.

"I did not!" I defend.

"Hold on." Lo grabs a cup and fills it with water. "Close your eyes."

I shut them tight as he starts washing away the shampoo suds, thick tension filling between us. It doesn't help that his frontal area is now grinding up against my ass.

"So what did he want in exchange for helping you cheat?" Lo asks.

I barely process this question. I'm a terrible multitasker, and right now I juggle my nefarious thoughts with rubbing soap from my eyes. There is no room to answer him properly. "Hmm?" I spread my legs apart, not enough that he'll notice.

At least, I didn't think he would.

He hooks my ankle with his foot and pins my legs back together like it's nothing, like this is our new routine. "Sebastian would want something in return," Lo says, his voice roughening as he pictures a not-so innocent bargain.

"He's not helping me cheat," I say again. He pours more water over my head, and I spit out a mouthful of soap.

"Sorry, love." His sweetness lasts only a second when I open my legs again and he pushes them together. "If he didn't help you cheat, what did he do?" Lo pauses as he wrings out my hair. "You do realize that having someone else take the exam for you constitutes as cheating."

"I know," I snap. He grabs a towel and starts massaging my scalp again. I close my eyes to bask in how it feels. Ugh, I can't even hate him while he does this.

He takes off the towel, and I finally stand up straight, my hair messy and wet around my face. But at least it's clean. Lo is still pressed up against me, and his hands even rest along my hips. Our eyes meet through the mirror, and I see the strength in them. "We can't," he says. "I'd love to fuck you right now, but we have to leave soon for the meeting."

I nod. It's not a healthy time, at least not for me.

I spin around to face him fully, and he backs away from me. Enough that my eyes drop to his pants. "How are you not hard right now?" I ask accusingly.

"I was just washing your hair," he says like I'm being silly, like that simple task wasn't sexual at all. I frown. Wasn't it? Or was the entire thing all in my perverted mind?

He tilts my chin with his finger, and I look back up into his eyes. "I spent three years as your fake boyfriend," he says. "I've had practice resisting you."

Ohhhhh. I like that answer better. I think he knows it too. Lo leans down and kisses me deeply, filling my lungs with his breath. I grab onto the back of his neck and reciprocate fully. We stay like that for at least a minute, but he retracts before we can go any further.

My eyes are glued to his pink, wet lips. My brain is only computing one thing: *Kiss. Kiss. Kiss.*

"How did you make an A? Or *think* you made an A?" he asks, popping my happy thoughts.

"Huh?" Can I play dumb? It should be easier for me, considering I'm relatively average on the smart scale. Lo doesn't buy it. He gives me a look and I crumble under his penetrating stare. "You can't tell Rose."

"So you *are* cheating." He realizes that Rose wouldn't care how I aced the exam unless I ventured to the dark side of academia.

"Not technically . . ."

His brows jump. "So what . . . you half cheated? What does that even mean? You cheated on the first page but not the last?"

I hold up my hands. "Whoa, can I explain?"

"Please."

"Sebastian gave me old exams, and I just memorized all the answers. I didn't bring the tests to class or copy the answers on my hand. I'm just beating the system. There's no harm in that."

Lo takes a moment to process this, and just when I think he's going to yell at me, he asks, "What did you make on the other exams before you did this?"

"44 and 29." Two *horrible* grades that I didn't think humanly possible. Actually, that's a lie, I've made a 7 on a test before—and I think the Penn professor was just being nice about that too. I reread my exam and it sounded like a planetary alien took the test and wrote in a different language. Honestly, the professor asked me if I was dyslexic. I couldn't really tell him the truth. *I'm so exhausted from all the crazy sex I'm having that I can barely process words let alone sentences. You're lucky I even showed up to this class, Mister.*

Lo is still thinking, so I add, "I've been getting C's in my other classes. Statistics is the hardest for me."

"You're right. It's not really cheating," he says. I can't help my smile, my face filling with glee. "But . . ." I don't like *buts* . . . scratch that, I remember that I do like *butts* with double T's. Like my butt. His cock.

Lo waves a hand in front of my face. "Did you hear me?"

"I lost you on *but.*"

"Jesus, you really want anal sex," he says with a grin. I open my mouth to ask him for it, and he quickly says, "No, love. Not right now." Boo.

Lo continues without missing a beat, "So Sebastian gave you old exams. What did you give him?"

"Nothing," I say with a shrug. "He said he was doing it because I'm Rose's sister and . . ." I taper off, knowing this is where Lo will get pissed.

"*And . . .*" Lo prods.

"And he told me that he doesn't like Connor and Rose together, and I think he may try to break up their relationship. Anyway . . ." I clear my throat. "I can't warn her about Sebastian, or else—"

"He'll keep the exams," Lo finishes and then nods.

Red-hot shame fills me, and this doesn't even have anything to do with sex.

Lo says nothing more. He takes a long time to process everything internally.

My nerves gather at his silence. "I need those exams, Lo. You know I need them. What am I supposed to do?"

"I don't know," Lo mutters. He rubs the back of his neck.

I shift uneasily. "Connor is the first real friend that we've ever had, and I'm standing over on Team Sebastian . . . unwillingly."

"We're going to have to think about it." He stares hard at the floor, plotting. "For right now, let's just keep this between us."

"Are you sure?"

Lo meets my gaze, recognizing the flash of guilt in my eyes. He pulls me closer to his chest and runs a hand down the back of my head in comfort. "Your priority is to pass this class. Try not to think about anything else."

"Connor—"

"He'll be fine for now. He's the most confident, self-assured guy in the world. He can handle Sebastian without either of us."

I think he's right, but we both also know it's not the moral path—the one that good friends take. Being sober isn't our only challenge. Becoming human, functioning people in this big vast world means making friendships and sustaining the very few that we already have.

There is no college course to "be a better friend" or "be a less shitty human being." Or else I would be signed up for both.

We're selfish, in every sense of the word.

I just don't want to fracture our friendships because of it.

Eighteen

Lily Calloway

The hardest part about being in a committed relationship with Lo isn't losing the sex with strangers. It's losing that moment where I become someone else. Where the shy, insecure Lily turns into a confident vixen. Where I'm completely and utterly in control and as my conquest looks at me with a heavy-lidded gaze, he knows it too. I was someone else during those moments. Someone better maybe.

The longer I'm monogamous, the more I forget what being *that* confident, brazen Lily feels like. It's like parting with a best friend for so long that their face becomes a blurry haze. I don't miss her enough to cheat on Lo. I just wonder if I'll ever see her again.

But I know who I never wanted to meet.

Sadie.

Connor's evil, orange tabby cat glares at me from across his apartment living room. All those grumpy kitties on Tumblr are not just photoshopped. Sadie is proof that felines can contort their face with such hot-tempered malice.

Lo and I sit on Connor's dark green leather sofa, his apartment decorated like a bachelor pad. Instead of red Solo cups lined on the bar, he has an array of expensive liquors locked away in a glass cabinet. Lo glanced at them once or twice, and Connor ushered us to a seat where our back is turned to the alcohol. That pissed Lo off a little. He doesn't want to be babied.

Afternoon light streams through windows that fill the entire back wall and the adjacent one. From floor to ceiling, Connor has a perfect view of Philly's old brick architecture. Like most expensive bachelor pads, Connor has art decor that makes very little sense to me.

There's just a porcelain ball stationed where a chair should be. I can't tell if it's an empty flower pot or a vase. There's no hole for lilies—okay that came out wrong. But really, it seems silly to have a ball thing just taking up space. I guess that's why they call it nonfunctional art.

The floors are concrete, but in the living area, he has a nice cream rug that Sadie apparently loves. Because she has yet to step off it. She struts in front of the couch, back and forth, her white tail wagging mischievously.

I have my eye on you, I say with a narrowed gaze.

Despite feeling violated by Sadie, I am relatively hopeful today. I want everything resolved with this blackmailer, evil texter, or whatever the hell he is. I want to move on and focus on getting healthy.

The bell rings, and Connor opens the door. "You're late," he says flatly, in a Connor Cobalt, *I dislike you* tone that very rarely presents itself.

Ryke's jaw hardens. "I'm the captain of the track team," he says. "I can't leave practice first."

"No, I wouldn't expect you to do anything first," Connor retorts.

Lo and I exchange hesitation. Something tells me that Connor is not Ryke Meadows's number one fan. And normally, I'd be suspicious that maybe Connor knows Ryke is behind all of this—that Lo's brother is the one we should be wary of. But their little heated looks began around the time Ryke dissed Connor in public. It wasn't one sole event. It was many things. Like Ryke calling Connor an ass kisser in front of his track buddies. Ryke can say those things in private, in front of us, and Connor just shrugs, but hurting his reputation in public crossed a line.

Ryke looks about ready to push through the doorway.

But Connor leads him in before Lo's brother becomes physical. Connor sits on a buttoned leatherette chair across from us, but Ryke plops right next to Lo on the couch. And I'm reminded that my sister isn't here to be on my team. Her schedule is too hectic to make the drive to Philly, so unfortunately, I'll have to carry on without her.

I didn't realize how much I relied on her support until I felt that uncomfortable dread when she told me she couldn't come.

Sadie circles the coffee table, but her harsh gaze never deters from me. "Connor," I say, "I think your cat hates me."

Connor picks her up in his arms. "She doesn't hate you."

Oh good. That's one less enemy.

"She just hates women."

Or maybe not.

Ryke lets out an incensed snort. "I thought Rose was making that fucking shit up."

"When you string together curse words, I go deaf a little in my right ear," Connor tells him. "What was that?"

Lo is trying really hard not to laugh, and I bite my lip to suppress a smile. It's too easy to pick on Ryke, especially since the guy takes very little to heart.

Ryke flips him off, mutters more swear words under his breath, and slouches in his chair. "Let's get on with this."

Connor strokes Sadie, and even though she purrs, she still wears a mask of evilness—directed right at me.

"I have bad news," Connor says, confirming that he is indeed the cat-stroking villain in this scenario. "My PI tracked down the phone number. It was a disposable, so we have no way of knowing the identity of the person on the other line."

Lo groans into his hands, hunching forward with his elbows on his legs.

I go the opposite route, leaning back into the couch like a tidal wave just struck my chest. What do we do now? "So should I prepare to be in the tabloids soon?" My voice comes out way too soft. Even the thought sends my heart into a dive pattern. I can't think about it without tears brimming. The shame that I'll bring to my family . . .

Lo straightens up and laces his fingers with mine. "There has to be something else we can do."

"Sure," Connor says. "But I need both of you to open up about things you haven't been willing to share. I need your top suspects that you believe could be threatening you. I can give those to my investigator, and he'll check them out."

"That can't be too hard," Ryke says.

Lo glares at the rug. Yeah, it took me hours just to go through our yearbook and circle faces—only to decide that over half of the student body hated Lo. And that was just prep school. We haven't even factored *college* into the equation.

"Seriously?" Ryke's brows rise. "How many fucking people did you piss off, Lo?"

"I wasn't well liked," he retorts. "We all can't be the captain of sports teams."

Ryke rolls his eyes.

"You can't be that surprised," I chime in. "You met us when Lo was being cornered by four guys wanting to beat his ass."

"People get upset over the stupidest things," Lo says, defending himself.

Connor tilts his head. "Didn't you steal a bottle of alcohol that cost forty grand?"

"I didn't steal," Lo says. "I drank from the bottle and set it back. And it was my birthday."

"How does your birthday strengthen your argument?" Connor

asks. "Unless they knew it was your birthday. Did they?" He knows they didn't.

Lo glares. "Shut the fuck up." His words come out lightly and they actually make Connor smile.

"What about those guys at the Halloween party?" I ask Ryke. "Do you think they could still be mad at Lo?"

"Yeah, what's the name of the guy who was really pissed?" Lo asks.

"Matt," Ryke says. We all stay silent, recalling the moment where Matt and his brothers chased Connor's limousine down the street as we sped away. He's also on the track team with Ryke. "I don't know if he's still angry or not."

"How could you not know?" Lo snaps. "You're the captain. You see them almost every day. Fuck, you *just* ran little loops with them."

Connor tries really hard not to grin, but if he wanted to hide his smile fully, I'm pretty sure he could. He's definitely gloating in Ryke's misery. I kind of like it.

"You run *little loops* with me," Ryke retorts, dodging the accusation.

"Only at your request. If it was up to me, I'd be running down the street alone." But there are bars along the sidewalk, and Ryke worries that he'll be tempted to run *inside*.

Lo's narrowed gaze pierces Ryke, and both speak through their hard features. Lo is egging Ryke to say the worst things to him—to bring up his addiction. But Ryke is not willing to go there.

"Look," Ryke says, "the guys on the team aren't going to tell me if they despise my half brother who just spent three months in rehab."

Oh. He has a point.

"Should I put him on the list?" Connor asks, scrolling through his electronic tablet. Sadie tries to sit on it, not liking his attention divided, but he moves the tablet to the armrest and she curls back onto his lap.

Lo pries his gaze from Ryke. "Yeah, sure." I think he wants someone to blame him again for that mistake—to yell and make him feel that pain, as though he deserves the assault. His father would do just that. But Lo needs to realize that's not the right way to deal with things. He shouldn't be punished every day for something that happened months ago. No one died. No one got hurt.

"Let's start with the people who have the biggest grudge against both of you and go from there," Connor advises.

Lo is staring at the floor again, his mind wandering in a thousand different places. I'm the one who poured over the yearbook, so I know better than him at this point.

"Aaron Wells," I start out. Both Ryke and Lo stiffen. They did something to Aaron, clearly, but I try not to think about it. "And maybe Mason Nix . . ." After the parking lot fiasco, I think there's a lot more resentment there than we realized.

"I have to give my PI motives to put with the names. So you're going to have to give me some details."

Lo sighs heavily. "You want to tell the stories?" he asks me. "I can if you're not up to it." But by his sharp jaw, I can tell he wants to share about as much as I do.

"How about equal opportunity," I say. "I call Wells."

Lo has lost a little color in his cheeks. He nods again, and now I regret my choice.

"Never mind, I can talk about Mason—"

"No you take Wells."

I pause. "Okay," I say in a small voice. I feel bad. Like I could ooze into the couch and not come back out.

"Aaron Wells," Connor says, his eyes lighting up in recognition of the name. "He attended the Fizzle event in January?"

"Yep," I say. Without Lo to accompany me, my mother called

Aaron Wells to be my escort (not the sex worker kind). She didn't know that he hated Lo or that he was hell-bent on making my time at the party miserable.

Lo turns to stone by my side, no longer huggable. He's upset that he wasn't there for me, but I would never want him to leave rehab on my account.

I begin the story as best I can.

Aaron Wells. Tall, brown-haired (almost blond), blue-eyed god of the Dalton Academy lacrosse team. He bled blue and shit gold. Even in ninth grade, he was held in high-esteem, a natural athlete that would grace our school with its first Lacrosse State Championship. Guys wanted to be him and girls wanted to fuck him. But Lo was the one guy who didn't care about being swathed in Aaron's circle of popularity.

In ninth grade, Lo and I denied our problems to ourselves and each other. Even after we had sex together for the first time, we just pretended it never happened. We were fourteen—naive and lost and trying to make ourselves feel better.

I remember the day after really well. I stuffed my books into my locker, and Lo's nearness caused my chest to tighten. That part was normal. He would wait for me with a strong arm against the dark blue locker, loosening the collar of his tie on his white button-down. He hated that prep school uniform, even if he looked sexy in it. He would linger by my side, wanting to walk me to class. He reeked of bourbon, and he wore sunglasses indoors to help with his tender eyes. Back then, before college, he felt more of the effects from a night of bingeing.

"Did you do that poetry assignment for Lit?" Lo asked.

"What?" My eyes widened. I must have forgotten. Not uncommon. Though, the teachers usually took pity on me. After being graced with Rose's supreme brain, they thought I was the stupid Calloway girl.

"It's fine, I have you covered," Lo said. I narrowed my eyes at him, skeptical. No way. "Roses are red. Violets are blue . . ." *Just great. I'm going to fail.* ". . . and if a jock asks, don't let him fuck you." He finished off the poem as his eyes wandered ahead. A group of lacrosse players passed us, Aaron leading the pack.

"Advice in a poem?" I said with a smile. "You're outdoing yourself, Loren Hale." My amusement was short lived though. Aaron detached from his pack and approached us. Lo stiffened and I tried to ignore the guy as he towered over me.

"You must be Loren," Aaron said. "We haven't met, but I've heard about you."

"It's Lo," he clarified.

Aaron barely blinked and continued talking as if Lo hadn't uttered a word. "I'm hosting a pre-season bash at my place."

"That's cute," Lo said with a wry smile, "not many people throw parties to celebrate spring."

"The *lacrosse* season," Aaron deadpanned, eyes cold.

"The meteorologists are inventing new seasons now? That's impressive."

I should have seen that coming, considering Lo wasn't in the best mood. Not after we had sex and ignored the event. Not after he guzzled straight whiskey from his flask on the ride here.

Aaron had kept his composure. "You can bring your girlfriend if you'd like."

"She's not my girlfriend," Lo said.

At the admittance, I turned around from my locker, books in my arms. Aaron sized me up, not crudely, and when his eyes landed on mine, he looked at me with such intense pity. Like he felt bad that I had to endure Lo.

Aaron didn't understand us. No one did.

"You're definitely invited," Aaron said directly to me. "And I can introduce you to some *nice* guys."

"Yeah, she's not looking for a nice guy," Lo said. He was right. If I wanted someone who would take me on a date, treat me right, and call the next morning—I'd date someone from Dalton. But I wanted the lay. The type of guy who could sleep with me and forget about it as soon as we left the room. I wanted easy. Nice guys were complicated.

I spoke up before Aaron could. "It's okay. I don't go to parties. I mean, Dalton parties." Rule number one: Do not have sex with boys from Dalton. Otherwise everyone would have figured out that I slept around.

Aaron frowned. "That's kind of weird."

"*Thanks?*" I said before turning to Lo, ready to leave.

"You both realize this is going to be the party of the year," Aaron said in confusion, his pride finally starting to ruffle. *Yes, Aaron, we had been serious about not wanting to go.* Though, I was positive it *would* be one hell of a party. Giant punch bowls. Neon lights. Good drugs. Maybe even a famous DJ. But I would choose to miss it all just to avoid being gossiped about the next morning.

Lo met my gaze, and I could see him cracking. Probably under the assumption that there would be *good liquor* too. I gave him a look. Dalton parties were my bane. The entire student population flocked to them, and so I would have to spend my time in the corner, trying to avoid leering gazes and making sure Lo didn't pass out.

He gave me those big pleading eyes, and I realized he was going to the party with or without me. So I just nodded.

Lo turned to Aaron and flashed a fake smile. "We'll see you Friday."

Aaron layered on his own mock happiness. "Perfect."

Only it hadn't been perfect. It was one of the worst parties in the history of parties. So bad, in fact, that the event blacklisted us from any social function related to Dalton. And I didn't even attend Aaron's stupid blowout.

I wasn't the one who opened all of Wells' expensive booze. I didn't grab a lacrosse stick and stumble around, somehow ending up in the wine cellar. I didn't take out all my frustration on two-hundred-year-old bottles that fractured and broke. I didn't drown the cellar and my pain in a pool of red.

But Lo sure as hell did.

And I should have been there. Sometimes I wonder if that would have changed the outcome. I could have stopped Lo, and then maybe Aaron and his friends wouldn't have hated him so much.

The wine-cellar debacle started their rivalry.

Then it mushroomed from there. First with silly stuff, like slapping Lo's textbooks from his hands. But then three of them cornered Lo, about to grab onto his arms and legs and stuff him in a locker. Lo ran before they could touch him. He was good at that. Running away.

Lo has admitted to me, and only me, that it was his fault the entire feud started in the first place, but he just didn't know how to end it once it began. Like dominoes that kept tumbling down and down and down. He wasn't big enough to step away, to back off. He had taken too much shit at home to let someone else run over him.

Over the next four years in school, they passively hated each other and sometimes the passivity turned to fists, but Lo was quick to dodge all attacks. It wasn't until our senior year that everything changed. I think, in part, Aaron had become tired of how teachers fawned over Lo and how he seemed to have special treatment that extended beyond athletes.

I was seventeen and in a fake relationship with Lo. For the first time, Aaron realized that there was a way to reach Lo without him running away.

He could mess with me.

Aaron started following me to class, and then a week later, he blocked me against a wall, ever so casually, with his lacrosse player friends in tow. To everyone else, they probably looked like they stood there for a quick chat, but whenever I met Aaron's eyes, I saw only hate.

The fourth time he cornered me, I was in the library, trying desperately to find a book on Renaissance art. Secluded in the back, between two book cases, I picked out a red spine and was ready to hightail it to lunch. When I looked up, my exit had been obstructed by a six-foot guy with athletic muscles and hardened brows.

Hatred is an animal you feed, and I imagined that after four years, Aaron's became plump and bloated. The seemingly nice guy who invited me to a party my freshman year of prep school had turned cold and mean. At least toward me.

His eyes were dark, and he stepped forward. My heart thudded against my chest as I stumbled back. He continued his stride and my back hit the wall.

"I have to get to lunch," I said in a small voice. I didn't know what he was going to do. He'd already laid a fist into Lo. (He got a week's suspension and Lo got a Friday detention), so I thought maybe he was preparing to hit me . . . or at least scare me.

Mission accomplished. I was terrified.

He came closer, not saying a word. I think that was the worst part, the unspeaking, unfeeling of it all.

He raised his arms, putting his hands on a Student Election poster beside my head, imprisoning me. His warm breath burned my neck, and it was then, at that moment, that I had the impulse. I wanted out. Away. Gone. I dipped down, small and quick enough to slip below his arm. I ran out of the library and then right out of school.

I didn't want to tell Lo what had happened, but Aaron's advances only became worse. One day when I was driving home, he tailed me with his lacrosse buddies. I drove straight to Lo's and they sped off. I kept my mouth shut, but I spent most of the school day stuck to Lo's side. No one harassed me when he was around.

I usually tried to skip when he skipped. But one abnormal day,

I actually slept at my own house, and he didn't tell me he was going to be late.

I tried to focus on the task at hand. *Get your books. Go to class. Done.* I tugged my World History book from the locker and the hardback spine tilted the mirror on the inside door.

And then I felt two hands on my waist.

I jumped: feet and heart. Then I spun around and Lo's eyes were wide.

"Hey *girlfriend*," he emphasized, seeing as how we were in our pretend relationship.

I wanted to smile, but I could barely catch my breath.

His face fell in a wave of concern, and he put his hands on my cheeks. "Heyheyhey," he said quickly. "Take a breath, Lil."

Tears pricked my eyes. I didn't realize Aaron had unraveled me until that point. *Game. Set. Match*, I thought. He won.

But I had forgotten who my "fake" boyfriend was.

"Lil, what's wrong?" His voice was heavy and serious.

I buried my head into his shirt and he held me there for a very long moment. We skipped class so I could tell him the truth, and it poured out of me like a flood.

"I'm going to fix this," Lo said.

I believed it too. He called Aaron and threatened his college career if he didn't stop harassing me. With the Hale name, Lo had plenty of contacts and one phone call from him or his father, and Aaron's collegiate career would be over.

Aaron called his bluff. And then Lo called the college.

So Aaron Wells was reduced to his safety school, losing out the lacrosse stardom.

He stopped following me after that . . .

Well, until the Fizzle party pretty recently (where he tried to scare me again). And not soon after, we received those texts. Maybe only a couple months separating the two events.

Connor's normal placid expression has been slightly overtaken by a wrinkled forehead and the hand that covers his mouth. I never thought I could shock Connor Cobalt—or that he'd let me see his surprise.

"In defense," Lo says, "Aaron Wells and I have hated each other since ninth grade. That's like an era of hate. None of the others are like that."

"We can only hope," Connor says.

"And our dad helped you tear up this kid's future?" Ryke asks.

"What can I say," Lo says with a bitter smile, "it's how we bonded."

Nineteen

Loren Hale

I couldn't talk about Mason. Neither could Lily. I think that one was too fresh for us. I mentioned what happened in brief to Ryke over the phone one day—about the parking deck and a little bit about the past—so I told him to just fill in Connor and that was that.

My head weighs a fucking ton and I could use a glass of whiskey. Hell, I'd settle for a beer at this point.

But we drive right on back to Princeton afterward. A couple times, I pull over at a gas station, telling Lily I have to pee. I avoid grabbing any six-packs in the foggy glass fridges, but the second time I park the car, Lily catches on and follows me into the convenience store. She finds me staring questionably at a case of Samuel Adams. Lily talks me down for a good ten minutes, telling me that beer tastes disgusting, that breaking my sobriety is not worth the small, insignificant buzz. She's right, but I just want to forget everything for one extended moment.

I want all of the memories to shut down so that I can sleep. But everything I did—every mistake, every fucked up word that spilled from my lips—replays on repeat. And I can't take it back. But I do have the power to drown it all out.

We drive again. Toward home. And I forget about the booze. I try to focus on things that I can do that won't involve alcohol.

"Maybe I should call Aaron," I say to Lily. My hands tighten on the steering wheel. "Apologize or something." What if he didn't do anything? What if I made it worse by going to his house and threatening him? My father's way to do things—it could be wrong. It's all I know. And it's what put me in this place to begin with.

I have so many regrets. I don't believe anyone who says they don't. How can you live life making mistakes and never wish you could take one back?

I destroyed the guy's *wine cellar*. If a person did that to me, I wouldn't be just a little ticked off. I would *despise* them. And I don't have much of an excuse. I was just . . . I was hurting, and I felt like I was screaming and no one could hear me. I was in the wrong, I get it, but my actions never gave him permission to terrorize Lily. For that, I just can't forgive him.

Lily runs her fingers over my hand that holds the gear shift. "I'm not sure that will help. He may not accept it."

If Aaron is the guy threatening us, we may be fucked.

We roll up to our gate, and I punch the security number into the keypad. We drive through, parking in the empty garage. Rose is late, not surprising with how much she juggles. When we walk into the house, I flick on the lights, half expecting Lily to turn around and ask me if we can fuck.

She usually does.

Tonight's different. Maybe because I openly confessed to thinking about a drink. Maybe she doesn't want to put me in a position where I have to tell her no.

Lily plops down on the couch like its normal for her to be more interested in the television than the bedroom. "I think they're playing *Thor* on HBO," she says, leaning over to grab the remote. My eyes drop to her knees, squeezed tight together. Yeah, she's struggling.

After pouring through all those memories, we both deserve a release. I mentally file through the therapist's blacklist. I've reread it enough times that every word is engrained in my head.

No masturbation.

No porn.

No public sex.

Stop when your partner stops. Helpful tips: Start with timing your sessions and have a set hour dedicated to sex. For the first few months stick to positions that won't elicit increased arousal after a climax. (This is subjective and you will have to experiment to discover what triggers you to keep going.)

Only engage in sex when both you and your partner want to. Helpful tip: Let your partner choose the time.

Healthy amounts—sex cannot interfere with daily routines. Helpful tip: Keep to morning and night schedules.

I know Lily thinks there are stipulations like banning anal and blow jobs. I've had lengthy conversations on the phone with Allison, discussing how far I should take Lily. We still have to be intimate, and banning sexual positions won't help that. So Allison and I agreed that the goal is to get Lily to a point where she doesn't expect sex.

Not asking me for sex is a good first step, and I want to reward her for it. But I also fear that she'll catch on to this. Over time she may pretend to be uninterested so she'll get a lay out of me. The point is to make her stop *thinking* and wanting sex—not devising strategies to get it.

Considering my mind circulates around hunting for a bottle of something alcoholic, I understand it's not a simple task.

"Ah, yes!" Lily says excitedly. "We didn't miss the part with Sif." Her eyes flicker to me briefly before they return to the TV. "You think we should go to Comic-Con this year? We can dress up as Thor and Sif."

I sit down next to her on the couch, giving her a cushion's worth of distance. I catch the instant frown in her eyes but it disappears when she focuses on the movie.

"I don't think I'd look good as a blond," I tell her.

She appraises my hair and then her eyes drop, lingering as she takes in my other features. She's stared at me so hard for the past couple weeks that I'm fairly certain in a year she could recall every freckle by memory. Her throat bobs as she swallows. "I . . . yeah, umm . . . blond . . . no," she stammers before turning back to the movie.

"How about we go as Loki and Sif?" I suggest.

She hesitates a moment before shaking her head. Her eyes meet mine again, and this time they stay right there. "How about Hellion and X-23?"

She never wants to dress up in the X-23 costume. It's skimpy black leather that exposes her entire midriff, and I practically have to beg her to cosplay my favorite mutant couple. She's offering this to me, and for some reason I have the sudden urge to take her right here.

So I do.

I bridge the distance between us and my lips find hers.

Her surprise stiffens her shoulders and freezes her arms, and I edge her mouth open, slipping my tongue inside. She wakes up, her hands swooping around my neck. I smile against her soft lips. My girlfriend is like a raunchy Sleeping Beauty, reanimating from a deep-throated kiss.

I run my tongue along the base of her neck, and she begins to writhe underneath me. She's unlike any girl I've ever been with. Little things set her off as if her body is made of a thousand nerves. She responds to every touch and lick like they're each the peak she wishes to reach.

Her hands fly toward my pants, and I have to grab them before she does anything. A moan escapes her lips, and her spine curves, her body arching toward me. I lift her up beneath her arms, and her legs instantly wrap around my waist. I press a strong kiss to her lips, inhaling the vanilla scent of her hair.

Even midway in the air, she starts to grind against me. She has to feel that I'm hard, but I need her to keep her hands off me. I have self-control, but it flits away whenever she starts rubbing against my cock.

I set her down on the rug, the couch to our left. My lips slowly brush the top of her ear, my teeth barely skimming the tenderness of her skin. She lets out a sharp gasp.

"Easy, love," I breathe. She settles again and I start, ever so slowly, undressing her. The light touch of the fabric sends her off as the shirt grazes up her belly and over her head. As I go for her jeans, she tries to sit up and touch me, but I put my hand on her shoulder, forcing her back to the floor again and give her a disapproving look.

She breathes heavily, and I wait to unbutton her until she nods, accepting that she must stay still.

When she does, I fish the button through the hole and slowly unzip. As I slide her jeans below her hips, down her thighs, I drink in her body and the way she responds to me. The little cries, the twitches of her legs and the curl of her toes. Every motion is filled with beauty that she won't ever understand. It makes me aware of how alive she is.

After tossing her jeans to the side, I kiss the tops of her breasts, and she shudders against me. I run my teeth playfully over her bra straps, and her chest rises and falls in quick succession, eager and wanting.

"Lo," she moans.

I stifle a groan in my throat, and I unclip her bra, freeing her of the clothing. And then I gently slip her panties down and off her ankles. While doing so, I lightly brush my fingers across the wet spot between her legs, so brief and powerful that the sensation immediately jolts her body. I have to remind her to stay still again.

"Lo, please," she says, her voice raw and raspy.

I kiss those reddened lips, and then stand to my feet, leaving her bare and naked on the living room floor. Her eyes widen in horror, thinking I'm no longer going to fuck her.

"I'll be right back, love," I say quickly, wanting that look to disappear from her face. "I have to get a condom . . . and lube." I grin at this, and I wait a second to watch her expression flip.

Her whole face lights up with delight. "But . . . I thought . . ." she starts.

I'm already backing away toward the bedroom. My dick feels like it might explode any minute, and I can't prolong waiting much longer to get my own fucking release. Fear crosses me for a brief second, realizing I'm leaving her naked, horny, and alone.

Halfway up the stairs, she's still watching me but her hands have edged closer and closer to the inside of her thighs. "Don't fuck yourself," I say roughly. "Or else I won't fuck you." It's a threat I don't like giving, considering my own arousal has almost peaked. I want to shove my cock inside her right now.

She nods eagerly, and I accept it, trying desperately to put faith in her. I just need her to be strong, but I know masturbation is one of her compulsions.

After reaching the second floor, I enter the darkened bedroom and quickly fumble around the desk drawer, grabbing a pack of condoms and lube. I haven't used up either in two weeks, which should be a record for us.

When I return to the living room, I find Lily still lying on the rug but she covers her face with her hands. She's concentrating too hard to hear me come in, and I take the time to kick off my pants and pull off my shirt. I lie down beside her and rub the top of her head easily. Her hands slide down, exposing her face and her eyes and the look that says, *fuck me now.*

"Lo, I almost touched myself."

I kiss her forehead and take one of her hands in mine. "But you didn't."

She shakes her head. "But I want to . . . so badly," she admits. "I can't remember what I feel like. Isn't that weird? That's weird, right? I mean it's my body, but I'm not allowed to touch really, and I . . . I . . ."

Jesus Christ. I take her in my arms, and she buries her head into my chest, near tears. This is not going as planned, and I feel like it's partly my fault. I shouldn't have left her alone and given her the opportunity to crawl inside her head. Maybe I can fix this.

"It's okay, Lil," I whisper. "If you want to touch yourself, just ask me."

With her hand in mine, I guide it down her stomach, past her belly button and in between her legs. She gasps as I rub her fingers over her clit and then down farther, letting her feel how wet she has become.

"Better?" I ask, pulling her hand and glistening fingers back up to her chest.

She nods, her shoulders relaxing, and I kiss the base of her neck.

I turn her on her side and lie right against her back. I can almost see her start to smile.

I rip the condom package.

"Can I put it on you?" she asks hopefully, hearing the paper tear.

"If you can do it quickly," I tell her, wanting to be inside of her more than she probably even knows. She flips over to face me, and I hand her the condom. Her eyes drop to my cock and I watch her entire expression practically glow. Her happiness is easy to bring, which I suppose is the problem, but I relish in sending her body into shock waves and seeing her face lit up like the city.

Not listening to me, she gently and *slowly* rolls the condom on my dick. I let out a heavy breath and then groan. Dear God. "Faster, Lil," I demand.

Her eyes flicker up, surprisingly, since it takes her great effort to look anywhere but my dick at times. She gives me a doe-eyed look and I can't help but smile, yet I don't give in. "Fast*er*," I repeat, stretching out the syllables.

She finishes rolling the condom up my shaft and then reaches for the lube. I grab her wrist and motion for her to turn around. I know she wants to be in control. I know she misses it. But she has to make me believe she can be on top and not get carried away. Right now, she's not even close to being able to handle that type of position without going crazy.

Before she flips over, she bends down and places a soft kiss on the head of my cock. Then she rolls onto her side, sticking out her ass for me.

I rub some lube on, and she squirms a little, but I hold her steady. My cock throbs and I know I can't hold out on going nice and slow. So when I have her ready, I thrust inside of her as fast and deep as I can without hurting her.

She lets out a long pleasurable moan and begins to writhe again. But I hold her tight, one arm around her neck and the other around her waist, grabbing her breast as I start pumping inside of her. Every thrust sends waves of ecstasy crashing through my cock and it feels too good to even stop for a second. I quicken my pace, her moans and half screams perpetuating my speed.

Within another few minutes, I can feel her reach her edge. I move faster and harder, closing my eyes as I try not to release. And after my hand descends between her legs, her body convulses in waves of pleasure. She shakes with each intense tremor, and then her breath comes out ragged and heavy.

I pull out, still hard and aching, and toss the condom off. Her eyes are heavy, but she reaches out to me. Quickly, I roll her onto her back and grab her leg, bringing it up over my shoulder. The new position reinvigorates her energy and her eyes hit mine. With one swift motion, I'm inside her soaked pussy and she's bucking up her hips.

I start thrusting harder, filling her deeply. My cock aches for release but I keep pulsing, keep feeding her needs. My free hand takes her chin and I lean down, our lips connecting. I kiss her while I move in and out, in and out. I hit something and she breaks away from my mouth, grinning. I smile back and then press my nose up against her cheek as I push harder, my lips parting once a noise catches. My hot breath on her neck, my hand across her lips, muffling her sounds and heightening her arousal.

Everything I ever wanted is right here in my arms. I wish I could stay like this forever, but eventually we come together—in a surge of bliss and longing.

Twenty

Loren Hale

We're on the floor, curled up in two throw blankets and a couple of pillows. Lily has fallen asleep in my arms, her steady breaths warming my bare chest.

She's never asked me why I can fuck better than the sloppy lay at fourteen. Granted, our first time together was actually *my* first. But I always knew I'd eventually get her back in my arms. I vowed to be better than all her other conquests. To keep Lily Calloway meant that I'd have to be able to satiate her every need.

So I practiced. I dated girls for a week or so, nothing too serious, but I made sure the sex was always about their desires, their pleasure, never mine. It helped figure out what would work for Lil—what sets off women the most. And I guess I just became good at it. So in most ways I succeeded.

I mean, I can satisfy my twenty-year-old sex addict girlfriend, for Christ's sake.

What I can't seem to do is fall asleep, but at least holding her takes my mind off finding a drink. Kind of.

Suddenly, I hear the back door open, and the kitchen light flicks on. Shit. Shit. Shit.

I forgot Rose lives here. How the hell did I forget that?

I glance down at Lily, completely naked like me. Oh . . . yeah. Her left breast is exposed, her nipple red and swollen from all the times I sucked on it. I cover her with the blanket and count the clap

of Rose's heels on the marble of the kitchen, waiting for that bomb
to explode.

Maybe she won't see us.

"Loren," she says coldly, in her normal octave.

I lift my head. Rose gives me a death glare that I'm sure has sent
children to tears. Her hands rest haughtily on her hips, and her
mouth is downturned in a perpetual frown. She is about to bitch
me out, but I put my finger to my lips and nod to Lily.

She's asleep, finally. Hours usually have to pass before she relaxes, but after she came a second time, she dozed right off. I could
have raced around the room and pumped my fists in the air. Sure,
sex—her vice—helped her sleep. It's not exactly a triumphant win.
But it's a small victory nonetheless.

Rose's eyes flicker between us. She points at me and then jabs
her finger at the kitchen. I mouth, *okay* and then carefully maneuver out from under Lily without waking her. She barely stirs, and
I readjust the blanket so she's covered completely.

"Loren!" Rose hisses at me.

I frown and look up to see her covering her eyes. Oh, right, I'm
naked.

I try not to grin as I grab my boxer briefs. Nope, can't find
those. I snatch a throw from the couch and tie it around my waist.
I walk into the kitchen and she immediately assaults me with her
leather purse.

"Okay, okay," I whisper, blocking the hits with my arms. "I forgot you lived here, my apologies."

She holsters her fucking weapon and uses her death glare again.
"You can't have sex in the living room, Loren. You broke a rule."

"What?" No way. I know that list front to back . . . but so does
Rose.

"*No public sex*," she reminds me.

"The living room is not public."

"It is now that you live with me. It's a public space." She motions around her. "Like the kitchen, and the garage, and everything that isn't shared by only you and Lily. I didn't think I had to explain that to you."

A pain shoots up in my chest and I sink down on the nearest barstool. "I didn't . . . I . . ." I frown. Holy fuck. I'm such a goddamn idiot.

And the urge to vomit rises.

"Loren," Rose says, her voice somehow soft. I meet her eyes and they look shockingly sympathetic. "It was one mistake. It won't happen again." Her voice is cold, but her optimism helps a little.

"It won't."

She lets out a small breath. "How did she do tonight?"

It's like Lily had a quiz she needed to pass, and I guess partly that's what sex is going to be like for her from now on—a test to see if she chooses to feed the compulsions or not.

"Better than usual," I say. "She listened to me more, and she fell asleep after the hour. But I think that may be because I finally took her from behind."

Rose talks about sex like we're in a psychology class, nothing more than science, health and the human anatomy, which makes it frighteningly easier to discuss. "Did you two have anal sex often?"

I let out a low laugh. "Every day."

I hear the garage door grind open or closed, and I immediately shoot to my feet.

Rose holds up a hand. "It's just Connor."

"He's sleeping here?" I say in disbelief and then my lips rise. "Are you finally popping that cherry, Miss Rose Calloway?"

She looks about ready to tear out my vocal cords. My smile only grows.

"He has an early meeting in New York," she says. Must be for Cobalt Inc., his family's ink and magnet company, which is almost as profitable as Hale Co. baby products, but not quite. "It was last minute, so I told him it might be easier if he slept here . . . on the couch." Oh. Fuck.

I grimace, not able to glimpse at the couch from the kitchen. But through the archway, I imagine pillows astray on the floor and one of the cushions perilously hanging over the edge. Basically I left the room a disaster with Lily swaddled in a blanket. A by-stander would assume we fucked on the couch, even though I was thoughtful enough to move her to the rug.

"There are two guest rooms," I say. "Why the couch?"

"He didn't want to cause a fuss after he left," Rose says. Her neurotic self would have to rearrange all of the pillows on the bed, wash the sheets, and probably iron the curtains just to be sure he didn't touch those too.

Connor walks through the door, a small duffel bag slung over his shoulder and his hand preoccupied by texting on his cell.

When he looks up, his eyes meet mine and then drift down to my nearly naked body, stopping at my blanket, and then right back up.

"Hey, beautiful," I say with a grin.

He barely blinks. "Pants have been invented in this century." He walks farther into the kitchen to give Rose a light kiss on the cheek. He must add the fact that I'm wearing a *living room* throw blanket because he says, "I thought you weren't allowed to have public sex."

Of course Rose told him about the list. She'll take any lengths to make sure Lily stays on track in her recovery.

"No one was here. It seemed private enough to me."

I can't read Connor's calm expression, but he looks to Rose. She already shakes her head—as though she knows exactly what he's about to say. "I told you that you should have clarified for them," Connor tells her.

"*I told you?* What are you, one?" Rose snaps, but she's just pissed she was wrong and he was right.

174 · KRISTA RITCHIE and BECCA RITCHIE

"Most one-year-olds can barely speak, let alone utter an entire idiom like *I told you so*."

She looks like she wants to slap him. "Why are we dating?"

"Because I asked you out and you said yes," he tells her with a burgeoning smile. "And you're madly in love with me."

"I never said such a thing."

He replies in French, and I can't even process the words.

She smacks his arm, and he whispers deeper in her ear, his arm spindling around her waist as he draws her to his chest. I don't think I've ever seen Rose so flushed before.

She puts a hand on his black button-down, making sure there's space between them. He kisses her on the head and keeps his arm around her, but he turns to me. "The couch isn't vacant then." His eyes fall to Rose, waiting for her to offer another solution. Like her bed, but she has solidified to stone.

She's not one-hundred percent ready to share a bed with a guy, which isn't a bad thing. I take pride in pissing Rose off, but causing her this type of fear—even unintentionally—makes me feel horrible.

Rose says, "The guest room in the basement is free. I put clean sheets on the bed the other day."

Connor nods, accepting the offer, and if he's disappointed, I can't tell at all.

I leave Connor and Rose to talk quietly among themselves, and I carefully lift Lily in my arms. I successfully carry her back to bed without waking her. She sighs, dreaming peacefully as I place her onto the mattress and tuck the comforter around her.

"Lo," she says in a sleepy voice and rolls over onto a pillow, hugging it tightly in her arms. I've never been so jealous of a damn pillow.

But I let myself smile.

A year ago it would have been another man in her arms.

Oh, how far we've come.

Twenty-one

Loren Hale

We made a deal not to put ourselves in stressful situations. Like the Sunday luncheon with Lily's parents. Like any communication with my father.

Today I'm breaking that deal.

Lily is busy with Sebastian, pretending to be tutored. I told her I was going to work out with Ryke at the Penn gym, but when I drive to Philadelphia, I make the turn into Villanova. Some of the houses have acres and acres of trimmed lawns, decorative fountains gushing in the front yard, and glittering Lamborghinis parked in the driveway—a place more suited for Beverly Hills than the suburbs of Philly. My nerves ricochet every mile down the road.

Before I talked to Connor last night, I had no intention of seeing my father. But I asked him about the probability of finding the blackmailer before the information leaked. He told me that I had the same chance as the sun exploding in less than a billion years. I looked it up, and apparently the sun won't explode for another four to five billion, so in Connor Cobalt's words—I'm fucked.

Then Lily's phone vibrated on the nightstand. She was in the shower, so I answered it. An unknown number texted her. The word pounding in my head. *Slut*. It felt like someone punched me in the ribs, and just before I went into the bathroom to talk to her, I had a sudden impulse to check her other texts.

Seventy-five of them.

That's how many times she'd been texted with insults—some more colorful than others. I'm not upset that she didn't tell me about them. But now she can't be upset when I talk to my dad. This has already gone too far. And I'm out of options. My father, he has more power in his right pinkie than I do in my whole body. And if this is what it takes to ensure Lily's safety, then so be it.

I pass the gates and park the car into the circular driveway. It takes a moment for me to muster the courage to ring the doorbell. I can hear the chime reverberating throughout the house.

After a couple minutes the door swings open, and I expect the staff to stand on the other side, ushering me in to see my father. Maybe Jonathan's assistant. Maybe the groundskeeper, who sometimes finds his way indoors.

But my father has done the impossible and answered his own door. His forceful posture fills the frame, nearly goading me to take a step down the stone stairs and plant my feet on the sidewalk in defeat. Somehow, I stand my ground.

He wears a tight-lipped expression, eyes darkened by booze and soul blackened by hate. I focus on the wrinkles by the creases of his eyes, weathered since the last I saw him. I think, in this moment, I should have a sudden undeniable resentment toward this man. He spit on me when I asked for help. He took away my trust fund when I told him I was going to rehab. He lied to me for twenty-one years.

My emotions tangle together, and yet, bitterness is so far from what I feel. Pity is closer to the surface. I realize that I could have become him. Hell, I still can go that direction and be alone in a mansion, drinking away my problems and wishing away the "could-have-beens" with the "nows." As much as I hate to believe it, he is me—without Lily. Without Ryke or Connor. He's my future if I drink again.

I don't say anything, partly because he should lead me inside without me asking. He can't pretend he never sent all those messages about wanting to meet up or have lunch. He wants to see me, even if he denies it, even if he's barely moved an inch from the door.

"You're on my fucking doorstep," he finally says. "Would you like to explain why, or are you waiting for an invitation?"

I hold in a strained breath. "I wanted to talk."

I think maybe he'll say something sharp like *calling me back would have sufficed*. But he pushes the door farther open and walks into the house, dapper in his charcoal suit. I follow him, closing the door behind me, and head through the long hallway toward the outside patio.

The house feels different. I grew up here. Ran through the hallways and slid on the waxed hardwood, nearly breaking my arm. Yet, being here sober, clearer, makes all those memories seem dark and hazy.

On the stone patio, I take a seat at the black iron table, overlooking the small pond that rests on sprawling acres of land. Two ducks swim in the murky waters, avoiding the lily pads floating beside them. My father mixes himself a drink at the black granite bar, glasses clinking together in a familiar tune.

I close my eyes, listening to the reverent sounds: the chirps of birds, the trickle of the fountain, the jingle of the wind chimes. Sometimes I think a part of me has been chipped away. I know I'm not completely the same person sober as I was when I was drinking. But what if the part of me that changed was a piece of my soul—a good piece? Or maybe I'm just making excuses to drink again. That's the problem, isn't it? Deciding what's right and what's wrong in my head. I just feel so confused all the time.

I open my eyes just as my father saunters over with two empty glasses and a bottle of dark liquid. He places the crystal glass in front of me, and I focus on his slow movements.

On impulse, I place my hand right over top of the glass before he can pour anything into it. My heart beats loudly in my chest.

His eyes darken. "So you can't even have a fucking drink with me now?"

My throat feels like lead, but I manage to find my words just fine. "It'll make me sick. I'm on meds." Thank God I took my pill this morning.

His jaw clenches tight, and he resigns by pouring himself a glass and sinking down in the chair across from mine. I take my hand off the crystal and flip it over.

"Are you here for money?" he asks, jumping straight to the point.

I stare at the table and gather my thoughts. Why am I here? For two things, neither of which revolve around finances or lack thereof.

He continues off my silence anyway, and I let him. "I know what I said before you went away—"

"Do you?" I snap.

"Yes, *Loren*. And maybe if you gave me some time to process everything, things would have turned out fucking differently." I'm not sure what kind of different he means. Not going to rehab? Having a relationship with him? Did he just take away my trust fund out of impulse? But if that was true, he would have given me money when I returned to Philly. He would have made a better effort to fix things.

My eyes narrow at the table in deep thought. He *did* try to call me. He was reaching out. I was the one closing him off—because Ryke told me to. He said I shouldn't open that door again, but maybe he was wrong. Maybe my father has been right all along.

He swishes his drink before downing it in one gulp.

My throat goes dry.

"You're my son," he says definitively, "and I'm not going to let you struggle because you make bad decisions."

"Rehab wasn't a bad decision."

"It was a waste of fucking time," he refutes. "Drinking isn't a problem, and you'll do it again. Don't fucking fool yourself." Before I open my mouth to retort, he says, "But that's beside the point." He pulls out his checkbook. "I want to help you get on your feet again."

"I don't want your cash," I say, even though I know that's a stupid choice. Because, really, what am I going to do? I can't keep living off Lily's inheritance. Sooner or later, I'm going to have to figure what I'm good at and make a living without crawling back to my father for rent.

"This isn't the time to start being humble," he tells me. "You can't try to be sober and work a job at the same time."

"What do you think normal people do? Not everyone has rich parents to fall back on."

"You do," he says. "And why the hell do you think I work so fucking much?"

"You have nothing better to do."

He glares. "I do it so that you won't have to struggle like this. So stop being a fucking idiot and take the damn money."

I believe him, even though Ryke would probably tell me that I shouldn't—that Jonathan Hale spends hours at his office because he's miserable and alone and likes all the riches that he can afford to buy.

There's a stipulation attached to that check too. I'll be indebted to him in some way. It's why he took away my trust fund in the first place. It's more than just him wanting me to enroll in college again. He wants that power over my life—to tell me what to do, to mold me as the son he always dreamed I would be. But I'm just a big fucking disappointment.

"That's not what I'm here for," I say, a weight bearing on my chest.

He sighs and shuts his checkbook. He pours another glass.

"What is it then?" He's more intrigued than he lets on. The curiosity glimmers in his dark eyes.

I take a breath, staring at the overturned, empty glass in front of me. Booze would help, but I have to do this alone. "I want her name."

"Who?" His voice has an edge, telling me that he knows exactly *who* I'm referring to.

"My real mother." The woman he had an affair with. The reason why he split from Sara Hale, Ryke's mom.

"She doesn't want to see you," he says coldly.

"And I don't believe you."

He lets out a low laugh and taps the table with his lighter, a cigar box not far away. "I knew you'd want answers. Where she lived, what she looked like, but they'll only upset you. And I didn't want to see your face twist."

"What are you talking about?"

"She didn't want *you*, Loren. I'm telling you not to waste your fucking time."

How can I believe him after all these years lying to me? But a part of me digests this information as truth.

"There it is." He brings the glass to his lips. I realize that my face has contorted in a multitude of emotions. Hurt, the strongest of them.

"You're wrong," I say under my breath, just so I can go back to being as hard and cold as him. "I want her name. After all these years that you told me Sara was my mother, I, least of all, deserve to have a semblance of the fucking truth."

He rolls his eyes dramatically, and to my surprise, rips off a check and flips it over. I watch him scribble on the paper and then he slides it to me. "I'm not the bad guy here," he says. "I'm just protecting you from feeling more pain. That's it."

I stare at the check.

Emily Moore.

"Did you love her?" Not, *where is she?* Or, *why did she give me up?* I have to ask the stupidest, most meaningless question there is—because my father doesn't believe in love.

"For all of fifteen minutes, sure," he says dryly. "Now you have what you want, can we move on from all this bullshit?" He wants to go back to the way things were, but I'm not even sure that's possible.

"I need something else," I tell him as I pocket the check. "And it requires discretion."

He laughs wryly and gets up to refill his glass. "Why am I not surprised? What the fuck did you do this time?"

I ignore the slight. "It's not entirely about me. It involves Lily."

He sits back down, hand cupping a full glass of scotch. I try not to focus on it too much. "I golf with Greg and have lunch with him every other day, so is this the type of discretion that requires me to lie to her father?"

Oh, yeah. "It will ruin the Calloways."

My father straightens up, his features hardening. He actually looks a little like Ryke. "What the fuck is going on?"

"You have to promise, and I want it in writing."

He gives me a look. "Don't be a little shit."

I glare. "I'm not being a *little shit*. You say you've done *all of this* . . ." I motion around me. ". . . the lying about my brother and my real fucking mother, because you were trying to protect me. Then understand that I'm trying to protect the girl I love. And I'd do anything to accomplish it. So if you don't fucking sign something that says you won't open your goddamn mouth, then I'm gone." I stand up, my chest rising and falling with sudden anger.

"Sit the fuck down."

I don't.

"*Sit,*" my father sneers. "I'll go get a piece of paper. I don't think I can write a contract on the back of a check."

I sink to my chair and watch my father leave the patio, muttering curse words under his breath. But I've won. This time.

. . .

He ends up typing it on his laptop. After an hour we have a contract written and signed, not allowing him to directly or indirectly tell the Calloways anything. If he does, he forfeits Hale Co. to Ryke. At first we had agreed that I would acquire the company, but he looked a little too pleased about the idea of me inheriting his business. Now stress lines crease his lips at the very thought that his kid—who despises him—could obtain his legacy. At least I know he loves me more, but really, that's not a very high achievement.

My father has a newly topped glass of scotch, and we're sitting on the patio again. His contract in his office, mine on the table.

"Now, what's so serious that I can't even tell my best friend?" he asks.

"When I got back from rehab, I received a text from an unknown number," I tell him. "He said he hated me and he basically threatened to expose Lily's secret out of revenge. So I don't think he's blackmailing us. He's not asking for money, but he did mention it once. He said he could get paid a lot from the tabloids if he told Lily's secret." The words pour forth before I have time to stop and evaluate each one. I'm scared, and if my father didn't see it before, he does now. I feel like a little kid blubbering about a bully at school.

"Slow the fuck down," he says sternly. "We'll take this piece by piece."

I repeat everything again, being vague about Lily's involvement and even going into more detail about the unknown number and how Connor's PI traced it to a disposable phone.

My father listens rather well, and by the time I finish I can see him reeling over the piece of the puzzle that I've purposefully avoided.

"Unless Lily is the ring leader of a drug cartel, I highly doubt it's anything to land Fizzle in a financial crisis. Really, tabloids have better things to do than gossip about heirs and heiresses. Look at you going to rehab, you didn't even make it in the *Enquirer*."

My addiction and hers are not proportionate. Not by a long-shot. I'm another notch on the rich-kid sob story who gets addicted to alcohol or drugs. Lily, a girl, is addicted to sex. Even if it does happen, people don't talk about it, but they will this time.

"Let's say people find her newsworthy, and not in a good way. What then? Do you think you could find this guy?"

"I could try," he says, eyes alight with interest. "What is it?"

And I just let it out. "She's a sex addict."

I watch him frown and then quickly the disbelief turns into humor. He laughs so hard that his fist subconsciously pounds the table, a pepper shaker overturning and clinking on the iron. I guess it's hard to believe that the girl he knows, shy and a little awkward, would have that kind of addiction.

"You got me. I'll give you that," he says, leaning back in his chair with a grin.

My expression never falters. I can't laugh with him or joke about Lily's problem. Not when I know how dangerous it has been. Before we were together, I found out that she was surfing Craigslist for a hookup. There are levels to sex addiction that scare the shit out of me.

My father watches my unwavering features, and his smile fades. "You're serious?"

"She's addicted to sex. She has been since . . . I don't know, since she lost it." I cringe, *never* wanting to talk to my father about this.

He rubs his mouth, connecting everything together. "Oh . . ." His eyes grow. "Oh . . . *fuck*." He glances at my contract like he's one second from snatching the paper and setting it on fire.

I pocket the contract, and his eyes lift to mine. "We have a deal," I remind him.

"Sex addiction—are you even sure?" he asks. "That's a serious accusation, something that would need *proof*."

"She's seeing a sex therapist," I tell him, "and not that it's any of your business, but she used to hire male sex workers, so yeah—she had a fucking problem."

"Had? Past tense?"

"We're working on it."

He lets out a low laugh that chills my bones. "You've been letting your girlfriend fuck other men?" He shakes his head, and I can practically hear his thoughts: *that can't be my pussy of a son*. He stands to pour himself another drink. I usually don't notice how often he refills, but this has to be the third or fourth time—an amount that would have most people sloshed. But he's a functioning alcoholic. Twenty-four-seven drunk. No one can really tell. It's there in his hard eyes, ready to lash out spitefully at any moment. He's just riding that wave, the edge to his life sandpapered down.

And I know if I had a sip, I'd be the same exact way. Maybe it wouldn't be so bad. I'm not aggressive, but sometimes I'm belligerent. I can make sure that won't happen. I'll be calm.

I have the sudden urge to flip my glass and ask for alcohol. *I'll get sick*, I remind myself. It's literally the only argument I can think of right now.

I try to focus on my father's eyes and not the glass in his hand. "I didn't let her fuck anyone when we were together. We only started dating seven months ago." I explain quickly about our fake relationship, cursing myself that everything has become so complicated that I have to reveal this too.

My father hasn't taken a seat yet. "You acted like you were together just so I wouldn't send you to a military academy?"

"Yeah," I say. "You were ready to ship me off, weren't you?" I had fucked up and vandalized some guy's house for messing with Lily. He mailed her a dead rabbit after his girlfriend discovered that he fucked another girl, and he blamed it on Lily, even though he was the cheating bastard.

I retaliated by dousing his door in pig's blood. It was one of my more creative efforts. And I was blackout drunk. I honestly remember very little of the whole ordeal. But I can recall everything afterward—how my father grabbed me by the neck and yelled in my face. *What did you get out of this, Loren? Did it make you feel better? Do you like being such a sick fuck?*

My father was prepared to kick me out after I dragged his name through the mud. I was the degenerate, the resident bad boy who would go to another school district just to mess with someone. I was suspended. I was a stupid kid who wanted to make Lily feel better—who wanted to change every horrible fucking thing. But I just didn't know how.

My father wanted to be proud of me, but I gave him nothing to be proud of.

"Maybe I would have shipped you off," he says, swishing his ice in his whiskey. "I was mad as hell back then. Your relationship with her was the only redeeming thing. So *maybe*."

I nod. Yeah it's why he let me stay. Maybe he would have missed me too. But he'll never admit that.

"So if you two weren't really together, what the hell were those noises coming from your room?"

I frown and then recognition hits me. I bury my face in my hands, mortified. "You heard her?"

"You weren't the only one living here," he snaps, "and you two were loud." No. *She* was loud. "It's not as if I was trying to listen. Believe me."

This is so fucked up. I rub the bridge of my nose, wanting so badly to wake up. *Wake the fuck up.*

He finally settles in his chair. "Don't tell me you let her fuck someone else in your bed."

I drop my hand and scowl. "Let's get something straight—you're not allowed to talk about her *fucking* anyone. Not me, not someone else, not anyone. Got it?"

He rolls his eyes. "You just told me she's a sex addict—"

"I don't give a shit," I say coldly. "She's still my girlfriend. She's still Lily. And I'm not anywhere near comfortable talking about this with you."

"Maybe she's just a slut," my father says, clearly ignoring me. "Ever think of that?

I could punch him. I think I could. But I don't. I use my words, just like he taught me. "I'm going to say this once, and then you will never *ever* fucking call her that again. Nor will we have this discussion." I'm standing up now. "She has a problem. She cries herself to sleep because she can't stop thinking about it. I hold her in my goddamn arms, trying to get her to quit. Sex is her drug." I point to my chest, my arms trembling. "I get it. I fucking get it, and you should too if you think for a goddamn minute how much you rely on *that*." I motion to his drink and he stiffens. "And if anyone is the slut, it's *you*." He paraded enough women in and out of the house that I could have easily obtained some complex. My chest rises and falls heavily as I finish speaking.

His voice softens considerably. "That still doesn't explain what I heard in your bedroom. If you two weren't together—"

I grimace. He's still on that? "I used to let her masturbate in my bed."

His eyes widen and he opens his mouth to speak. I cut him off. "No way," I snap. "You don't get to ask any questions about that. Our relationship—even fucked up—is between us. It has nothing to do with this situation." That's a lie, but I'm not discussing that shit with my father.

He keeps his lips tight now and then sips from his glass.

"If the tabloids found out—" I start, but it's his turn to interrupt me.

"Lily would be in the tabloids, being called names that you don't like."

"What about Fizzle?"

"It would suffer, and because you're linked with her, so would Hale Co." He rises from his chair. "Let's find the bastard."

Part Two

We all have secrets: the ones we keep, and the ones that are kept from us.

—Peter Parker, *The Amazing Spider-Man*

Twenty-two

Lily Calloway

hate flying.

Not like Superman flying. But plane flying—trapped in a metal tube in the air.

Add in my fear of heights and the prospect of being in a small, confined space for a long period of time, and I begin to freak out a little. I need the option to dash into a room and burrow underneath the covers, to hide from everyone and escape to my sanctuary.

Privacy, that's my bread and butter (besides porn).

And now that I'm on the road to recovery, I can't even join the mile-high club. I should already be in the prestigious sex-on-flight club. Being denied for the umpteenth time aggravates me and cranks up my already intolerable sexual frustration.

Lo doesn't fare much better. He used to love flying because of the mini bottles of vodka. Now he just looks like someone stole his favorite toy.

The only upside is that we're flying somewhere fun for spring break. Initially, I didn't want to go anywhere. Traveling to a party locale during the wildest week of the year seemed like a disaster zone for a recovering alcoholic, but Lo basically forced me to concede. He said he wants to test himself, and there's no better place than Cancun—with Ryke tagging along. Because we all know his half brother would stand in front of a bus before letting Lo drink.

I would too. But I haven't been put in that kind of situation yet.

My father's private jet resembles a presidential living room more than a commercial plane. I lounge on a long plush couch with blue pillows. A television is mounted on the wall and plays a newer thriller film with Nicholas Cage.

Lo is sprawled out longways, his head in my lap as I give him a mediocre head massage. He reads a comic on his tablet, flipping the pages with his finger every so often.

Over on leather recliners, Rose slides her rook across a chess board. Connor leans forward with his fist to his lips in contemplation before he makes a move with his measly black pawn. The little alcove is nice for four people. And there's another set of chairs and a tabletop to our right.

My eyes drift from the movie to the bathroom, hidden behind the same wall that the television occupies. "She's been in there a long time," I tell Lo in a soft voice. I am jealous of everyone in that bathroom. I just want to drag Lo by the arm and let him do whatever he wants to me in there. Preferably something that makes my back arch.

Lo expands a panel of his comic, his attention absorbed by persecuted mutants. I stop rubbing his temples, and then he follows my gaze. "Maybe she has to actually use the bathroom."

"True." An insensible part of me thought that tall, athletic volleyball players are immune to natural bodily functions.

I pause and glance over my shoulder, expecting to find Ryke in the right set of chairs. But that alcove is empty, only a couple bottles of water and splayed magazines. My eyes widen in realization. I gasp. "Ryke is missing." I point to the bathroom door. "They're screwing."

Lo sits up, rising off my lap. I realize I am done giving him a terrible head massage. I'm surprised he hasn't fired me before.

"They are dating," Lo reminds me, powering off his tablet and tossing it on the cushion.

Ryke brought his "somewhat" girlfriend on vacation with us. In truth, Ryke doesn't have real girlfriends. He just *dates,* which is a loose term for seeing someone and having sex for a short period of time. At least, that's how he explained it to me when Melissa stood at the airport with her rolling suitcase in tow.

Really, if I think about it, that's what Lo used to do before we became an official couple.

I squint at the bathroom door, wondering when my X-ray vision will kick in.

It doesn't.

"Why do I have the sudden urge to put my ear to that door?" My eyes grow big. Did I just say that out loud?

"You're staying on the couch." Lo tugs me onto his lap and kisses me lightly on the neck. I smile into our next kiss, his mouth meeting mine, but he draws back before I can deepen it. Damn.

My eyes flash back to the bathroom. "Can we? Later?"

He shakes his head. "I'm sorry, love." He places a small kiss on the edge of my lips.

The bathroom door swings open, and I watch as Melissa struts out first, combing her fingers through her shoulder-length, honey-blonde hair. I spring from Lo's arms and rush to the bathroom as though I have to pee.

I don't.

I just really want to catch Ryke red-handed. I think both Lo and I can agree that it's overly fun trying to make his brother uncomfortable. I have yet to be successful. But one day, I'll figure out what makes Ryke Meadows squirm.

When I look through the doorframe, I find Ryke at the sink, washing his hands. He doesn't even recoil in surprise.

"You are so busted," I say. "I just saw Melissa leaving here." I waggle my eyebrows for further effect, but he stays unblinking. Catching someone in an incriminating deed is not as fun when they don't act like they've been caught.

"So?" He dries his hands on a cotton towel.

Being a cop can't be nearly this annoying.

He says, "I'm sure you've spent plenty of time in a plane's bathroom with someone else." I have tried. None have been successful. But that's not the point . . . right?

"We have a no-sex policy on this flight."

"For you." He gives me a stern look, and then his eyes float over my shoulder.

"You're making her paranoid," Lo says from the couch. "Wait until we land."

My cheeks redden. Maybe confronting Ryke wasn't the smartest idea. But at least Melissa has stuck earbuds in and flips through a magazine, settling in her chair among the empty alcove.

I shake my head at the guys. "No, it's fine. Ryke, you can fuck Melissa all you want. Do it in the bathroom. On the couch, well not *on* the couch, I'm sitting there. The point is . . ." I take a breath. "Don't let me stop you." Because really, it's my only distraction right now. Or maybe I just really want to hear it or something. *No, I don't.* Okay, I miss porn way too much.

Ryke stares at me for a long moment, and I wonder if he senses my longing for porn too. Then Lo says, "Unless you want to start being in her fantasies."

Ryke grimaces. "It won't happen again."

He slides out of the bathroom, and I return to the couch, and slap Lo lightly on the arm. There's no way that Ryke would ever fill my fantasies, desperate or not.

Only when my gaze drifts, do I realize that the couch is lower than the chairs that Ryke, Melissa, Connor, and Rose sit on. I can clearly see their legs underneath the table. And while Connor's knees knock with Rose's, her ankles are modestly crossed.

Melissa and Ryke are a different story. It's like the angels on my left side and the devils on the right. I should watch Connor and Rose's chess tournament. Connor has won two games and Rose has won three. By Rose's pursed lips, I can tell she's losing the current round.

But I can't deny the call of the bad.

Melissa may think she's stealthy, but her hand runs up Ryke's leg and toward the inside of his thigh. I even catch her unzipping his jeans. They sit side by side, and I have a worse view of Ryke, but his hands aren't on the table either, if you know what I mean.

A sudden burst of jealousy infiltrates me. Because she can have sex on the plane. Twice. Or three times. She can even grope her somewhat-boyfriend, and he can run the bases with her.

"Try not to think about it," Lo says. "And that probably starts with not looking at it."

I turn to meet him, and he gives me a sympathetic smile. But he looks just as tweaked as me. "How are you doing?" I ask.

"I'd feel better if I knew you were okay."

"When we land do you think we can . . . ?"

He doesn't answer me. He just pulls me to his chest and strokes the back of my head, his fingers lost in my hair. He finds the remote and turns the volume up on the television. I take his silence as an answer anyway.

I'll have to wait.

The gold ornate lobby has dark green floors and large Mayan statues along the tiled walls. Decked out with four pools, more than a dozen restaurants, and even more clubs, the resort is much fancier than I feel.

Melissa waits with me by an ornate fountain while the others join the line to the front desks, hoping to check us into our rooms in a reasonable hour. Ryke's somewhat-girlfriend runs her fingers through her blonde hair again. She wears no makeup, which reminds me a little of my youngest sister. Daisy can pull off that fresh-faced look but still be pretty enough to pose for a magazine. Melissa looks prepared for the cover of *Sports Illustrated*—perfectly toned arms and clear complexion. Beauty and brawn.

I'm still trying to nail down the beauty bit, and with my chicken legs, I don't think I'd stand a chance to achieve the brawn part.

"Do you have a brush?" she asks. "My hair always tangles in the humidity." She flashes an outgoing smile, and I suddenly feel badly for never instigating a single conversation before now.

Lo and I mostly kept to ourselves on the plane. I did cheer on Rose at one point—that was before she lost her chess tournament and knocked over Connor's king in frustration. Connor tried not to gloat, but even the appearance of a smile irked Rose. She called a Scrabble rematch, which she won. So in Harry Potter's epic final words, "All was well."

But even in a tight, cramped space, Lo and I blocked out the rest of the world and whispered to ourselves. We have to work on that. So from this moment on, I make it my goal to be a better friend . . . or person . . . whatever you call someone who needs to work on her social skills.

And that starts with a brush—that I don't have. I cringe. "Sorry, I didn't pack one." Has she seen my hair? "I'm sure Rose does."

Melissa shrugs. "I can wait." She snaps a blue band off her wrist and ties her hair into a small bun at the base of her neck.

"So . . . how did you meet Ryke?"

"At the gym. One of the machines wasn't working, and he helped me."

"Sounds like Ryke," I say with a nod. He's a fixer. "Did he punch the machine into submission too?"

She frowns, and I immediately regret my words. Oh my God. I'm an idiot. "I mean, because he's kind of aggressive . . ." I cringe again. What is wrong with me? "Not in like a woman-hitting way. I don't think he'd ever do that. He just, you know, punches first and asks questions later." *Lily, shut up!*

She looks mildly freaked out—which isn't too bad. She could be horrified to the point of darting away. "We haven't been going out that long, but I've never seen him hit anyone."

"Oh yeah, me too," I lie, trying to find an out from this situation. She frowns again, because I'm obviously not making any sense. But it's better that she now finds me insane and not Ryke.

I have seen Ryke throw a punch. First to protect me when some guy didn't understand the word *no*, and then to protect Daisy at an out of control New Year's Eve party. In fact, the only time I've ever seen him be aggressive is when women are treated badly. But I don't tell Melissa this. I've already dug myself a big enough hole.

"What's going on over there?" Melissa nods to the front desk. A long line spindles across the lobby, the place jam-packed from the spring break festivities. Three hotel staff in green collared shirts left their posts to talk to our group, and Rose's hands are moving wildly in the air.

Something is definitely wrong.

I pay one of the bellhops to watch our luggage, and Melissa and I make our way to the front desk, weaving in and out of angry stares that think we're cutting the line.

"Sorry," I apologize a couple times.

I don't dare go near Rose, who is having some sort of verbal battle with the hotel staff, Connor right by her side with a narrowed gaze. Instead, I slide next to Lo and Ryke who stand off to the side. "What's going on?" I ask Lo.

He runs his hands through his hair like he's fixing it, but I think he's more anxious than anything. "There's a problem with the room," he says casually. "It should be resolved soon, or so they say."

"What kind of problem?" Melissa asks.

"They double booked," Ryke says, leaning an elbow on the counter.

"Is there another room?" I ask.

"That's what Connor and Rose are trying to figure out."

Just as he says this, Rose pulls out her phone and walks off toward the exit. I frown. Where the hell is she going?

Connor slips past hordes of sweating tourists who just want their room keys, and he stops in front of us. He looks about ten times less stressed than my sister. "So bad news. The three-bedroom suite that we had booked is unavailable due to scheduling issues. Rose is going to call other resorts, but the probability of getting a last-minute suite during college spring break is slim to none. This resort, however, does have a room available. Two queens and a pull-out, so it sleeps six."

His eyes flicker to Lo and me as he delivers the last line.

The bottom of my stomach drops down and down and down.

I can't have sex.

I hate, hate, hate that I'm most worried about *that*. I hate that Connor and probably my sister are concerned about my sexual cravings. I don't want to make this a big deal.

"That's fine," I say quickly, adding an assured nod. Even though I fiddle with my fingers and focus on *not* biting my nails.

Melissa's lip twitches. I bet that she's peeved by the change of plans. She says, "Well, this sucks." Yep, I knew it.

Ryke's features harden. "You realize that if you went with your volleyball team to Panama City, you'd be sleeping on top of each other in some dingy motel room anyway."

"I just qualified for the Olympics," she reminds him. "I'm pretty sure I can afford to rent a condo in Florida."

Ryke tugs her into his arms and then whispers something soft (and I imagine sexy) into her ear. She sighs exasperatedly, but her shoulders relax.

Connor ushers Lo and me away from them and over to the fountain. His voice lowers. "Rose is trying her best, but seriously, we can go anywhere else. The Alps. Canada. Bermuda. We don't have to stay here if it's going to make you both uncomfortable."

Running away from this situation sounds enticing. I've never even been to summer camp. And as a girl who likes her privacy and avoids social interaction, I do not take pleasure in the idea of sleeping in *one* room with *five* other people for an entire week. Add in my sex addiction status and everything becomes a big pile of *this is going to blow*.

Lo reaches out and takes my trembling hand in his. His gaze tells me to be strong. "It's up to you."

I don't want to run. I don't want to put other people out because of my stupid addiction. It's time to work through this instead of scampering away like a squirrel caught in traffic. "We should stay."

"Are you sure?" Lo puts his hand on my neck and a breath hitches in my lungs. Maybe we can have sex in the bathroom or . . . on the beach at night. We can find somewhere to do it surely. It won't be that bad. I just nod over and over as I try to convince myself.

"Lily," Connor cuts in, "where did you leave the luggage?"

"With the bellhop . . ." I turn to look at the place I stood. Which would be *right here* by Mr. Fountain.

"What bellhop?"

"Um . . . the one I paid to watch it." My heart sinks and my palms go clammy.

"You mean the guy you paid to steal it."

Oh no.

Twenty-three

Lily Calloway

After two hours and a police report later, we come to the conclusion that our bags are officially lost—or rather, *stolen*.

Lo, Ryke, Melissa and I have to spend one of our vacation days at the US Embassy to replace our passports before we can return home. It's not by luck that the only two people responsible enough to keep their passports on them were Rose and Connor.

Losing our bags is just another headache, and I've apologized so much that my throat has gone sore. Rose is mostly upset that she no longer has all of her clothes and her products and everything that makes her feel comfortable away from home. To make matters worse, our room doesn't even have a pull-out couch with a bed underneath.

It's a normal sofa.

And to rectify the situation, Connor called room service to bring up a cot. Ryke offered to sleep on it with Melissa on the couch. But she wore the "I hate this" expression that she had in the lobby. She did not want to be volunteered for the sofa and cot. She planned to cuddle with her somewhat-boyfriend, and that's unachievable if they're on separate pieces of furniture.

I can totally understand her frustration right now. Even though I was lucky enough to snag a bed, Connor and Rose's queen sits not even five feet from ours. It's not as if I can have a quickie without them noticing. And Melissa would catch us too. The couch faces the beds, and Ryke somehow wedged the cot between both.

It's as if Ryke Meadows is sleeping at the foot of our mattress. Such an unsettling thought.

The silver lining has to be Rose and Connor. During disaster situations, they're the two people you want in your squadron—able to think under fire. They both went to the gift shop and bought essentials like toothpaste and toothbrushes. For pajamas, Rose picked out extra-large neon shirts that say I LOVE CANCUN.

When she showed me those, I immediately remembered how this week was supposed to be a big step in her relationship with Connor. She asked him to sleep in the same bed as her, and when we had the three-bedroom suite, her plan didn't seem as scary. But now that the sleeping arrangements have altered drastically, and everyone will be in clear sight of their bed, she's more nervous. Tackling this level of their relationship in front of other people is not something she had imagined.

Even in my twenties, I still find sleeping in a bed with a boy a kind of intimate affair. Maybe because it usually coincides with sex for me, but I think Rose can agree that the act is not so friendly.

Darkness blankets the room, but I can still distinguish the outline of bodies. Rose and Connor lie underneath their maroon comforter, facing each other but not touching. They were whispering softly before, but their voices have quieted, leaving the room in an uncomfortable stillness.

I flip over and turn to Lo, his arm wrapped around my waist.

His eyes are already open, and his foot slides against the bareness of my ankle. The silence envelops us and makes me hyperaware of every small noise, my breathing too loud in the quiet. I'm sure Ryke believes all my little movements coincide with me attempting to screw Lo.

But I just . . . can't sleep.

Anxiety crawls under my skin like a bedbug. I start playing scenarios in my head of being denied sex over and over. Where I can't do anything for an entire week. Where I can't escape to a bedroom to disappear from other people for five minutes. I'm surrounded. Suffocating.

"Lo," I whisper, trying to be as silent as I can. But my voice sounds like a megaphone in the quiet.

He tugs me closer, and his hands lower to my hips and then lower. He cups my butt with one palm and rubs my back in a circular motion with the other.

He tries to be quiet, even as he kisses my lips gently, encouraging me to relax with each one. But his tender kisses do the opposite, building need so deep inside of me. And a horrible part of my brain clouds the reasonable side. I fling my leg over his waist, and then his lips immediately depart from mine. I wonder if I'll ever be able to touch them again.

After a couple minutes of Lo stroking my hair and watching my breath begin to calm, my eyes grow heavy and I think I'm finally about to drift to sleep.

And then my phone glows and vibrates on the pillow that I've abandoned to be closer to Lo. I roll away from him, and he props an elbow on the mattress, worried about me.

"I'm fine," I whisper and cradle my phone in two panicky hands. I swipe the lock on my cell, and I'm met with a brand new text.

Have fun sucking cock in Cancun.—Unknown

I blink a couple times, the brightness from the screen hurting my eyes. Bile rises to my throat as I reread the words. I'm less affected by the "sucking cock" part as I am by the "Cancun" bit.

He knows where I am . . .

Quickly, I shut it off and swing my legs off the bed. My heart pounds in my chest and I really just need to think for a second. I try to navigate the room in the dark, but I end up tripping on the end of the cot. I fall to my knees.

"Fuck," Ryke groans. "That was my foot."

"Sor-ry." My voice shakes and I pick myself back up, stumbling to the bathroom. I feel a hand on the small of my back as soon as I retreat inside.

Lo closes the door behind us, and I flip on the lights. He squints from the blinding fluorescence, and I splash some water on my face. The bright neon-blue Cancun sweatshirt stops at my thighs and feels so hot on my body right now.

"What's wrong?" Concern laces his voice. I haven't told him about the texts. I meant to, but every time I'm about to mention it something else comes up.

Tears prick my eyes, and I manage to hand him my phone anyway. I turn back around to the mirror and the sink, not wanting to watch his face as he reads them. This already feels so out of my control. Every breath falls heavy against my chest. I just want to be unsaddled from this anxiety. Is that at all possible?

Yes it is, the bad part of me says.

I'm not wearing any pants or shorts, and my hand just seems to naturally direct itself to my panties. I slip my fingers below the hem while I have an elbow planted on the counter, hunched over with my forehead buried in my arm. Everything feels so, so, so wrong and out of my control and I just want to feel good again.

"Lil," Lo says behind me. He drops my phone, the cell clattering to the floor. He instinctively grips my arm and presses his chest hard against my back. "Shh, you're okay, love."

I want to listen to his voice, but I'm more focused on how *that* feels, my ass rubbed against him. He removes my fingers from my underwear, and I let him bring both of my hands underneath the warm water. He washes them quietly.

I sniff a little, emotions bubbling, things I really hoped I wouldn't feel at all on this trip. Guilt, shame—failure. He brushes the tears from my cheeks, and I finally hear his voice.

"We're going to find this guy. You don't need to worry about it, Lil."

"He knows we're in Cancun . . ." My voice comes out in a whisper.

Lo spins me around after he dries off my hands. He cups my cheeks and tilts my head a little to meet his eyes. "No one is going to hurt you. I promise."

I love—more than anything—that he doesn't bring up the fact that I just touched myself. That I fucked up in a tiny immeasurable way. He brushes it off, moves on, and makes me feel like I should too.

Twenty-four

Loren Hale

J ust drink more water."

That happens to be Ryke's brilliant advice whenever I tell him that I feel like a car ran over me. This morning is no different. I stand on the patio, the crystal-blue beaches in the horizon, but right below lies the congested pool. Sloshed college students splash in the clear waters to the beat of some techno rap remix. Amps sit beneath a white stretched canopy, shaded from the dangerously hot sun. Sometimes a DJ arrives to fuel the crowd's drunkenness, but right now, the station stays vacant. The leathered-skin DJ downs tequila shots at the tiki bar with two girls in G-string bikinis.

It's definitely spring break.

I chug more water, but it doesn't cure the pounding headache or the exhaustion that aches my muscles. By the time Lily and I went back to bed, it was near three in the morning, and I couldn't stop thinking about the text and calling my father. I replayed an entire conversation about what I would ask him. How I would frame my words . . . just to check up on the progress of everything.

"Are you okay?" Ryke asks.

If I say yes, he'll know I'm lying. So I don't know why he asks me. "I've had hangovers that have felt better than this." I stretch my arms and legs, loosening up my joints.

Ryke sits on the patio chair and smears cream cheese on the bagel that he ordered from room service. "But this type of pain isn't accompanied by horrible drunken memories. Consider your-self fucking lucky."

"Yes, I'm feeling overwhelmingly lucky right now," I retort bit-terly.

"We'll find that guy," Ryke tells me. I showed him the texts this morning before Lily woke up. "And then I'm going to put my fist in his fucking face."

"HEY! THIRD FLOOR!"

I lean an arm on the balcony railing and spot two American girls in string bikinis, their breasts hardly contained. Like the locals, they've tried to adopt the scarce bottom look, asses fully exposed. Both girls hold brightly colored plastic cups, their hair braided across their shoulders.

Ryke stands and puts his forearms on the railing, taking in the sight. He bites into his bagel nonchalantly, watching as the girl in the green bikini waves us down.

"Come swim with us!" she shouts with a smile.

"Remind me why I came here with a girl," Ryke says with a longing look. He checks out her ass, and the girl only grins wider.

"Because you didn't want to be the fifth wheel." I smile at his distress.

A loud scream echoes from the room, and we both quickly peel away from the balcony and rush inside. Without much room, I bump straight into Connor's back. He almost trips over the cot that blocks the hall, but he grabs onto the dresser before falling.

"What's going on?" I ask, trying to maneuver around the fold-out bed.

Ryke is so annoyed that he kicks the entire thing. It slams into the wall and somehow efficiently makes room for us to walk.

"Daisy is here," Connor says.

"What?" Ryke goes rigid. Probably thinking the same as me—that was a *happy* scream?

I frown and search the room with a hesitant gaze. But I only spot

Melissa on the couch, eating a bagel and typing on her cell phone. Her lips are downturned, not having as much fun as she probably imagined.

"They're in the bathroom," Connor explains. "Rose wants to put makeup on and use Daisy's flat iron. She's actually excited, but the luxury of name-brand hair products will probably wear off when she realizes that her sixteen-year-old sister just arrived to Cancun during *college* spring break."

"So no one knew she was coming?" I ask.

Connor shakes his head. "She wanted to surprise her sisters."

"She can't stay," Ryke says roughly. "I nearly died trying to chaperone her sweet sixteen in Acapulco."

I heard the story from Lily, who also chaperoned Daisy's birthday. Apparently the fearless Calloway jumped off a cliff into the ocean and Ryke felt the need to jump in after her.

"I won't let her jump off anything," I tell him. "I happen to be a damn good chaperone."

He glares. "You couldn't chaperone a fucking sloth. And that requires remedial skills like sitting and watching."

I shoot him a hard look. I honestly don't care if Daisy stays or not. One more person in an already crowded room won't change anything. "Daisy blends in. You won't even notice she's here."

His brows harden and his jaw sets, equally as firm. "When's the last time you've fucking seen her?"

I want to say *last week*, but I'm certain that's wrong. I strain my mind. I guess I haven't seen her since I've been back from rehab. In fact, I don't think I ran into her at the Christmas Charity Gala last year. Granted, I didn't stay long. The last time I saw her must have been during the yacht trip to the Bahamas—when Lily and I became a real couple. Jesus.

That was a long time ago.

"Daisy doesn't blend," Connor says.

"When have you seen her?" I snap accusingly. I don't like that these two guys have spent more time with my girlfriend's sister than me. I've been around the Calloways longer. I've known Daisy since she was a kid. I'm supposed to be the interim "big brother" figure. Though, I've done a pretty shitty job of it so far.

"I go to the Calloway Sunday luncheons with Rose," Connor tells me. Oh. Shit.

If I marry Lily, I am easily going to be the worst son-in-law.

And then I pale at the idea of Connor and Rose.

Connor Cobalt cannot marry Lily's sister. He'll set unattainable standards that I will never be able to meet.

Loud, happy squeals resound from the bathroom. I relax at the mere thought that Lily is smiling. Last night she was near tears, and anything that can change her mood is something I wholeheartedly approve of. "I'm going to check on them," I say.

Ryke takes a seat on the edge of the bed, scowling at the carpet. He seems deep in thought. About what—I have no clue. Could be Daisy. Could be Melissa. Could be me.

As I pass, I point at him, "You know what would make you feel better?" I open my mouth to finish, but he cuts me off.

"I'm fine." And then he crosses his arms.

"Sure." I give him a once-over. He's probably pissed that he's stuck with Melissa. The girl wears impatience like it's her job. "A beer."

"A what?"

"A beer would make you feel better."

He glares. "That's not funny."

"It wasn't a joke."

"You better go to the bathroom before I punch you, which *will* actually make me feel better."

I mock gasp. "But I thought you were fine."

He actually stands off the bed. I don't badger him anymore. But Christ, his annoyance made *me* feel better. Sans beer and all.

With a wide smile, I walk over to the bathroom. The giggles grow in octave, and I rap my knuckles against the door.

"Who is it?" Rose calls from inside.

"Lo." I glance over my shoulder. Ryke and Connor watch me in curiosity by the balcony doors, not attempting to infiltrate the exclusive club that the Calloway girls have. For the first time, I'm a little nervous that the girls won't invite me in. I've always been allowed to be with them. I'm Lily's other half.

But things have changed, I realize. Rose has a boyfriend. I have a brother. Two more guys have been added to our dynamic, and I could easily be grouped off with them.

So when the door swings open and Lily grabs my shirt, pulling me inside, I can't help but grin. I feel kind of fucking special. I kiss her almost immediately and while my tongue slides into her mouth, she pushes the door closed with her foot.

Rose clears her throat, and I break away, wrapping my arms around Lily's waist. She leans back into me with a deep breath, and I finally take in the room. Hair products and makeup have exploded across the counter. Rose sits on the bathtub ledge with a flat iron in one hand and a tube of lip gloss in the other.

"Did Saks Fifth Avenue vomit in our bathroom?" I ask.

They all laugh, and Rose is even too happy to retort with her usual ice. She looks like someone saved her from a deserted island. When Lily untangles from my arms and kneels down over a huge suitcase, I see Daisy for the first time.

She sits on the other side of the suitcase where clothes upon clothes pile high, the stack threatening to topple over. Shopping bags are smashed into available corners of the luggage.

"Hey, Lo," Daisy greets with a warm smile.

And as I truly look at her, my face slowly falls. All I can manage to say is this, "You're . . . blonde . . ." A million other thoughts cross my mind. Most of them circulate around one thing: Me, warning Daisy to stay far away from *every* guy on the fucking planet. And I have a flash of having to beat the shit out of someone on this trip—just to protect a girl who easily looks as old as her two sisters. She can fit in with our group of college-aged kids. And she shouldn't. She's *sixteen*, despite being a high fashion model.

Great.

Now I know exactly why Ryke was scowling. He knew she was going to be trouble. Not because of her personality. But because . . . she's beautiful and too young to be here.

Daisy runs her fingers through her insanely long hair. "The modeling agency wanted it blonde." She drops the strands, and they splay past her breasts. *Fuck*. I hate that I'm even looking there. I fix my gaze on Lily instead.

She tosses bathing suits from the shopping bag. She looks like she's digging to China through clothes. It's kind of adorable.

"So what are you doing here, Dais?" I ask, my eyes staying on Lily. It helps keep my mind off dragging Daisy to the nearest airport. I just want to make sure she's safe. Three years ago, I'm not sure I would have even cared. Being sober definitely shifts my priorities.

"Well," she says, leaning against the sink counter. "I always miss out on spring break with Lily and Rose. Seeing as how this is Rose's last official college spring break, I thought I'd just kind of tag along. But don't worry, you won't even know I'm here. Promise."

I must be glaring because she smiles again for sincerity. I believe her. That's not what I'm worried about.

"What about high school?" I ask.

"The teachers gave me extensions on all of the assignments like they do when I have a photo shoot out of the country." Before I can protest, she adds, "And Rose texted me last night about the stolen luggage, so I had time to stop at the mall and pick up some clothes for everyone." She grabs a Macy's shopping bag and hands it to me. "I picked out some swimsuits for Connor, Ryke, and you. I didn't think you guys would want to suffer through shopping on your first day at the beach."

"Yessss!" Lily cheers from the floor.

Everyone turns to see her raising a one-piece bathing suit like it's baby Simba.

"I thought you would like that," Daisy says. "It's Billabong."

"You need sun," Rose says flatly. She claps her iron at Lily. "Drop. The. Suit."

Lily clutches the black one-piece to her chest, half the suit multicolored with layers of diamond patterns. "I have Daisy on my side," Lily reminds her. "She'll tackle you."

Daisy nods confidently. "I will."

Rose is in such a good mood that she concedes. "Fine." Her eyes flicker to the one-piece that Lily covets. "It is cute in a beach bum, 'I'm going surfing because I can't read' type of way."

I dig through the Macy's bag that Daisy gave me, and I pause.

There are five swimsuits, all different bright neon colors but the same style. A Speedo. Pretty much a mankini.

"Uh . . . Daisy." I raise my brows. I hold up the banana hammock on the end of one finger.

Daisy tries not to smile too wide, but she's enjoying this. "The store clerk said those were the most popular."

"For children maybe. I'm not sure my dick can fit in this." And I instantly wince at my choice of word. "I mean, my stuff."

Lily is distracted enough that she drops her bathing suit, her eyes gleaming between my crotch and the suit. Her imagination is just too fucking vast. I cannot keep up.

Daisy looks at me like I'm the weird one. "It's okay to curse in front of me. I won't tattle on you." Yeah, she definitely makes me feel stupid for trying *not* to warp her young, fragile mind. But she's a model. I can't even begin to understand what goes on after a photo shoot, during one, or before. I'm pretty sure they talk about dicks and breasts and a whole lot of other shit that would be inappropriate around easily influenced kids.

She's not twelve, Lo, I remind myself. She's sixteen. There is a difference. She's in high school. Hell, she's probably had sex.

I stop myself. There are some things I just don't want to know.

I twirl the suit around and focus on Lily. I fling it at her and she catches the mankini in her hands.

"Yeah," she says, far away with her naughty thoughts that I definitely wish I could hear. "I don't think he'll fit." She flushes like she didn't mean to say that aloud. I just want to kiss her.

"Unnecessary information," Rose says.

"Actually, that was necessary," I say. "If I can't fit, then I need another bathing suit."

Daisy bends down and starts digging through the suitcase beside Lily. While she rummages around, I remember that she shouldn't be here in the first place.

"So she's staying?" I look between Rose and Lily, waiting for one of them to be the mature older sister and set guidelines, rules, whatever and send Daisy back home.

But the most responsible girl—maybe in the entire universe—gives me the worst kind of reprimanding glare and says, "She can stay."

I think they've gone nuts. They obviously don't understand what Daisy looks like or realize her age and the fact that just outside our window are hundreds of horny fucking guys. "Can I talk to you and you"—I point at Lily and Rose—"in private. Thanks."

From the suitcase, Daisy glances up at me. "I'm sorry about the swimsuits. It was just a joke, honestly. Here." She tosses a new shopping bag to me, and I hesitate, mostly because I see how much Daisy wants me to be okay with her here. She doesn't want to put anyone out since she's essentially crashing our spring break. And I think if I told her that she's not welcome, she would be on the next flight without argument.

Before I search in the plastic bag, I keep my gaze trained on Rose who has the most sway in whether or not Daisy stays in Cancun. "What happens when a guy offers her a drink?"

"I'll turn it down," Daisy answers. She rocks on the balls of her feet, prepared to answer more questions.

"Are you going to drink?" I ask her.

"If it upsets you, then no."

My muscles twitch. I don't like the idea of people being sober just because I am. That's ridiculous. "It doesn't upset me, but you're underage, Daisy, even in Mexico."

"Since I was fourteen, my mom has always let me drink during vacations. Ask Rose."

Rose unplugs her flat iron and brushes her glossy hair. "Just the fruity drinks," she says. "And only because Mother trusted you not to go crazy."

"I won't," Daisy says. "And if it makes you feel better, I won't drink at all."

I shake my head and wear a deep frown. I'm not sure what the right call is. I know that most kids drink at sixteen. And I wouldn't want to baby her just because I'm an alcoholic. But is twenty-one the magical safe age or something? I don't know.

I internally groan. She may not be staying here at all so it won't even matter. "What happens if she breaks from our group, Rose?"

"She won't," Rose retorts. "I'm not going to leave Daisy alone in a foreign country. While the big brother routine is flattering, Loren, she has two sisters in Cancun who care for her just as much, if not more. She's safe with us."

I watch Lily glance between me and Daisy, and I see the worry so apparent on her face. She wants her little sister here just as much as Rose does. Maybe they want to spend time with her, to reconnect together in ways that they haven't in a long, long time. And if Daisy can put a smile on Lily's face, then maybe the hassle will be worth it.

"Okay," I nod.

"Are you sure?" Daisy asks. "If you're upset, then I can go . . ."

"No," Rose cuts in.

I glare at her. "So glad to know that you consider my feelings, Rose. We now know who the nicest sister is."

"I thought that was me," Lily pipes in with a coy smile.

"You're the best everything, love, that's unspoken and true."

She bites her lip, and I can practically hear her chanting for me to come over there and kiss her. I would, but Rose is searing holes in my forehead.

"What about Connor and Ryke?" Daisy asks hesitantly.

"Connor won't care," Rose tells her.

Ryke will. I flash her a comforting smile that feels a bit false for me. I just hope I'm not grimacing. "If Ryke isn't nice to you then I'll take care of him." I actually turn to Rose for approval, not sure why hers means so much to me. But she nods in appreciation, or as close to the sentiment as that girl can come.

"Thanks, Lo," Daisy says.

Lily stands up and sidles to me. I wrap an arm loosely around her shoulders while she sinks into my body. This is a hug that should turn into something more. I can feel her aching for it as her fingers dig deeper in my waist. But she can't. I just hope she can withstand a week without sex. She'll need to be satisfied by kisses. Whereas normal people take a kiss as real affection, Lily sees it as nothing more than teasing if it's not the means to a good fuck.

I rub her back while I dig through the plastic bag with one hand. I find three appropriate male swimsuits in black and navy-blue. "Are these the only other guy suits you bought?" I ask Daisy, a wicked thought crossing my mind.

"Yeah. Are they bad?" She comes to my side and peeks in the bag. "These Ralph Lauren ones should fit."

"I know. I'm just thinking that you only bought two of them . . . for me and Connor." They all catch on to my ploy.

Rose shakes her head repeatedly, but Lily is nodding fiercely. Daisy's lips pull into a devious smile, definitely up for a bit of harmless fun.

If Ryke and I are going to be brothers, I might as well start reaping the benefits. And it begins with a prank.

Twenty-five

Loren Hale

We took one step onto the beach, and I thought my eyeballs were going to burn out of their socket. The sun was inescapable, too hot to even breathe properly. And all the beach cabanas are first come, first served, so we have to wake up earlier to claim one tomorrow. We end up finding seven lounge chairs around the crowded pool. On the elevator ride down, Daisy asked me again if it was okay if she drank around me. Personally, I feel worse if people stop having a good time on my account. I've forced Connor to order wine—his drink of choice—on numerous occasions.

But I thought I'd be a little more creative in my reply to Daisy since she is sixteen and I'm still trying to understand what's appropriate for teenagers. I told her that I didn't mind if she drank, but she shouldn't drink more than Rose. In fact, she should try to loosen Rose up this week. If there's anything I'd pay good money to see, it's Rose Calloway drunk.

Daisy easily agreed. She seems to want to please other people, and I wonder just how much of her life has been dedicated to appeasing her mother.

Both Daisy and Rose wade in the pool with piña coladas in their hands. An engulfing rock fountain swamps one circular alcove where a poolside bar lies, but we're a good distance from that mobbed area.

Ryke climbs out of the pool and nods to the rest of us who idly stand in the water. Lily is the only one on dry land.

She lies alone on a lounge chair, not wanting to join us. I get it. She touched herself the first night, and I've been repeatedly telling her that she's not going to have sex this week. Now we're at a pool with half-naked guys, a half-naked *me*.

I can spot several couples groping underneath cabanas, and even a few cling to each other in the water, making out, the guy's tongue deep down the girl's throat. There's no shame there either. And I think she's probably just as jealous of that too.

She's craving sex badly, and I understand wanting to drift off with music and take a nap in the sun. So I let her have her space and try to talk with our friends.

"I'm going to go buy some tacos," Ryke says. "If you want to eat one, you better come with me." He stands confidently in his hot-pink mankini. When I told him it was the only suit left, he literally shrugged and put it on. Tan skin, ripped abs, and stylish wayfarers—he instantly looked cool even wearing that damn thing. And the girls playing water volleyball even gawked at his ass.

That's not exactly the reaction I was looking for.

Melissa swims to the edge and climbs out, always attached to Ryke in some way. And whenever she's forced to untangle herself from him, her mood flips. A part of me wonders if that's what Lily and I look like when we're in someone else's company—bored and aggravated. Probably. I guess it's something we're working on.

"Ready?" she asks, hooking her pinkie with his fingers.

He lets go of her hand and nods to the pool again. "Calloway," he calls. All three girls turn to look at him, even Lily on the chair. He rolls his eyes and points at the tall blonde. "Daisy. You coming?"

She shakes her head and sucks on the straw of her piña colada.

For lunch, we all ate handmade pizza, but Daisy picked at a salad instead. I think it's a success that she's even sipping a fruity drink that contains a shit ton of calories, but knowing Ryke, he no doubt believes alcohol is the equivalent of bark on a food pyramid.

"Come on," he prods, gesturing her to follow him. "You'll like the taco, I promise."

"I probably will," she says, "but that still doesn't mean I should eat it."

Melissa clutches Ryke's hand and begins to pull him toward the outside grill behind a set of palm trees. "She doesn't want a taco," she says, tugging him like a child would a parent. "Let's go."

Ryke's jaw locks, and I think he would try to convince Daisy until she relented, but not with Melissa yanking his arm. So he leaves with that failure. Ryke inserting himself in other people's problems is nothing new. I'm not surprised that he would take interest in Daisy's diet, one that she maintains only to please her mother—I've known that since she started modeling.

Connor holds a mojito low in his hand and watches Melissa disappear behind the palm trees with Ryke. "He's going to regret bringing her."

"He already does," I say. I didn't think being around alcohol would affect me as much. My attention zones in on the plastic cup, and it takes a great deal of energy to concentrate on other things. Like my brother's sex life, not that I particularly care about it.

"What'd you do last year for spring break?" Connor asks.

I strain my mind and shake my head. "I can't remember." I'm sure I spent my nights at a bar while Lily fucked other guys. Our old routine. It's all so hazy, even trying to crawl back through the memories is like walking through fog. "Probably something stupid," I mutter under my breath.

Connor takes the hint and doesn't prod. "If it makes you feel any better, my last three spring breaks were in Japan trying to convince angel investors to capitalize in Cobalt Inc."

I let out a short laugh. "Now I just feel like an underachieving loser."

"I tried," he says with a casual smile.

Rose swims over to us and she elbows me in the ribs.

"Hello, Rose," I say with a grimace.

She points to our lounge chairs where Lily lies.

"Do you see what she's reading?" Rose asks me, not even slurring yet.

I frown and study Lily. Sure enough, in her hands is a *Cosmo* magazine. "Where did she get that?"

"Daisy probably bought it from the airport."

"Is she not allowed to read trashy magazines?" Connor asks.

Rose tilts her head like he asked a stupid question. "Not ones that describe sexual positions and have romance stories in the back."

I raise my eyes at him. "You've never read *Cosmo* before?"

"I never needed to know the top fifty ways to pleasure a man."

I splash him, and he lets out a laugh, and I actually smile. I swim to the ledge, knowing full well that if I had whiskey today, nothing would have stopped me from uttering a biting response. And for once, I truly feel like I achieved something.

I hop out of the pool. Lily doesn't even see me coming, too immersed in a dirty magazine.

Twenty-six

Lily Calloway

5 *Sex Toys Perfect for Traveling.* My little bullet vibrator survived the bellhop-impersonating thief since I stowed it in my purse, but there's a slim chance I'll be using it anytime this week.

Vibrating panties even made it on the list. I have those too (back home), but I never actually tried them out. I flip the page and land on the sex tips from guys. Some make me laugh, while others are actually helpful. I skim the list and smile at the advice from Brett, 24. *Wet your lips. Then tell me you can't wait to taste me.* Thank you, Brett for making it seem like girls have to give blow jobs to please a guy. Not true. In fact, if I didn't like giving Lo head, I wouldn't do it.

"Hey."

I jump a little at the voice and press the magazine to my chest, flushing in a rosy shade. I relax when I see it's Lo, dripping wet in his swimsuit. I try to focus on his face and not his body, but even the striking jaw and dark, wet hair looks extremely sexy right now.

I lick my bottom lip and say, "I can't wait to taste you."

He narrows his eyes, not amused, and grabs the magazine from me. My shoulders slacken as his eyes flit over the page. They roll dramatically when he reads Brett's advice. Lo folds the magazine in his hand and sits down on the foot of the lounge chair. I realize I'm probably not going to be getting that *Cosmo* back.

"It's not porn," I defend immediately.

"You still shouldn't read it. You're trying to go a day without thinking about sex, and flipping through a magazine that highlights the ten best ways to go down on someone is not going to help."

I just nod, and then my eyes drift to Ryke who walks back toward our area with an aluminum foil–wrapped taco. He licks his fingers, so I assume he already ate one on the way here. Melissa says something, and she leaves his side, heading back to the hotel room. It's strange that she would ditch him when she's made it clear that he's the only reason she's withstanding the rest of us.

My gaze drifts to the bright pink Speedo that leaves nothing to the imagination. He fills it out too well. One wrong move and everything may just pop out. "That kind of backfired, didn't it?" I say to Lo with a smile.

Lo places a hand on my bare calf, which sends tingles down my spine. Even the simplest touch right now, I covet. "How was I supposed to know he was so comfortable in a banana hammock?" Lo says loud enough for Ryke to hear when he approaches. "We've only been brothers for four months."

"We've been brothers for twenty-one years," Ryke refutes. He sits on the pool ledge beside our chair, sticking his feet into the water. "You only knew about me four months ago."

"And that's supposed to make me like you more?"

Ryke flashes a dry smile and nods to the magazine in Lo's hand. "Beach reading?"

Lo tosses the magazine on the wet cement beside Ryke. "Here, maybe you can learn how to go down on Melissa. She seems incredibly displeased by you."

"I can lick her just fine. That's not why she's mad."

I tear my eyes off the hand that Lo keeps planted on my ankle. I would like, dearly, for his fingers to run up to my thigh. Especially after all this sex talk.

"Why is she upset?" I ask.

"Same reason you are."

"She's a sex addict too?" I say brightly. I'm not the only one out there. Wow, that feels good.

"No, she's just a normal horny girl."

Oh, damn. My shoulders droop.

Lo starts rubbing my calf. *That* feels even better. I sink against the back of the chair, relaxing. Lo scrolls through his cell phone for a moment, and I watch as Ryke motions to Daisy in the pool without calling her name.

She swims over to his spot by the pool wall, and since he sits out of the water, he towers above her and hunches slightly to look down at Daisy. He holds the taco out to her.

She sets her empty cup beside the sopping magazine. "I thought you said I could only have a taco if I went with you."

"I'm making an exception."

Her eyes flicker between the taco and Ryke, and I don't like where this is headed. It reminds me of the time where he tempted her with a piece of chocolate cake. She ate it, but only after a string of inappropriate events. Lo didn't see that. And he's too focused on his phone to look up and watch Daisy and Ryke.

But maybe . . . maybe it's all in my head. I mean, my thoughts circumnavigate to sex all the time. Maybe these past three months without Lo, their time together has been innocent and not as bad as I believed. And I *do* want Daisy to eat that taco.

"What will you do for me if I eat that?" Daisy asks, a scheming smile lifting her lips.

"We're bargaining now?"

She swims a little closer to him, her shoulders the same height as his knees. "It's only fair. You want me to do something. So I think I should get something in return."

"You get the nutrients of this fucking taco," he tells her. "That's a win-win."

She tries hard not to smile and just shakes her head. Oh, she's learned how to play his games since the last time. I should break this up, I think. But I'm hypnotized by their easy banter.

"What do you want?" he asks.

I nudge Lo with my foot. He needs to see this! They're about to strike some deal that is not going to be pretty. I try to find Rose and Connor too, but they've drifted over to the poolside bar.

Lo reluctantly tears away from his phone and follows my gaze, watching my sister and his brother.

And then Daisy's sly smile falters. "I don't know what I want," she realizes.

"Well that's a problem."

Lo gives me a stare like *that's what you're freaking out over? Really? It's all in my head, isn't it?*

"And I don't have time for you to figure it out," Ryke tells her. "The taco will be cold by then." He peels the aluminum foil back and holds out the end to her. "Come on, just one bite." His tone isn't kind or soft. It's rough and forceful, something that Daisy is not used to, I think. Her curiosity twinkles in her eyes.

Daisy stares at Ryke for a long moment. "Why do you want me to eat this so badly?"

"Because your body needs something more than fucking rum, ice, and piña colada mix."

"My agency would disagree."

"Your agency fucking sucks," he says.

"You would try to make every model eat cake, wouldn't you?" He doesn't deny it.

She smiles. "You know they'd just throw up afterward."

"You better not—"

"I'm not bulimic," she says. "I'm not even anorexic. I just know what I should and should not eat. And trust me, when I'm not counting down the days to a photo shoot, I'll pig out. But I have a runway in three weeks. Everyone will be pinching my fat, and you won't be there to see their disappointed, disgruntled looks. I will."

"I think," Ryke says slowly, trying to process the words, "you need to realize that this taco isn't going to add an inch on your waistline. If you have as great willpower as you say, then eating this won't cause you to binge tomorrow."

I kind of want to clap. He actually makes complete sense, and Daisy contemplates his whole statement with high regard. And then she nods in acceptance.

"Okay," she says. "But just one bite."

"Unless you love it."

"Like I said—"

"*You like many things, that doesn't mean you should eat them,*" he finishes. "I heard you."

"You listen," she says mockingly. "What kind of guy are you?"

"The rare kind."

My shoulders tense. Are they flirting? Does Lo see this? He is watching, but I can't read his expression at all. His muscles, however, pull tight.

"Okay," Daisy says, eyeing the taco. "I'll eat it."

"Stop talking about it and do it," he says.

She sets a hand on his leg and the other on his wrist as he holds out the taco. She leans forward to take a bite, and I swear, her eyes connect with his the entire time. There's something incredibly dirty about this—I see it, does anyone else?

Lo says nothing.

When she takes a bite, her eyes flutter closed and she lets out an audible moan. "Oh my God," she mumbles, chewing.

Ryke wears a satisfied grin, like he won the best prize, seeing her happy (or making an orgasmic noise, I have no idea). Sauce leaks onto her chin, but her head is tilted back, too absorbed in food bliss to notice. He uses his thumb to wipe the sauce right below her lip.

"Good, right?"

She swallows. "The best."

Okay, maybe I'm the only one processing the event in a phallic way. Ryke and Daisy act completely innocent about the entire ordeal. Maybe they don't even realize how sexual it all was. (At least it wasn't a hot dog.)

"Here." He holds out the rest of the taco.

Surprisingly, Daisy accepts the food, taking the foil from his hands. "Thanks," she says in genuine appreciation. And then she swims off toward Connor and Rose.

Lo opens his mouth, and I wonder if he's about to chastise Ryke. But how can he when Daisy ate something healthy for once? That has to be a win, right?

Before Lo says a thing, Melissa returns and we all go quiet. Well, technically Lo and I were already quiet, but the air stretches in an uncomfortable way.

Melissa sits beside Ryke on the cement, and she leans a shoulder into him. He wraps his arm around her.

"The maids are done with our room," she tells him, practically batting her eyelashes.

That's where she went—to check on the status of *our* room? If I'm not allowed to have sex there, then why can she? I look to Lo for answers, but his gaze has permanently fixed on Ryke.

"I already talked to you about it," Ryke says evenly.

"Yeah, but the public bathrooms are so gross." She looks up at Lo and me. "You guys don't care if we fool around for a couple minutes back in the room, right? We'll stick to the cot."

"Daisy is sleeping on the cot tonight," I remind her. Daisy offered to sleep on the floor, not wanting to ruin our arrangements with her impromptu arrival, but Ryke refused to let her crash on the ground. He was nice enough to take the worst spot.

"Then we'll use the couch," she says with a shrug. "You two are free to go back and have fun whenever. Really, it doesn't bother me." Hope surges through me. This is my opportunity to have sex later this week. Just when I'm about to tell her to frolic right on over to the room, Ryke has to speak.

"It bothers Rose and Connor."

Her face falls. "Oh."

An awkward silence soaks the air, and Daisy swims over to cut it right up. "Rose and Connor are fighting," she exclaims. She lifts her body out of the pool and sits on the chair next to me. "It's kind of scary. I don't understand half the words coming out of their mouths." Her hair looks almost brown now that it's wet. She wrings it out in her hands.

I glance at the poolside bar. Sure enough, Rose and Connor square off, their mouths moving in such rapid succession that they look as if they're on a debate team. People surrounding them watch in amusement and even awe.

"Anyone want a refill?" Melissa asks. She stands and waves her empty cup.

"I could take a daiquiri," Daisy says.

"Virgin, right?"

Daisy doesn't even blink. "No, I'm drinking rum."

"I don't really condone underage drinking. You're what, seventeen?"

"Sixteen," she says, still unaffected by Melissa's edgy words. "In some countries, I'm old enough to be married and sold into sex work, so hey, I think a couple of drinks won't necessarily kill me."

"Well, life is different here. We're in America."

"We're in Mexico, actually."

Melissa's throat bobs, but she tries to brush off her snafu with a shrug. "Yeah, whatever."

Ryke hardly suppresses his grin, and when he meets Daisy's gaze, she gives him a look like *you're going to get in trouble.*

Ryke does not care what anyone thinks of him, even his somewhat-girlfriend.

Melissa sets a hand on her hip. "Want anything, *babe*?" she asks Ryke with a little force.

He doesn't drink. We all know that, and so her power move is completely obvious.

"No, I'm good," he says. When she struts off in her black bikini, Daisy tilts her head, watching Melissa's butt bounce all the way to the tiki hut. "She does have a nice ass."

"Yeah?" Ryke says casually, eyeing Daisy as she observes Melissa.

"Oh yeah," Daisy says. "But I'd put my ass in contention too." I think she's testing Ryke.

Lo stiffens beside me, and he waits to see how his brother is going to respond. *Shut it down, Ryke*—I can hear Lo recite in his head. Or I'd like to *think* I can hear him. I still haven't developed that superpower yet.

"Her ass is better. Sorry," he says, but he never looks back at Melissa. Daisy has stolen his attention.

She shrugs. "You're probably right, but if I had to rank asses, Rose's would be number one. She has the best hair too."

"Your hair is pretty," Lo tells her.

"Don't," Ryke warns him with the shake of his head. If Daisy is insecure about anything it's the hair she cannot cut or dye, per her agency's rules.

Lo's face sharpens, resentful that Ryke knows more than him. Being out of the loop for three months has been a disadvantage. Ryke saw exactly what went on when Lo was in rehab. Lo did not.

I scoot to the foot of the lounge chair and rest my head on the crook of his shoulder. He draws me into his arms. But my presence isn't enough. I can't give him back all those days he missed.

"My hair is fine," Daisy says. But she braids it subconsciously. Then she rises and sets her toes on the pool edge. She splashes into the water, and surprisingly, Ryke joins her, dropping in. He breaks the surface and runs a hand through his wet hair. Both of them cling to the wall, facing us.

"Is she good in bed?" Daisy asks him.

My eyes widen to saucers.

"Why, you want to fuck her?" he asks.

"Sure, why not," Daisy says. I can barely tell she's sarcastic, and Lo grinds his teeth a little. Ryke, however, finds it way too amusing.

"Then have at her, Daisy. She's all yours."

"You would just ditch your girlfriend like that," Daisy says with the cluck of her tongue.

"She's not my girlfriend. I'm just passing through."

"Wow," Daisy says flatly. "I hope for her sake she knows that."

"She does, but I may have promised her a week of mind-blowing sex in exchange for ditching her volleyball team." No wonder she's so grabby.

"You better find a way to make good on your end of the deal," Daisy says, her gaze past our chairs. I turn my head and spot Melissa coming over with two drinks.

"Why is that?" Ryke asks.

"If that's how pissed off she looks now, imagine what she'll look like on the seventh day of abstinence." For some reason, I only see my distressed, manic face staring back at me. "I'm glad I'm not you," Daisy tells him with a laugh.

He gives her a bitter smile and then puts a hand on her head, submerging her underneath the water. She splashes underneath, trying to surface.

Lo shakes his head at him.

"What?" Ryke says.

"You're walking a thin fucking line."

"I always am, little brother." And then he releases Daisy so she can come up for air. When her head breaches the surface, she spits a mouthful of water right at Ryke's face.

He splashes her back, and underneath the water, Daisy must

hook her ankle to his because he almost slips backward. Instead, he grabs ahold of her so he stays above the water.

"Hey," Melissa says. Little umbrellas are plucked into both of the piña coladas. She scrutinizes Ryke and Daisy, the way Ryke is basically hugging her in the water, but it's really accidental. Or so I keep telling myself. It makes me feel better about the situation.

Ryke drifts from Daisy, and she swims to the ledge where we sit. They both look completely innocent again, as though no flirting just occurred. Maybe it didn't. Maybe I'm just the pervert, thinking with my downstairs far too much.

Yeah, that has to be it.

Daisy holds out her hand for the drink.

"It's a virgin daiquiri," Melissa says, passing her the white slushy-like mixture.

"Oh." Daisy holds the clear plastic cup. "Why is that?"

"They didn't understand me when I told them my order. We're in a foreign country." I can't tell if this is a ploy to keep Daisy sober, but I don't see what she would have to gain from that.

Daisy hikes her body out of the water and stands from the ledge, sopping wet. She's dripping water onto the foot of my lounge chair, and she glances at Ryke. "How do you say in Spanish, *no virgin drinks*?"

Melissa frowns. "How would he know?"

"He's fluent," Daisy says. She discovered that during her sweet sixteen in Acapulco. Ryke has a proficiency in Spanish due to his prep school upbringing.

He climbs out of the pool and grabs the cup from her. "I'll order you a fucking drink. Wait here." He leaves, and whatever Melissa was expecting to happen, this was not it. She pout-glares, which is a scary combination.

While I love that I'm not the only one who's going to be sexually frustrated this week, Melissa is like a storm waiting to break. And with Lo being surrounded by never-ending drinks and the threat of the blackmailer still lingering, this trip teeters on the brink of chaos.

My only hope is that Rose and Connor, the two levelheaded people of our group, can keep us afloat. My gaze hits the pool again. They're still bickering.

God, help us.

Twenty-seven

Lily Calloway

Sleep hates addicts. At least that's my theory on the matter. While everyone else is well rested and off to explore Mexico, Lo and I have to drag ourselves out of bed.

My frozen muscles barely even stir when a burst of water douses me in the lukewarm shower. I raise my half-asleep arms to scrub the shampoo in my hair, and I find myself leaning a hip against the coldness of the tiled wall for extra support.

Being late sleepers means having the room all to ourselves. We haven't had sex (and aren't planning to) but the privacy is nice for a little while.

As I rinse the shampoo, the bathroom door creaks open. Even though I know Lo is the only one still at the hotel, I cling to the tiled wall, wondering if the fog will magically hide my naked body.

I spot Lo through the shower glass door, not enough mist to conceal me. And if I can see him, surely he can see *me*. I even catch a glimpse of his sharp cheekbones and devilish smile, his eyes flitting up to mine for a brief moment. Then he turns to the sink.

My mind switches into imagination mode. Thinking about all the ways he can do me.

"Morning, love," he says, watching me through the mirror. He combs two hands through his disheveled brown hair.

That's so not helping.

"You could have knocked," I tell him as he pulls off his T-shirt.

His muscles ripple down his chest, and he even has those defined ridges that lead toward his cock. "Or, you know, announced your entrance like they do on *Downton Abbey*."

He steps out of his drawstring pants, now completely naked. He walks toward the glass shower door and stops. And then he knocks on it.

I am petrified by the tiled wall.

"It's Loren Hale," he says, a smile spreading across his lips. "May I come in?"

"We can't . . ." I hesitate. *No. I do not want to finish that sentence.*

"We can't shower together?" he says in disbelief. "Says who?" *No one. Definitely not me.*

"You may enter, but I have to warn you the water is being stubborn. There are moments where it'd rather be cold despite my demands."

He opens the glass door. *Don't look, Lily.* My eyes plummet against command, and once I'm staring, I can't stop. Sensitive places pulse as I imagine him inside of me. His fingers press against my chin, lifting my gaze.

"If I have to, I'll take a shower with my bathing suit on," he tells me.

I shake my head fiercely. "It's okay. I won't look." But even as I say the words, I impulsively glance down. *Shit.* The magnetic force pulls and my eyes betray me for a split second. I look back up, and I throw my hands in the air. "That's the last time! I swear!"

His lips rise in amusement before he sidesteps to grab the washcloth and soap off the ledge. I now have a perfect view of his butt.

"Same goes for my ass," he says with a small laugh, his back still turned to me. The lightness and humor in his voice relaxes my shoulders.

"I like your ass," I tell him as he rotates to face me, a washcloth in hand.

"I know you do," he murmurs. He laces his fingers with mine and draws me to his body. My thigh brushes his cock, and a breath catches in my throat. "You're okay, Lil," he whispers. That's not what it feels like.

He runs the cloth along my arms and in between my fingers, soaping my skin. I am hypnotized by the slow, lingering movements. And then the cloth dips to my belly and rises to my breasts, circling each one with meticulous care. I stagger forward a little and grip onto his arm.

"Easy," he breathes. "Think of this as a test."

"Showering with you?" My eyes widen.

"Showering with me," he confirms with a nod, "without sex at the end. I'll wash you and then you can wash me, okay?"

I don't know what comes over me. I just . . . don't think this is real. So I reach out and pinch his arm.

He flinches. "What the hell?" And he retracts his hands. *No, come back!*

"I-I was making sure this wasn't a dream," I explain. "I'm sorry!" I lean down and plant two soft kisses on the reddened skin.

His chest rises and falls with full-bellied laughs. "You're supposed to pinch yourself, dummy," he tells me.

Oh, right. I squeeze the skin above my elbow. Ouch, that *does* hurt.

He draws me back to his chest, and his hands slowly skim my arms, lighting every part of me. His eyes flicker to mine. "Am I real enough for you?"

Dear God, yes.

He talks easily as he returns to soaping my body, as though he didn't just blanket me with Loren Hale seduction. "Today we can do touristy stuff alone together. Whatever you want."

It's our first vacation where Lo is sober and I'm in recovery. Our last trip by ourselves, we spent the weekend in Prague. We never even made it to a museum or Prague Castle. Lo wouldn't let me wander the streets alone, so our time was spent in the hotel bar where I could pick up a guy and he could drink without us dying in the process. Now the memory just seems sad. We missed out on all the good aspects of traveling.

"We should see the Mayan ruins," I say, excitement bubbling in my stomach. "Oh and turtles! I want to see turtles."

"Sounds like a date."

A date. A date in a foreign country with my boyfriend. A date in a foreign country with my *sober* boyfriend. It sounds amazing.

And then the washcloth descends and all my thoughts whoosh right from brain. I hold on to Lo's arms as he rubs the cloth on the spot between my legs. It aches for a deeper touch, for my body to burst with that familiar euphoria. But I remember something: This. Is. A. Test.

I plan to pass it. No matter how hard it is. I focus on his eyes and not his hands. "Hey, boyfriend," I say easily, testing out the word. I rarely say it aloud to his face. Maybe it will distract me.

"Hey, girlfriend," he replies. "You okay?" His brows rise, a little teasingly. I think he understands my physical state better than I do at times.

The washcloth ascends, leaving my tender flesh, and I nod in reply, words escaping my head. The water beads our skin and caresses us in its warmth, provoking me to take him every which way. But I won't. My sex life is in his hands. I won't jump him. I won't hike a leg around his waist. I'm restraining myself. Willingly.

I feel a little good with the fact.

And then the shower chooses to have a manic episode, the water spurting in ice-cold sheets.

Holy shit!

I shriek and spider Lo's body to avoid the chilly spray. *So much for* not *jumping him.*

His feet slide against the wet tiles, and he almost falls. But he catches his balance and rights himself, his arms wrapping around my hips to keep me from toppling.

I just realize that my arms are flung around his shoulders and my leg is most definitely midway up his waist. The position is not so innocent. But any arousal is smothered by Lo. He is laughing his ass off, his voice echoing in the boxed shower.

He cannot stop. Seriously.

"It's not funny. This shower is a demon," I tell him.

He tries to hide his smile, but fails. "If you're scared of a little cold water, how are you going to pet snapping turtles?"

"I'm not petting *snapping* turtles," I say, lowering my leg to the floor. "I only want to pet the cute ones."

He passes me a bottle of shampoo from the ledge. "Oh, so the ugly ones don't get any love from you? They're left out all alone, cold, un-petted?"

I frown deeply. He's right. I should pet all of them. Even the scary ones. "Okay, I'll pet the snapping turtles, but only if someone holds their muzzle." Before I run my fingers through his hair, I soap his abs with the cloth and follow the taut ridges across his body, being methodical but not too focused on where this could lead—which is *nowhere*. I tune into our conversation instead.

"I don't think turtles have muzzles," he says with another laugh.

"Snouts?" I ask, a little confused now. What *do* you call the nose of a turtle?

"That's a pig." We debate the existence of a turtle's nose and the difference between Mayan and Aztec ruins while we finishing washing, and then we both step out of the shower and dry off. After a long moment, I realize that I'm okay. That I'm more excited about spending the day with him than I am about having sex.

I don't know if I'll feel this way tomorrow.

But today . . . it feels nice.

Twenty-eight

Loren Hale

My Nike soles sink into the sand, digging hard into the uneven surface as I run. The sun beats against my bare chest, and I hope that I sprayed enough lotion to avoid a nasty burn.

Even in the boiling heat, Ryke sprints beside me, keeping up with my lengthy stride. I try to run every morning. It helps with my cravings, especially in Cancun. I can't take one step out of our hotel room without seeing a sloshed college student or a bottle of beer. Seventeen bars are on this resort alone. I knew coming here would test me to the limit, but I never anticipated how I would feel.

Yesterday with Lily was literally the only day that alcohol never crossed my mind. Not once. We snorkeled with the turtles and climbed to the top of a Mayan ruin. She never asked me for sex, and I never craved a drop of whiskey. But that was one good day out of many shitty ones. I want to improve our statistics, to lessen all the bad days until they're nothing but a dream.

I push harder, the humid air squeezing my lungs. Sweat beads my skin, and the pain that ripples through my muscles feels better than my nagging thoughts. So I keep driving farther. I keep bending my knees and pumping forward. And Ryke never breaks from my side.

I know that if I didn't care so much about Lily—or have Ryke here to glare at me—I would have already broken my sobriety.

And then Connor makes me want to be a better person—however lame that sounds.

But today we all split up.

Lily is shopping with Rose and Connor, which gives her a break from obsessing over having sex. Surrounding ourselves with other people is still new for us, and kind of exhausting, but we're making it work.

I glance over my shoulder, and we slow down to a jog almost immediately. Melissa and Daisy are barely a speck in the distance. They were the only two who wanted to join us on a run. Unsurprising, since Lily looks like the Big Bad Wolf huffing and puffing after a minute sprint, and I've never seen Rose wear sneakers in her life. Connor would have come along, but he didn't want to leave Rose and Lily shopping alone in Mexico.

Our feet slow to a complete stop. "Connor's investigator still hasn't come up with anything new?" Ryke asks, wiping his forehead with the back of his hand, shirtless like me.

"Connor says he's looking into it as quickly as he can." And if his contacts don't pan out, hopefully my father has better luck. But I wouldn't tell Ryke that I'm talking to Jonathan Hale. Nothing good can come from that.

"Let's say, worst-case scenario, it gets leaked that Lily is a sex addict," Ryke says, uncapping his water bottle as we wait for the girls to catch up to us. "What happens then?"

My stomach churns at the thought. "I don't even want to entertain the idea." All I picture is Lily sobbing and unable to be consoled. Watching her in that kind of gutted agony would kill me, but if we do go down that road, I can't resort to booze. For once, I have to be there for her. She's my best fucking friend. And she deserves the type of guy who can make her feel better, not worse.

If I can't do that, then we really shouldn't be together.

Ryke studies me. "You still taking Antabuse?"

I give him a bitter smile. "One pill a day keeps the demons at bay."

"You didn't answer me."

"Yes, Dad." I stretch my muscles, pulling my arm over my chest, trying to relieve this built-up pressure. If the pill bottle wasn't in my pocket—if I had left it in my suitcase with the other stolen luggage—I would have more temptations to drink. I was lucky for once.

I also hate talking about that medication. Talking makes me think and thinking makes me want to fucking drink.

"I wish you would have told me about Mason Nix sooner," Ryke admits, changing the subject once again, this time to one of our top suspects. Ryke is good at that—talking and revolving around different topics. I find myself zoning into something, being immersed by his roundabout discussions like a whirlpool.

"Why is that?"

"We share the fucking gym at Penn. I see him almost every day. If I knew what he did, I wouldn't have . . . tolerated him."

"So what does you not tolerating him look like?" I ask with furrowed brows. I picture him ramming his fist into Mason Nix's conceited face. Granted, I already did that.

"We may have had words," Ryke says.

I still imagine a fist fight.

"You know," I mutter, staring at my water bottle, "for the longest time after our freshman year, I kept thinking that I was in the wrong. I can't even tell you how many tires I slit. And Lily told me that she didn't expect what happened that night, but she didn't mind it either." I shake my head, thinking back to our first year at Penn. We both went to a frat party, the entire soccer team in attendance. Most of it is still a giant blur. But I do remember hearing guys near the kitchen discussing some girl on the second floor. Someone named Mason convinced a freshman to screw each guy on the soccer team.

One after the other.

I didn't have to be told it was her. I just knew.

I grabbed a bottle of Jim Beam, pulled out my serrated hunting knife, and paced in the parking lot. I lost it on any car with a fucking soccer sticker, badge, identification, whatever. They would have to find another ride home.

That morning, she was dazed and hung over, but somehow I pulled the truth from her. Mason Nix asked if she wanted to have the night of her life, and she agreed as long as no one watched. As long as each guy came in and went out like a factory line.

It was one of her fantasies, she told me. And it came true, but I saw how much shame gnawed on her after that. She shrunk into herself and waited for me to stare at her like she was gross and dirty. But I just wanted to hold her and tell her that she was worth so much more than whatever she was searching for.

But I was a selfish prick back then. I wasn't willing to change our dynamic just yet. I thought if she overcame her addiction, then she'd make me overcome mine.

And now that's all I want for us.

"I remember how you explained it," Ryke says. "But fuck that, Lo. I didn't know Lily before you two became a couple, but it doesn't matter if she wanted it or not. No self-respecting man would offer something like that to a girl, especially one that's drunk. You had every right to be upset and go after the asshole."

"Yeah . . . maybe." But now Mason Nix could be the one terrorizing Lily.

Melissa bounds over in a steady jog, not winded in the least. She's closer and closer to us, but Daisy doesn't run beside her. My stomach knots, and I scan the beach quickly. I couldn't have already lost Lily's sister. It's barely been an hour.

"Ryke . . ." I slap his arm and gesture to Melissa who's alone.

Ryke searches the beach with a hard gaze, on alert. But we don't show panic. We both look like we're about ready to enter a UFC match, muscles flexing, spine straightening. Must be a Hale thing.

He taps my shoulder and points to a spot by the shore where the waves lap into the sand. I can barely make out the head of a tall blonde, chatting up two local guys who carry strings of jewelry looped on their arms.

Shit.

Before I can even move a foot, Ryke has taken off. I follow close behind, hoping he doesn't antagonize the locals. That image that I had of protecting Daisy—yeah, I thought the fight would be between drunk, stupid guys. But these two probably wouldn't mind whipping out a knife if things turn heated. I don't want to be thrown in jail in a foreign country without a fucking passport.

Luckily, Ryke slows once we reach them, his eyes dead set on Daisy, not the guys.

I join them as Daisy holds up two chain necklaces with silver Mayan coins on the ends. "These are supposedly handmade. I can't tell though." She shrugs. "I think I'm going to take Pablo's word for it."

My gaze drifts to the two Mexican guys, standing passively back with their backpacks and strings of jewelry, skin dark and weathered from walking up and down the beach. They look harmless, and I have a suspicion that Daisy approached them first. She's a little wilder than I remember. Crazy, even. I've missed so much since rehab—or maybe she's always been like this and I was just too drunk to really notice.

"You can't run off and talk to strangers," I tell her. It sounds stupid and parental—nothing I would normally say. When did I become a person who lectures someone else on responsibility? Fuck—I'm turning into Rose.

"We're not strangers," Daisy says quickly. "That's Pablo and . . ." She squints in thought. "Ernesto . . . I think."

The bigger set guy nods at this and holds out a plastic bag to Daisy, filled with more pendants and stones. "Onyx. Rubies. Sapphires."

I narrow my gaze. "Do you have a gold brick in their too?"

Ryke catches Daisy's wrist and tugs her to his side. She shrugs off Ryke's hold, and her eyes flicker behind her. "Melissa is glaring at you."

Ryke doesn't even check over his shoulder. "Don't worry about her." Melissa is about twenty feet away, arms crossed over her chest, waiting for Ryke to rejoin her. But he's abandoned his girl-friend to help me with this situation. I won't admit it out loud, but I'm pretty thankful.

"I'm just trying not to get you in trouble," Daisy tells him.

"I can take care of myself." His eyes bore into hers.

I cut in, "Daisy, let's go."

"Wait," she says, raising her hand to show off the two necklaces. "Which one do you think Lily would like?" And now I feel like an ass. She just wanted to buy her sister jewelry.

Lily doesn't wear necklaces often, and the fact that I know this over Daisy makes me feel kind of good. But an uneasiness spins my stomach—because it means that our isolation has strained her relation-ship with her sisters. And I have to remind myself that this trip is about rebuilding everything we've ignored.

I think Lil would like anything that came from Daisy. I inspect both necklaces, one with a black rope and the other with a chain.

Daisy brushes her finger along the rope necklace. "This pendant has a guy sticking out his tongue. I thought she'd get a kick out of it."

"Definitely," I say.

Daisy spins back to Ernesto and hands him the chain necklace. "Just this one." She holds up the rope necklace to buy. "How much?"

"Two-hundred-and-sixty," he says with a thick accent.

She gapes. "What?"

"Pesos. Pesos. Pesos," he says quickly, afraid of losing a sale. "Twenty dollars. Two-sixty pesos."

"Ohhh." Daisy's eyes light up. She laughs like she didn't know any better, but she spent all morning helping Lily understand the peso-dollar conversion before she went shopping. Daisy said that she became an expert at currency calculations in Europe during shoots and Fashion Week.

"Daisy," I warn. And here I thought Ryke was going to cause trouble.

Ryke cocks his head at me, brows raised like *I told you*. Yeah, he told me she jumped off a cliff, I didn't think that equated to conning a local on the beach.

Daisy waves me off. "One minute, sweetie."

Ryke stiffens and I just frown. What the hell is going on?

"I only have . . ." She pulls out a wad of cash from her bikini top like it's nothing, like Ernesto's eyes haven't just zoned in on her breasts. She counts the bills one by one, really fucking slowly. ". . . Two-hundred pesos." Her big green eyes rise innocently to Ernesto, but he's still looking at her tits.

I step forward, irritated beyond belief. "Hey." I snap my fingers at him. "Two-hundred pesos?"

Ernesto finally looks to me and begins to shake his head.

"Oh no," Daisy says quickly. She wraps her arm around my waist and presses her head against my chest. I immobilize. "We're on our honeymoon, you see, and I promised my sister I'd bring her back something. She'd just love this. I know it. Could you make an exception just this once, please?"

My eyes widen at Ryke, but he's just glaring, and when I mean glaring, I mean he has the whole Frankenstein's monster routine down. Hard set jaw, clenched fists, taut shoulders, and tight lips. He looks about ready for a fight. But I'm not sure who he wants to pummel.

"No. Two-sixty," Ernesto repeats.

Daisy's shoulders slacken and she turns to me, her hands on my chest. "Do you have any pesos on you, sweetie?"

"No, so maybe we should cut our losses, *dear*."

"Give me your money," Ryke says, holding out his hand to her.

Her face lights up and she thankfully steps away and returns to Ryke, out of earshot of the locals. I follow close behind. "Are you going to haggle in Spanish?" she asks him, sliding the bills into his palm.

"Sure," he says. "First give me the rest of your cash."

"It's all in your hand."

"It's in your boobs."

I scowl, not wanting him to say anything about her boobs. *Ever.* She's Daisy Calloway.

Daisy looks down at her breasts with a frown, and I turn my grimace to the sky. *I'm blaming this situation on you, God. For allowing little sisters to have breasts.*

"I don't see anything in there."

"I would check myself, but I'm here with a girl," Ryke says dryly.

Okay. No. If there's one thing I'm good at, it's speaking my fucking mind. "There are actually a million other fucking reasons you shouldn't," I say coldly, my blood turning to ice.

Daisy just ignores me and says, "Melissa left three minutes ago when you refused to go to her side. What's your excuse now?"

She challenges him.

And he's the type of guy willing to take it.

I stand between them before Ryke can answer her. I raise my eyebrows at Ryke in disbelief. I seriously thought I was dreaming what happened at the pool. *It wasn't fucking anything*, I told myself. He was being nice, prodding her to eat a taco, even though he should have passed it to her rather than let her bite it from his hand. He shouldn't have rubbed sauce off her chin. He shouldn't have joked with her about fucking Melissa. There are so many things he should *not* do. But I let myself believe that he's just an idiot. He doesn't understand boundaries. That is Ryke's biggest problem.

But now, how do I explain *this.*

"What?" Ryke growls in defense at me. "I'm trying to get us out of this fucking situation." He locks eyes with Daisy again and steps forward to try to reach her. I put my hand on his chest to stop him, and then I quickly turn to Daisy.

"Give me the rest of your money."

"I don't—"

"Now." I can't even hear my own voice or how mean it sounds. All I hear is my half brother offering to feel up my girlfriend's little sister. I don't even fucking care if it was a joke or sarcasm or fucking anything. I think I'm going to kill him later.

Daisy's smile instantly vanishes and she reaches into her bikini top again. I look at the sand, the sky, anywhere but her breasts until she places the money in my hand. I grab the rest of her cash from Ryke and start counting out two-hundred-and-sixty pesos.

"I was just trying to have fun," she says softly, her voice layered with guilt. "I'm sorry."

She's apologized, and I know I should drop it. But I'm fuming. "There are other ways to have fun." I hand Ernesto the money. Both guys nod in thanks and they walk off toward the resort near the string of straw huts and white cabanas. I look back to Daisy, and my nerves haven't settled yet. "You're the fucking daughter of a multibillion dollar mogul. Bartering with a man that makes a thousand times less than you is the equivalent of stealing."

Her eyes go big and round and a little glassy, and it hurts to know that I'm causing her distress. The pain in my chest only intensifies because I can't stop speaking. I don't know how. "Next time rent a fucking jet ski."

"I just wanted to do something normal."

"You're not normal. None of us are."

"Lo," Ryke says, his tone warning. But his voice sends razor blades down my back.

"Don't you even fucking speak to me," I snap. I hate him right now. I hate me, most of all. I hate that I just bitched out Daisy, who didn't really do anything wrong. At least, nothing that warranted my harsh words. The remorse tastes like acid, and I usually drown it with whiskey.

My next breath comes out ragged and Ryke focuses on me for a long moment. But when Daisy inhales strongly, staring at the sand with tears brimming, trying to bottle her emotions, he turns his gaze on her. I watch his face change. If he was concerned for me, I don't even know what to call the expression he has for her.

What the hell did I miss when I was in rehab?

"I have to get out of here." I cringe when I realize I said it out loud. I start walking.

Ryke awakens and follows me. "Where the fuck are you going?"

His anger fuels me and I stop suddenly. He nearly knocks into my chest. "What the fuck is wrong with you?" I hiss. "She's sixteen." I see Daisy in my peripheral, standing off to the side, looking on but not wanting to interrupt.

"I'm not doing anything," Ryke refutes.

My forehead hurts from frowning so hard. He can't be serious, but I think he believes he is. That's fucking terrifying. "Don't be stupid."

Ryke sets his hands on his head for a second. I've never seen him unravel, and I can tell he's trying hard not to. "I'm blunt and abrasive," he says. But he knows that's not the answer I want to hear. "I can't turn that off."

"You're going to turn it off around her," I sneer. "And you know what, I invited you to Cancun, and I can uninvite you."

"Are you uninviting me?"

"No, but I don't want to talk to you or be around you right now."

He grabs my arm before I turn around. "Wait."

"What? You're going to blame everything on the fact that you're blunt? When Connor wants to be, he's just as honest as you, and he would never say the things you do."

"Because I'm a fucking asshole," Ryke says.

"That's not good enough."

Ryke's nostrils flare and he points to his chest. "I was raised by a single mother, Lo—"

"So was Connor," I retort. I give Ryke such a hard time. I make him hurdle the highest walls, and he's taken each test without complaint, but I can tell this one is tearing him inside. And a little part of me likes that he's finally breaking down. The other part hates that I take pleasure in someone else's pain.

"Stop comparing me to him," Ryke sneers. "His mother was the head of a corporation. My mother sat around all day and plotted ways to fuck over my father. I spent years being torn between the two of them, having to choose sides, and I chose her." He points at his chest again, his eyes blazing with heat. "I was made to believe that she was a saint and he was the sinner, when they're both guilty of things that I can barely even stomach. Do you know what that's like—to defend someone so vehemently out of love and then realize they were no more innocent than the man you hated? It fucking sucks."

My chest is so tight that each breath takes force.

Ryke steps forward. "I *love* women and care about them more than you even fucking realize, Lo. But I saw my mother turn callous from that divorce. I say things that I shouldn't because I stopped giving a fuck what people thought of me. I stopped trying to play the doting son—the role that *that* girl is going through right now. And it's fucking killing me to watch it happen."

I'm assaulted with so many emotions that I almost can't see straight. I just keep nodding, trying to understand his point of view, trying to get it. "I need some space . . ." *to think*.

"I can't leave you alone like this." Ryke breathes heavily, and he hesitates to put a hand on my shoulder. If he sets one finger on my body, I'm going to jerk away. I'm so full of hate, resentment, and blackness—everything that normally sends me right to a bar.

"I'll go back to the room with Daisy," I say. "You go find Melissa.

You know, the girl that you came here with." I don't want to butcher him anymore, but it's so easy to cut people, especially my brother.

Ryke takes the hit, not moving one inch. "You almost made Daisy cry. You really want to spend time alone with her?"

"It'll give me a chance to apologize," I say. "Either you take that scenario or I'm walking out of here on my own." My hands shake, and I clench them into fists. Ryke would never leave me alone right now. I want to relax. To sit at a bar and just float away.

Ryke motions to Daisy, and she jogs over. When she stops by his side, he says, "Don't let him drink."

"Okay."

He hesitates before heading farther down the beach. We walk toward the resort in a heavy silence that weighs on my chest.

"I'm sorry," I end up muttering while we wait for the elevator.

"No, don't be," Daisy says. "You were right. What I did—it was wrong. Sometimes I just forget about money. I'm going to try to be better about it."

"Yeah, but I do it at times too. And I'm not your dad. I shouldn't be lecturing you." Or anyone.

She smiles. "It's nice to know you care."

We stop on our floor and she walks in front of me, leaving me to think about that.

I do care. Is that because I'm sober or is it just because things have changed? I wish I knew.

Daisy waits by the door, and she suddenly pales with worry. "Are you going to tell Lily?"

She'll ask me what's wrong as soon as I get inside. We've been around each other enough to pick up body language, and mine says I'm losing my shit. I hadn't intended on lying to her. "Yeah," I say, "but I don't think she'll be mad."

"Really? Because I don't think I've ever seen Lily in beast mode, like Rose's eternal setting, and I've always been kind of scared to see that."

I smile as I try to recall an angry Lily. She does kind of look like a little monster, but I find it more adorable than frightening. "You'll be fine."

I don't know if Daisy thinks I'm actually this upset just because of the bartering, or if she realizes I caught onto her flirting with Ryke, both at fault, I believe. But I will never have that conversation with her. Lily can handle her sister, and I'll handle my brother.

Daisy lets out a breath of relief before edging out of the way. I slide in the keycard, and we enter the room.

Rose refolds clothes on the nearest bed while Connor organizes various bags that surround the room. Between what Daisy brought and now what Rose purchased, I think we've officially clothed seven people for the week.

"How was the run?" Connor asks.

"Hot," Daisy says.

I scan the room for Lily, unable to find her, and then I look through the glass door to the patio. She's curled up on a chair, her legs to her chest, watching the birds or something.

I move toward the door, and Connor suddenly blocks my exit like he wants to have a conversation. All I really want to do is talk to Lily. I need to know if she knew about Ryke and Daisy's . . . Jesus, I don't even know what to call it.

"What?" I snap.

Daisy focuses on us, filled with curiosity, and this causes Rose to pat her mattress. "Daisy, come help me fold," she insists.

Daisy answers her sister's call—reminding me of what Ryke said about her. And I cringe a little, not wanting Daisy to be affected by her mother. All these girls have complexes, and I can see how most people would get one just from the freedom of our lifestyle and the pressure to maintain it. I feel like we're all a little fucked up in our own right.

Connor leads me to the farthest wall from the girls. And I instantly understand what's going on. He's moving me away from

Daisy so she can't hear. Whatever Connor wants to tell me—it's about Lily.

The worst thought crosses my mind.

She cheated.

She slept with some cashier at Bloomingdales.

She fucked another guy.

I feel the color drain from my face.

I feel my stomach roll in on itself.

My world slowly begins crashing down. I should have been with her. I try to move past Connor and reach the patio, wanting to talk to her, wanting to make this right, wanting to be alone again.

Connor steps in front of me once more and puts his hand on my shoulder. He reads the panic on my face, and says, "Nothing happened, not like that." I don't know Connor well enough to know what *that* entails and this just heightens my nerves.

"What *did* happen?" I ask quietly.

He stays resolute, calm, and for some strange reason it feeds into me. His casual attitude makes me believe it's not that bad, and I wonder if this is a Connor Cobalt gift. To pacify people with his demeanor rather than words.

"Look," he says easily, "Rose didn't want to tell you, but I convinced her, I think." He lets himself smile at the accomplishment. "She wants Lily to handle these things on her own. In a feminist's perspective, I guess it seems like when you help Lily, you don't give her a chance to be strong on her own."

It feels like he knifed me, even though those are Rose's words. "I'm not her fucking cure, I know that," I say, trying to mimic Connor's easy tone, but my voice comes out strained and edged. I've let Lily succeed on her own, but I am the person having sex with her. All I can do is tell her to stop, to guide her. She's the one actively making the choice to ask me to have sex, to want to have sex, to give into cravings enough to let them control her thoughts. That's on her.

"I know, and Lily will never be completely on her own. That's what I told Rose. You're sleeping with her, and sex addiction is a two-person recovery process. She sided with me on this one." I think he keeps gloating to postpone the news.

"Connor. Just tell me."

He nods. "I noticed that Lily can sometimes zone out," he says, "and I actually thought she was just a little slow. But then I found out she was a sex addict, and I know fantasizing can be a huge issue with the addiction."

I know where this is headed, and I shouldn't be relieved. But a pressure lifts off my chest. "And?"

"And it was fine. She zoned out a couple times and Rose would reengage her with conversations. Then Rose had to try on practically every pair of heel in her size, and we both forgot about Lily . . . until we heard her."

What? She wouldn't masturbate in public. That's beyond what she's ever done. My chest starts to hurt again. "Heard her? Was she masturbating?"

"No," Connor says quickly. "No. Not at all."

Good.

"But we heard her orgasm."

What? "I don't understand. How is that possible?"

"There have been numerous studies about the female orgasm. It's not fully understood, but many scientists have shown that it can be brought on by thought alone."

She fantasized and had an orgasm. Out loud. In a fucking store. I know how embarrassed she must feel and it floods me, seizing my ability to even form words right now.

Connor takes my silence as an opportunity to keep speaking. "Rose made her call her therapist."

I nod, but my feet are glued to the floor. I want to go outside and be with her, but Rose's words—or Connor's reiteration of them—

haunt me. I want Lily to be strong on her own. I can see her through the blinds, hiding in her body, and it doesn't seem like she's looking at the birds anymore.

She's looking for a way out.

I turn to Connor, suddenly so relieved that he's here. That I have someone that I can ask this, "Should I go out there?" I want someone to tell me what's right. To put me on the correct path. I don't want to keep making bad decisions.

"She needs you," he tells me in a single breath. "Just don't have sex with her. Easy enough, right?"

"Yeah, it'd probably be difficult on that chair," I say, trying to smile, trying to lessen how much I empathize with her hurt.

"Not for you two." He taps my shoulder, unfreezing me from my state and I find myself moving onward. Toward the door. Toward her.

Twenty-nine

Lily Calloway

The door opens and I don't move, don't breathe, don't speak. I want to disappear from this chair, this country, this planet.

Lo walks in front of my view of the balcony ledge, where I had literally considered testing my ability to fly. He's shirtless, but not even the curve of his abs could entice me right now. He remains a few feet away from me, not closing the distance that draws tension like a black hole.

I finally look up to meet his gaze, my body numbing.

His eyes have become glassy, and he grips the railing behind him for support. On a normal occasion, before rehab and before recovery, he'd be sweeping me up into his arms. I'd wrap my legs around his waist and wish for sex to take away my humiliation, to remind myself that I'm good at something. I'm not worthless or alone. With every thrust and every climax, I'd be gone.

But now, the thought of doing that drives a hammer into my heart. I know with certainty that it's wrong. I wonder if he's keeping distance, afraid of that path that I might choose for us.

I don't want it.

So I say, "I don't want sex." Tears gather in my eyes. "I just want you to hold me."

They are magic words.

In one quick motion, he is in front of me and then I'm in his arms and on his lap. He blankets me with his body, wrapping his arms around my small frame. I bury my head into his chest, the tears pooling out as he rubs the back of my head. I feel safe here.

We sit like that for a good while, until his heart steadies and my breathing evens. What happened feels like a failure on my part. I screwed up and let my addiction win.

"I'm sorry," I say softly, breaking the peaceful silence.

"You don't need to apologize to me, Lil."

"I feel like I let you down . . . let us down," I admit. "We're supposed to be getting better."

"And there will be roadblocks and setbacks," he tells me, "just because you hit one doesn't mean you let me down. If anything, I'm proud of you for handling it like this."

"Because the alternative is me attacking your body."

He smiles. "Something like that, yeah." He tucks an escaped piece of hair behind my ear. "What did your therapist say?"

Connor must have told him more than I thought. I'm glad. It saves me from reiterating the most embarrassing moment of my life.

"She said that I need to start coming up with ways to stop myself from fantasizing. Like focusing on homework or American presidents."

"Basically what every teenage boy does to avoid a hard-on."

I frown. I didn't think about it like that. "I guess . . ." Then I shake my head. "But it doesn't sound that simple. I understand how to stop myself from looking at porn and from self-love, but how do I stop myself from thinking. How does someone control that?"

"Practice," Lo says. "I'm trying too. Believe me."

I nod, knowing it can't be much easier for him. At least thinking about booze doesn't lead to an involuntary orgasm. I flush at the memory and groan into my hands.

"Maybe I'll just remember the look on Connor's and Rose's

faces. I think that will keep me from fantasizing about anything for the next solid two-hundred years."

He pulls me closer, rubbing my back soothingly, and then he kisses my lips in one quick second, testing it out.

We're worse together when things are out of control, and during these moments we have to be careful. It'd be so easy to enable each other just to make us feel better again, but being a couple also means being intimate. Comforting someone normally involves touch—a hug, a kiss, a hand on a leg—things that send me off the deep end. We just have to find a balance.

"How was that?" he asks.

It felt simple and right. "Good."

"I have a question, and I want you to know that I won't be offended if the answer isn't what I want it to be. I just . . . I'd like the truth."

"Okay."

He takes a small breath and then his eyes drop to my lips again. He plants another soft kiss, longer this time. I don't move or force it into something else. I let him take the lead, and I don't wish for anything more either. What he gives me is enough.

He draws back and looks from my body to my lips to my eyes, taking in every detail. "You okay?"

I nod again. "Just waiting for your question."

"Right." He takes another trained breath. "Your fantasies—who was in them?"

"Me," I say. "And you."

"You answered so quickly," he says in worry.

"That doesn't mean I lied. I haven't fantasized about anyone but you since you left for rehab. You're like . . . the best I've ever had."

His face seems to glow at the last line, taking it as truth and fact. As it is. His hand glides to my neck, caressing me gently. For the first time, I feel in a different state of mind when he touches me. In part, it has to do with my talk with Dr. Banning. I asked her what

I should expect when I see Lo, and she told me that he'd want to touch me, to comfort me. And that's what I have to accept it as. Not all touching leads to pleasure.

A hug is just a hug, not the pathway to sex.

This type, it's new to me because I've never allowed myself to be touched this way, at least not without the desire of it progressing to other things.

I think I like it.

His lips press against the tender skin below my ear, and I can feel the hesitation in his body when he pulls away. "How was that?"

"Good."

"You don't want anything more?"

"No," I say sincerely, "not unless you do."

He kisses my lips again, but this time parts them a little with his. I don't deepen it. I wait, and he deepens it himself, his tongue gently slipping in. His thumb strokes the back of my neck. When he breaks the kiss, he slowly rubs my wet bottom lip with his finger. I don't even shudder.

I'm letting him comfort me without having sex, without the fear of enabling me. We're trying to be a better couple, and I think this is what progress feels like.

His eyes glimmer with possibilities. "Is this your new superpower, Lily Calloway?" he asks me sweetly. "I can touch you now without feeling guilty?"

"It may not last forever."

"Then I'll enjoy it for now."

For now.

I like that too.

Thirty

Lily Calloway

We remain on the patio to watch the sun set. The only time someone disturbs us is when Rose comes out to ask if we want anything from room service for dinner. I fear that they're only eating in because they're nervous to leave us alone, but I don't question her about it. Instead, I tell her to order us a couple burgers, and then she slips back inside.

Lo still has his arms wrapped around me as I sit on his lap. The sun fades into different shades of oranges and yellows. The opulence must spark my memory. "I forgot to ask how your run went," I say.

"Oh . . . that." His tone is dry and edged, not at all what I was expecting.

I swivel a little so I can see his face. He's glaring at the sky. The pretty sky. This can't be good. "What happened?"

He grimaces. "I feel like if I say it out loud it will come true. Can you try to inherit some telepathy in the next five minutes?"

"I can try to guess."

"That doesn't sound like a fun game either."

I narrow my eyes at him and try to put the pieces together. He was on a run, a perfectly normal run, with Ryke, Melissa, and . . . oh shit.

"Daisy. What did she do?" My little sister has a habit of seeking danger. I know I land on the right answer because tiny stress-wrinkles crease his forehead. It takes him a quick minute to tell me about the bartering on the beach, but when he finishes, he doesn't look relieved.

"There's something else, isn't there?"

"Yeah, and it's the part that makes me want to jump off this balcony." He stops before spoiling the news, which only makes me curious and nervous.

"Are you going to tell me?"

He lets out a long sigh and rubs his eyes in slight distress. "I don't even know what to call it, Lil. There's so many words for it, but none of them really describe the situation. Inappropriate and fucked up are my favorite ones though."

I frown. "Are we still talking about Daisy?"

"And Ryke."

His eyes flicker to mine, taking in my reaction as he lets this sink in.

"Wait, what?" It can't be what I think. That was all in my mind, wasn't it?

"Daisy had cash in her bikini top," Lo says. "Ryke made some offhanded comment about it and it led to . . . other comments." His jaw tightens at the memory and then his eyes land back on me. "Why the fuck are you smiling? I just told you that my half brother was flirting with your little sister."

I press my lips together, to try to hide it, but I soon surrender to the fact that I'm happy. "Do you know how long I've thought it was all in my head?"

This doesn't amuse him. In fact, he straightens up like he's ready to go assault his brother. "*How* long?"

I put my hand on his chest to calm him. "January . . . but I didn't want to worry you if it wasn't true."

He lets out an angry breath.

"Do you know how many times Ryke has called me a pervert?"

I continue. "I thought this was just another illusion from my dirty mind, like I was interpreting something out of nothing and making it all up."

"You're not. Now move past that achievement and bring your-self down to my level." He turns his body a little more, so that we're looking straight on at each other. "My twenty-two-year-old brother is flirting, apparently not deliberately—I'm not even sure how that fucking happens—with your sixteen-year-old sister." He waits for it to sink in.

"Shit."

"Yeah, shit. So what are we going to do? I'm worried that your sister is going to like him in a bad way. I mean, most girls are like babbling fools around Ryke. The fact that she's not . . . I can't even." He runs a hand through his hair. "All I'm saying is that Ryke is smart enough *not* to make a move on her, but Daisy prob-ably doesn't know any better."

"I've already talked to her." On numerous occasions, but she keeps saying the same thing to me. "She knows that she can't do anything with him. And"—I snap my fingers at the realization— "Ryke brought Melissa here, so he is clearly putting off the right signals." Showing up on vacation with a girl screams "taken" and should let Daisy know not to act on her feelings, if she does have any that extend beyond a friendship.

I kind of hope we're blowing this all out of proportion and no chemistry really exists there. Because they have to know that noth-ing can ever happen.

Our mother would be more than just furious if she learned that Daisy even had a crush on Ryke Meadows. For one, his age. And two, he's the spawn of Sara Hale. After the separation between Jon-athan and Sara, my parents chose a side—Team Jonathan all the way. And with our mother's incredibly high standards, I can see her wanting something more for Daisy. Something better.

Someone as affluent as Connor Cobalt or Loren Hale. Someone

who has more to offer than a trust fund inherited out of a quiet divorce and hurt feelings.

Lo tilts my chin so that I meet his eyes and come back to the present, pulled straight from my thoughts. "Then Ryke needs to stop ditching Melissa for Daisy," Lo tells me. "I'll have another conversation with him . . . when I'm not picturing tearing his head off his shoulders." His jaw locks at another thought. "He's older. He has to be the one to take responsibility."

"Can you blame him though?" The words tumble out of my mouth before I can catch them. I'm so not used to defending Ryke Meadows, but being in his company for three months maybe opened me up to his ways.

My eyes widen, and Lo looks equally shocked by the words. "Explain," he says.

"Well, it's just . . ." I stumble. "Daisy is a high-fashion model. She's always around older people, and she doesn't look sixteen. She has a career. She makes money and travels the world. Sometimes she acts her age, sure, but most of the time she's basically twenty." There are moments where I even feel younger than her. I'm less worldly, less cultured, and less experienced (not sexually but for everything else, sure). "I can understand how that might be confusing for someone who's attracted to her."

Lo presses his hands to his face, more distressed than I've seen him in a long while, at least in moments that don't involve craving booze. "That word, don't say that word."

"What?"

"*Attracted*."

Oh. "I think my fear is that the more we keep telling them to stop, the more they'll just do it to spite us." And what if nothing's there but friendship and we involuntarily push them together. ". . . like two rebellious teenagers or something."

He groans. "She is a *teenager*." He drops his hands and lets out another breath. "This is so fucked up."

I smile at this and nudge his side. "Doesn't it feel good to not be the only ones?"

He meets my gaze with a tilt of his head, and his lips try hard not to rise. "No, I like being alone on the *fucked up* island with you." He nuzzles his nose into the crook of my neck. I laugh, a sound that I didn't think possible an hour ago, and he responds with two light kisses on my collarbone.

"So what do we do?" he asks me, intertwining his fingers with mine. I appraise our hands for a moment, trying to come up with a plan.

"Maybe . . . maybe we just keep them separated for the rest of the vacation. Or try to."

"But what about when we go home? What do we do about them then?"

"How many times are they really around each other?" Daisy has school, and modeling occupies most of her time. Without her knowing about my sex addiction, she's invited to less and less outings with our group. Sometimes I imagine telling her, but I don't think it will improve our relationship. And that's what I'm trying to repair.

"Then we have a plan."

He extends his palm like we're closing a business deal. As I go in for the shake, he drops his hand and plants a surprise kiss on my lips. It takes me aback, but it sends little happy flutters in my stomach. The kiss lasts longer than the others as he cups the back of my head and gently opens my mouth with his. I feel the brush of his tongue and more flapping fills my belly.

He edges back after a moment and I curl up in his arms. One thing is certain.

Surprise kisses are the best.

Thirty-one

Loren Hale

Four days of pool and beach have left me a little sunburned, tan, and tired. Lily and I have succeeded in separating Ryke and Daisy for the majority of the trip, at least enough where they haven't had any opportunity to really talk.

Tonight we're all eating at an authentic Mexican restaurant in the city. Chips and dip overflow the table, and the noise gathers by a stage, which sits close to the bar. I draw back at Daisy's threat to make us all do karaoke later tonight. Not going to happen, even if the youngest Calloway girl can be highly persuasive. She seems to bat lashes, give us those big green puppy-dog eyes and everyone falls under her spell. The frightening part is, I think she knows she has this power too.

If I was Greg Calloway, I'd have her ass on the next flight home. But I know her father: a workaholic who pours his time in business, who believes love equates to money and the luxury he can provide his family. I've watched Lily accept that kind of love and move on, as I've done in a sense. My father wasn't always around. You don't achieve this lifestyle without sacrificing something.

I ask Daisy what her mother thinks of her being in Cancun. Lily confirmed that she has permission, but I'd like to hear it from Daisy's mouth.

She hasn't touched a single chip. Her hands busy themselves

with folding a paper napkin into a flower. The one downside to separating Daisy and Ryke is she seems less inclined to take bites of food without pressure from him. His persistence is useful sometimes. And I've tried to do the same "eat this" bit, but she gives me a look like I'm crazy for suggesting an avocado, and then she dodges me with word games that spin my head. Ryke can keep up. I can't. My lingo is clearly meant for sex addicts, not adrenaline junkies.

"Well, you know . . ." Daisy starts and trails off as if I didn't ask a question. She looks around and taps a waiter on the back. "Hey, can we get a margarita pitcher?"

He stares at her blankly, and with Ryke in the bathroom, Connor takes the lead and translates for her. Apparently, I'm the only guy who slept in Spanish class.

"Daisy," I say. "You didn't answer the question."

We sit at a circular table, so it doesn't take much strain for Daisy to turn back to me. "Oh, sorry, what was it?" she asks innocently.

"Samantha, your mother," I say dryly, already knowing where this is headed. "She doesn't mind you being out here all week?" Samantha's ways have always eluded me. She digs her nails into Poppy's daughter, Rose's fashion line, and Daisy's modeling career, but leaves Lily alone. It's strange and something I couldn't quite comprehend before rehab. Being around them, I'm starting to understand it even more.

Daisy is about to answer when Ryke and Melissa return from the restroom. No shame on their faces. Way less guilty than Lily and I ever were when we screwed during a meal. Melissa plops into her chair and grabs a napkin, wiping her lips.

Daisy sits between her sisters, and she basically stares straight at Melissa and Ryke across the circular table. I try to read her expression, but she stays guarded and nudges her rice with her fork.

Ryke motions to the suddenly silent table as he takes a seat beside me. "Don't let us interrupt you," he snaps. His eyes land on Daisy, who stares blankly at her rice, very interested in a pea that she unburies. It's the first time Ryke has shown interest in Melissa with Daisy present. Usually Melissa just hangs all over him.

"Daisy," I say, urging her again to answer the question. My arm slides around Lily's shoulders beside me, and she surprisingly keeps her hands to herself. Normally she'd have me unzipped by now. Yes, even at a restaurant. Her restraint is admirable, but I can't deny that a horrible (mostly horny) part of me wishes for it.

Daisy blinks a couple times. "Right. And no, my mom doesn't mind. She was really happy that I could have a whole week to bond with my sisters. I just have to abide by my normal rules." She shrugs at the last bit and claps her hands. "Should we start karaoke early?" She begins to rise from her chair, but both Lily and Rose put their hands on the frame to stop her. Rose pushes her back in.

"What are we talking about? What rules?" Melissa asks. She reaches into the basket of chips.

Lily cringes beside me, and I can see Rose's icy demeanor turn even frostier at the topic.

Daisy eyes the chips longingly before putting on another smile. "It's nothing."

Ryke is slouched, leaning back on only two legs of his chair. He looks like an asshole. "You brought it up," he reminds her. "So clearly you want to talk about it."

Melissa rubs his thigh, smirking now that he took her side for a change. I should feel good about it too, but for some reason, I just feel really fucking awful.

"I did bring it up," she nods to herself. And then she shrugs. "I guess the rules are simple. You know, *no getting fat. No ruining your hair. No getting too tan. And no tattoos*." Her lips twitch. "So good news is—I'm free to contract an STD."

"Jesus Christ," Ryke says under his breath, only loud enough for me and Melissa to hear.

"That's not funny," Rose tells her, "and our mother may not kill you, but I would."

"Only joking," Daisy says, sporting a goofy face before she turns to Lily. "How's school?"

Bringing Lily into any conversation usually deflects attention, and it's like watching a little perceptive mastermind at work. Daisy's good, and I wonder who else has caught onto her tricks. Which is why I look to Connor.

He watches quietly, observing everything like some analyst ready to type the social dynamic into a spreadsheet. He probably knows more than he lets on. I wonder if he's predicted the outcome of everything, if our lives are neatly mapped out in his head with probabilities and statistics. Then again, he didn't figure out that Lily was a sex addict.

Regardless, I think being inside Connor Cobalt's head would be both terrifying and strange, and yet the most expensive amusement ride there is.

Lily begins to spout off some story about a professor with a bow tie and lisp, trying to avoid any topic about Stats and her exam grades.

". . . so he was old."

"That's not a story," Rose tells her pointedly.

"It is. Just not a good one."

"How are you doing in classes, grade-wise?" Connor stirs up the topic. "Sebastian is still tutoring you." He doesn't ask it more as confirms what everyone already knows.

Lily's eyes dart to a man carrying a huge bottle of liquor. "Tequila!" she exclaims.

He turns to the table.

"You don't drink," Ryke reminds her, almost growling, even though the alcohol was, obviously, a distraction. I don't think she wants it, but I'm feeling a little defensive today.

I shoot him a look. "She can have some if she wants." I don't want her to think she has to be sober because of me. I wouldn't ask her to do that.

"No," she says, wide-eyed. The waiter comes over and she physically pushes him away.

I grab her arms. "Keep your hands to yourself," I tell her easily, not wanting her to get in trouble.

"You're on Antabuse, right?" Melissa asks me. "My step-mother took that for a while. She couldn't even kiss my dad when he had a glass of wine. It made her so sick." She motions to Lily. "Is that why you don't drink?"

"What? No," Lily says roughly, offended. "I never liked drinking, really. But if I did, I wouldn't care if I couldn't kiss him." She cringes. "I mean, kissing doesn't matter to me. In general. Not just with Lo. So . . . yeah. I could give up kissing."

"I think she gets it," I tell her with a smile. She turns bright red and takes my hand in hers. I lean over and whisper, "I'm glad I can kiss you." I put another soft one on her temple. Ever since her involuntary climax in public, she's been allowing me to touch her without desiring more. We've even slept in bed without a pillow wedged between my cock and her ass. She doesn't grind on me or ask for more. It's just sleep. In a way, something amazing came out of something terrible.

The waiter starts taking everyone's orders, and when I place mine for the fish tacos, I just barely catch Daisy's words.

"I think kissing is overrated."

Oh no.

Ryke tenses beside me, and I hope he's hearing my fucking voice raging in his head right now.

"How so?" Melissa takes the bait.

Rose chokes on a bite of rice. She clears her throat and puts a hand to her chest. "This isn't appropriate dinner conversation." Rose isn't a complete prude. She swears and talks dirty like the rest of us. I've heard her curse out a three-hundred pound redneck for slapping a girl's ass. Her language was vulgar and kind of hilarious. Rose just knows this is headed to a bad place.

Melissa rolls her eyes, not the biggest Rose fan, considering Ryke blamed her and Connor for shutting the room down for sex. "I, for one, would love a sixteen-year-old's perspective," Melissa says, turning right back to Daisy. "I want to know how the younger generation feels."

"Totally," Daisy says with a head bob. "So my theory about kissing—"

"There's a theory?"

"Oh yeah. And my theory is that *not* kissing is sexier than actually kissing." She holds up her hands. "Just go with me on this. Say you're with a guy and you can tell he's interested. There's some heavy petting, some under-the-bra fondling."

"We get it," I snap.

"And then," she continues without missing a beat, "he goes in for the kiss. You pull back, refuse him an intimate piece of you. Tension builds, and every other touch, flesh against flesh, feels illicit and intoxicating."

"So you're a tease," Ryke says.

I'm about to curse him out, but Daisy cuts me off. "No, we end up having sex."

Ryke doesn't even flinch. "If I'm not fucking mistaken," he says, "you mentioned sex being overrated as well." When?! *Rehab.* I fucking hate rehab. I missed everything.

"That was until I took your advice."

This is a train I cannot stop, and I selfishly want the information I lost more than trying to halt it. "What advice?" I ask, my voice edged.

Lily taps my leg repeatedly in fear. She knows, but I don't want to wait until later to hear myself.

Daisy opens her mouth and Ryke interrupts, seeing my anger begin to boil. "We don't have to talk about it."

It's bad. Whatever he said to Daisy involved sex, and my mind is already reeling. "No, I'd like to hear," I say, motioning for Daisy to continue.

"Me too," Melissa adds, shooting Ryke a side glare.

Lily buries her head in her hands. She's the only one who knows what they said to each other. She was the only one who went to Acapulco besides Daisy's friends.

Daisy hesitates now, and she tries to backpedal. "Just so you all know, my sexual experience before was less than stellar, and I had planned on warding off the male species entirely before Ryke talked to me."

"That's comforting," Connor says flatly. He has a finger to his cheek in contemplation, but his gaze is directed on Ryke, not Daisy.

I turn to my half brother. "Thank God for your advice, Ryke." I wear a bitter smile and slap him on the back, hard.

He jerks forward and almost tips over his glass of water, but he grabs it before it spills.

"Honestly, his advice worked," Daisy continues, trying to dig him out of a hole, but he's buried too deep. "So really, you can't fault him for saying it if it helped me in the end."

"Seriously," I say between clenched teeth, "if you don't fucking tell me what he said, I'm going to flip the table."

Ryke winces and gestures to Daisy. "Just say it."

He gave her permission, but she's still wary. Slowly and cautiously, she says, "You shouldn't let any guy fuck you until he makes you come at least twice."

The table practically silences with Rose giving Ryke an unparalleled death glare.

Ryke and Daisy are both in the wrong. I know this, but I'm putting all my frustration on Ryke. I don't even know what to do or say, but if I look at him, I think I may lose my mind.

Melissa breaks the quiet. "What great instruction for a sixteen-year-old." She crosses her arms over her chest.

Ryke lets out a breath. "What can I say? I give good advice."

Melissa slaps him across the face, the sound like a gunshot, and most of the restaurant quiets.

Ryke sets his chair legs on the ground, his cheek red. That had to sting like hell.

"I need to talk to you," Ryke says. At first I think he's speaking to Melissa. "Lo."

I shake my head, unable to meet his eyes.

Melissa lets out a low laugh. "Really?" She rises and throws down her napkin. "I'll be back at the hotel, not that you'd care."

"Wait . . ." Ryke stands up but he glances at me and falters.

"I'll talk to her," Daisy says, rising from the table. Melissa hates Rose. She's not that fond of Lily either, but I'm pretty sure it's Daisy that she despises. And I can't say a word. I sit in my chair, replaying Ryke's advice to Daisy. I don't care if it helped her or if it was good—there's a line there that I think he knows he crossed. Like he told me before—he just doesn't give a shit.

"You won't be able to," Ryke tells her. "Just let her go. I'll talk to her when we go back to the hotel."

Daisy shakes her head, not taking this as an answer. She sprints after Melissa.

"Fuck," Ryke curses, running his hands through his hair. He turns to me. "Please, just give me a fucking minute, Lo."

I'm about to curse him out when Lily says, "Go on." She nudges my side, and I find myself rising off the seat and following Ryke into the bathroom.

When the door closes, he turns to me and opens his mouth. But for some reason, I have to be the prick who has the first word.

"You could have told me that story about your stupid advice on the beach when we were having a fucking heart-to-heart," I fume.

"Clearly it wasn't stupid if it helped her, and I didn't think you'd take it well, obviously."

"I am *so* close to punching you, and I can promise that it will hurt a hell of a lot more than Melissa's bitch slap."

He holds up his hands in peace, which doesn't ease my temper.

"Let's hear your apology," I say.

He glares. "I wasn't going to apologize."

I make my move toward the door, *fuck this shit*, and he steps in front of me. "You can't be that angry at me. Not over this," he says coldly. "She's not your little sister. You couldn't even tell me ten facts about Daisy if you tried."

"Fuck you," I shoot back. "She's Lily's little sister. I remember her in diapers, so don't try to defend yourself based on a goddamn family tree."

Ryke has had enough. His fists clench and he looks ready to fight me. Instead, he actually uses his words.

"Don't make me into the villain because you're upset you lost out on a human fucking relationship with her," Ryke almost screams, pointing toward the door. "Blame booze, blame our father, but don't you ever fucking blame me."

I stand my ground, seething. He's right. I'm partly upset over all I've lost by drinking, and maybe I am being too hard on him. But I can't stop what happens next.

"Do you want to fuck her?"

He doesn't hesitate, and his tone softens, less defensive. "No. I don't," he says. "She's the last person . . . ever. I promise, Lo."

This is where I have to trust him.

"Can I explain at least?" Ryke asks. "There is a reason I said those things to her."

I run my tongue over the bottom of my teeth and shake my head, a laugh caught in my throat. "Since when do you have to have a reason?"

"Usually, I fucking don't," he agrees. "But that time, I did. So can I talk now or am I going to get the third degree?"

I motion for him to continue.

"It was Daisy's sweet sixteen and we were on the boat. Her friends were discussing sex, and I was not a part of that conversation, believe me. They roped Lily into it, and she looked ready to fling herself off the yacht. I mean, she's a fucking walking oxymoron: a sex addict who's uncomfortable talking about sex."

"She's working on it."

"That's what I thought too, but she ran away from the girls. And when Daisy confronted her to talk about sex, she was flustered again. I was just trying to show her that it's okay. That people can be comfortable about it. I knew I was going to cross a line, but I thought it was going to be fucking worth it. For Lily . . . and a little bit for Daisy too." He pauses. "It just happened, Lo. I can't take it back, and I honestly wouldn't."

I think that should be Ryke's motto. *It just happened.* Or better yet, throw in his favorite word. *It just fucking happened.*

I'm strangely calmer—mostly because I can picture Lily turning a shade of red, crawling into herself over all discussions about sex. Even with her sister.

"Are we good?" he asks hesitantly.

Saying yeah feels like a complete defeat, so I just nod.

When we return to the table, everyone is gone. The plates are scraped clean and the chairs are empty. We exit the restaurant and spot Rose and Lily by a taxi van that hugs the curb. They hold Styrofoam to-go boxes and wait for us. Connor has the passenger door opened, speaking to the driver over the seat.

Daisy climbs out of the cab, her eyes set on us. She jogs to reach our sides. "So Connor couldn't get the limo service to come pick us up early," she says, catching her breath. "They were all booked, but I hailed a cab—"

"Why'd everyone leave?" Ryke asks.

Daisy gives him a stern look. "We weren't going to let Melissa go home by herself. We're in *Mexico*."

I can't help what I say. I'm so pissed at everything and everyone. "That's funny, last time you were in Mexico, you had no problem leaving Lily and your friends to go jump off a fucking cliff."

Ryke shoots me a glare to drop it.

"That was different," she says to me. "I wasn't storming off angry. And I already apologized . . . I didn't mean to upset anyone."

"It's fine," Ryke tells her. "Where's Melissa?"

"In the back of the cab, waiting for you," Daisy says, "I calmed her down a little. She's no longer looking at flights to go home, and I think if you make out with her, she'll forgive you."

Ryke rolls his eyes. "Are you serious?"

"She wants to know you care."

"I do care!" he shouts, frustrated.

"You don't act like it," Daisy says. "Girls want to be the sole focus of your attention. They want to be all you think about, all you look at and see. You're more fixated on chicken tacos than Melissa." She pauses. "But if you're sick of her, you know, you don't have to do anything. She'll just leave . . ."

Ryke stares at Daisy for a long moment, his features hardening.

I think he does want Melissa gone, but that will give Daisy the wrong impression—that he's saying goodbye to Melissa *for* the youngest Calloway girl. And I don't think that's it at all. I think Melissa is annoying as hell, and he'd rather be alone than deal with her any longer.

He meets my hot gaze. He only has one choice, and the fact that he's considering leading Daisy on makes me want to go back into the bathroom and strangle him.

"Fucking fantastic," he says under his breath and walks past both of us toward the cab.

Daisy shakes her head repeatedly, but she stares at Ryke's back, her eyes pinned to the spot even after he climbs into the cab. Maybe

Lily is right—the further you push two people away, the more they'll pull together.

When we reach the cab, I kiss Lily on the cheek and take the box from her.

"I saved your fish tacos," she says.

I'm glad since I had *nothing* to eat. I was too concentrated on unnecessary drama than my food. She keeps her hands cupped in front of her, but I'd like nothing more than to wrap her in my arms and kiss her for a long, extended moment.

She bites her bottom lip, which shallows my breath and beats my heart. All my anger suddenly depletes as I imagine what I can do to her. How I could take her so hard and so fast that she'll cry in such searing pleasure.

I am used to having sex with her every single day. And I know she fears that I'll resent her for withholding sex, but the new frequency only makes the next time we fuck even headier.

I draw her to my chest and lean my head low, my lips brushing her ear. I want to whisper how she makes me feel and how I plan to take her so many different ways. But I can't promise her things that won't happen. I can't even bring her to the beach to screw because that would be considered public sex.

So I just land on the truth, "I love you," I whisper.

She stands on the tips of her toes and kisses me sweetly on the lips. I run my hand through her hair and then bite her shoulder playfully before setting an equally chaste kiss on her neck. She shivers in my arms, and I don't tempt her anymore. I fear that one kiss may drive her to want more. It hasn't since her public humiliation, but I know it can be all too easy to go back there.

We climb into the cab, Lily and I on the middle seat, and Daisy squeezing beside her sister. Rose and Connor take the front, and Ryke and Melissa are happily snug in the back.

Ryke has Melissa pinned against the back of the seat. I can barely see her behind his broad shoulders. Sitting up, her legs wrap around his waist, and his body melds into hers. His hand disappears underneath her shirt, and his lips devour hers hungrily. She can't stifle a sharp breath as he sucks her neck.

She grips his back, lost to his hands and his tongue. Lily is going to be jealous. Fuck, *I'm* jealous. While Melissa has her eyes shut, Ryke's are open, and he meets my gaze while he bites her bottom lip. And he glares at me, basically saying, *I hate that I have to do this.* But it's the right thing to do. And frankly, I don't care that he's pissed about it. Leading Melissa on—that's fine (all she wants is sex anyway). Leading Daisy on—that's not okay.

I turn my back to him just as Daisy leans over to slide the door closed. If she notices Ryke and Melissa's make-out session, she doesn't say a word about it.

The cab bumps along the uneven street, the strip lit up in the darkness, club signs blinking and twinkling. Constantly calling me.

I open the to-go box and pull out a fish taco, taking a bite while Lily rests her head on my shoulder.

Connor spins around in his seat to face us. "Did you get your test score back?" he asks Lily.

She sits up immediately. And I curse him for causing her to drift from me. Even though Lily is technically the cheater here, studying old exams. "I'm doing well," she says vaguely.

"That's not really what I asked."

Her cheeks redden. "Yeah, I got the test back."

"That bad, huh?" He turns to Rose. "I told you that Sebastian isn't that smart. He bought his way into Princeton. You should have let Joseph Kim teach her."

"Sebastian *is* smart," Rose refutes. "You don't know him like I do."

Connor wears a blank face, but if he'd show true emotion at all, I think he'd be upset by that.

"I actually did well," Lily says.

Connor can't hide his frown. "What's *well*? A 75?"

I cut in, hating to beat around this bush, but Lily is too nervous to come out and say it. "She made a 95 on her Statistics exam." Before Connor opens his mouth, I add, "She didn't want to hurt your tutoring feelings."

Rose beams and tilts her head at Connor. "What were you saying about Sebastian?"

"Wait . . ." Connor holds his hand at her face. Rose's eyes grow, incensed by the hand. I think she's going to bite his fingers off. "Was there a curve?"

"No," Lily says.

Rose grabs Connor's hand. "Why can't you believe that Sebastian is a good tutor?" she asks.

He covers her mouth with his other palm, not done grilling Lily. "Did you take Adderall?"

Rose smacks her purse at Connor's chest, beating him with the damn clutch until he drops his hand from her mouth. "That was unnecessary." She points a finger at him.

And I swear, he tries not to smile. I think he'd like nothing more than to tackle her on the seat and make out with her as much as Ryke is doing to Melissa. "Rose, darling," he whispers. "Let's not jump to conclusions because of personal bias. I don't know Sebastian like you do."

"Exactly," she says as though she won.

He ignores that and nods back to Lily. I think he may be smarter than Rose. If I told her that, she'd probably rip out my lungs.

"Lily, did you take Adderall?" Connor asks again.

She shakes her head quickly. "Nonono," she slurs together. "I studied, Connor. The normal, natural way like you taught me."

"And Sebastian clearly helped," Rose adds.

Connor shakes his head. "No . . . something's not right."

Rose pokes his arm. "You can't admit that you're wrong. That's the problem."

"I know when I'm wrong, Rose, and I don't think I am here."

"How many times have you even talked to Sebastian?"

"A couple," Connor says. "He runs out the door the minute I walk in, and he barely looks me in the eye. Only liars and cheaters can't meet my gaze."

Lily sinks deeper into her seat.

"Lily didn't cheat," Rose snaps back, her glare darkening.

I chime in, afraid that we've suddenly fissured their relationship, "Lily isn't as stupid as you think. Is that really so hard to believe?"

"Yes," Connor says. "I spent months tutoring Lily, and she never did better than a C."

"Maybe I'm just good at Statistics," Lily shrugs.

"You bombed your first two exams."

Rose raises her hand to cut in like we're in class. "Or maybe," she says, slinging her cold voice back at Connor, "Sebastian is just a better tutor than you."

Connor cocks his head at her like she's being foolish. "No, that can't be it."

She lets out an exasperated growl. "You're impossible."

"You love me," he says matter-of-factly.

She gapes. "I never said such a stupid thing." That's her go-to response. But she has turned bright pink.

Connor raises his brows at her and then pins his attention back on Lily. "Did you cheat?"

Oh shit.

Instead of interrupting, Rose waits for Lily to answer this time. Lily needs to stay strong here. Even if we're inadvertently siding with Sebastian rather than Connor, those tests are important for her future at Princeton. We spent years lying to people about our addictions. We're fucking good at it, but I remember all the times where I had to calm her down, to placate her anxiety about fibbing in front of Rose and her parents. Lying eats her up inside more than it does me.

Lily clutches my hand tightly, and with a steady voice, she says,

"I'm being honest, Connor. No cheating, no drugs, no nothing." She nods to herself. "Things have changed. I'm just more focused now." Her tone is sincere, something hard to reject.

I put my arm around her shoulder and watch Connor go quiet. But he doesn't look a hundred percent satisfied. I'd say he's at least forty percent, which is good enough for now.

Before he says something more, Rose smacks Connor on the arm, and the two begin arguing in French. I can't make out any of it, but I'm sure they're flinging curse words.

Lily cringes, watching Rose's eyes puncture holes into Connor, her words sounding nasty. And he's quick to retort back. Lil leans into my side and whispers, "I don't like lying to her."

I squeeze her arm. "We'll make it right." Eventually.

And then the cab hits a pothole and my stomach starts to twist in on itself, sending a shooting pain right through me. I touch my abdomen as it intensifies. I retract my arm from Lily and grip the door handle of the cab. What the fuck is happening?

"Lo?"

I open my mouth to speak, but a wave of nausea crashes into me.

"Lo?!" Her high-pitched voice quiets the car.

"Pull over," I hear my brother say. "Pull over *now!*" My head is a blur. I plant my hand over my lips, and as soon as the cab stops and the door flings open, I am on the road retching. My throat sears and my muscles burn.

Everything starts coming up. But for each heave, my head pounds, my body aches, and I think some animal wants to crawl out of my stomach. It claws and scrapes and tears up my insides.

"Did he drink?" Rose's cold voice pricks my ears in the background.

"What the fuck did you drink?!" Ryke yells at me, his voice louder.

I shake my head and puke again, cars whizzing by and honking their horns like I'm another drunken college student on spring break. But I didn't have one fucking beer. Not even a drop of whiskey. I don't understand. I don't get it. I did nothing wrong.

Lil clutches my arm, and I briefly meet her eyes, and the flood of disappointment feels worse than this pain.

I did *nothing* wrong.

But I don't have the voice to say it.

I'm too busy throwing up.

Thirty-two

Lily Calloway

spend the entire night with Lo in the hotel bathroom, wiping his clammy forehead with a warm washcloth and making sure he isn't sick enough for a hospital.

I think we all overreacted in the cab. But it was clear that his illness wasn't from food poisoning. He literally just took a bite of his fish taco. Food poisoning doesn't work that fast. So we all figured Antabuse was to blame—which meant one thing.

He had alcohol.

Ryke yelled at Lo while he puked his guts up on the side of the road, but I didn't believe that Lo could have been secretly tossing back whiskey shots or some other concoction. Not when we were all sitting at the table. He's not that stupid.

But there was an inkling of doubt creeping in. The *what if* taking over my mental process. Addicts lie. I just never thought Lo would start lying to me too. We have been a unit for so long that I didn't realize I could be pushed out so easily—and without warning. I wondered, for a short moment, that if he could lie all this time about being sober, then he could be keeping other secrets from me. And I wouldn't even know it.

Connor was the one to shush everyone's doubts, including mine. He said there was a high probability that the fish was beer-battered, a detail that Lo may have overlooked before ordering. So

Rose called the restaurant, and sure enough, the fish was not only fried with beer but tequila too.

Lo moves sloth-like this morning, brushing his teeth, practically hunched over the sink. He looks a little like he used to before his sobriety—like he just woke up after a night of bingeing.

"Are you okay?" I ask softly. "We can stay here if you want."

A stage is set up on the beach for an outdoor spring break concert, and we're all supposed to be headed down there soon. I can't imagine the chaos and noise being pleasant for him.

While I wait for his answer, I start the bathtub to shave my legs, normally I'd just do a quick shave-and-go in the sink, but we share it with five other people.

He spits into the sink. "No," he says and wipes his mouth on a towel. "I want to go, and honestly I feel better than I did last night."

The bathroom door opens, and Ryke slips in, already outfitted in a neon blue Speedo. Lo confessed about the bathing suits a couple days ago, and oddly Ryke would rather wear the skimpy ones than the trunks that Connor and Lo chose. He claims he gets a better tan, but I think he likes the way all the girls stare at his ass.

I grab a razor, focusing on my prickly calves rather than his . . . area.

"How are you feeling?" Ryke asks as Lo starts applying sunscreen along his abs.

"Like shit. Must have been that bottle of whiskey I guzzled while you were all sitting around me," he snaps. "Oh wait, no, that's what you accused me of."

"I already apologized." His voice remains rough and he looks to me, distracted. "Lily, what the hell are you doing?"

Lo follows his gaze and rolls his eyes. "She's just shaving her legs."

"What he said," I say, trying to concentrate so I don't knick my kneecap or ankle. Those are the tricky spots. And since I'm only lathering my legs with a bar of soap, I have less suds to work with.

"Why don't you take a shower?"

I let out an exasperated breath. "That's so much more work."

"You're as lazy as Lo."

I shrug, not denying it. Ryke puts his attention back on his brother. "Did you take your pill yet?"

"Yeah." He holds out the sunscreen bottle to me. "Can you do my back when you're finished shaving?"

"I'll do it right now. I'm done with this leg." I rinse off my right leg and spin on the porcelain ledge. He sits down beside me so I don't have to get up to reach his height. I squirt some lotion into my hand and start rubbing it along his bare back.

A sinful thought creeps into my head—of Lo turning around and taking me right here on the ledge. I'm straddling it already, the spot between my legs against the coldness of the tub. This is just bad. I try to smother my longing and any attraction quickly. *No sex*. Not today. Not this week. The words don't devastate me as much as they would have before.

Ryke keeps his gaze on Lo, skepticism creeping into his eyes. "Where's the pill bottle?"

His shoulders tense. "Under the sink."

I smooth out the white streaks along Lo's skin, my fingers dancing along his back. I wish I could touch him other places, which I realize is my problem. I shouldn't want to have sex when I'm just rubbing lotion on his back. Right? Maybe it's not so weird, but I know my persistence to go further is wrong.

I'm not supposed to *go* at all.

Which just sucks.

And not a good sucking, mind you.

Nope, this is a bad suck, which I didn't think could exist. But it does. This is definitely a bad kind of suck.

Ryke rises from the cabinet a second later with the orange container in his hand, and then he pops it open, spilling the pills on the counter.

"What the hell are you doing?" Lo asks.

Ryke moves them out into little piles, and I suddenly realize "what the hell he's doing"—counting.

Lo goes rigid as the same thought strikes him. But he shouldn't have anything to fear. Unless . . .

Ryke starts shaking his head and scoops the pills back into the bottle. "Why do you fucking lie to me?"

"When did you start counting my pills?" Lo asks, brows furrowed.

"When you got them."

"You had no right—"

"I have every right. You're an addict, Lo. You lie, you cheat, you fuck around the rules to get what you want. I go behind your back because I fucking care, not because I'm trying to undermine your privacy."

"Tell me what I haven't already heard!" Lo yells. "I'm a cheat. I'm a liar. I get it. And if that bothers you so damn much, there's the fucking door."

· Uh-oh. I should go back to shaving my leg. But I can't stop watching.

Ryke's face turns to stone. He grabs a bottle of water off the sink and hands it to Lo, along with a pill. "Take it."

"Did you not hear me?" Lo sneers. He pushes Ryke's hand back. "I don't want it."

It hurts to watch him deny something that helps him. "Lo," I say softly. "Just take it."

He jumps off the tub ledge like I electrocuted him, and then squares off with Ryke and me like we're the enemies now. "You two don't get it."

I stand up, not caring about shaving my left leg at this point. "What don't I get?" I ask, choking back my hurt.

"Last night, I puked my guts up from mediocre fish tacos. I couldn't even taste the tequila or beer batter or whatever the hell was on them! Like hell am I going to have that accidentally happen again."

"So read the fucking menu next time," Ryke tells him. "Ask the waiter, ask the fucking chef. Don't make excuses."

"I'm not making excuses, but staying sober shouldn't be this much goddamn work. I shouldn't have to set an alarm clock to remind myself to take a pill. I shouldn't have to spend five hours a week in therapy." Lo's chest rises and falls heavily. "And you . . . it's not fair that it's so goddamn easy for you. Drinking your water every day, making it look like it's nothing."

"I'm not you, Lo. Don't try to compare us."

"How can I not?" Lo says, running two shaking hands through his hair. "You stand there telling me what to do, what's best for me, like you've been through this all before. You've never even taken Antabuse, Ryke. You don't know how this fucking feels!"

I'm not sure what to say or do right now.

"I'm just trying to help," Ryke says. "Stop pushing me away."

Lo grips the sink tightly.

I agree with Lo, staying sober takes more work than either of us thought possible, and obviously Lo and I are the type of people who only give ten percent of our energy. I don't know if it's because we've always been lazy, or if we're just apathetic. But right now, in this moment, I care. I just hope Lo does too.

"It doesn't even make the cravings stop," Lo says, motioning toward the pill in Ryke's hands.

"No, it doesn't," he agrees, "but you just felt what it's like to drink when you're on it, and I'm pretty sure that's enough to motivate you to avoid booze."

Lo hesitates. "Fuck," he curses, rubbing his eyes.

"You should take it," I tell him. "If I had a magic pill that made me puke whenever I looked at porn, it'd probably help."

I don't know if it's me, or Ryke, or his own warring conscience, but something wins out. He turns around and accepts the pill from his brother.

Thirty-three

Lily Calloway

The remixed rap song bleeds into the crowded area, swimsuit-clad college students pumping their fists in the air and chugging vodka straight from water bottles. I have the best seat on the beach.

Right on Lo's shoulders.

The height gives me an advantage from the sweltering body heat and sweaty stench. I also have prime view of the stage, where the rapper in shiny shades saunters around and jumps in unison with the riled crowd.

Lo hasn't left my side the entire concert. Not to buy a beer, go to a bar, or to find his way to liquor. I haven't made a move on him or asked for sex.

We're having unadulterated fun.

The song ends and I stick my fingers in my mouth, letting out a loud whistle as everyone claps and cheers and hollers. Below me, the rest of our group tries to remain together and not be pushed too far away.

Rose wears a black sheer bathing suit cover-up and stands rigidly among the crowd, petrified by the closeness of so many bodies. Connor couldn't be more composed. He's like a chameleon, adapting to the drunken, party-like atmosphere with ease. He keeps her close, his hands on her hips, and normally she'd probably push him off. But I think the fear of ramming into someone and beer being spilt all over her cover-up and chest outweighs her fear of intimacy with Connor.

Melissa has all but forgiven Ryke. The make-out session helped in the cab, but the below-the-panties groping solidified her plans to stay in Cancun. I would have been more jealous last night if Lo wasn't sick. But his clammy skin and pale hue literally rerouted my whole mind. Even as I heard Melissa's giggles from the deck, pitch black outside—I didn't care all that much. I just wanted Lo to feel better.

Melissa is in a good mood now. She sits on Ryke's shoulders, clapping beside me as the next song starts.

A gust of smoke plumes up by my nose, and I sniff the salty air. Joints are lit all over this beach, the smells overpowering, but this one is so near that I look down. Daisy stands directly in front of Ryke and Lo, a cigarette pinched between two fingers. At least it's not pot. So there's that.

She effortlessly keeps the cigarette from burning anyone in close proximity, and she lifts her head to blow the smoke into the air away from other people. Except me, of course.

I've let Daisy smoke on numerous occasions. I didn't know if it was my place to tell other people to *stop* when I can barely stop myself. I hate the thought of being a hypocrite. But I'm under the impression that Daisy only smokes recreationally. I imagine that recreation turning into a habit, which turns into an addiction. I just can't bear for Daisy to go through what I am.

Before I can say anything, Ryke plucks the cigarette right from her fingers and tosses it to the sand.

I don't see her reaction because the rapper has stopped singing and starts talking, the music still going on behind him. "Now I want to see more ladies in the air! On shoulders now! Let's go!" Girls start climbing on random guys' shoulders, being lifted into the air like Melissa and me.

Connor doesn't even ask Rose, probably knowing she would

prefer to keep her feet planted firmly on the ground. Daisy taps a bandana-wearing guy in front of her. He gives her a long once-over from head to breasts—mainly staying on her breasts, which fit in a neon green bikini, the fringe accentuating her boobs from a small B to a C.

"I'm light," she tells him. And then she whispers in his ear.

Melissa is watching Ryke with the utmost scrutiny, but he doesn't say a word.

The guy breaks into a big dopey grin, which is not good. I am thinking sexual things—like Daisy whispered to him that she will return the favor of sitting on his shoulders. Sexual favors, of course. But maybe that's just my dirty mind playing tricks on me again.

I put my hands on Lo's head and glance down at him. He is *glaring* at the guy. So . . . maybe everyone is just as dirty as me. I grin at the idea.

The bandana guy bends down to let her on his shoulders.

When she's at my height, she turns a little and gives me a high-five, oblivious to the overprotective guys below me.

"Ladies! Say *yeah*!" The rapper chants.

"YEAH!" This is kind of fun. My smile takes over my face.

"Guys! Say *fuck yeah*!"

"FUCK YEAH!"

He continues a portion of his song, the beat pumping and my view officially gone with the amount of girls on shoulders.

"Now, ladies!" He goes back to his talking. "It's spring break! Let's see those titties!"

Wait. What?

I go still while the girls around me respond by flinging off their bikini tops as though the rapper said a magic word.

All I heard was *titties*, which has the opposite effect on my willingness to free-boob. Everyone hollers in drunken excitement, eyes wide at the sight of nipples and springy parts.

Boobs of all sizes jiggle and bounce around me. I'm slapping

Lo's face, his nose, his cheek—*get me down*. Down. I need down. Now.

Beside me, Melissa has already pulled the string to her top. Which is cool. She has pretty boobs. She drops her top on Ryke's head. He grabs it and looks up, exactly what she wanted.

I have nothing much to show off, and I am easily embarrassed. Clearly.

I do see a few other girls lowering from the air, not wanting to take part in this either.

"Daisy!" Rose screams from the ground.

Just as Lo sets me on my feet, I crane my neck and spot Daisy fingering the clasp on her back.

"Daisy!" I shout with wide eyes, equally as mortified as Rose. I do not want anyone to see my sixteen-year-old sister's boobs. If she wants to tear off her bikini top in two years, then so be it—but not now.

Lo plants his hands on my shoulders. "Jesus Christ," he curses, trying to divert his eyes.

Daisy just looks at me, grinning from ear to ear.

Rose is about to swallow her anxiety and push through all of these bodies to reach Daisy and wring her neck. But then Daisy drops her hand with a laugh.

"Scare you?" she asks, waggling her brows.

Yes. She scared me, but at least she had no intention of doing it. That has to count for something.

Her eyes flicker beside me. Not to Lo but to Ryke. His normally hard features are darkened slightly. And I think he's trying really, really hard not to call Daisy a tease, just to piss her off and start something.

It's what he does.

The longer she stares at Ryke, the more her smile fades. She turns her back to us, hunches forward, and says something to the bandana guy. He lowers her to the ground, safely on Earth, and before she returns to our group, she continues talking with him, even with the loud music.

She nods a lot. He smiles even more. I don't like it. Because he looks in his late twenties and she's just a teenager.

And then his hand rests on her hip and starts traveling to her ass.

"I'm thirty seconds," Lo says under his breath, his eyes flickering to Ryke.

"I'm fifteen."

I frown. For what? To intervene?

Connor looks between them. "You both can't be serious."

Ryke glances at his watch. "Five . . ."

"She's a smart girl," Connor reminds them.

"She's sixteen," Lo says.

"Three . . ."

And then the guy slaps her ass, and Ryke is about to drop Melissa on the ground. But Daisy just smiles and waves goodbye to the guy and comes over to us. When she meets our faces, her smile contorts into a frown, confused like I was. Now I'm pretty positive there's too much testosterone pumping in this area.

"What's up with all of you?" Daisy asks. "Lo, you look like you're going to pop a blood vessel." He does. But she tries to shrug it off. "That guy told me a good place to swim with sharks. Anyone up for it?"

Everyone stays quiet.

And she deflates again. "What? What did I do?"

"That guy practically stuck his hand down your bathing suit," Ryke tells her, "and you didn't care."

Melissa has her arms crossed over her chest. Her mood is slowly tanking.

Rose shoots me a harsh look and mouths, *Girl time.* Yes. Definitely.

I take Daisy's hand, wanting air too but mostly wanting Daisy away from their judgmental gazes for a second.

"Wait, I didn't do anything wrong," she says. "He was just being nice."

"Are you really that naive?" Lo questions. "Because if you are, we should consider sending you home before something terrible fucking happens."

"I'm not naive," she says. "He was happy."

Ryke cringes. "You let him slap your ass because it made him *happy*?" Yeah, that doesn't sound right.

"Okay," I interject. "We're leaving. Right, Rose?"

"Yes." She sets a glare on each of the guys.

Connor raises his hands. "I didn't say a word."

Her eyes soften at him. "You're exempt."

"Daisy," Ryke says with so much emotion to the name that shivers run down my arm. And it's freakin' hot out here. I think he wants to say a lot of things to her—give her some sort of pep talk about how she doesn't have to please other people to make herself feel better—that doing so will hurt her in the end. But Melissa leans her head down and starts whispering in his ear, deterring him from speaking his mind.

So Daisy says, "I'll see you around." And she actually drags me off toward a tiki bar that sits on the beach. Rose races behind us, wanting out of the mobs of people too.

We rest our elbows on the counter, and I buy a water bottle while Rose and Daisy wait for the bartender to blend their margaritas.

Rose raps her nails on the counter, antsy as always. "Daisy," she says. "Do you have something you need to tell us?"

Daisy stands between Rose and me, and she rocks on the balls of her feet. "I'm not going to sleep with that guy," she says. "I wouldn't. I just told him I thought he was good looking, and then afterward, I asked him about sharks."

I frown. "Really?" It was that PG? Maybe all of us are so focused on sex. We're the gross ones.

"I mean, he said some suggestive things, but I wasn't trying to flirt back. Honest." She shrugs like it's nothing. "I'm used to it."

"Which part?" Rose asks icily. "The touching or the flirting? Because if you're going on photo shoots where the crew is putting a hand on you—"

"Nonono," she says, slurring the word like me when I'm trying to cover up a lie. "That has never happened. Mom comes with me. She wouldn't let anyone touch me inappropriately."

Rose believes her. She nods, but I stare at Daisy for a long time, not as trusting. Maybe because I have lied for so long that I can see right through it.

Daisy meets my worried gaze and she wraps an arm around my shoulder. "I'm okay, Lily."

I don't feel like she is.

I remember being young, trying to navigate what's wrong and what's right in a place where lines blur so very often. But I had Lo to fall back on—to make sure I didn't fall off the deep end and drown.

Daisy is thrust into this modeling world without all of us there to catch her. She's alone and confused. And I'm not sure how to fix that without telling her to quit. But she would never leave—not because of the money but because her career is related to our mother's happiness. And keeping our mother happy makes Daisy happy.

My phone vibrates, and I check the caller ID. Poppy.

I click off the phone and slip it back into the pocket of my jean shorts.

"Who was that?" Daisy asks, talking over the loud blender.

"Poppy."

Rose glares at the bartender for being so slow, and Daisy's forehead wrinkles in confusion. "Why would you hang up on her?"

"I just don't feel like talking." It's the truth. And anyway, my relationship with Poppy is distanced at best. She's six years older, so by the time I entered ninth grade, she was two years into college and engaged.

Rose's phone rings, and she answers the cell on the first chime. "Hello, Poppy." She gives me a sharp look, but nothing nearly as upset as Daisy right now.

"Is that why you don't answer my calls?" Daisy asks. "You just don't feel like talking?"

The accusation hurts when I remember Daisy is four years younger than me—five years in August, when I turn twenty-one. Almost the same age gap as Poppy and me.

But any ability to heal a relationship with my eldest sister has sailed long ago. She's married. She has a baby and started a family of her own. I have a chance to be a sister to Daisy, and I'm trying my damned hardest.

"No, that's not it, Dais."

"Yes, Poppy, we're having fun. The mojitos are weak, but the margaritas are usually good." Rose's sight is still planted on that sluggish bartender, taking ages to squeeze lime into the frozen slush. "Yes, Lily is with us. She couldn't hear your cell because of all the noise."

Daisy bumps my arm. "Then what is it?" she asks, waiting for a viable excuse. *This is it*, I think. This is the moment where I should come clean and tell her that I have a sex addiction, and that, in the past, I preferred sex over anything else—even talking to her.

My throat tightens for a minute, and then I say, "I'm just all awkward on the phone. I guess I prefer texting." The lie tastes bitter and rolls my stomach.

Daisy stares at the bar, quiet, which I'm not sure is a good or bad sign.

"What?" Rose says over the phone, perplexed. "Are you sure it was addressed to Lily?"

"What's going on?" I ask.

"Hold on, let me ask." Rose cups a hand to the receiver and tugs me away from the bar, separating from Daisy a little, but she joins us, curious. I would be too if I was her. "Did you mail a package to the Villanova house?" Rose asks. Villanova . . . my parents' house? Why . . .

"Why would I do that?"

Rose's bony shoulders stiffen in sharp angles.

"What package?" Daisy asks.

"Here, talk to her." Rose hands me the phone.

I press the cell to my ear, my nerves spiking. "Hey, Poppy. What's going on?"

"Lily, I'm at the Villanova house for Maria's birthday party," she explains in a hushed tone, as if she's afraid someone will hear. "Harold just brought the mail in, and there's a package addressed to you. It's from a website called *Kinkyme.net*. There are literally X's all over the box. He was going to give it to Mom, but I stopped him before he could."

"I didn't order that," I say quickly, my heart beating out of my chest.

"It's fine if you did," Poppy says gently. "I'm just wondering why you would mail something like that here. Mom would have your head."

"Honestly, I really didn't."

Rose seems a little skeptical, and I wonder if she thinks I sent the package there to hide it from her and Lo or something. She trusts me about as much as Ryke trusts Lo.

I make a sudden decision. "Poppy, can you open it and see what it is?"

Rose's eyes go wild, but now she can't possibly believe I sent the package.

"Yeah, hold on," she says. I hear her fumbling around and then the rip and tear of tape. Her voice lowers to a whisper. "It's a dildo."

I grimace.

"Wait, there's a letter." She pauses and the silence is agonizing. "Oh my God."

"What—What does it say?" I stammer.

Rose taps her foot, annoyed that she can't hear. Daisy rests a hand on my shoulder, comforting me even though she's blind about the origin of my distress. The guilt starts creeping in almost immediately. *I should have told her.* Maybe not. *Yes.* No . . . I don't know. My head hurts.

Poppy reads quietly, "*Dearest Lily, here's something to keep you full at night.*" She pauses. "There's no signature. Is it from Loren?"

"Why would Lo buy me a dildo?" I say out loud, unthinking.

"Dildo?" Daisy's mouth falls open, connecting some of the dots.

"Who else would send something like this to you?" Poppy asks.

"It must be a stupid prank," I say. From the blackmailer. "Can you throw it out before anyone else sees it? And can you tell Harold not to mention it?"

"Of course," Poppy says. "If you're having problems making friends at school—"

"It's not prep school, Poppy. It's college. No one is stealing my lunch money."

"Then why would someone do this?"

"They must think it's funny. I don't know," I say quickly. My throat is starting to close up with a lump and my voice threatens to shake. "Hey, do you want to talk to Rose?"

"Sure."

I hand the cell to Rose, and she engages in a cordial conversation.

"Hey." Daisy squeezes my shoulder in a side-hug. "It's probably just some loser from Penn who's pissed you never put out for him or something."

Tears prick my eyes. She couldn't be any further from the truth.

"Oh no, please don't cry." Daisy spins me around and grabs my hands, swinging my arms like she could dance with me at any second. "We're in Cancun. Spring break. The best week of the year. Don't let some asshat get the best of you."

She's right, so I sniff and wipe my eyes. She pulls me in for a real hug, and her fingers go through my hair. She sighs enviously. "So short and pretty," she says with a smile.

I rub my nose as we separate a little. "It's greasy."

She waves me off and her eyes wander toward the stage. I follow her gaze and spot the guys plus Melissa retiring from the huge crowd. I'll have to tell Lo what happened. Not only does the blackmailer know I'm in Cancun, but they know my parents' address.

He's trying to unnerve me.

It's kind of working.

Thirty-four

Loren Hale

On the balcony, the music blasts from the pool below, but at least it's more private than the bedroom. Everyone throws on nice clothes for the club tonight—our last outing in Cancun before we travel back to the real world with responsibilities and commitments.

I stare at the screen of my phone. Five missed calls from my therapist. I should call him back, but talking to Brian makes me feel like a failure. He carries this hypersensitive tone like I've already fucked up, and I can't listen to that. I don't want to hear him try to calm me down or to tell me that I should be tucked in my bed at home where alcohol doesn't exist, where my vice isn't staring me in the face.

Lily has made a better effort to stay in touch with her therapist. When I see her on the phone, Allison is usually on the other end.

I sit on the plastic chair and open a text message that my father recently sent.

Emily Moore

789 Huntington Drive

Caribou, Maine 04736

Whether he was feeling particularly generous, forthcoming, kind—he spontaneously gave me my birth mother's address. I asked him for it only once. When he denied my request, I wasn't about to grovel for it. Now that I know where she lives, I don't know what to do. Seeing her will open new gates that may crash me backward.

I'm not sure I'm ready to handle that.

My hand trembles, and I glance over my shoulder. No one watches me, but if I dial a number, they'll believe my therapist is on the other end. No one will disturb me. That's my hope at least.

I punch in a familiar number, and when the line clicks, he speaks before I have a chance. "Long distance calls aren't fucking cheap. How do you expect to pay for it?"

My father's words drill into me, bringing up an insecurity with such ease. "That's really not your concern."

"Greg Calloway gives his daughters an allowance. Lily can't afford to support your apathy forever."

I clench my phone tightly in my hand, trying so hard to focus. I had a reason to call him after all. "Well, since I am paying per minute, can you stop talking about money and let me speak?"

"Make it quick, I have to get back to a meeting."

He stepped out of his meeting to answer my call?

That's all that processes. Greg would have never stopped a meeting for one of his daughters. If Lily needed her father, he'd send an assistant and then find her after his work was finished. My father— he dropped everything for me growing up. If I called him at school, he was the one walking into the principal's office. But I only needed him when I was in trouble, and he'd yell at me for causing it.

"Have you found the guy?"

"These things take time, Loren," he says curtly. "Answers don't just fall down from the goddamn sky."

I pinch the bridge of my nose and take a sharp breath. "Look, something else happened," I say quickly. "He sent a package to the Calloways' house."

I hear rustling on his end like he's looking for pen and paper. "Okay, give me the details."

I explain the dildo and the note, trying to be specific, even though all I want to do is find this guy and make his life a living hell. He's torturing her.

"He hasn't asked for anything? Not a dime?"

"No."

"This sick fuck is making it clear he doesn't care or want to be found, but I'll try my best." He pauses. "How is she?"

I laugh bitterly. "Since when do you care?" He wasn't fond of Lily when we were teenagers. He believed having a female as a friend was like girl repellent, and if she wasn't putting out for me, then I should kick her to the curb. But I knew once I started a fake relationship with Lily, he'd be pleased. And he was. Only because she suddenly became of use to me.

I never saw her like that—an object that I could fuck or toss away. My father's perception of women is demented.

"Please, she's practically my daughter-in-law," he says defensively. "And if Greg and Samantha Calloway ever find out she's a sex addict, don't think they won't react accordingly."

"What is that supposed to mean?"

"It means when you're both fucking broke and homeless, I'll be here to pick up the pieces. Just like I've always done with the two of you. Cleaning up your goddamn messes."

I narrow my eyes at the ground. That's his fucked-up way of saying he'll be there for me when everything goes to shit.

"Just find this guy," I snap.

"Of course." Voices puncture the other end and then he says,

"I have to go. The partners are getting restless. Impatient fucks. I'll see you next week?"

I don't know what for, but I just end up saying yeah. We hang up, and I feel as paranoid and anxious as I did before. Obviously, that did not help. No conversation with my father ever really does.

Thirty-five

Loren Hale

The nightclub transforms into a live show, complete with impersonators, dancers, and flying trapeze artists. A huge square-shaped bar fills the center floor where girls dance and take body shots. Ever since I was ill from the fish tacos, I don't even flinch when a drink passes by. I have no desire to be sick again.

The Calloway girls made a goal to drink and dance tonight, which I translated as: *We're getting shit-faced*.

Connor, Ryke, and I promised them that they could go crazy and we'd be the responsible ones, fit to take care of them. For once, I'm on the other side of things. And it feels pretty good.

I like knowing that I have the power to keep Lily safe. Before, all of that seeped away with each whiskey I downed. So yeah, this is new. But it's a good new.

The crowds aren't as large as the concert yesterday, and Connor bought a balcony table so we can keep an eye on the girls. We're seated on the highest level, and the psychedelic lights strobe around us—well, around Connor and me. Ryke is still in the bathroom.

I have a clear view of the three Calloway girls, all of them hovering around the square bar. Rose carries two glasses of some pink concoction, handing one to Daisy.

"Have you ever seen Rose drunk?" I ask Connor. The event has to be like a lunar eclipse or something.

"I don't think she'd allow herself to exceed her limits."

I nod in agreement. I've never even seen her beyond tipsy. "She's probably too afraid she'll get wasted and lose her virginity to a guy with an IQ less than hers."

Connor breaks his usual placid expression, his mouth opening in slight surprise.

Oh shit. "What did I say?"

He takes a small sip of his wine and his face resumes its normal composure. "I didn't know she was a virgin."

Shit. Fuck. Shit. Lily is going to kill me. Hell, Rose is going to have my balls first. I should have known better than to open my goddamn mouth.

"I'm sorry," I say slowly. "I thought you knew." I scratch the back of my neck.

He stares at his glass and shakes his head. I can't even begin to guess what he's thinking. So I have to ask. "Is this a bad thing?" My heart crushes instantly at the thought. As much as Rose and I bicker and fight, I'd never want to ruin her relationship. Especially not with Connor, a guy who is pretty damn perfect for the girl.

He doesn't say anything, and all my guilt suddenly morphs into anger.

"Hey, she's a virgin, not a fucking leper." I point a finger at him. "And if you dump her because of this, then you're a fucking prick. There are a *million* guys who would gladly be with Rose. For whatever reason, you met her incredibly high standards, and if you hurt her because she's not experienced, I swear to God, Connor, you are going to wish you never met me." I finish my rant, surprising myself as much as Connor.

I've learned a lot about myself being sober.

I guess I'm kind of protective of Lily, Daisy, and even Rose.

"Lo." He says my name like I'm five years old and just threw a tantrum. "I don't care that she's a virgin. I care that we've been dating for six months and she hasn't told me. Obviously, I've over-estimated the progress in our relationship." His eyes flicker down to Rose as she sways to the music beside Lily, and then he looks back to me. "And while I appreciate the sentiments behind that threat, it's really unnecessary. I have no intention of hurting Rose."

He pacifies me with a few sentences as if his words are liquid morphine, but I still feel obligated to defend Rose since I divulged her secret. "She likes you," I say quickly. "She's just . . ." She's Rose. I don't know how else to explain it.

"I know."

Of course he does. He knows everything.

"When she was twenty, I had a suspicion that she lost her virginity to someone on her Academic Bowl team," he opens up, sharing information that he usually keeps to himself. "She used to slide out of hugs, but she let him rest an arm around her shoulder. I even saw him kiss her in a hallway. She didn't recoil." He shakes his head, staring at Rose from far away. "Turns out she was playing me."

"What do you mean?"

"She knew I was watching. She knew that I could tell how in-experienced she was, so she stomached whatever revulsion she had toward male contact—just so I would form the idea that she was no longer a virgin." He sips his wine. "I shouldn't be surprised. She was never ashamed of it as a teenager, but whenever her virginity was brought up in front of me, she'd get defensive. I think she as-sumed I'd use it against her."

He sounds more genuine than usual. I wonder if this is the real Connor Cobalt, a guy not saving face for investors or future con-tacts. Just him. "You knew Rose when she was a teenager?" I ask.

Connor sets down his empty wine glass. "Since she was four-teen. We both attended the circuit of academic conferences with our schools, Model UN, Beta Club, National Honor's Society." I feel like I hardly know him. We've been friends for months now. How could I not know *this?* "I'm a year older than her, by the way."

"Wait, what?" I frown. "I thought you're twenty-two."

"Twenty-three."

"Were you held back as a kid or something?"

"Fifth-year senior," he says. "I triple majored, so I had to stay an extra year at Penn to finish my courses." He keeps his gaze on Rose.

"Why haven't you told me this before?"

"You never asked. And really, is it that important?" I'm beginning to think that Connor Cobalt only lets people into his life halfway. Maybe he's more like us than I believed.

We drop the subject as Ryke returns from the bathroom. Melissa rejoins the girls on the dance floor, which she wasn't willing to do when we first arrived. She was clinging to Ryke pretty fiercely, so I assume Ryke went down on her in the toilet stall. She seems appeased at least.

I want to change the topic off of Rose's sex life, so I say the first thing that comes to mind. "What kind of a name is Ryke?"

He sinks into the seat beside mine, a can of Fizz Life in his hand that I'm pretty positive doesn't have any alcohol in it.

"It's a middle name," he says like I don't know. But last year at the Christmas Charity Gala, when he admitted to being my brother, I made him show me his driver's license. *Jonathan Ryke Meadows.*

"What kind of a *middle* name is Ryke?" I clarify.

He lets out an aggravated noise. "What the fuck did Jonathan give you as a middle name?"

"I don't have one. I think he realized sticking me with Loren was torture enough." My name was the target for teasing in elementary school, despite the guy-version spelling.

"Ryke," Connor muses. "From Middle English, a variant of the word would mean *power* or *empire*. Though, your spelling is a little off."

"Yeah, my father is an egotistical douchebag," he says roughly. "My name literally means *Jonathan empire*."

I can't help but laugh into my next sip of water. For the first time, mine doesn't seem so bad.

"I don't know why you're fucking laughing. You have a girl's name and no middle name."

I flip him off.

"Speaking of names," Connor says casually, and yet, I sense his mischief as his eyes set on Ryke. "You realize if you ever married one of the Calloways, she'd have a porn star name."

"And which Calloway would that be?" I snap. "Poppy is married, I'm dating Lily, you're dating Rose, and Daisy is sixteen."

"Hypothetically."

I don't like hypothetically, but maybe this will deter Ryke from even thinking about a possible future. So I play into it. "Daisy Meadows," I say, inwardly cringing at the idea. "Sounds like someone who knows her way around a—"

"Don't even finish that sentence." Ryke glares.

"I was going to say *camera*. Why? What were you thinking?" My voice remains edged and cold.

The lights flicker as the show begins to start and we both sit back, trying to calm down. We know how to push each other's buttons, and I wonder if that's a brother thing or just because we're both products of Jonathan Hale.

The room darkens except for the stage and the servers—the latter of which walk around with flashlights to take drink orders. An Elvis impersonator struts on stage and starts singing with dancers gyrating beside him. The oldies song is remixed so it beats with the hypnotic atmosphere.

I sit a little straighter, watching Lily, who dances in a small space with her sisters and Melissa. The lights flash brightly, illuminating the dance floor in a wave of colors.

It doesn't take long for some guy to approach Lily from behind.

I stiffen but stay in my seat, trusting her as I should. His hands slide along her hips, and all these memories of seeing her dance with strange guys flood me cold. I would settle at the bar, keeping a trained eye on Lil so she wouldn't get hurt, watching as she led some half-witted man to the bathroom. And I'd drown my misery in Maker's Mark.

As soon as his hands plant on her, his fingers slipping underneath the hem of her blouse and another falling to her skirt, she flinches and darts right into Daisy's chest. I can't help but smile. Some months ago, she would have played into his advances. Finally, she's chosen me.

But my happiness is popped when the guy approaches her, not taking the clear hint. His half-lidded, droopy gaze drives worry into my gut. He is drunk and definitely prepared to dance right on Lily's ass again.

I'm about to rise and descend to the dance floor, but Daisy shoves his arm hard and points a finger in his face—a Rose move that I wouldn't think possible from the youngest Calloway.

I glance at Ryke, and he rubs his lips, curiosity swimming in his eyes. She intrigues him as much as her actions concern him. The mix is not good, and I don't need to remind him of that. He's heard me shout it in brutal warning.

Lily slinks behind Daisy's body and then spins around, looking up and meeting my gaze. She gives me a small wave and then turns back to her sister. Daisy physically moves him out of their area. He has his hands up in peace, but he's staring at her breasts, which are pushed up in a short strapless dress. He licks his bottom lip.

"This is killing me," Ryke says under his breath.

"You can't play hero to her," I remind him. "If she was in trouble, I'd go down there. You can't."

He runs his hands through his hair and sits forward with his hands on his legs, watching carefully.

Daisy thrusts the guy back again, and then she gestures to a group of girls in bandage dresses about ten feet away. She breaks from Rose and Lily's side to bring him over to the girls who bounce up and down. He's too obliterated to protest, and it's not long before he's mesmerized by four more sets of tits.

He forgets about Daisy, and she leaves him to return to her sisters easily.

Lily hugs Daisy in thanks and whispers something in her ear. Both girls smile wide before they laugh.

"Do you trust her?" Connor asks me. I'm sure I look ready to spring down there and glare at any guy who so much as hits on Lily. But I don't want to be that guy, the one who is so insanely over-protective that he suffocates a woman. There's a happy medium somewhere. And it does come with trusting her.

"She's a sex addict," I remind him.

"Does correlation warrant causation in this instance?" Connor asks.

"English."

"Does being a sex addict automatically make her untrust-worthy?"

"I don't know," I say, "but I've spent more time seeing her with other guys than being with her, so I guess I can understand how it might be natural—for her—to just fall back into that."

"To cheat," Ryke clarifies.

I give him a glare. "Yeah," I snap, "but if it happens, it hap-pens, right?" Even the thought, though, devastates me.

"I don't think it will," Ryke says.

I jerk back in shock. He's never been an advocate for Lily. "And why is that?"

"Because I think she loves you more than she loves sex. And you love her more than you love alcohol, but you two just haven't let yourselves believe it yet."

Maybe he's right, but allowing myself to process that is harder than it seems.

Female servers start carrying out blue glowing bottles on the dance floor, flashlights held underneath the bottom to add the luminosity effect. They offer willing guys and girls straight shots. One of the servers stands in front of Rose and Daisy.

"They aren't . . ." I say with furrowed brows. Do they know what they're about to drink? I thought they wanted to get crazy-fun wasted, not "holy shit, what's that" wasted. But they have to know what they're drinking. Rose probably has the highest IQ in the club—not counting Connor. If I recognize the alcohol, she would too.

I watch Daisy nod excitedly, and my stomach tosses as she leans back against the bar. We're going to have our work cut out for us tonight . . .

The server pours the liquid into her mouth, and Daisy spills not a drop. She licks her lips and motions to Rose. She goes next, without much prodding from Daisy. Maybe all the lights and music have warped her mind.

She finishes off the first shot, and surprisingly, she leans back for another.

One of my short-term goals is coming true. Rose Calloway is definitely going to be drunk tonight.

I'm not as happy about it as I thought I'd be.

"What kind of liquor is that?" Connor asks. My whole face falls. Wait, if Connor can't tell . . .

"Look who doesn't know something," Ryke pipes in, capitalizing on Connor's question.

"Types of liquor aren't high on my priority list. But that's sweet of you, Ryke, to think I know everything in the world."

"Absinthe," I tell Connor. "It's blue absinthe." How could he not know? If he doesn't, then what's the probability that Rose *does*?

As soon as the words leave my mouth, Connor is on his feet, and he can't hide the concern on his face this time.

"You worried, Cobalt?" Ryke calls, but I can tell Connor's sudden ruffled composure is making Ryke equally alarmed. Because Daisy is the other girl downing the liquor—and she doesn't have a boyfriend here to look out for her. But she does have me.

Even so, my eyes latch on to Lily more, hoping she doesn't join her sisters if she doesn't know what she's getting herself into.

"Absinthe contains thujone," Connor tells him.

"So you don't know what it looks like, but you know what chemicals are in it," Ryke says.

"It's usually green, and it's also banned in the United States because thujone has hallucinogenic properties."

"Yeah," I say, rising to grab his arm to stop him. *Rose has to know*, I keep telling myself. She wouldn't drink something foreign to her. "I'm sure Rose knows what's in it."

His concern doesn't waver. "The bottle isn't labeled."

What? I look back down to the girls, where Daisy is taking another shot of absinthe. The bottle glows from the light underneath it, and sure enough—there's no label on the slender glass.

They don't know it's absinthe.

Shit.

Thirty-six

Lily Calloway

Daisy steps forward for another shot, and she stumbles a little. I do not want her to be sick tonight. I put my hand on her shoulder and wave *no* to the server. "We're good here."

Daisy doesn't fight me on the decision. When the server saunters away, I snatch Rose's arm, and she *wobbles* in her four-inch heels.

My eyes bug.

I've only seen Rose break her stride once. Her heel caught in a metal grate in New York, and she burned those shoes afterward to rid herself of bad juju. I think if Connor knew that she's *truly* superstitious, he'd tease her for a solid century.

Melissa sidles next to me, and I must be giving off a distressed look because she says, "Your sisters are sloshed." Announcing the obvious does not help.

The music changes into the theme song from *Superman* and it totally disorients me. I whip around, and impersonators on the stage are now dressed as various superheroes. Superman and Captain America stand on the tall balcony, a spotlight shining on them.

People start trying to edge closer to the stage, and someone bumps me from behind, almost making me lose my grip on Rose. "Watch it, buddy," I snap at him, but it really loses its effect when my focus is on the superheroes. It's my catnip.

The tempo starts to speed up, and as the crescendo hits, Superman and Captain America leap from the balcony and fly to the square bar only feet from us.

Bullshit.

Cap cannot fly.

I'm so angry that they made Captain America have a superpower he really doesn't possess that I don't see the incoming body from my right. His arm rams my side so hard that I teeter, and Rose's heels slide out from under her. She completely falls, dragging me with her. We're both on the ground before I can make sense of anything else.

My bony hip digs into the hard concrete floor, and my skirt soaks in sticky alcohol. I don't even want to think about what else could exist down here. I sit up and lose sight of Rose. Has she risen to her feet? But that's unlikely considering she could barely stand on her heels.

My heart thuds. "Rose!" I call. The bodies cage me in, and I suddenly fear being stepped on and squashed like a little bug. But more than that, I fear the same thing happening to my inebriated sister. Before I make a move, two pairs of hands slide underneath my armpits and lift me right off the ground like I weigh as much as a bag of apples.

It has to be a guy.

A guy is touching me.

Abort. Abort. My mind has flashing signs, picturing some flirtation on his part as soon as I turn around. He helped me up, after all. I'm sure he'll expect the damsel in distress to kiss him for his chivalry.

I contemplate running off, but he spins me around and places his hands on my cheeks. I jerk away on impulse.

"Lil."

"Lo." I take a breath of relief and willingly slide into his arms, my heart practically beating out of my chest. When my thoughts realign, I pull away quickly. "Where's Rose?"

As soon as I say the words, confetti bursts from cannons, blocking my vision and coating the floor in slick paper. I take a step and slip again, Lo reaches out and catches me before I fall to the floor.

His arms are tucked behind my back, and the music pumps and streamers fly. I feel like it's midnight on New Year's Eve. He stares deep into my eyes, and he says, "Did you drink anything?"

I shake my head. I wouldn't. Because then I wouldn't be able to do this. I lean forward and kiss him on the lips. He pulls me into his body and lifts my back completely straight, swept up in the way our tongues dance together. But I retract first.

Even though I love Lo, even though I'd like nothing more than to kiss him—my sisters are lost somewhere. And I need to find them.

Lo sees the panic in my eyes again, and he gives me a look like *I won't let anything happen to them.* I believe him. Now, more than ever, I believe that he's here for me.

He grabs my hand and leads me through the congested area that's teaming with bodies. "They're really drunk," I tell Lo over the music.

His cheekbones sharpen.

"What?" My pulse speeds up. "What is it?"

He tugs me in front of him, his hands on my shoulders as we move, and he lowers his head so that his lips brush my ear. "They were drinking absinthe."

What?! I don't think the server mentioned what was in the glowing bottles. Rose would never be crazy enough to drink absinthe, something that's too crazy for America.

On Halloween, Lo's eighteenth birthday, we took a plane to Amsterdam just to buy a bottle. He claimed he wanted to get drunk with a green fairy, thinking he'd hallucinate. He ended up passing out within the hour, leaving me to watch over him in our hotel room.

I go into sister-mode and walk faster, my eyes open and alert for any signs of my effervescent blonde sister and my fashionable brunette one.

We find Rose first.

By a high table littered with empty cups and bottles, Connor holds her tight around the waist while she presses two firm hands on his shoulders, unsteady in her heels. He whispers in her ear, probably trying to convince her to take them off.

But a tiger would birth a baby lama sooner than Rose would be barefoot in a dirty club.

We approach them, and I hold on to Lo like a kid clutching the wall in a skating rink. "Is she okay?" I ask.

"I'm just fine, thank you," Rose says. "But we need to contact the staff and have this mess cleaned up. The floor is filthy." She motions to the floor that's covered in sticky liquor and now little strips of confetti. Her nose crinkles at the table nearest her. The staff already starts sweeping streamers so that people don't slip. "Ah, right on time." She sways with a loopy smile, and then she stumbles without even taking a step. Connor rights her back up.

Lo can't stop grinning.

"What's so funny?" I ask.

"For once, that's not me."

I can't help but smile too.

"Don't . . . patronize me, Loren!" Rose points her finger at him. "I'm calling my lawyers. Have you arrested for . . ." She hiccups. ". . . public indecency."

"I'm pretty decent right now, actually," Lo says, still smirking.

"How about we call it an early night?" Connor asks, his hands firmly on her hips. She doesn't even seem to care. In fact, she leans back into him. This is probably the closest they've ever been, and yet it looks so natural.

"Yes, we have to tuck you into bed," she tells him.

"No, darling, I'll be tucking you into bed."

She lets out a puff of air. "I'm perfectly fine. Look." She holds out one hand and it shakes like she's on crack. "Steady as a rock."

Connor looks to us. "I'm taking her to the car."

"Connor Cobalt," Rose says with a cluck of her tongue. "Is that a made-up name?"

He sweeps his arm underneath her back and then, in one motion, lifts her effortlessly into his arms.

She plants her hand onto his chest, her eyes going wide. "Whoa. We need to tell the manager to slow down the carousel."

His lips rise as she swings her legs and inspects the style of his buttons. I watch him carry her through the exit, just to make sure she's safely out.

When she leaves, I spin around again, scanning all the girls, but none are blonde or tall enough to be my youngest sister. "Where's Daisy?" I ask Lo. The last time I remember seeing her was before the superheroes took to the stage and hypnotized me.

He searches the club with a narrowed gaze. "I don't see her."

I spot Ryke by the bar, discussing something with Melissa.

And this one time, I do wish Melissa wasn't here to distract Ryke from Daisy. Because he would have kept an eye on my sister during that confetti madness and the rush of people pushing to the stage. But instead, he was busy placating his somewhat-girlfriend. Just like we told him to.

This is our fault.

I am frantic with horrible feelings. I push my way ahead to Ryke, and Lo braces me with a hand on my waist so I don't slip again.

"Hey," Ryke says, turning to us when we arrive. His eyes flit around us really quickly. "Where's Daisy?"

"We were going to ask if you saw her," I say, more frightened now. He didn't even go looking for Daisy as soon as he came down from the balcony. That would be a Ryke thing to do. Did we really scare him off that much? I bite my nails. We made a person who is so *deeply* caring become uncaring. How is that possible?! I am freaking out. Just a little. "I thought that you would know where she was." My high-pitched voice causes his face to break.

And then he turns his attention to Lo. "You said you were going to get Daisy."

Lo rubs the back of his head. "Lil fell on the ground. Everything was crazy . . ."

"*Fuck*," Ryke curses, the word harsh on his lips. His muscles tighten.

Lo keeps rubbing his neck in anxiety.

"It's okay," I tell Lo before he's assaulted by guilt. "No one is to blame." We'll find her. Hopefully.

He nods.

And before we can go search for Daisy, Melissa chimes in, her expression sour. "She's probably running around here somewhere. I'm sure you and Lo can find her yourselves."

No, we need Ryke. Lo will be worried about me falling on my ass so much that his attention will be split. I need someone who's focused solely on finding her. And I'm too short to see much of anything in the crowd.

"Come on," Melissa says, tugging Ryke toward the stage to dance.

He scowls darkly. "If you're not going to help, you can go to the car."

Melissa drops her hands. "Are you serious?"

"I'm not leaving a sixteen-year-old drunk girl in a fucking club!" he shouts at her like she's not listening.

"They can take care of her! She's not your sister or your responsibility, Ryke!"

"You don't know me," he sneers. "You don't fucking get it."

She steps into his face. "I didn't come here to babysit!"

"Then leave!"

"*Fuck you*," she snarls. Then she storms off, pushing through the mass of people with ease.

My heart is about to spring from my chest with every second we lose. "Let's go."

"Wait." Ryke looks between Lo and me. "If I help, this is it. You two can't be hounding me about her anymore. You can't have it both fucking ways. I'm either ignoring her or I'm her friend. That's it."

"You're her friend!" I exclaim, practically throwing my hands up in the air. I don't want to waste any more time. "Okay, let's go, please!"

Ryke doesn't move. His eyes pin to Lo, waiting for his answer. I am tossing daggers into his eyes. I don't have time for this. Daisy may not have time for this. I picture her drunk in the bathroom being gang-raped by other people high on the green (or in this case blue) fairy. I shouldn't have lost her. I should have kept her tethered to my arm.

"Lo!" I yell.

"Fine," he says. "Fine."

Ryke revives like someone struck him with a hot torch. He moves faster than I could have ever imagined. He slams bodies out of his way, on a mission from hell. *Thank you, thank you, thank you*, I chant each time he makes a new path for us.

"Don't let go of my hand!" Lo shouts over the music, his fingers intertwined in mine.

We wind through the people, following Ryke to the bathrooms, where a long line swerves. He walks toward the men's bathroom and ignores the angry stares as he passes the line.

"Hey!" a guy shouts. "I've been waiting for fifteen minutes!"

Ryke glares. "I'm not pissing; I'm looking for someone." He reaches the door, and the guy grabs him by the arm. Ryke literally throws his body weight at him, just to push him off. The guy topples backward, giving Ryke enough time to open the door and disappear inside.

"I'm going to look in the girl's bathroom," I tell Lo, leaving him in the hallway. The girls stare with hot anger, their lips up-turning snidely. My explanation blows over just about as easily as Ryke's, but no one physically assaults me.

When I make it inside, the line extends here, the girls crammed in a row, waiting for an open stall. "Daisy!" I shout, checking each face. *No, no, no.* I peek beneath the stalls, searching for her gold sandals.

Red heels.

Black flats.

Sparkly platforms.

No, no, no.

I run back outside at the same time that Ryke exits the bathroom—without Daisy on his arm. He doesn't hesitate or stop. He guides us to a long, narrow hallway that appears reserved for staff.

"We should check outside," Lo tells him. "She may have found the exit."

"I want to be sure she's not here," Ryke says.

A door ends the hallway. And it's literally marked *Employees Only.* Lo grabs Ryke's arm before he rushes inside.

"We're going to be thrown out of the club, and then we're never going to find her."

I pale.

And they both look down at me. I realize I squeaked, a petrified sound escaping.

"You two stay out here, then," Ryke says. "I'll go in. If some-one throws me out, then you run down the fucking hallway and disappear in the crowd."

"Fine." But I hear Lo mutter, "I'm going to have to bail my brother out of Mexican jail."

Ryke turns the knob, and he peeks inside a little. His chest rises in a strong inhale, and he motions for us to come inside with him.

We trust Ryke enough to listen, heading through the doorway. And then we stop.

The door clicks shut behind us.

We must be in some sort of break room. Red couches fill the large space, a television and pinball machine on one side. Graffiti— or really nauseating neon-colored artwork—is sprayed on the walls.

The room is empty except for one blonde girl who has her feet on the couch cushions. She bounces a little and slaps the graffiti image of a window on the wall.

I'm just really, really glad no one else is in this room. And that all of her clothes are on.

Ryke nears my sister. "Daisy," he says slowly.

She glances over her shoulder and smiles weakly. "Hi, Ryke." She points to the painted window. "Did you know this window doesn't work?" She tries to grab at the picture. "It won't open."

"How are you feeling?" he asks.

She plops on the couch and touches her head like she's spinning. "Well . . ." She swallows hard. "I learned that the blue stuff was absinthe . . . so . . . I think I might be high."

"No shit."

"Yeah . . ." She blinks a couple times, trying to force open her heavy eyes. "And that door . . . that door was not the exit." A spike of fear breaches her voice. She knows she's not completely coherent and she was all alone.

My fearless, daring sister is afraid.

Because this was not her choosing.

I'm about to go to her, but I stop. Ryke has already reached the couch, and when her gaze trains on him fully, her face begins to break into slow, liberating relief.

"Hey," he says, gauging her state.

"Hey." Her eyes fill with tears.

"Dais, it's okay. You're okay." He brings her to her feet, and her legs quake.

She nods repeatedly, trying to believe it herself.

Lo lets out a breath. "It's weird," he says softly. "I thought Rose was going to be the one like this."

I frown. "What do you mean?"

"Terrified," he clarifies, "of not being in control."

Daisy is naturally wild, but I don't think she was expecting to be this drunk. I don't think she wanted it, and that was a different kind of unknown than jumping off a cliff or house or plane.

Ryke cups her face. "Hey, you're safe, Dais."

She nods again, biting her bottom lip to stop it from trembling.

And then Ryke shifts uneasily. "You didn't run into anyone before you got here, did you?" Oh my God, he doesn't think . . . no one touched her, did they? I am going to throw up with worry.

She shakes her head, a couple tears falling. "I don't know." She rubs her face before anymore tears slide down.

Ryke is more concerned than I've seen him in a while, and that includes when Lo was puking on the side of the road.

Daisy stares at her hand as though it leads to a magical portal. "I think . . . I think I'm high," she repeats what has already been said.

"Fuck," Ryke curses under his breath. He gently leads her to where we stand. She looks up, and her face brightens a little when she sees me. "Lily. Lo."

I hug her instantly, and she clutches onto me, her hand disappearing in my hair. "Whoa!" She shrieks and jerks backs into Ryke's chest.

"What?" My eyes widen.

"What's wrong with your face?" Daisy asks, panicked. "Ryke, something's wrong with her face."

"You're high," he reminds her.

"Oh . . . yeah."

"The sooner we get out of here, the better," Lo says.

Daisy breathes heavily. "I can't feel my feet."

"Great," Lo says, a nervous hand combing through his hair.

"Anything else you can't feel?" Ryke asks.

She runs her tongue slowly over her upper lip before saying, "My face."

Ryke rests a hand on Daisy's spine. "Daisy, look at me."

She can't find the source of his voice. "Ryke?" He's standing right in front of her.

He pinches her chin and turns her face so she meets his eyes. "I'm going to pick you up, okay?"

"Okay."

He lifts her in his arms—one on her back, the other underneath her knees.

And she clutches his shirt. "Don't leave me," she whispers. "I can't find the exit . . ."

"I have you," he assures her.

We navigate our way out of the club, and I constantly glance back at Daisy to make sure she's okay and not ill. She buries her face in Ryke's chest, and when we pass the threshold of the club, safe on the sidewalk and out of the hazy atmosphere, we can talk more freely.

"Daisy," Lo says. We head to the parking deck, and Lo has his arm tight around my shoulders.

Her head rises to look at Lo. Her eyes are bloodshot, and Ryke's shirt is wet with her tears. She's upset, and I wonder how much she's going to remember in the morning.

Probably nothing at all.

Maybe that's good.

Lo hesitates to ask her something.

"What?" she murmurs.

He gives in. "What did you think you were drinking if you didn't know it was absinthe?"

"Curaçao."

Ryke readjusts his hold on her, and she rests her cheek on his arm. "How the hell do you know what that is?" he asks.

"A Brazilian model." Her eyelids flutter a bit, hopefully just out of sleep.

Ryke lets out a low breath. "He sounds like a winner."

"*She* was pretty awesome," Daisy says sadly. And then more silent tears start streaming, her gaze far away as though she's lost in a very bad trip.

Lo's face twists in guilt and hurt. I squeeze his hand, worried that he's going to be possessed to drink now. Alcohol is not the answer to fix his pain of not finding Daisy sooner, but I'm sure he's fighting the temptation.

Ryke looks between his brother and my sister, and then his eyes fall to me, and I think he sees a girl who can possibly help his brother rather than send him down that dark road.

I won't let Lo drink.

I am here for him, just as he is for me. So I turn to Lo and poke his arm. "Did you see Captain America?" I ask.

And his face lights up. He stares down at me as we walk, and the guilt begins to wash away. "Yeah, who the fuck thinks he can fly?"

I smile. I love him. More than sex.

More than anything.

Thirty-seven

Lily Calloway

Seven days of abstinence, being surrounded by drunken college students and booze, and we've survived. The private jet flies us back to Philly. My panic and worry has subsided into a puddle. After enduring spring break in Cancun, the biggest obstacles seem like little hurdles.

Not everyone had a pleasant experience.

Melissa has officially broken up with Ryke. I secretly think she'll make a hate-shrine of him once we return home. Partly, I'm sure it's because he whiffed on his deal to give her mind-blowing sex. But last night at the club was what really cemented her anti-Ryke status. She gave him the classic ultimatum. Me or her. And he chose to protect my sister.

So she isolates herself to a corner chair, flipping through a magazine and wearing earbuds, tuning out the rest of us. I suspect she'll call a taxi when we land, putting considerable distance between herself and Ryke.

The source of her agitation sits by the window. Ryke plays poker with Daisy. She woke up this morning remembering nothing from the club, and no one had the heart to tell her what happened—that Ryke had to carry her home, that she was crying. I think the truth would have shattered her spirit more than any of us could bear.

And after last night, Lo and I have no say in separating Ryke and Daisy without turning into hypocritical monsters. All we can do is trust them at this point—the same way they've tried to trust us with our addictions.

Rose is passed out on the bed in the back cabin, working off her killer hangover. Connor slips in the room every so often to check on her, but right now, he types away on his laptop on a plush seat and table. He's working on his thesis to graduate with honors.

His diligence reminds me that I have to start memorizing old exam questions for my next Stats test. A task I have been avoiding. While memorizing isn't as hard as studying (or writing a thesis), it still takes a great toll on my poor brain. Last exam, I thought it might explode from being gorged with numbers.

I flip aimlessly through the channels on the television, sprawled on the couch with Lo. My head rests on his chest and a slow contentedness washes over me. I never thought I'd be able to feel so . . . still. He tucks a piece of my hair behind my ear, and I feel his warm breath on my forehead. "We made it," he murmurs.

I smile as he plants a kiss on my temple. Tonight, we'll be home. Alone again. Free to have sex.

I don't want Lo to think I've been obsessing over it, so I don't say a word about sex. Even though the thought has crossed my mind. I fantasized a little in the shower this morning, but I tried really hard to just wash and step out. No self-love. And that accomplishment feels sort of good, but I know sex would have made me feel even better.

"You know what tonight means?"

He's bringing it up?

"Lil."

"Huh?" I turn my head, my eyes wide with anticipation. If he instigates this conversation, then I'll gladly take part in it.

"Tonight," he says again. His eyes stay on mine, never leaving. I don't break our gaze, filled with seven days of need and want and tension. I refuse to stare at his lips or his abs or any other part of him. I want Loren Hale. The man, the lover, the guy who fills me with happiness and bliss. Not just the body.

His hand reaches out and cups my cheek, his thumb skimming slowly over my lips. I wonder if he's testing me.

I want to pass.

His thumb pulls gently on my bottom lip, and I let out a short, ragged breath. His hand slides down to the back of my neck before he whispers, "I'm going to fuck you." Oh. God.

Now? No, that can't be right.

He must sense my confusion because his lips quirk. "Tonight, love."

"Right." I nod, flushing from the foolish presumption. I don't think it would go over well with everyone if he took me right here on the couch. Even the image—of Lo on top of me, of his hardness pressing so deep inside of me—steals the air right from my lungs.

He holds me tighter in his arms and lowers his head to murmur dirty things in my ear. My arousal grows, and he must believe I have the strength to last the whole plane ride and the drive to the house. So he's tempting me little by little. My peak tonight will be so freakin' intense when we finally do have sex—the walls will not be able to silence my screams.

I squirm a little, the tension a good kind of tension, the kind where I know I can wait to release it. Months ago, I don't think I could have. But I'm learning restraint.

I flip through the channels while Lo holds me on his lap. I try to find a movie that won't put me to sleep or a television show that won't draw my attention back to Lo's cock or my nefarious thoughts.

Lo rubs my shoulder, and his gaze drifts to his half brother. "Are you losing?" Lo asks, a smile at the idea. I perk up a little with equal amusement.

Ryke stares at his cards with pinched brows. On the table is a pile of hundred-dollar bills, what looks like his Rolex, and her hemp bracelet.

"No," he snaps.

Lo laughs under his breath. "Hey, *bro*, did you fail remedial math? That watch is worth five times more than that bracelet."

"Can the peanut gallery please shut the fuck up?" Ryke says. "I'm trying to concentrate here." He accidentally flashes his cards at Daisy.

She covers her eyes quickly. "I didn't see anything."

"Fuck," he curses, shooting us another glare like we made the fumble. He goes back to concentrating really hard. Brain power must hurt Ryke as much as it does me.

Daisy puts her cards to her lips, trying not to smile too hard. She glances at us. "There's a diamond in my bracelet, by the way."

"Well, then, I take it back," Lo says. "Ryke is only half the idiot I thought he was."

Ryke flips him off.

Daisy says, "You should fold."

He stares at her for a long moment. "You're bluffing."

"I'm not. I saw your cards, remember?"

"You said you didn't see a fucking thing."

"I lied." Oh, she is good. I can't tell if she's bluffing.

"Fuck it." Ryke slides off a gold ring from his middle finger and throws it in the pile. "That's worth two grand."

Daisy pales a little. She has to match that or fold and then he'll take what's in the pot.

"Let me see . . . hold on a sec." She searches in her nearby bag.

And Ryke looks a little worried. He thought she was going to fold.

But her face falls. "I don't have anything worth two thousand, *but* . . ." She snatches her journal and scribbles something on a piece of paper. She tosses that into the pile.

"Lo," Connor calls from the back of the plane, still staring at his laptop. "Can you come here?"

"In a second," Lo says, entertained, like me, by the poker game.

"Now would be best." Connor's voice pitches from its usual steady tone.

Lo sighs and slides out from beneath me. "Catch me up when I come back?"

I nod, and he kisses me tenderly on the lips. As he retracts, he has that twinkle in his eye like *more later.*

Yes.

When he leaves, I prop myself on my knees to try to see the paper in the poker pile. "Read it out loud," I tell Ryke.

"She's tossing in her two Ducati Superbikes." His eyebrow quirks. "I already have a motorcycle, Dais."

"These are faster than your Honda." Clearly they have talked "motorcycle" before if she knows what sits outside his apartment.

"Wait," I interject. Ryke said *her* two Superbikes. That means she already has them. "When did you get a motorcycle? And why would you buy two?"

"A client at a shoot bought them for set decoration, and he gave them to me."

"He just gave them to you?"

Ryke fingers the piece of paper. "That's what I said."

"It was a *thank you for doing a good job,* is all. It doesn't happen often, but it did then. And now I have two motorcycles begging to be ridden. I've only taken the red one out on the road, so I put some miles on it."

"You don't have a motorcycle license yet," he tells her flatly.

"Yeah, I know. But in order to get a license, I have to practice."

He lets the paper go, and I see a sort of longing for those bikes in his gaze. They must be really nice. "You do realize that these are worth a lot more than my ring?"

"You don't have to match me. I'm not trying to up the bid, but it's really all I have that you could want."

I glance at the rear of the plane. Lo's back faces me, but he's hunched over, his hand to his eyes. Something . . . something's really wrong. What happened? Is it his father? I go to stand, but Connor meets my gaze and shakes his head as though I should sit back down.

I do. He has some sort of power in his assuredness. It's like Jedi mind control.

But I want to go comfort Lo. My chest hurts just watching the back of him. I bite my nails, catch myself, and drop my hand.

"What the hell, let's do it," Ryke says.

I turn back to the poker game. Maybe it'll keep my mind off something horrible. But I'm so antsy that I start scratching my arm. I catch myself doing that too.

"So the motorcycles are fair, then?"

"Sure. Just don't cry when I take them from you."

She grins. "Okay. Let's see your hand."

He turns over two cards and compares them to the ones flipped on the table.

My attention is split between the game and Lo, and I don't want to focus on him anymore. I'm about to go against Connor's wishes and dart to the back of the plane. In order to stop myself, I switch the television channels to find a show that can preoccupy my mind.

"So you have two eights," Daisy says, a smile to the words.

"You beat me, didn't you?"

"Two jacks," she says.

"You were dealt two fucking jacks?"

"You shuffled."

He groans.

"You can have the ring back if you want."

Boy Meets World? No. *Sabrina the Teenage Witch?* No. Soccer? Definitely not.

"No, you won it. It's yours."

"I'm going to feel weird if it's a family heirloom or something." She tries to shove the ring into his hand. He holds them up in the air.

"It's from a jewelry store, and I was going to retire the thing anyway."

"Why?"

"It's ugly."

"So, you gave me an ugly piece of jewelry."

"It's worth two thousand fucking dollars."

She smiles wryly. "Oh yeah."

Ryke crumples the paper with the Ducati arrangement on it. He lost those bikes, and there's a bit of disappointment in his eyes from not being able to snatch one. I wonder if they're rare.

"How about . . ." Daisy folds the cash and stuffs it in her wallet. ". . . I'll let you keep the black Ducati if you teach me how to ride."

Law & Order? No. *X-Men* cartoon? Possibly. I hover on this channel a little, watching Wolverine in his original yellow and blue spandex.

Ryke taps the pen to the table. "I'm not going to teach you how to kill yourself."

"That's dramatic."

He glares. "Knowing you, you'd run the fucking bike off a damn cliff for the hell of it."

She spreads her arms. "Then teach me how to stay on the road."

He shakes his head. "No, if I show you how to ride, you're going to do something stupid on the interstate."

She touches her chest. "I would never."

He throws a hundred-dollar bill at her face. And it flutters into her lap before hitting her nose, not the effect he was looking for.

X-Men is not helping take my mind off Lo. I glance back at him again. Same hunched position. Same sadness. What is going on? I sigh and switch channels quickly.

"I'm not killing you," Ryke repeats.

Her smile fades. "Ryke," she says, "I'm going to figure out how to ride a motorcycle with or without you. I was just giving you the opportunity to have one of the bikes. I know you want it."

He stares off, deep in thought, and then he shakes his head repeatedly, cringing. "Fuck."

"What?"

He covers his face with his hand. "I can't stop picturing you flipping the bike over."

"I haven't fallen off yet," she reminds him.

"Have you tried to do a wheelie?"

She stays quiet. "No," she mutters.

"Jesus Christ," he says, not believing her one bit. "You're going to kill yourself."

"You keep saying that."

"And is it not processing in your head or you just don't give a fuck?"

She unfurls the crumpled piece of paper slowly. "I think . . . that I'll be okay," she sidesteps his question with more confidence than I could even possess. "But if you change your mind about the bike, here's my number." She writes down her cell on the paper.

I wonder if a premium channel is playing a Marvel film.

Before I click into special programming, I land on a newsfeed.

I see the word *sex*.

Huh.

It's like a big flashing light in my eyes. I stay on the channel in curiosity. Maybe some senator had a sex scandal.

"Lily, wait!" Lo shouts.

My heart stops as my mind tailspins, trying to digest the program and Lo. *Wait, wait, wait*. Tears brim. Lo was upset.

And that's not a senator.

He was upset because of *this*.

It's me on the screen.

I shrink into a ball on the couch, my knees tucking to my chest. My hands are fixed on my mouth, my eyes too wide to shut.

I think . . . I think . . . I don't know what I think.

The news stations are congregated outside Penn, and the bottom of the screen reads: *Fizzle heiress has over fifty sexual partners and counting. Rumored sex addict.*

Is this national news? How is this a national issue? What the hell is going on?

I don't hear Lo call my name again. I turn up the television, and I'm shaking so badly that I have to hold the remote with both hands.

The news anchor is a petite blonde woman with bright red lipstick. "We just confirmed from a source that Lily Calloway, daughter of the founder of Fizzle, is a sex addict. As well as the fifty-plus known men she's slept with, she's also been known to hire male sex worker."

My throat closes up, but I manage to barely breathe a word. One word. "Lo."

He doesn't come to me, and I can't tear my eyes from the television.

"Lily, what's going on?" Daisy asks, her voice tight.

Daisy, my parents—oh my God, my father? His company . . . the guilt plows through me. They're watching this. Everyone is watching this.

Melissa stirs from her corner, tugging her earbuds out and eyeing the screen. Oxygen refuses me. I shake my head again and again like this is a dream. I want to wake up. This can't be real. But the words on the TV run through my head over and over and over. *Sex addict. Sex addict. Sex addict.*

This can't be happening.

How much shame have I brought to my family?

"Lo," I say a little louder, fixated on the TV as tears begin to scald my cheeks. "Lo!" I cry, terrified about what this means, as I process just how badly this is going to hurt everyone.

My phone buzzes beside me, and the first text sends a knife in my gut.

Whore— Unknown.

It begins to explode in a rapid-fire wave of inflammatory messages. My eyes burn, and I choke on either a breath or a sob. "Lo!"

"I'm right here, Lil." How long has he been on the couch? He turns me so that I face him, no longer absorbed by the newsfeed.

His hands touch my face, and he tries to wipe away the tears, but I can't stop crying. My chest constricts, and I sob into my palms. He draws me to his chest.

"You're okay," he says, rocking me a little, but there's pain in his voice.

The plane feels too small. I don't have enough air or space or lungs to battle this kind of affliction. I have ruined my family. It's all I can think. It's all I feel. I have spent years keeping my addiction a secret so that they wouldn't bear the humiliation and disgrace. Their daughter is disgusting. I'm disgusting . . .

My mother . . . how will she look at me after this? How will Daisy?

"Lo, it hurts." I try to take full breaths, but they're sporadic and filled with so much desperation. I just want it to end. I want to fly the plane back and start over. We were headed home in triumph. We defeated spring break without giving into our vices.

Tonight was supposed to be about Lo and me together. And now . . . this . . .

I want to disintegrate, to flutter away and never wake up again.

"You're okay," Lo says, pulling me onto his lap. His arm swoops around my waist as he holds me tight to his chest. I can't look anywhere but at my hands. They seem so empty all of a sudden. And then he grabs them and squeezes tight. "I have you."

But I am falling so quickly.

I am drowning, Lo.

I don't think I want to come up for air this time.

I'm not sure I can.

"We have a former captain of the Penn soccer team, Mason Nix, here to give a statement about Lily Calloway."

This can't be happening.

"Turn it off!" Lo yells.

But as Lo and Ryke struggle to find the remote that is lost in the depths of the cushions, I hear the past bleed into my ears.

"I slept with her when she was eighteen. My entire team did. She wasn't just willing—she wanted it." This is his payback. Was he the leak? We still don't know. This one statement could just be revenge for being thrown over the hood of my car.

I can barely move. A single tear slides along Lo's cheek. He wipes it quickly as he catches me watching. "Hey," he whispers. "It's okay, Lil."

But my tears brim and burn. "You can't be sad if it's true," I whisper back.

He stays strong and reaches out to touch my cheek. He kisses my lips, but I don't feel the power in them that I usually do. My heart does not flutter. I am just sinking.

"And was she dating Loren Hale at the time, the heir of Hale Co.?" the news anchor asks.

"Lily, come on, love," Lo pleads, kissing me stronger. "I'm right here."

"Yeah," Mason says. "She's cheated on him this whole time." The news anchor wears a look like *what a poor bastard. I feel so sorry for him.*

I turn my head from Lo, crying, my lips separating from his as I bury my head into my knees.

"Lily." His voice breaks.

What have I done? I didn't realize that my addiction would hurt him if it became public. He's now the sad sap who was fucked over by the slut. By me. How do I make this right? There's no way to change this. How do I erase years and years of mistakes?

I want to go back in time. I want to tell myself that I don't need to sleep around to satisfy this emptiness in me. That the guy I love is right there in front of my eyes. That he can be more than a friend. That I don't need anyone else in the whole universe but Loren Hale.

And if I had just done that, everything would have turned out right.

I would not be sitting here listening to my past mistakes. I would have spent four years with Lo like I'm doing right now. Committed. Fulfilled.

Happy.

My voice is stolen, and the words stay in the back of my throat. But I manage to say something.

"I'm sorry," I tell him, muffled into my knees and incoherent with my sobs. *I'm so fucking sorry, Lo.*

He rubs my back. "Lil, it's okay."

It's not okay.

Someone finds the remote because the voices silence. My phone vibrates manically on the floor, and I cover my ears with my arms now, a ball that cannot be unfurled. The noise pierces me, each rumble is another *slut* or *whore* that I have yet to read.

I truly want to disappear. I want my superpowers to kick in, right now. I want to never, ever exist again. I want Lo to live in a world where I don't hurt him. *Please, someone, make that come true.*

Lo untangles me a little. He kisses my forehead and tries to let me cling back to him and not my bony legs. I slowly crawl onto his lap and press my cheek to his chest, listening to his unsteady heartbeat. I remain hidden, not vacating the safety of Lo's shirt and avoiding the look of hurt and betrayal on Daisy's face that I am sure exists tenfold.

I should have just told her on the beach.

And I don't know what propels me to do it—maybe thinking that one simple thing, maybe feeling the regret—but I pop my head from my burrow. "Daisy?" I look around and find her standing by her chair.

She is crying.

And I'm not sure if it's because I am or because she's mad at me.

"I'm sorry," I tell her. "I meant to tell you."

"It's true?" she asks, wiping her face quickly like Lo had, not wanting me to see. It's as though they can't cry because I am. I hate that. It makes no sense, and it drives me to dam my waterworks sooner rather than later.

"I'm . . ." I can't say it. *Why* can't I just say it? My sister deserves more than me weeping and hiding away. I wipe my nose with the back of my arm and sit up straight. I slide from Lo's lap, but he intertwines his fingers with mine. It helps. It makes me not want to drown so much.

"It's okay," Daisy says what Lo has been repeating. She rubs all of her tears away. "It's fine, you don't have to explain." Daisy hates to see people upset. I forgot that about her. She just wants everyone to be happy.

But all the pain that it's going to take to admit this to my sister—I need to feel it. Telling Rose was the hardest thing I've ever done, but this is worse. Because I told Rose on my own accord, but in this instance, someone has played my hand, forcing me into it.

There is no compassion in telling her my secret. It's just . . . necessary.

Very softly, I say, "I'm a sex addict."

Her tears have dried up. And she nods. My strong, fearless sister. "And Mom . . . does she know?"

I shake my head once.

"Dad?"

"No."

Daisy glances at Ryke. "You knew."

"It's complicated."

Daisy nods again, trying to understand, I think. Her eyes go to Connor. "And you knew."

"And Rose. That's it," Connor says.

Rose. My eyes flicker to the back cabin door where the bed lies. I wish she was here. She's like a prickly iron chair that will weather any battle.

"But not Poppy?" Daisy asks me.

"Not Poppy," I say, "and I only told Rose six months ago. I would have told you sooner, but I was . . . am—I'm ashamed." Tears build again. "You're my little sister. I didn't want you to see me like this." I am the fuckup. The broken, pathetic one now. I can no longer dole out sisterly advice and expect the same admiration in return. Everything will change.

Her dark eyebrows bunch together, such an ugly expression for someone so beautiful. "You're still the same person, Lily. I just . . . I have to get my head around this." Her eyes flicker to Lo. "How long have you known?"

We meet each other's gaze. How long has he known? How long have I known? Setting a date seems like trying to pin down when a growth spurt begins and ends. Immeasurable time.

Thinking about it reminds me of all the moments we've shared. From childhood to adolescence to adulthood. We have lived together, loved together, and fucked up together. I'm not sure many people can truly say that about someone else.

His eyes soften and he turns to Daisy. "Awhile."

Awhile. That seems right.

Daisy opens her mouth to ask another question, but a Bob Dylan song starts playing from her pocket. She pulls out her phone at the same time something vibrates near my leg. Lo fishes out his own cell.

A chime and another vibration go off and both Connor and

Ryke look at theirs. We must have hit an area in the sky with good cell reception. Who knows how long people have been calling?

"It's Mom," Daisy says.

"My therapist," Lo tells me.

"My mom," Ryke adds.

We all look to Connor. His eyes flit up to Lo's. "The private investigator. I have to take this." He retreats to the back cabin where Rose sleeps. We still don't know who leaked the information, but maybe we will now—not that it matters. What's done is done.

Daisy's phone keeps playing "Shelter from the Storm," and everyone sits on edge the longer they ignore their calls.

"Go talk to them," I say.

Daisy sniffs and stares at her phone. "I just like this song."

Ryke puts a hand on her shoulder. "Rose should talk to your parents first anyway."

She shakes her head. "No, it's okay." She clicks the green button and puts the receiver to her ear. Daisy risks sitting by Melissa since she's secluded in the most private alcove of the whole plane. (Besides the bathroom, that is.) Melissa stays frozen in her seat, uncomfortable and a bit stunned by everything.

"I have to go pee," I mutter, about to stand up. I can imagine the sheer horror on my father's face. On my mother's. I don't think I can ever confront them.

Lo grabs my wrist before I rise from the couch. "You shouldn't be alone right now."

"I just have to pee," I tell him again, tugging his hand off me.

He gives me a look like *do you really?*

No, I don't. I want to cry in solitude. I guess he knows this, and I understand his fear that I'll avoid my emotions with self-love like I've done in the past.

It's tempting.

I stay put and stuff my face into a pillow. The news replays in my head again, and I'm on the verge of tears once more.

"Hey, Lily." Ryke comes over and nudges my side. "I don't want to talk to my mom, so how about we play cards?" He glances to Lo. "And you need to talk to your therapist."

"I can stay here."

Ryke gives him a firm look.

He sighs, resigning more easily than normal. I must have drained him of energy. Lo rises and disappears to the bathroom.

"Lily? Cards?" He pulls out the deck from his pocket and shuffles.

I lower my pillow, sensing his tactics to distract me. "What kind of card game?"

"Whatever you want."

"Go Fish."

He looks like I've almost stabbed his soul.

"You said whatever I want," I remind him, trying to wipe away silent tears that keep falling against my will. I need permanent tissues stuck to my tear ducts. Like when you staunch a bloody nose. Would it work?

"That's not even a two-person game," Ryke tells me.

"But it's still possible to play with two people." I want the distraction without having to bust my brain learning a new game.

"Fine," he says, relenting when I sit on the floor since there's no coffee table. He deals the cards on the carpet, and I try not to dampen them with my tears.

"We're flying over Georgia right now," I hear Daisy say. "We shouldn't be long." Her voice shakes really badly. I don't like that she's talking to our parents first.

Ryke's concerned gaze flits between Daisy and his cards. "Do you have a king?"

"Go Fish."

"Lily's taking a nap," Daisy says.

Ryke picks up a card and then kicks my knee. "Your turn."

Right.

"Do you have a . . ." I stare at my cards. "An eight?" I look at the bathroom door, not hearing a peep from Lo. But he leaves the door cracked so we know he's not doing something rash, like chugging alcohol or . . . worse. My chest hurts, like someone decided to stand on my diaphragm.

Ryke hands me his eight and grumbles under his breath about how this is the stupidest fucking game. But he's partially concentrated on my sister in the corner.

"I can't wake her up," Daisy says, her voice growing more frantic and low. "Wait, please . . . I don't want to . . . *Mom*."

Ryke stands up before I can find the strength to put weight on my gelatin legs. He goes over to the four-chair alcove. He has to lean over a glowering Melissa to reach Daisy. "Give me the phone," he whispers, but I can still hear his hostile voice.

"Mom," Daisy says. "I have to go . . . But . . . I . . . Wait . . . I . . ."

Ryke grabs the phone from her before she has a breakdown. And at the same time, Rose is halfway across the plane aisle, her eyes dead set on me with so much confidence and power that I immediately wish I was her. Strong and built like a fortress—able to withstand anything that's thrown at me.

I meet her gaze, but I point to Ryke, who now clutches my mother—or the phone that contains my mother. Rose understands. She grabs Daisy's cell from him and immediately goes into crisis management mode.

"Mother, calm down. No," she snaps. "*No*." And that's all I hear before she struts back to the cabin to talk in private. She said the one word that Daisy couldn't.

I'm not sure I could either.

Daisy stares out the window. Ryke whispers something to her, and she just nods and gestures to me.

Ryke comes back to the floor, collecting his cards and fanning them in his hands. "It's my turn, I think," he says. "Do you have a ten?"

"Ryke?"

"Yeah?"

"Whatever happens, you'll take care of him, right?"

He goes rigid. "I don't know what that fucking means."

"It means what it means," I breathe. "He doesn't have anyone besides you and me. I just need to know you'll be there."

"And so will you," he snaps.

"Not if my parents force me into rehab or halfway across the country." My mother will want to bury away this problem by transporting it to a different time zone.

"You're almost twenty-one. You're a fucking adult. Your parents can't make you do shit, Lily."

"I owe them—"

"For tarnishing the Fizzle name? For bringing you up with cash and luxury?" He keeps shaking his head. "You and Lo have it so warped. You think you're indebted to your parents because they gave you everything you have. But they didn't give you what fucking mattered. They owe *you*. They owe you for not asking why their daughter isn't home. Why she looks distant and sad. Why she has barricaded herself in a fucking apartment with her boyfriend. They have failed you, and if they tell you to get on a fucking plane or go to rehab—where we all know you shouldn't be—then you need to tell them to go to hell. And if you don't, Lo and I will. I promise you that."

The right words stay at the back of my throat—*thanks, Ryke*. It's a hard phrase to produce, especially when he delivers his opinions with such fervor and force.

I land on something, though.

"Go Fish."

He lets out a short laugh as he reaches for the deck. "You'll be fine, Calloway."

At least one of us believes it.

Thirty-eight

Loren Hale

I lean against the bathroom wall, staring at my pallid face and sunken eyes. I look like utter shit. I feel even worse. My left hand keeps shaking, and I have to clench my fingers into a fist just to make it stop. My father bitches me out on the other line for ignoring his previous calls.

"I'm in the goddamn air," I remind him curtly, keeping my voice low so Ryke doesn't hear. "Unless you'd like reception to magically be invented over the ocean."

"Hey, I'm just as fucking livid as you are."

"I don't think that's possible," I say, my voice slightly breaking. I don't want to be talking to him while Lily looks one second from opening the hatch and jumping from the plane without a parachute. And every time I picture her crying like that—goddamn, I can't start. I rub my eyes to push back the emotions. I want to kick the wall so fucking hard, and I swallow a scream that needs to escape.

"Whoever this motherfucker is," my father says, "I will personally rip him a new asshole, Loren. You hear me? He's not getting away with this shit."

I have to ask. "Did you do it? Did you leak it?" One week after I told him, the news exploded across the globe. Is it really all a coincidence?

There's a long pause. And then this: "You have got to be fucking kidding me. Did you not hear what I just said? I have busted my ass trying to find this fucker." He growls a little. Yeah, it's not him.

"Then who?" I ask. "Who would do this? What do they possibly have to gain?"

"Money," my father says flatly. "We're still working on some leads."

I bring the phone away from my mouth and struggle between not shouting and screaming my head off. No sound escapes, but I catch myself in the mirror, and I look like I'm fighting an invisible battle against a shadowed enemy. I look crazy and tortured.

"I have to go," my father says quickly. "Greg is on the other line. I'll talk to you soon. Keep your head up." Words of encouragement from my father. Those don't come often. So I take them.

We hang up at the same time. I lean over the sink and splash some water on my face. Trying to get my shit together.

I should call Brian, the therapist that Ryke and Lily believe I'm talking to about my deep inner thoughts. But I can't discuss alcohol. Even the thought makes my stomach turn. Because Lily shouldn't be worried if I'm going to relapse. The world is crashing down on her shoulders, and I don't want to add to that weight.

I let out a long breath, bearing her pain that feels so much a part of me. We've become entangled, years and years of lies and childhood memories and stories all wrapped into one. I know her better than her sisters. I know her sometimes better than she does herself. I know just how much this is killing her inside.

And then one thought punctures me.

I'm here.

I could be at a bar. Passed out cold.

I could be in rehab. Away from her.

I have the chance to be by her side through all of this.

So go, you stupid bastard.

That's what it takes. I'm out the door.

Part Three

One day, you're going to have to make a choice. You have to decide what kind of man you want to grow up to be. Whoever that man is, good character or bad, is going to change the world.

—Jonathan Kent, *Man of Steel*

Thirty-nine

Loren Hale

No one speaks in the car, from the tarmac to our house in Princeton, New Jersey. Melissa calls a taxi to bring her back to Penn, so at least we don't have to deal with that.

Connor's black limo gives us all plenty of room. Lily rests her head in my lap, trying to play cat's cradle with my shoelace. She stopped crying sometime between our fifth game of Go Fish and when the plane landed.

I want her to call Allison, but she keeps saying she doesn't want to talk to anyone. And I guess I have no right to force her to speak to her therapist when I've been avoiding mine. Regardless, I plan on calling Allison tonight whether Lily does or not. I have to ask about medication for Lil.

No one understands lows like an addict. And I fear the one she's about to hit when she confronts her parents.

She holds up the intertwined shoelace in her fingers. "Your turn," she tells me. "Go under my hands and grab it."

"I'm going to mess it up."

"No, you won't," she says. "Just make sure to grab the right ones."

Problem is, I don't know which are the right ones.

Rose sits stiffly beside Connor, her cell clutched in her steel grip. Lily told me that Rose has been in "damage control mode"—she even yelled at a reputable news producer for an hour before Connor pried the phone from her fingers. She's been texting and emailing gossip magazines and lawyers since we landed.

Rose isn't taking the leak very well. She keeps fixing her hair and smoothing her dress. Connor has to grab her hands to stop her. And as I look between the three Calloway girls—Rose in a frazzled state, Daisy drifting far away, and Lil with a sad, soft voice—I get it. I get what Ryke sees and what he feels. I have this insane wish to just make things right again, to plug all the cracks in our lives—just for the small sliver of hope that these girls will be able to stand up on their own for one more day.

I think the six of us—we're all strong. We're each just a different kind of strong. But we all have a different kind of weak too. And I'm figuring out how to bottle my weakness to help them all.

I'm not going to be the villain of my own story. That shit is done.

Rose's phone buzzes. She stares at the screen, Connor reading the text too. "We have a little hiccup," she says.

Lily's hands fall to her lap, tangling the shoelace herself. "What?" Her worry cracks her voice. I rub her arm, and she holds on to my bicep for support.

"Our parents are at our house," Rose says. "They're waiting for you."

Lily bolts upright, shaking her head fiercely. "I can't, Rose. I need another day."

Gilligan, Connor's driver, remains quiet behind the wheel, leading us down our street. Only a couple blocks away, news vans line the curb, most likely camped out by the gate.

Daisy presses her nose to the window. "Holy shit."

Lily's eyes widen at the scene.

She can't handle this right now. That much is certain. I look to Ryke and he just nods once. "Gilligan," I call to the front and tap the privacy screen. It lowers so I can see his bald head. "Change of plans. We're going to Philly."

. . .

Ryke's off-campus flat has brick walls and hardwood floors, a Philadelphia 76ers poster hanging in the dim living room, fit with leather beanbags, a big-screen television, and a decent-sized sound system. I've been here only a few times before, and it's hard to remember that this isn't just another random apartment. It's my brother's.

After a quick call to Allison, I get an approval to give Lily a sleeping pill. She falls asleep in the spare bedroom, quicker than I thought she would. Crying must have exhausted her already.

When I return to the living room, I take a swift glance outside. No news vans or camera crews. Not many people know that Ryke Meadows is related to me, and in this instance, it comes in handy.

Connor and Rose talk in hushed whispers on the couch, sometimes even switching to French. He told me that the private investigator is still working on finding the leak. Same thing my father said about his connections. A part of me feels hopeless by the news—like maybe we'll just never know. Another part of me thinks maybe I shouldn't know. Because I have a penchant for hurting people who hurt Lily or me. And I don't want to be the guy who threatens someone else's future anymore. I don't want to become my father.

"I just got off the phone with a friend," Connor says.

"You have other friends?" I ask with a frown. Why, out of everything, does this bother me? Maybe I'm too fucking emotional right now. I rub my eyes, trying to pull myself together.

"Acquaintance, contact," Connor tells me, "whatever you want to call him."

Ryke walks over and hands me a glass of something amber colored. I stiffen and give him a look. "Are you crazy?"

"It's tea."

I barely relax but take the glass anyway.

Connor continues, "My contact told me there are cameras outside my apartment. I just wanted to let you know that they're seeking all avenues to get information." Even Lily's sister's boyfriend—a far fucking stretch.

Daisy sits on the hardwood floor, the remote control in her hands as she stares at the blank television. I can see her curiosity. She's the one still halfway in the dark, and all the answers lie in that box. She offered to be brought back to her house, but Lily and Rose refused. Their parents are as bloodthirsty for information as the media, and we all know they'd sink their claws into Daisy if they had her.

So she stays with us for now.

I stare at the floor, trying to piece together a semblance of a plan. First things first. I turn to Connor, who relaxes against the couch. His arm stays around Rose's shoulders, and I realize that he's subtly massaging her neck so she'll be more at ease.

I didn't want to drag him through all of this, and with his usual impassive expression, I can't tell if it bothers him that paparazzi have invaded his apartment building.

"You're not related to Lily or me. If you want out, you should probably leave now before things worsen."

I expect Rose to spit at me for untethering her own boyfriend from this complicated matter. Because it'd mean that Connor would have to leave her too. But she's busy texting on her cell, inhaling sharp breaths every so often that sound like knives slicing her lungs. I even saw her pop some kind of medication.

"Rose already showed me where the door is," Connor says. "I'm fairly capable of knowing when and how to walk out of it."

"The media may get worse," I remind him, but I forget that Connor has probably weighed all the possibilities in his head, and maybe even created a mental spreadsheet of the pros and cons of the situation.

"Yes, and you'll need someone who doesn't curse every five words to handle the press."

Ryke rolls his eyes, the dig clearly referring to him. "Journalism major," Ryke says, pointing to his chest. "I know the press better than you, Cobalt."

"And do you really plan on doing anything with that degree?"

Ryke says nothing.

"Exactly."

"What about your mother's company?" I ask Connor.

"Cobalt Inc. isn't a household name. People don't associate us with our products like they do Hale Co.—your name is on the label of every baby shampoo and diaper package. We deal with manufacturers and subsidiaries." Like MagNetic, I remember. "My affiliation with you or Lily won't hurt the company, and for that, my mother won't care. And plus, if she's outside of the scandal looking in, she enjoys the drama from time to time. It keeps her days interesting."

I wonder if that's how he sees us sometimes. Interesting. Entertainment. Something to make each day unpredictable.

I also can't imagine the woman who spawned someone like Connor. She seems as fabricated as a character in one of my comics.

"Like I said, Lo," Connor finishes, "I know how to use the door."

Ryke nods to me. "You going to give me an out too?"

"No, if I'm going down, you're burning with me."

"Does that qualify as a brotherly obligation?"

"For me, yeah."

Daisy fumbles with the remote and it drops loudly on the hardwood. "Sorry," she mumbles and continues to stare at the black television.

I want to watch the news and figure out how much the media already knows. Finding the leak has become a second priority. Our first task is to clean up whatever blowback we're about to receive. I suspect Greg Calloway and possibly my father are already working with a team of lawyers to subdue the crisis. One of the many reasons they'll want to talk to us.

I don't trust them. But I do trust the people in this room, and that's enough to put me at ease for the current moment.

I realize Daisy is still in the dark—about a lot of things. It's not fair to her, especially since we'll be talking freely now. "Do you have any questions, Daisy?" I ask, slouching on the couch.

She places the remote carefully on the coffee table and sits cross-legged on the floor.

"I do have a beanbag," Ryke says.

"I see it." But she hugs her knees loosely, making no effort to move. Her eyes flit to me. "I have hundreds of questions, but I can wait to ask Lily. I don't want her to be upset if you reveal something that she wants to keep secret."

"You're going to hear it on the television or the tabloids anyway," I tell her. "She would prefer if you knew the truth from me."

She hesitates. "I can ask anything?"

Anything is a strong word, but I'm confident in my ability to deflect the too-personal questions. I agree with a nod.

"If this is going to be a Q&A, then I have a couple questions as well," Ryke says.

I smile bitterly. "Of course you do."

Daisy throws the nearest pillow at him. "This is my Q&A."

He catches the pillow. "Now you're throwing my things, but you won't sit on the damn beanbag?"

"You're pushy—did anyone ever tell you that?"

"I do all the time," I say. "He never listens."

Ryke raises his hands like *what the fuck*. "I'm sorry if I can tell that there's an uncomfortable girl on my fucking floor, and I know how to fix the problem."

"Don't," I warn him. We're not opening those floodgates ever, ever again. I can withstand him being friendly to Daisy in tiny microscopic doses, but when he starts talking about girls on floors and fixing shit, it makes me nervous.

Daisy asks the first question, which doesn't necessarily lessen any tension in the room. I'm not sure anything can after the leak. "Have you and Lily been in an open relationship?"

I like to refer to what we had as a "fake" relationship, but when we became a pretend couple, we *were* a couple. I had everything with her that a boyfriend would have. Except the sex. But when I think of open relationships, I picture swingers and people who have multiple partners. I'm sure the term is vague enough to encompass a variety of situations. Just not ours.

I don't have a yes or no answer for Daisy, so I have to go into explaining what we did. How we lied to her and everyone around us. How our friendship turned into something more but still remained something less.

"Wow," Daisy says when I finish. "All to hide your addictions? Couldn't you have just, I don't know, moved to Europe?"

"We contemplated it."

Her face falls. "I was joking."

I shrug, indifferent about it all. "Lily and I never ignored you because you're younger. The phone calls we didn't pick up, the lunches we canceled, all of that was because we'd rather drink and have sex than be around people. Especially ones that we'd have to lie to."

"That's messed up," Daisy tells me.

"So I've been told."

"Actually, I told you it was fucked up," Ryke clarifies.

Daisy ignores him. "Why is she a sex addict? Is there something that caused it?"

My throat goes dry and my eyes flicker to the bedroom door.

Lily and I haven't discussed the cause of her addiction, but I know she's been trying to parse through the past with Allison.

Lily shuts down when it comes to her childhood, refusing to look at her relationship with her family for what it truly is. I can touch her painful memories without being terrorized by the hurt, and in turn, she can focus on mine without bearing the guilt. It's a symbiosis that I've come to recognize after hours and hours of therapy.

Whether we allow ourselves to open up to our own feelings— well, that's something we're both working on.

My silence lingers in the air as I try to focus on a suitable answer.

Ryke grows restless by the quiet. "I've read that eighty percent of sex addicts are abused as a child. Did Lily—"

"No," I cut him off, my tone defensive and edged. My eyes bear the same heat, and I wonder if this is why Ryke has never asked me that question before.

"I'm not the only one who will fucking ask that," he snaps. "You're going to have to start being less sensitive."

I glower at that word . . . *sensitive*. It makes me sound weak and fragile. It's one of those words in my father's arsenal. I wasn't living up to my potential when I failed a sixth grade math test, when I had to do a group project alone after no one picked me, when I lost a Little League game. He told me I was worthless, and as a kid, I didn't know how to stop those tears. *Don't be so sensitive, Loren. You're being too sensitive, Loren. Why are you so goddamn sensitive, Loren?* So I stopped crying. Now I just get mad.

My eyes are on Ryke and my mouth moves before I can stop it. "I'm not sensitive," I deadpan. "You're the one who flinched every time I called your mother a cunt." Granted, that was before I knew Sara Hale was his mom. I just thought she was mine, the one who abandoned me.

On cue, Ryke cringes at literally the only curse word he can't stand.

I watch the way his face flips through emotions, and in a quick second, he settles on one: *Guilt*.

I expected rage, a battle of words, something to perpetuate the

turmoil spinning in my stomach. Not his eyes to cloud with remorse, as if he was the one who spitefully slandered his mother.

*He knows me. He knows what I was thinking, why I say the
things I do.* Between the aggressive attitude and foul language, I
often forget Ryke has a brain, probably one that works better than
mine.

"Not sensitive," he says softly, almost hesitant. "I think *guarded*
and *defensive* are better words."

His eyes fill with apologies, not wanting to hurt me like my
father does. Ryke doesn't have the same fear as me, the one where
I turn into Jonathan Hale. But for a moment, Ryke must have
tasted what it was like to be him. I personally know it isn't pleasant.

After a deep breath, I say, "I can't help it. I'm always going to
be defensive when it comes to Lily."

"We're her sisters," Rose pipes in. "Everyone in this room loves
Lily *and* you. We are the last people you should be guarded around."

Something burns inside of me, words that ache to be released.
I've never talked to any of Lily's sisters about their childhood. I only
know what I've seen and what Lily has told me. If anyone can fill
in the blanks and help me answer Daisy's question, it's Rose.

"Why was Lily allowed to spend nights at my house?" I ask.

"You were her friend."

"Rose. What friends at twelve, thirteen, fourteen, *fifteen, sixteen, seventeen years old* spend the majority of nights at someone
else's house?"

She narrows her eyes. "It was usually on the weekend."

Holy shit. Someone has taken a sledgehammer to my stomach.

By the look on her face, she has no idea how many nights Lily
slept at my house when we were children. But how many activities
did Rose's mother bombard her with? Ballet, horseback riding,
piano, French.

Off my shock, Rose starts shaking her head fiercely. "I would have known. I would have seen her walk through the front door in the mornings . . ." Her face falls, and Connor reaches for her hand while she stares off dazedly.

"You never saw her in the mornings," I say what Rose is thinking. "My father's driver always took us to school from my house."

"I had club meetings in the morning. I left early all the time, so I just thought she was asleep." It wasn't Rose's duty to take care of Lily. She's only two years older. "How many nights did Lily sleep at your house?"

"In middle school, about four days a week, and then she just kept coming over more and more until high school . . ." I shake my head and cringe. It's my fault. A huge part of what happened, I know, I caused. ". . . in high school, she slept over almost every night."

"I didn't know that either," Daisy admits. I'm not surprised. Daisy is a lot younger, and when she turned about eleven, her mother started pursuing acting and modeling agencies for her. And for the majority of Daisy's tweens, I remember how she always looked exhausted, eyes heavy-lidded and yawning more than talking.

"Our parents couldn't have known about your sleepovers," Rose says. "They would have never allowed it."

"Are you sure?" I ask.

This is where my chest constricts, where vile resentment starts to pound in my head. I didn't have these feelings toward Samantha and Greg Calloway until I went to rehab. Before that, I thought they were the coolest parents for letting their daughter, my best friend, spend an exorbitant amount of time with me. Sitting in therapy for three months and becoming sober has cleared the dust.

I'm beginning to understand what happened.

Connor's mouth slowly parts in realization, letting me know he's put the pieces together. Why Lily is the way she is.

Rose is clouded by her own relationship with her parents. She sees a mother who inserts herself into her daughters' lives to the point where compassion transforms into suffocation. She sees a father who loves his children, buying them fancy things and sending them to exotic places to show his affection.

"Loren," Rose says, "finish what you have to say."

"Every day, Lily asked her mother if she could spend the night at my house. The answer was always the same. And then when Lily was fourteen or fifteen, Samantha finally told us to just stop asking, that she'd approve no matter what."

I remember Lily crying onto my pillow that same night. She never told me straight out, but I knew the only reason she even asked her mother in the first place was because she wanted to hear the word *no*. A single sign that her mother cared about her the same way that she did Poppy, Rose, and Daisy. That she wasn't undeserving of her mother's time and attention. Her mother doted on her other sisters. She put all her excess energy into them, skipping right over Lily as though she was worthless of that affection.

And so she tried to find it down the street. With me. And when that wasn't enough, she tried to fill it with other men. With sex. With a high and an intense burst of emotion.

"You know why Lily was allowed at my house at night?" I ask Rose, starting from the beginning again.

Her cheeks become concave, her back goes rigid, and a familiar chill fills her eyes. "Because you're a Hale."

That's what I thought.

"What does that fucking mean?" Ryke asks.

"Lily didn't need to be good at anything," I tell him. "Her mother passed over her because she was my friend. I was her future." The heir of a multibillion dollar empire. Her mother concentrated on Daisy, on Rose, who could be more successful in other facets. But Lily—her worth centered on a guy. Me. And I think, somewhere in her head, she believed it herself. That she would never amount to anything more than pleasing other men. That she was destined for a life less than her sisters'.

Daisy frowns. "I thought Lily just got a pass since she was kind of average at everything. I've always been jealous of the freedom she gets."

I nod. "Lily thinks she should be grateful for the freedom too." That's why she has trouble admitting to herself that she's been hurt by her mother. She could have been suffocated like her sisters. And she wasn't.

But there should have been a happy medium between what Lily had and what Daisy is now enduring.

I pause for a second, these words some of the hardest to produce. "Your mother outwardly loved you, Daisy, and you, Rose," I say, looking to each of the girls. "Even Poppy was showered with this type of overbearing maternal affection. And Lily . . . she was denied all of that. She was like the runt in the litter."

Rose's eyes glass like she may cry. I've never witnessed tears from her. I always imagined that they'd ice over. Her voice, however, is strangely stoic. "I didn't realize . . ." She shakes her head. "My mother wanted the two of you to become a couple. I knew that, but I blamed you more for taking my sister away from me. I didn't realize that she really had nowhere else to go."

Well, that kind of makes me feel like shit. She makes it sound like I was Lily's only option. "She could have stayed home."

"She would have been alone, Loren. I was barely around because of school and ballet."

And then a wave of guilt just annihilates me. "Yeah, well, maybe she should have been alone. Look what good it did being around me." I shake my head, running my hands repeatedly through my hair. My leg starts to jostle in anxiety.

"You didn't do this," Rose tells me. "Our mother should have told her that she loved her for something more than being with you. She could have found her something to do, something to achieve." A dream, a passion, a hobby, a fucking sport. Sex became all of those things for Lily. And I never stopped her. Not once. I was so consumed with my addiction that I didn't care what the hell she did, as long as she was breathing at the end of the night. As long as she was by my side—my best fucking friend.

"You don't understand," I mutter. I led her here. Unknowingly, I brought her to this place in her life. If I never even existed, she would have received that love from her mother that she craved.

"Then tell me."

"You don't get it."

"Loren—"

"She slept in my bed!" I shout, my eyes welling. They burn so badly. "I let her sleep in the same bed as me. Okay, this wasn't *Dawson's Creek*. I never kicked her out after we hit puberty."

Rose whispers to Connor, "I don't understand the correlation."

"Dawson and Joey stopped sleeping in the same bed together in the first episode. She said that he was old enough to get an erection."

Rose looks back to me. "You didn't have sex with her every night, did you?"

"No, but—"

"You can't compare your life to a television show." The fact that Rose is defending me does not entirely help. I'm used to her tearing me down, not building me up. I keep waiting for someone to thrash me with their words, with their feelings. With hate. I deserve that pain. It's my fucking fault.

"You don't get it!" I'm on my feet somehow. "I could have stopped her. I should have walked her down that road every night. I should have done *something*." Instead I gave her a bed to sleep in, a place to fill her vice.

"Loren," Rose starts.

"Stop," I say, placing my hands on my head, these thoughts swarming me in a tidal wave, the guilt so unbearable on my chest. "You should hate me," I tell her. "I deserve that." I nod. "I broke your sister." My face contorts in pain, a hot tear escaping. I want to punch something. To go run until my heart stops, until the breath just leaves me cold and dry.

No one says a thing. They wait for me to collect my bearings.

My breathing slows, and I rub my face. When I drop my hands, I say softly, "I wish I could take it all back." I want to reverse time. To walk Lily right out of my house, down the street, and to her own bedroom door. I would tell her that it's okay if her mother doesn't love her because her sisters do. And she doesn't need to avoid her house by being in mine—that she shouldn't keep searching for love in sex because it will only leave her empty and miserable.

I should have told her all of these things, but I didn't know any of them back then. And I was too goddamn drunk to care.

"It's not your fault," Rose says. "You were a kid. We all were."

"And you have a shitty fucking father," Ryke adds.

"And no mother," Daisy says.

"And you were an alcoholic," Connor concludes.

It's like they're my conscience, and yet, they're only my friends. For the first time, I have them, and I feel tears build at the words that I never thought I'd hear.

It's not your fault. Yeah, I'm getting there. I can believe it one day, I think.

I have weathered the most painful answer. I can manage any others now.

I look to Daisy.

"Next question."

Forty

Lily Calloway

A full week has passed. And I haven't left Ryke's apartment. School is an afterthought, even though my last test is in a few days. I'll just show up and pass and then be back to my reclusive state before finals begin. I have no intention of seeing my parents, and if Lo and Ryke would let me, I'd be a hermit for the rest of my life.

But Ryke is not the kind of person who coddles, and Lo refuses to enable me anymore. So they have awarded me a seven-day "grace period." Or what they like to call "the time it takes to get my shit together to face my parents." It may have taken God seven days to create the world, but I think I may need more time to screw my head on right. I am not Christlike. When I mentioned this to Lo, he told me I could have an extra sympathy day. I think he said that word on purpose—*sympathy*. I crinkled my nose and decided to take the seven days instead.

I'm on Day Seven. Judgment Day. The one where I'll have to face my mom and dad.

The majority of the camera crews remain at our house in Princeton or the one in Villanova. Rose and Daisy have been staying at Connor's since the cameras are sparse around his neighborhood. Plus, he has more room at his bachelor pad.

My parents have opted to stay silent when it comes to the media.

They paid their lawyers a hefty sum just to utter the words "no comment." There will be a press conference at some point, especially since Fizzle and Hale Co. stock have dropped considerably.

After home visits and lengthy phone calls with Dr. Banning, we agreed that I need to read and watch what's being said about me. Her words were, "Don't internalize your feelings when you hear what people are saying. If they upset you, then let it out." She also told me to make light of every painful situation—to uncover a silver lining and humor in all the bad. Anything to soften the gut-wrenching blows.

I sit on the leather couch and perform my usual morning ritual. Turn on the television to the morning news and flip open my laptop to the gossipy tabloid websites.

"We still don't have an official statement from Lily Calloway or her family," the news anchor says. "But we have a psychologist here today to talk about sex addiction and the dangers." Boo. I spend hours in therapy; I do not want to listen to this. I mute the TV and focus on the computer.

I type my name into the search engine. Various articles titled *Sex Addict* pop up. One even says, *Sex Addict or Slut?* And there's a lengthy debate on whether sex addiction is truly an addiction or whether I'm a whore in disguise. I stay away from that one.

Dr. Banning says that the more I hear and see the two words, the more I'll become desensitized to them.

It hasn't happened yet.

I shudder when I click into a new site. *Daughter of Soda Mogul Sleeps with Soccer Team.* I close out quickly and enter another webpage.

Lily Calloway Reviewed by Princeton after Allegations of Hiring Male Sex Workers.

Apparently being a frequent client of an escort service doesn't bode well in a university's eyes. I'm trying not to worry about it until after I talk to my parents. Tackle one issue at a time.

I make the mistake of logging on to Twitter and typing in my name. How do I make light of someone saying my vagina must be stretched and ugly? I haven't checked lately, but I don't think it looks that bad.

Besides, who stares at that body part and thinks, *wow, that's the most beautiful vagina I've ever seen?* Likewise, penises are not all that pretty. I may enjoy them, but I'm not about to snap a picture and decorate my wall. Eyes are beautiful. Sex parts are functional.

My fingers click away and land on Tumblr—my bane. I'm about to search for *Lily Calloway*, but I hesitate above the keyboard. And on impulse I type in something bad.

Sex gifs.

The magic words open Pandora's Box, and animated "moving" pictures cascade in an infinite scroll. Girls and guys are tangled lustfully, some positions sexier than others. And a few images are pure close-ups of naughty bits. I shouldn't be thumbing through anything pornographic, but I begin to relax at the familiar routine.

I hover on a black-and-white picture with pretty shadows. The girl's mouth forms a perfect O as a cock thrusts inside of her. I can't believe it's been two whole weeks since I've had sex. I try to remind myself that I lasted ninety days without Lo, no sex in sight. But that feels different than this.

After my addiction went public, Lo wavered on having sex with me. And he chose not to feed any compulsions that he thought would arise. He believes I'll turn into a wild, sex-crazed monster. Those are actually my words, but when I said them, he never denied it. Sex has been a coping mechanism, the tool that I use to deal with tough situations. And for the first time, I have to confront a hard-hitting issue without a boost of my natural high.

It's not like we haven't done *things*. We just haven't done *it*. He fingered me the other day, and last night, he let me give him a blow job. So that was nice.

I sigh. I am desperately envious of a two-dimensional girl's orgasm, worthy of fireworks and sparklers and red velvet cake.

Suddenly, the lock to the front door clicks, and since Ryke's apartment resembles a flat (the living room connected to the kitchen), I have a direct view of anyone who walks toward the couch. I quickly shutdown Tumblr and log on to *Hollywoodharlots.net*, a site that has been incredibly gossipy about my addiction. They even snapped a blurry photo of Daisy exiting Connor's apartment and captioned the pic: *Younger Sister of Lily Calloway: Future Sex Addict?*

It makes my stomach churn.

"She wasn't hitting on you," Lo says as the door swings open.

"Are you sure?" Ryke asks. He shuts the door and pockets his keys. "She looked like she knew where she was going."

"She was definitely lost."

Both shirtless with only running shorts, sweat glistens on their toned bodies. Morning runs relax Lo, and all week I have been searching for my anxiety-reducing activity. But those funny positions in yoga revert my mind to sex, and meditation causes me to fantasize. So I started looking at porn again, but I've been economical about my usage. I won't get carried away this time.

Lo plops down on the couch beside me, his eyes flickering to my computer screen. "You read anything interesting?"

"Besides the fact that I've officially screwed up my sisters' lives . . ."

"Rose and Daisy can handle it," Lo reminds me. But the whole point of pretending to be in a fake relationship for three years, of keeping this giant secret, was to avoid all of this from happening. I never wanted to hurt anyone.

"I rewatched the SNL skit," I admit. "I think I found it funnier the second time around." On Saturday, a comedian impersonated me. She drank so many cans of Fizz that she acted drunk and stumbled into a brothel. A few humorous quips later and I sufficiently turned into a caricature.

"You have to admit, the comedian nailed your hair perfectly," Ryke says with a grin.

"Yeah, but she gave me a terrible accent." I don't have a regional dialect, but she layered on a thick, obnoxious Philly drawl. I've also zeroed in on the least offending thing about the entire skit.

"To her credit, she's probably never heard you speak."

"Whose side are you on?" I ask him, but I already know the answer. If anyone has been making it easier to make light of the situation, it's Ryke and Lo.

"I think your first press release should be in that accent," Lo tells me. "How funny would it be if everyone thinks you actually speak like that?"

I smile. It would be a good prank.

Lo leans over to grab my computer. "Let me see this for a second," he says.

My guard rises and fear spikes. I grip the console as if I'm trying to protect a fairy kingdom from goblin invasion. "What? Why?"

He edges back a little bit, eyes narrowed with skepticism. "I want to see if my dad had a press conference yet." It must be hard to stay silent toward his father throughout all of this, but it's probably best that they're not on speaking terms. Jonathan Hale has always been Lo's trigger to drink.

"Uh . . . I can check." I type quickly into the search engine. It's not that I have anything incriminating on here, but I fear random pop-ups from a porn site that I visited yesterday. When the time is right, I plan on telling Lo that I've found a way to be a healthy porn-watcher. Definitely not now, though.

"No," I tell Lo after a couple minutes. "He hasn't even released a statement." Same as my parents. I wonder if they're both waiting to speak to their children first.

And right as I turn, the computer leaves my hands. Lo sets the device on the coffee table. My heart slows down when his lips touch mine, and then it speeds up again when his hands dip to my waist. I lose myself to the way his tongue slides into my mouth and the way he sucks on my bottom lip. Out of the corner of my eye, I catch Ryke entering the living room and bending in front of my computer.

Oh no.

I've been tricked!

I pull back abruptly, my bottom lip caught between Lo's teeth. I tug away and jump off the couch, charging for my laptop before Ryke can. But Lo grabs me by the hips and throws me over his shoulder. Oh man.

"Hey!" I yell, lifting my body off of Lo by pressing my hand on his back. "That's mine." Ryke doesn't seem to care. He takes the laptop casually and sits back against the couch. "Lo, put me down!"

He pats my ass. "You don't like it up here?"

"Are you taking me to the bedroom?" I ask, rethinking my dislike of hanging upside down. If it ends with me on a bed and having crazy sex, then I wouldn't complain.

"No, love."

"I can give you head," I offer.

"I'm still in the room, Lily," Ryke reminds me, his eyes on my computer screen. I flush only a little. I have become terrifyingly more comfortable mentioning sex around Ryke.

"You don't care, do you?" I ask Ryke, egging him on a bit. He has my computer after all.

"I care," Lo replies instead. "It's almost noon."

"That's why they call it a nooner."

"No, Lil."

I clench my teeth, hating that I'm making him say the word *no* over and over. I should be better like I was in Cancun. But ever since the leak, I feel like I've regressed a little. I just . . . need to figure out how to return to where I was, but finding that path proves harder every day.

Ryke taps the keyboard, the clicking incessant while his eyes dance around the screen. "I don't really understand why you're so fucking obsessed with blow jobs anyway. You're a sex addict. What the hell do they do for you?"

"Ryke," Lo snaps.

"What? It's an honest fucking question."

I don't want to tell Ryke the truth. That before I dated Lo, it was just a means to an end. Foreplay. Getting a guy hard. Pure and simple. Now, since I'm not even allowed to be on top (lest I become too compulsive) giving head is really the only thing that makes me feel in control. And I just really, really like making Lo come.

I smile at the thought.

"You're not going to answer me?" Ryke asks. "I thought we were friends now."

I may be comfortable saying *some* things in front of him but definitely not that. "What are you doing on my computer, then?" I ask. "And why am I being held hostage?" I try to wiggle out of Lo's grip.

He slides me down to my feet, and before I dart to the computer, his arms slip around my waist again, pinning my chest to his. He stares past me, and disappointment and dread begin to fill his amber-colored eyes.

What? I crane my neck over my shoulder. Ryke grimaces at something on the screen. My heart flip-flops and somersaults. "What's wrong?" I say in a small voice.

"Your history is fucking filthy," Ryke tells me in a serious tone.

But . . . that's impossible. I clear my history. All the time. Lo lets go of me, cold replacing his warmth, which stings the most. I stay frozen by the coffee table, and he joins Ryke on the couch, scanning the long list.

"I don't understand . . ." I mutter.

"I checked your history yesterday," Lo says, his eyes grazing the screen like Ryke's. "It was all erased. I thought that was suspicious. So I told Ryke this morning, and he said there's a backup installed on expensive computers to revive it." He finally meets my gaze, and before he speaks this time, I interject.

"I can explain," I say quickly. "I started looking at it a few days ago, but only for a few minutes at a time. I'm learning how to portion control. I was going to tell you after I talked to my parents. It's a good thing actually. I can watch it like a normal person now." My voice becomes unnaturally high.

Ryke, surprisingly, keeps quiet and turns to Lo.

I've already framed his response. He won't condone my porn usage, that I'm sure, but he'll tell me he understands how hard it is for me and that I have to do better. I wait for his sympathetic words.

"I hope you enjoyed it," Lo says with edge, "because that was your last time on the internet."

My mouth falls open, too shocked to speak. He closes my computer and snatches it from Ryke's lap. I imagine him tossing it in the trash, and my voice suddenly reanimates. "Waitwaitwait!" I throw up my hands. "I have school. I need to write papers and do research."

Lo walks to a cabinet and places my laptop inside. "Then I'll sit with you when you do them, but obviously you can't be trusted with a computer right now." His eyes hit mine. "Have you been looking at porn on your phone?"

I stare at the cabinet in a fog. I can't believe this is happening. Lo has never practiced tough love with me. The only love I know is either the sweet kind or the kind that makes me come.

"Lily!"

I blink. "A little."

His chest rises and falls heavily, hurt or angry or maybe a bit of both. "There is no *a little*," he says roughly. "It's either yes or no."

I shake my head. "I was making it work," I defend.

"Porn is not like sex. You're not allowed to look at the photos for an hour and be done."

"Why not?" I ask. "If I'm not being compulsive about it—"

"You're *addicted*. It doesn't feel like a compulsion now. But two days later, that hour on your computer turns into three. A week later, you're losing sleep to the habit. Then in a month, all your free fucking time is consumed by checking your phone, logging on to websites, falling asleep to movies. Lily . . ." He walks over and cups my face, brushing fallen tears from my eyes. "I have watched porn eat away your time and your life. I'm not going to let it happen again."

Before I can wrap my head around my feelings, his hand slips into my back pocket, and he retrieves my cell phone. "On the way to your parents, we'll stop and buy you a flip phone. One that doesn't have internet."

He slides the cell into his own pocket. His eyes fall to mine, still serious.

"Have you been masturbating?"

I feel the heat of my rash-like embarrassment flooding my face. I glance hesitantly at Ryke, not wanting to discuss any of this with him in the room. They have banded together, and I can't deny that Ryke has made Lo stronger.

"Lily, you asked to give me head in front of him," Lo reminds me. "You can't be embarrassed now."

"I'm not . . . I haven't." I don't mention how I've contemplated the act and almost succumbed to the temptation (more than once) in the shower.

"You promise?" he asks, still disbelieving. "Because there are ways I can check. I could smell your fingers right now or go through your box of toys."

I scowl. My stomach turns in a mixture of anger and hurt. "You don't have to do that," I say. "I'm telling you the truth."

"This . . ." He motions from me to him. "*Us.* We can't work unless we're honest with one another. You'll be able to tell if I drink, but, Lil, I'll have no idea if you've relapsed until it's too late. I don't want there to be distrust between us."

"I don't either."

"Then talk to me," he urges. "Don't reach the point where you're watching porn or masturbating again to speak up. It's not okay, Lil."

He's right, but that doesn't make hearing those words, from him, any easier. Maybe I need a good kick in the ass, though.

Ryke clears his throat from the couch, and Lo rolls his eyes dramatically. He grabs his wallet from the table and fishes out a twenty. Ryke smirks as he takes the bill.

"Did you bet on me?" I ask, dumbfounded.

"Yeah," Lo says, unabashed. His eyes fall to mine. "And I'll always bet on your side."

He probably suspected I had watched porn all along too. I should be more offended that they bet on my addiction, but it lightens the mood and helps me not curl up in a ball of guilt.

"And I'll gladly take your money," Ryke tells him.

No way. The prospect of Ryke winning off my failure motivates me to do better.

I open my mouth, about to tell Ryke that he'll never win again, but a glimmer in the window catches my eye. I sidle to the panes and peer through.

Across the street, a van has pulled onto the curb. Cameras flash, the lens directed at Ryke's living room. I duck to the floor. How did they find us?

Lo sees me hugging the hardwood, and he comes over to glance out the window. I shoo him with my hand. "Cameras," I say.

He squints in confusion and then quickly grabs the remote. He flips on the television while Ryke hops over the coffee table and comes to my aid. He snags the blinds, and they close the room in afternoon darkness.

A familiar voice blares through the sound system, and my head whips to the flat-screen.

"I spent an entire week with her during spring break."

Oh. My. God.

I go to Lo's side in a daze and plop on the couch. Melissa talks candidly with a camera crew outside of what appears to be Ryke's apartment complex.

"And what was she like?" the news anchor asks.

Melissa lets out a short laugh. "Wild."

"Liar!" I yell and grab a pillow from the couch, ready to fling it against the television.

Ryke points a finger at me. "Do not break my TV."

I motion to Melissa and her fake smile. "The one time I actually didn't even have sex, and I'm being blasted for it. It's not fucking fair."

"She's not the first person who's been on camera lying about you," Lo reminds me. Yesterday a kid from prep school claimed I had sex with him, and since I was particular and choosy back then, I can recall most of my high school conquests. He was definitely not among them. But this feels different. Melissa is the first person who has proof that she's been in our company, and not only that, she's discussing events that didn't take place four years ago.

It happened last Friday.

As far as they know, she has no reason to lie.

The news anchor asks her to elaborate, and Melissa wears another complacent smile. "Well, let's just say Lily and Loren Hale have an *open* relationship."

"What does that mean exactly?"

"Loren Hale has a half brother," Melissa says. Yeah, the media revealed that not too long ago, and Sara Hale was finally painted as the hero, divorced out of adultery, which she was forced to keep quiet after the end of her marriage. She's no longer the money-grubbing gold digger that my own mother used to call her. Although, I suspect my mom still knew the truth about Jonathan's cheating all along like my father did.

"Do you know who his half brother is?" the anchor questions.

Ryke's identity has not been confirmed. By anyone yet.

"Of course," Melissa says. "He tells almost everyone that he's related to Loren Hale. I think he likes being associated with money."

Ryke rolls his eyes and sits on the armrest of the couch beside his brother.

Lo pats his back. "Nothing like a woman scorned, huh, *big bro?*"

"Fuck off," Ryke says lightly.

Lo smiles, but it fades as soon as Melissa answers the news anchor's whole question.

"His name is Ryke Meadows."

"And there goes my anonymity," Ryke mutters. He sighs and curses under his breath as Melissa discusses the apartment building, his affiliation to Penn and the track team . . . it's a lot to digest.

"And there goes those morning runs around the block," Lo adds.

Melissa divulges more secrets, like which coffee shops he frequents, the gyms he likes. Ryke groans into his hand.

Lo's voice softens. "You really pissed this girl off."

"I didn't mean to. Honestly."

Melissa stares straight into the camera, delivering her next lie. "Lily Calloway liked to do it a lot, but *especially* with both of them." She pauses. "*Together.*"

None of us move, not at all expecting *that*.

"Fucking fantastic," Ryke breathes.

I can handle guys lying about sleeping with me. I can handle comedy skits about my sex addiction. I can handle the *sluts* and *whores* that are blasted my way. But having someone else—someone who has only helped me—being dragged into these lies, well, that sets me off.

I storm toward the door, not even caring that my hair is unwashed, that my clothes are wrinkled from all the lounging around, and that I look one second from joining the trash in a garbage can. I'm a girl with a fucking mission.

"Whoa!" Lo wraps his arms around my waist before I reach the door. "Where are you going, love?"

"To the street. I need to set things straight." They cannot think I've slept with Ryke. They cannot think I've had sex with Lo and his brother. That is beyond wrong.

Ryke stares at me from the couch. "So your first fucking statement is going to be *Melissa is a big fat fucking liar?*"

"You can't point fingers," Lo clarifies.

"I can't just be quiet," I say. "This is getting bad."

"You have to talk to your parents first," Lo reminds me. "They have money. They have lawyers."

But every second that Melissa's lie is accepted as truth is another moment where Ryke and Lo suffer because of me.

Ryke gives me an annoyed look. "You honestly think I care what people say about me?" No, he wouldn't, but I still feel horrible. "I'm more pissed that she's told the press where I rock climb."

I picture lenses swarming him as he grips a mountain with his fingers, and the cameras distract him as they flash repeatedly, so much so that he tumbles to his death. I wince. "I'm sorry."

"I don't want your apologies, Lily," Ryke refutes. "I only want one thing."

"What?"

"When your parents tell you to go to rehab, what do you say?"

We talked about this on the plane. I can't go to rehab. That would entail leaving Lo and a brilliant therapist, both of which I love, and all of that would be replaced with anxiety-ridden group sessions. I can't form the words Ryke wants me to until Lo laces his fingers with mine, courage filling me.

"I'm going to say . . . go to hell."

Ryke tilts his head at me, appraising my tone. I said the right words, but maybe not in the most confident way. He turns to Lo.

"We'll work on it," Lo tells me.

I nod. At least I have their support. Ryke and Lo, as a team—for however strange that would have seemed months ago—it's the best thing for me.

Just not a sexual team.

Purely chaste here.

Okay, I'll stop now. I think porn has fried my brain. I blame Melissa! I'm going to use that excuse for the rest of the day.

I do feel a little better.

Forty-one

Lily Calloway

haven't told my parents to "go to hell" yet, but that's partly because they really haven't spoken to me. When we arrived at their Villanova mansion, Lo and I were ushered into one of the dens. My parents were there, along with his father, but so were four lawyers that squeezed onto a single couch. The lawyers asked us questions, and I tried to explain everything without becoming too much of an emotional mess. I failed on multiple occasions, blubbering so much that Lo would have to finish talking for me.

But my mother and father never said a word and avoided my gaze as much as possible. They might as well have been listening from another room. The hardest part was going through the video clips that many guys posted and claimed as sex tapes. Some blurry ones I couldn't be certain were me or not, but others were clearly fabricated. I don't have any cute freckles on my butt.

Four hours later, my throat has swollen from talking and bearing as much of the truth as I could. We even came clean about our fake relationship. Now Lo and I wait in the living room while the lawyers and our parents deliberate about the next steps. Rose and Ryke offered to be here, but we both wanted to do this on our own.

"What if they never speak to me again?" I say, rubbing my puffy eyes. I spot Harold, our butler, walking rather quickly past the doorway with the mail in his hands. The staff, most of whom

I've known for years, have all had the same skittish reaction around me. Like I'm contagious.

"That wouldn't be a big change, would it?" Lo asks.

My heart twists a little at his words. They haven't been the most active participants in my life, but I always thought it was my own doing. I purposefully alienated myself during college. But then again, my father was never around when I was a child, and my mother brushed me away pretty easily. But Rose said my mom bought self-help books to learn how to reconnect to her children, so maybe . . . she's trying? I don't think there's a black-and-white answer. I think I've been swimming in the gray state of things for so long.

They're still my parents. I love them because I believe they truly love me. My father has given me so much, and even if Ryke says otherwise, I can't just abandon this life with my family or walk away from what I did. I don't want to be that insolent child, stomping on my parents' livelihood and then telling *them* to clean it up. It's my fault. I need to take responsibility.

I just hope that I haven't done irreparable damage—to the company, our family, and my relationship with them.

"It's going to be weird talking to them through lawyers," I rephrase. "It's already weird."

"Yeah, that's kind of bullshit," he agrees and takes my hand in his. "Whatever happens, we're in this together. You and me."

"Lily and Lo," I say with a weak smile. It hurts to lift my lips, but I try my best. I've avoided this day for a week now, and every minute I'm here reminds me of all the harm I've caused.

He kisses my cheek and the doors to the den open. The lawyers and our parents file out in a large wave. I haven't been able to apologize to either my mother or father. Every time I tried to digress from the lawyers' questions, they snapped me back on track with a sharp tone. I fear this may be my only chance.

I walk quickly around the couch, my parents heading in the

opposite direction down the long, narrow hallway. "Mom!" I shout, scooting past one of Jonathan's burly lawyers.

She doesn't look back. "Mom!" I yell again, nearly reaching her as I walk faster. She ignores me, and I rest my hand on her shoulder to stop her.

She spins around on her heels, my father padding ahead.

Her cold eyes puncture me, filled more with malice than anything else, and it takes me a moment to remember what I was even doing in the first place.

I stumble back a little. "I'm sorry," I choke. "I'm so sorry."

"You can be sorry all you want," she says with a chill. She touches her pearls across her sharp collarbone. "It won't repair the damage you have done to this family." She takes a step forward, and I take one step back so we don't bump chests. "You have everything a girl could ever want, and you had to spread your legs for every boy who gave you an ounce of attention. I didn't raise you to be so disgusting."

Tears cloud my eyes, and I disobey my therapist's orders and internalize everything she says. I deserve her hate. I've ruined everything my father has ever created. Years and years of hard work have been tarnished by me and my stupid fucking decisions.

Her eyes flit to Lo as he comes to my side. Coldness blankets me, and my hand feels numb to his palm. My mother looks him over in one long gaze before she says, "You could do better."

I try to disentangle my hand from his, but he grips fiercely, holding on. Tears spill down my cheeks as I focus on prying each one of his fingers off mine. He directs his attention to my mother.

"You don't know us," he says. "If you did, you would realize how guilty she already feels, so stop tearing her down."

I shake my head. He doesn't get it. I want to hear her anger and disappointment. I'm so tired of people telling me it's okay when it's not. It's not okay that my little sister is being theorized as a future sex addict. It's not okay that my father's company has lost investors.

I don't want to lock myself in an apartment and pretend that everything is fine anymore.

There is no one else to blame but *me*.

Lo squeezes my hand with extra force, making it impossible for me to let go.

My mother purses her lips. "It's late. You both need to talk with the lawyers." She spins on her heels, and they clap all the way down the hall.

I breathe in sporadic, choppy inhales, and my head spins so much that my vision starts to whirl with it. Lo presses his hands to my cheeks, cupping my face with strength that I do not possess. Months ago, he'd probably leave me on a bench in the hallway to go collect bottles from the liquor cabinet. Now that he's here, I try to ingest some of his power to stand upright. But all I see is a boy who's good and whole and a girl who's broken and weak.

I want to be him.

I want that.

But those are my parents. And they hate me.

I think I hate myself more.

"Lily," he says, very softly. "You're going to have a panic attack if you don't slow your breaths."

Going to? This isn't a panic attack?

"Lily," he snaps. "Breathe. *Slowly.*"

I try to listen to him and focus on his chest, the way it rises and falls in a stable pattern. When my lungs feel less strained and my breath steadies, we both turn to the team of lawyers that lingers in the corridor. Exhaustion sags their eyes, and they each hold stacks of papers that they'll be sifting through for the next forty-eight hours.

The head lawyer, Arthur, holds the largest stack. "We need to discuss what should happen in the upcoming weeks."

I don't know what my parents have decided to do. Send me to rehab? Fly me to Switzerland? I'm supposed to tell them to go to hell, but after confronting my mother, all I want to do is make this right.

And that means giving in to whatever they want. Whatever they need. I'll repair the damage I've done.

Jonathan Hale steps forward, already clutching a crystal glass of scotch. Surprisingly, like my parents, he didn't utter a word during our briefing in the den. "I can take it from here, Arthur," he says easily. "I think Loren and Lily have had enough of this intermediary bullshit."

Arthur sways on his feet, hesitant to leave.

"You don't need to relay information," Jonathan snaps. "You need to get your ass back to your office and make phone calls and fact-check the hell out of those stories. It's time for you to go. Now."

They disperse quickly, and Arthur hands Jonathan a couple files before he leaves. A burst of envy pops in my chest, and I'm frightened that I covet Lo's father and want to trade mine in for the Jonathan Hale version, wishing mostly that my dad could be more supportive.

The world has gone mad.

Jonathan looks to us. "We should do this at my house. The staff here is getting on my last goddamn nerve." On cue, one of the groundskeepers walks into the house from the back door and then speeds off in another direction. Jonathan mumbles something that sounds like *ridiculous motherfuckers*. But I really can't be certain.

The farther I am from this house, the better, even if it means that we have to drive through mobs of camera crews again. Lo and I climb into my car, and before he puts it in drive, he faces me.

"I have to tell you something, and you're probably going to be mad."

I frown, not having a clue where this could go. I watch Jonathan's car exit the gates, cameras flashing and clicking, the light glinting off the tinted windows.

"What is it?" I ask, my voice smaller than I like.

He licks his lips, guilt lining his face. Uh-oh. "This isn't the first time I've seen my father since rehab."

The truth washes over me in a freezing cold wave. I shiver and nod, letting this sink in fully. Okay. He's lied. But he just opened up, so that has to count for something, right? Still, no matter how much I make excuses for him, I can't help the sadness that pours into me.

I lift my legs to the seat and bury my head in my knees, hiding from *Lo*, not the paparazzi.

"Lil," he says, his hand hovering above my head, hesitant to touch me. "Say something."

I can't speak, the words tangle, swollen in a pit midway up my throat. So Lo pulls the car out and navigates past the cameras. He explains his conversations with his father and how he went to him specifically to find the blackmailer and to learn more about his mother.

By the time we reach the street, away from the paparazzi and news vans, he has finished spilling all these secrets. After a long, tense silence, he asks, "Are you mad?"

"No," I say softly, silent tears streaming down my cheeks. I don't lift my head from my knees. *I'm just sad.* I should have known and busted him like he did me. He was able to go to rehab and come back a little stronger than before. I didn't have that. When he returned, I started back at day one, trying to figure out how to cope with my addiction and him in the same room. And I'm just realizing how much of a rock he is for me, and how much I may have let him down if he relapsed and I didn't stop him sooner.

"Lily, please talk to me." He tails Jonathan's car and slows down when we reach the gate.

"Did you drink?" I murmur.

"No, I promise, Lil. I mean . . ."

My chest collapses. I don't like *I means*.

". . . I thought about it, but I didn't. I couldn't. I'm on Antabuse," he says. "The idea of vomiting stopped me more than once. Being around my father does make me want to drink. I can't deny that." He pauses. "But I'm at a point where I can say no." At least he's being honest now.

I raise my head, rubbing my cheeks on my sleeve. "You didn't tell me because you knew I'd disapprove."

He nods. "But, Lil, he's my *dad*. He's my fucking family."

I can't tell him what I think. That even if his father shows heart one minute, he'll cut Lo into pieces the next. I've seen Lo walk away a shell of himself after his father screamed at his face for half an hour.

He parks the car and lifts my hand. "You're my family too." He kisses my knuckles. "Always." He wipes away a stray tear. "Please don't be upset over this."

"I just don't want to see him hurt you," I say softly.

"He won't."

Lo is not built of armor. He goes into every fight without the padding. He lets people hurt him because he believes he deserves that pain. It's sick. It's something I think I'm coping with right now.

I breathe heavily and just nod. "Okay." I feel so ripped open. The extra dagger just fits in place with the others. I have to believe that Lo will be fine in the face of his father, that he can handle all the verbal onslaughts and the sudden disparaging comments. The *why aren't you living to your potential? Why are you such a fucking disappointment?* I have to believe he's stronger than me.

I think I can do that.

We enter the house, and I skid to a stop by the grand staircase, absorbing a home that I spent most of my childhood in. It's quieter and darker than my parents' place and carries a somber quality. Maybe because I have more memories here. And not all of them good.

"Can we do this in the morning?" I ask. Postponing the inevitable sounds nice. I could take another sleeping pill too, or Lo might even go down on me tonight. I shouldn't be thinking about sex right now. I shake my head to try to reset it. I'm a spin-cycle revolving backward.

Lo strokes my hair. "My father is impatient."

Oh right. He leads me to his father's office, where I've been many times before. Jonathan is already pouring himself scotch when we walk in. I settle on the brown leather sofa, and Lo scoots close beside me.

I remember kissing Lo on this couch. We'd have these hot and heavy make-out sessions, complete with over-the-clothes caressing, just to be caught by Jonathan or the staff. We weren't really together, but we made excuses to kiss each other. We said that we were "reinforcing our relationship," even though it was just pretend. I liked the stroking and the groping more than I should. And Lo did too, I suppose. He just never declared, outright, that he wanted to be with me.

Jonathan lingers by the liquor cart, examining his bottles. "Greg and I agreed not to speak during the briefing. If it felt formal, it's only because we didn't want the thing to last all fucking night." He raises a crystal bottle of amber-colored liquid. "Would you like a glass or are you still being obnoxious?"

"No, thanks," Lo says, his voice firm.

Jonathan returns the bottle and slumps in the plush leather chair behind his desk. He shuffles the three files out along his desk as he takes a slow sip from his glass.

"From here on out, the goal for both of you is to reform your images. You will become upstanding individuals who can proudly wear your last fucking name." He flips open a file and scans the page. "We'll start with Lily. The easiest solution would be to deny all the claims, but no one would believe that sixty men were lying."

I already knew I couldn't deny the accusations, and I wouldn't want to. Most are true. I wait for the word, the one that will seal my fate—*rehab*.

"So your parents and the lawyers have drawn up a list of things you must do. It'll help restore your reputation, and in effect, that of our companies. Simple, easy, seamless, yada fucking yada."

"What if she doesn't do them?" Lo asks.

Jonathan shoots him a sharp look. "I was getting there. Hold your fucking tongue for a second." His eyes fall to me. "Starting today, you no longer have access to your trust fund. When you complete all the tasks, your inheritance will be restored to you in full."

My money is gone.

I'm broke. Just like Lo.

I wish I could talk to my parents. I would have completed their list without putting my financial security up as collateral. The guilt motivates me enough.

Jonathan stares at Lo, and I know he wants him to ask for his own trust fund back, especially now that we're both penniless. But Lo remains resolute and tight-lipped.

His father switches his attention back to me. "I must admit, your father didn't like this idea all that much. He preferred you keep your trust fund, but your mother convinced him otherwise." I wonder why Jonathan tells me this, maybe to vouch for his best friend. I'm not sure.

"What's on the list?" I ask softly. "Do I have to leave?"

Jonathan lets out a short laugh. "Running away doesn't solve anything. In fact, it makes you look guilty. No, you'll stay in the city, preferably Princeton after the lawyers get done with the university."

I'm not going to be expelled? Hope surges through me, only to be smothered by Jonathan's next words. "You will apologize publicly during a press conference, and you will start seeing a psychiatrist handpicked by your parents." He narrows his eyes at the list. "They also want you to stop visiting bars and clubs, but really, the three of us in this room can agree that you can go, just don't be seen. This is about your image, not a fucking path to morality."

He taps his pen on the folder. "The most important and last item on the list . . ." He reaches into his suit jacket and reveals a small black box. I don't look at Lo. My eyes zone in on the case as Jonathan opens the lid, a shiny diamond ring inside. "Congratulations," Jonathan says, his voice more rough than enthusiastic. "You're now engaged, and the wedding will be held in a year."

My joints don't work properly, even though all my thoughts scream violently for me to take the ring. It's a small price to pay for what I've done. But to turn what Lo and I have into bait for the media, cheapening our love, hurts beyond words.

More tears pool.

"Lil," Lo says, squeezing my hand. "We can find another way."

We can't.

This is what they want, and we've been selfish long enough. I shake my head, grab the box, and pluck out the ring that glitters. It's larger and more extravagant than anything I'd ever want. I take a small breath and slide it onto my finger.

It fits perfectly.

I can't stop staring at the way it sparkles and dwarfs my small hand. It's gaudy and feels cold and wrong.

"I'm sorry," I tell Lo. He's fixated on the piece of jewelry as much as me, and I already know what he's thinking. This isn't what he imagined for us either, a proposal by his father in his office.

Maybe . . . maybe we're just not meant to have a happy ending.

Maybe we don't deserve it.

Forty-two

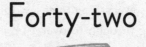

Loren Hale

When I was in rehab, I had plenty of free time to let my mind wander. Stupidly, I started thinking about how I would propose to Lily. Not any time soon, but when we were both healthy and happy. I even envisioned the ring I would buy her—a small pink sapphire. Simple, nontraditional. I think she would have liked it.

Now I'll never know.

I glare at my father, hating that he has hijacked my proposal. It's not entirely his fault, but if we're being coerced into marriage, I'd rather have something on my terms. He could have given me a day's notice. Anything.

Instead, I'm going to shelve this memory with all of my other black, inky tarred ones, ruined by something larger and nastier than me. Lily quietly appraises the ring with sad eyes. I wish I could fix this, but rejecting her parents' pleas will hurt her more. The shame she caused is tearing her from the inside out, and doing nothing to repair the damage would rip her soul.

"The wedding," I say, breaking the tense silence. "You said it's in a year."

My father nods and sips his scotch.

I itch to taste it, but I focus more on Lil, and any ache for alcohol subsides. For once, I truly feel strong enough to help her. "She has to complete all the tasks before her trust fund is returned. Does that mean she'll have it again when she agrees to the wedding?"

"She gets it when you're married."

My stomach caves. *A year?* She'll be broke for a whole fucking year even if she does everything they say. Lily can't hold down a job while she's going through recovery. I remember how I found her hiding underneath her desk in Rose's office, afraid of the male models. She's not ready to handle the stress of a workplace environment with her addiction at bay. That anxiety is what causes her to go crazy.

"We'll get married sooner," I offer. Why prolong the wait? She'll have money. The cameras will stop hounding us. She won't be gossiped about in blogs anymore. All will be right again.

"Really?" Lily asks, her eyes big and glassy.

I wipe a fallen tear with my thumb. "Two weeks or one year, it doesn't make a difference to me, Lil. I'd marry you tomorrow if it'd make you happy."

She nods once and lets me hold her close.

"It actually does make a difference," my father cuts in, chilling my bones. "It can't look like a shotgun wedding designed to coax the media. It has to look real. One year. No sooner and no later."

He strangled my only alternative.

My father closes a file and opens another. "Now for you, Loren," he says, "the media has modeled you as the pathetic boyfriend, cheated on and discarded. You will publicly release a statement about how you and Lily have had an open relationship, something *new age*. You have been sleeping around with other women, and you knew she was sleeping with other men. But since your *romantic* engagement, you both have decided to commit to each other fully."

Lily holds in a breath, probably believing I'll refuse this stipulation. She wants this to be easy, for us to agree and move on. I'm accustomed to lies. If this one helps, I'll gladly carry it. I nod in acceptance and my father closes the file.

"That's it?" I ask.

"You're not the sex addict," he reminds me with a dry smile and the raise of his glass. He takes a long swig, and my mind lapses back to the money issue.

I have to ask him.

For Lily.

For me.

So we have one less problem to solve. So we can stop taking handouts from our siblings.

"About my trust fund . . ."

Lily bristles beside me. "Lo, you don't have to—"

"I want to." Whatever the repercussions, whatever I have to do to please my father, I'll work out. A part of me screams *failure*. I'm giving up by crawling back to this man. But the other part says *this is the right way*. And I'm listening to that side of my brain. Whether it's the dumb fucking side—that's to be seen.

"What about it?" He swirls the scotch in his glass, creating a small whirlpool.

He'll make me ask. Beg. Plead and grovel. I'm not about to drop to my knees, but I'm close. I'm almost there. "You told me I could have it back," I remind him, but I'm not an idiot. I know there are strings attached. "What do you want me to do?" *Not college. Not college. Not college.* I cannot go back to school, surrounded by booze, surrounded by fully functioning twenty-somethings. It drives me to a bottle more than Lily knows. It's a reason why I opted not to return.

Every sane, happy person is like a reflection of what I could have been, like being met with Christmas Future every day. I don't want to be haunted by my problems like that.

"What I want you to do," he says, "is be a fucking man."

I glare. "Last time I checked, I was one."

"Having a dick doesn't make you a man," he replies. "You've been an irresponsible little boy all your life. I give you things and you shit on them. If you want your trust fund, you have to use the money to make something of yourself. You can't fuck it away."

"I'm not going back to college."

"Did I say anything about college? You're not even *listening* to me." He throws back the rest of the liquor into his mouth and smacks the glass on the desk.

I flinch.

And he stays silent, not about to divulge the details. Apparently I'm supposed to know what being a man really entails. In my father's head, that could mean anything.

"Okay," I accept blindly. He just wants me to meet my potential, not squander away his wealth with apathy. His terms should be in my power. Hopefully.

His brows jump in swift surprise, but it slowly washes away, replaced with a true, genuine smile. I think I just made my father happy.

That happens . . . well, almost never.

"I'll call the lawyers. Your inheritance will be back by tomorrow morning," he says, "and I expect a business proposal by next week."

"A what?" My stomach tightens.

He rolls his eyes and his mouth downturns. That smile lasted point-two seconds. "For Christ's sake, Loren. A *business proposal*. You don't have to be involved in my company, but you better create your own. I don't even fucking care if it succeeds. Just get off your lazy ass." He stands and hovers over the liquor cart to refill his empty glass. "It's late. You two should spend the night here."

I don't want to step into my old bedroom, a haven for bad memories and shitty mistakes. I shake my head. "We're staying at Ryke's tonight."

He stiffens at the name. "Then get going. I have work to do." As we walk toward the doors, he says, "And when I find the leak, he's going to wish that he never fucked with our family. I can promise you that."

Forty-three

Lily Calloway

We're all back at the Princeton house, and I haven't spoken to Rose in three days. She leaves the house early and returns late. And every time I call, her automated message clicks. Usually Rose answers on the second ring.

H&M and Macy's dropped Calloway Couture from their stores, citing the "negative attention" as reason to pull the garments from the hangers and shelves. I apologized over text, and I caught her once in person to utter the words, but she patted me on the shoulder and said something about a meeting and hopped into her car.

She texted me this morning. *I'm just busy, and I'm sorry I don't have more time to talk. I don't blame you. Keep your head up.* —Rose

I'm not feeling very sprightly today, but the text helps ease the weight on my chest. My last test is today before finals start next week, and it marks the first time I'll set foot on campus since the scandal. I shouldn't go. I didn't study or memorize the answers from old exams. I just plopped on the couch and watched reruns of *Boy Meets World*.

My limbs sag heavily, an anchor that tethers me to the bed, to the floor, to the couch. Morning, noon, and night. The urge to disappear, a superpower that I have always wanted, strikes me more often. Dr. Banning would tell me that I'm depressed, maybe even prescribe medication for me. But I haven't spoken to her since my meeting with the lawyers.

I'm not allowed to see her. I have a new psychiatrist now. Dr. Oliver Evans. I'll meet him next week.

The shower is my one solitude: a place where self-love exists, where the steam and my prickling nerves combust and ward off anxiety. The guilt accompanies the high. And IknowIknowIknow. I'm technically not allowed, but I'm monitoring how long I spend touching myself. This isn't the same thing as porn. I can't masturbate in public. I'll never overdo it if I just restrict myself to self-love shower time.

And anyway, after last night's attempt to have sex, Lo will probably steer clear of me for a good thousand years. It started fine. I was ridiculously excited to finally sleep with him after two weeks of abstinence. The hour sped, tricking my mind into believing we only fooled around for five whole minutes, not sixty. I needed more time.

He kept telling me *no*. And I even tried to spider him and ensnare him in my sex web, which (now that I think about it) couldn't have been all that sexy. I turned into the compulsive sex-monster that we both feared. Then, something worse happened.

I burst into tears.

So not only did I whine for sex, but I cried when I didn't get it. I'm ashamed to the point of reclusiveness. I never want to show my face, to anyone. I don't blame Lo if he never wants to sleep in the same bed with me ever again.

I glance at the kitchen clock. Lo and Ryke can no longer run at the Penn track or jog down the block without being bombarded by paparazzi or nosy students. So they've resorted to sprinting around the land at our house in Princeton. At least it's gated.

But they shouldn't come inside for another ten minutes. My damp hair wets my shirt. I think I can squeeze in one more shower before they enter the house. I hop off the barstool and race to the bathroom. I retrieve a small bag of tampons from a cabinet in the way, *way* back. Stuffed in between all of them is a pouch with my waterproof mini-vibrator. I take it out and shove the bag back.

Shower or bathtub?

I hate that we don't have a combo bathtub-shower scenario. This would be a lot easier then. Self-love standing up is not my favorite, and that's what I've had to do in the shower.

The bathtub calls me. Bubbles. I can have bubbles too. But I only have . . . ten minutes. I think I can make it work. Bubbles have to be worth it.

Quickly, I turn the faucet, test the water for the perfect warmth, and squirt in bubble mix (of course) and toss in one of those pink soap balls (not really sure what they do). The water swishes into a pale pink hue, and I breathe in the flowery aroma, the scent pretty close to lilies.

So I call it a success.

I shed my clothes and sink into the water, gasping at the way the warmness skims my thighs and up to my breasts. I hold the vibrator in one hand, anticipation and glee filling me first. I close my eyes, lean back, and let my mind wander while my hand moves.

I focus on a particular memory, one with Lo during our sophomore year of college. We were roped into attending my parents' holiday party back at their Villanova mansion. Since we planned on spending the night, we both decided to get drunk off the eggnog. My mother shooed us upstairs so we didn't disrupt any of the other guests, and we locked ourselves in my room for the rest of the night.

Standing by the foot of the bed, he kissed my neck and lips with an intoxicating gaze, inhaling every part of me, a look that devoured my body in a single second. Even though we were alone, he didn't stop.

I was aroused. He was drunk. And he gladly lent me his mouth, and I accepted (at first) because my mind was on a super rush. His lips pressed against my collarbone, tender and then deep, sucking. His fingers slid down my waist, lower and lower.

"Lo." I let out a ragged breath and tried to hold on to his white button-down, trying to keep my body upright. But the world was dancing, and I wanted nothing more than to be swept up in it—preferably with a thrust and a high.

He retracted and held my cheeks, his amber eyes carrying a strong haze, but not enough for him to be completely gone to booze. He was still with me. Here. For now.

I was sure I resembled the sloppy drunk between the two of us.

"Lily." His lips lifted into a crooked grin. "How do you feel?"

"Wobbly," I admitted. "And horny." The alcohol repressed any embarrassment because I added, "Really horny, actually." But I couldn't find a one-night stand at my *parents'* intimate party. Besides the fact that most were in their fifties, the few young people knew my family too well. I was not in the market to scatter rumors that I cheated on Loren Hale. We were still pretending to be a couple, after all.

He kept smiling. "Is that how you get guys hard? Blunt honesty?"

My eyes immediately fell to his groin. "It doesn't seem to be working on you," I countered. I slipped out of his arms and found his stowaway of Macallan in my desk drawer. I uncapped it and took a quick swig. His face darkened, and he yanked the bottle away from me. He put the rim to his lips and drank a large gulp, his throat bobbing three times.

He set the bottle back on the desk. "You're always horny. I'd have an eternal hard-on if that's all it took."

My mind started to wander to sinful places, thinking about what exactly would get Loren Hale off. But this was Lo. My best friend. A relationship I couldn't devalue with a quick lay. We've crossed lines a few times before, but I was determined to never jump over the ultimate line—the one that ends with him inside of me, with the highest, brightest climax.

"I usually don't say things," I admitted. "I just *do* things."

He gave me a bitter smile. "I bet you give a spectacular blow job."

I was about to offer one, but I remembered who he was and my throat went dry again. I held out my hand for the Macallan. "Hit me," I said.

He laughed as he pressed the bottle to his lips again. "Cute." He took another long sip. He was always so territorial over his booze.

I stomped back over to the drawer and fished out an airplane bottle of vodka.

He raised his eyebrows. "You don't have anything to chase that with, big shot."

I shrugged, screwed off the cap, and tossed the liquor back in my throat.

"Hey!" he shouted and rushed to my side just as the liquid burned its way down my esophagus. I coughed roughly. *I'm on fucking fire*, I thought. He snatched the bottle away from me, but eighty percent was already invading my stomach.

My nose crinkled in disgust. "Why do you do that?" I asked. I've seen him drink straight liquor. I rub my hand on my tongue, trying to get rid of the taste. *Ugh.*

He just laughed and let me complain for a few minutes, and then the alcohol slowly began to warp my mind, turning my lustful thoughts on overdrive. I craved *touch*. For hands to slide up and down my legs and thighs.

I plopped on the edge of the bed, my eyes drifting over Lo's body. My gaze fell to his ass as he stared out the window, where he was mesmerized by the twinkling Christmas lights and the flutter of snow.

I wanted sex.

I wanted to feel as good as he was feeling. Alcohol made him relaxed, at ease, and I yearned for that type of temperate peace.

"Lo," I breathed. "Are we still pretending?"

His eyes met mine. "I'll be sleeping in your room tonight because we're supposed to be dating. So . . . yes."

"Can I do something?" My eyelids felt heavy from the liquor, and hopefully my voice was not so slurred.

He didn't even hesitate. "Sure," he said. "I can wait in your father's study. I don't think there's anyone there."

He moved toward the door, about to give me privacy for self-love. But that's not what I wanted. "Wait," I called out, my heart beating rapidly. His feet halted in the middle of the floor, and he spun around, facing me with the tilt of his head.

"You can stay," I told him. "Right there. Just . . . stay right there."

I slid underneath the covers and tried to avoid his gaze as I fumbled with my dress. I pulled the fabric over my head and threw it to the floor—along with my panties. I had enough sense to keep my strapless bra on at least. Not that it was covering much.

Now situated, I looked back at him. An amused expression danced across his face. "How drunk are you?" he asked.

Truthfully, I hoped I wouldn't remember doing this in the morning. That didn't end up happening, though. "Enough," I said. *Enough to touch myself in front of you.*

He licked his bottom lip and held up the bottle to his mouth. He waited to see if I'd go through with it. My fingers dipped between my legs, finding the soft, wet spot that ached for touch. My breath deepened as soon as my fingers pulsed along my clit, and I basked in the way it lit up my core.

I stared longingly at his pants, imagining his cock that I never really saw during our college years. I never wanted his penis to spike my temptations, so I avoided eye contact with it most days. But that night, I didn't care about any of that. Sex was on my mind, and it wanted something *more.*

His fingers traveled to the button on his pants, and my breath hitched as he pushed it slowly through the hole.

I looked at him questioningly. What was he doing?

"If you want to watch me while you get yourself off," he said, "you might as well do it the right way, love." He tugged down his pants to his ankles and slowly stepped out of them. My mouth hung open, and I stopped moving my own fingers in shock.

He was hard.

Not completely, but definitely more firm than before. His tight black boxer briefs exposed every muscle and curve and, of course, the bulge that I fixated on.

"Keep going," he urged.

My fingers reignited at his words, and I moved them faster, my hips writhing and pumping in animation. His cock slowly grew. I was beckoning it to me, like I had become a little snake charmer. I loved that control . . . that power.

I stole a glance and caught Lo drinking in my features, the way my lips parted and my eyes fluttered back. But when we locked gazes, I dropped my focus, his hand disappearing below the hem of his boxer briefs.

A moan caught in my throat as I watched him rub himself beneath the fabric. I couldn't see his cock, not really, but that felt even sexier. More sinful and wrong and just about right.

His heavy breath became deep and rough, as ragged and wanting as mine. "Lily," he groaned. My climax arrived in that idyllic rush, in a tidal wave that blew me over in staggered successions. My body shook and my toes curled, my high blistering me from the inside out. Lo grunted, his breath sharp, and he came right along with me.

The usual shame was absolved by the booze and the reminder that we hadn't broken any rules. I convinced myself that he's probably heard me come in the next room thousands of times. Seeing the act couldn't have been much different. And I had never done something like this with any other guy before.

It felt special.

I turned to ask him if we could do it again. Once was never enough.

He saw the desperation before I uttered a word.

"If you do it in front of me again, I'll have to fuck you," he said.

"Have to or want to?" I asked in confusion.

He smiled easily, but never gave me a clear answer. "I may not get hard when you tell me you're horny, but I'm still a guy. And you still have rules. Ones that I won't take advantage of when you're drunk."

"So when I'm sober?"

His smile turned mischievous. "I'm going to take a shower."

He gripped the neck of the Macallan. I must have looked disappointed still because he went to my closet instead of the bathroom. He pulled out a pink Victoria's Secret shoebox from the bottom and set it gently on the bed beside me. He knew it was filled with some of my toys. The gesture was kind.

He tucked a stray piece of hair behind my ear and kissed me on the forehead. "Merry Christmas, Lil," he said and left for the bathroom.

He never came back. I spent the next four hours in a self-love coma until I passed out. In the morning, I found him asleep on the tiled bathroom floor hugging an empty bottle. We never spoke about it again. I buried the memory with my fantasies, and I've always believed he lost the memory to his booze.

Forty-four

Loren Hale

can't believe you're fucking engaged," Ryke tells me.

We stretch by the small koi pond at the edge of our property, trying our best to run without nearing the wrought-iron gates. Paparazzi camp on the street, peering through the gate that does little in terms of privacy. Rose already called a landscaper to plant tall hedges, but they won't be finished for a whole month.

"In a scandal management perspective, marriage is the clear solution," Connor says. He stretches his quads on the ground.

"Yes, because now people will think Lily's an adulterer and not just cheating on her college boyfriend," Ryke retorts.

Connor stares him down. "Society believes marriage shows commitment, a stronger bond." He stands to his feet. "Not to mention gossipmongers eat up a good love story. And what's better than love uniting a sex addict and an alcoholic?"

"Aren't you supposed to be in New York right now?" Ryke snaps back, surrendering the fight. Everyone has an opinion about the engagement, but the only one that matters to me is Lily's. "I thought Rose was running around with her fucking head off her shoulders."

All of our family's companies have been hit financially from the scandal, but unlike Fizzle and Hale Co., Calloway Couture is a young business already on shaky ground. The blow toppled it over. The menswear line that she's been slaving over for months—the one I briefly modeled for—is being reviewed for Fashion Week. Even Connor said that the likelihood of the line surviving is slim to none. So she's going to be pulled from the show, two department stores just dropped her, and she had to let go her assistants, including Lily. Rose won't tap into her trust fund to pay her employees, and she's losing money too quickly to keep them.

"She called and told me not to come," Connor admits. "She doesn't want me to be in the way."

"Is Sebastian there?" I ask. I can see that scheming motherfucker trying to whisper his awful opinions about Connor into Rose's ear. With the slow annihilation of her company weighing on her, she must be vulnerable.

"He's been helping her with the line. I'm sure he's there. Why do you ask?"

I should tell Connor that Sebastian is not fond of him, but he probably already picked up those signals. I should *definitely* mention how Sebastian is most likely plotting a way to cut him out of Rose's life. But Lily still needs those tests.

"No reason," I say with a shrug.

He stares at me for a long moment, disbelieving, but he doesn't prod further. We start walking back toward the house, our shoes crunching the stones on the path.

"Speaking of Calloway girls," Connor says, "I read that Daisy is doing a spread in *Vogue*. Is that true?" After Lily and I talked with the lawyers, Daisy went to stay at her parents' house again. Her modeling career catapulted because of the scandal. Magazines and photographers are lining up to book her for five-page spreads, labeling her as a "sex symbol" in ads that transform the sixteen-year-old into a man's wet fantasy. They call her a young Brooke Shields, but comparing her to another teen icon doesn't settle my stomach. And my blood is on boil, angry that anyone is willing to exploit that girl.

What's worse, her own mother booked her the jobs. But it's not my place to stick up for Daisy. I often wonder whose it is. Poppy has taken sanctuary at her small house in Philly, trying to protect her four-year-old daughter from the paparazzi. Rose is frazzled enough with her fashion line, and Lily and I are just trying to keep our heads on straight.

So who's protecting Daisy?

Her parents sure as hell aren't.

"I'm not sure," I admit. "I haven't talked to her in a while."

"She's doing it," Ryke says. "She says it's tasteful or whatever." He shakes his head, disgruntled by the situation. "She was a high fashion model and overnight she became a fucking supermodel, and instead of sheltering her from the media, her fucking mother is pushing her into it. I think I hate that woman."

"You and me both," I say, "and since when are you talking to Daisy?"

He gives me a glare. "Don't get onto me about that shit," he snaps. "She needs a friend."

"You know, I heard about that recession of sixteen-year-old girls," Connor says. "It must be difficult for her to find a friend her own age."

I smile and Ryke glowers. "Fuck off, Connor," he snaps. "You know what all her prep school friends are doing? They keep asking her if she's a sex addict too. As if it's genetic. She needs someone who knows Lily, who fucking understands what's going on."

"So she needs you," I say like he's an idiot.

Ryke throws up his hands and stops walking. "For fuck's sake," he exclaims. "I'm giving her rock climbing lessons, not taking her on a date. We're *friends*. The perverts who stare at her in magazines may forget she's sixteen, but I won't." He starts uncapping his water bottle. "I also thought we talked about badgering me. We made a fucking deal in Cancun, remember?"

I won't admit it, but there's a piece of me that's lashing out in guilt. I should be the one talking to Daisy and being a friend to her, yet I'm swamped in my own bullshit. If I was a better person, I'd probably actually thank Ryke. She does need someone to talk to, even if that someone has to be my hotheaded half brother.

When we start walking again, Ryke ignites a conversation I thought we dropped at the beginning of our run. "Maybe you should start a company about pissing people off. You can call it Bastards-R-Us."

I knew I shouldn't have told him about accepting my trust fund or being obligated to build a company from scratch, like I'm a little kid playing with Legos. Ryke is vehemently against anything that puts me in contact with my father. He even went so far as offering me half his inheritance.

I turn around and he walks right into my chest. He takes a step back and glares. "What? You can dish it out, but you can't take it?"

"I'm not taking your goddamn money," I sneer. "Stop bringing it up."

"Children," Connor says, breaking our feud. "As entertaining as this is, doesn't Lily have a Stats exam in a half hour?"

I glance down at my watch and curse. We're supposed to be escorting her to her class, since she refused to accept the bodyguard her father wanted to hire for her. It was a generous offer that Poppy and Daisy accepted. Rose was too fucking stubborn, and Lily didn't want to be "shadowed by a big beefy guy," which I took to mean she doesn't want to be tempted by someone that isn't me.

We jog back to the house quickly, but Lily isn't in the kitchen where I left her. She's become sedentary since the leak, moving at a snail's pace. So I can't imagine she wandered too far. I'm about to check the living room when I hear the pipes groan through the walls.

"Do you hear that?" I ask, turning to Connor and Ryke for clarification.

"Sounds like someone's taking a Jacuzzi bath," Connor tells me. That doesn't make any sense. Lily took a shower this morning. Why would she need to bathe again?

Holy fuck.

My first thought: she's masturbating. My second: she slit her wrists. The second thought propels me into hyper-drive. I am running up the fucking staircase before I can think anything else. I must look scared out of my mind because Ryke and Connor are right behind me. Maybe they fear it too.

I'd like to believe Lily couldn't reach a low like that, but I'd be fooling myself. I've been there. I know she has too. It's what happens when you hit a bottom that you can't crawl out from.

I push through the door, envisioning her cold, lifeless body. She jumps, and I don't have time to breathe in relief. Because if she's not dead, it means she's masturbating.

I can't believe this is how my world works.

Bubbles cover her naked body but don't hide her cheeks that burn bright red. Connor and Ryke stumble in behind me and then Connor swivels right back around. "Sorry."

Ryke blocks the door so Connor can't leave.

"Get out!" Lily yells at them.

I haven't moved closer, but she is bathing in guilt. You don't just shower and then fifteen minutes later hop into a bubble bath.

"No, stay," I tell them.

I've chastised her about porn.

I've pleaded with her to be honest with me.

Obviously, I need to find different fucking methods to make her stop doing this shit. I don't want to embarrass her, but how else is she going to stop?

Ryke spreads his arms in the doorway, sufficiently blocking Connor's exit.

"Really?" Connor raises his brows.

Ryke shrugs, and Connor shields his eyes with his hand as he backs into the counter.

I keep my gaze on Lily.

She avoids me and the two guys. "Make them leave," she says, looking anywhere but here. "I have to get changed. What time is it?" She acts like nothing's wrong. Like she's innocent in all of this.

"Why are you taking a bubble bath?" I ask, sitting on the porcelain ledge.

She shrinks back and begins descending, her chin disappearing beneath the suds. "I dropped my ring into the trash. And then after I fished it out, I smelled like our leftover sausage, which is not a pleasant stench. So I decided to take a bath, but I dozed off. Baths do that, you know. They're like nap-whisperers or summoners or whatever."

"Is the shower broken?"

She shakes her head. "You know that pink soap ball—I saw it on the counter just before I hopped in the shower. And curiosity just kind of overtook me. I was hoping it'd turn this thing pink." She holds up her left hand, flashing the diamond. "But alas, soap chemicals are inferior to shiny rock." Her eyes flicker nervously to Ryke, who stares at her, unflinching. "This is awkward."

"Not for me," Ryke replies.

She points to Connor, who still covers his eyes. "You're making Connor uncomfortable," she tells me. "You have done the impossible."

"I'm not uncomfortable, Lily," Connor says. "I'm just not looking forward to the two-hour lecture from your sister about female privacy." But he must know what I'm trying to do because he stays here, and when he lowers his hand, he nods to me like I'm doing something right.

Lily pales a little, realizing *Connor* is not going anywhere. "Don't you think you can give me more privacy if you went in the other room?"

"Believe me, you don't want to know what I think right now."

Her eyes flit around the room again. She knows she's been caught, but she won't admit it. Normally, I'd yell, maybe say a few encouraging words, and then dial Allison's number so she could give Lily a proper lecture. But yelling does nothing, and Allison isn't her therapist anymore.

I know what I have to do.

"You have an exam to get to," I remind her. "So why don't you finish what you started and then we'll head on out."

She blinks a couple times. "What—what are you talking about?"

"Finish up and then we'll leave," I repeat, unwilling to clarify. She has to admit it herself.

"I'm done, so can you hand me that towel?"

"You're done?"

"Yeah."

"Are you sure?"

"I don't smell like garbage anymore, so I call it a bathing success."

"Maybe you misunderstood me," I say dryly. "Finish fucking yourself." I'm angrier than I thought. In my head, I meant to say *finish pleasing yourself,* but my mouth had a different agenda.

Her eyes bug in horror, and I refuse to back down. *Stay strong. Be tough.* She doesn't need a hug or to be coddled anymore.

"Can I talk to you alone?" she asks, refusing to look at the two guys that make this situation really fucking uncomfortable. That's the point, though. This isn't supposed to be easy for her.

"No," I snap. "I know what you were doing. *You* know what you were doing. And Connor and Ryke do too. It's not a fucking secret."

Her nose dips below the water, and in seconds, she's about to submerge to hide from us. I reach out and put my hand underneath her arm, holding her upright to face her problem.

She stares dazedly at the bubbles, and a part of me wants nothing more than to climb into the bath and pull her into my arms. To hug her and tell her that everything is going to be okay. But that's how it begins. She self-medicates her sadness and anxiety with sex, and I let her do it too many times before. I have watched this girl fall into the cycle of addiction, and she's jumping onto those tracks again.

"I can't be around you twenty-four seven," I tell her. "You have to figure this out, Lil. You can't masturbate." How many times do I have to say the words for her to understand them? How many times did I have to hear *no more booze* to fully accept it? It never gets easier. This is going to be a long-term battle. And I'm prepared to be there for her every fucking step of the way. Even if she wants to drown in this water, I'm going to pull her back up until she's healthy. Until she can stand on her own two feet.

"You don't understand," she starts.

"Lo," Connor cuts in. "If we don't leave soon, she's going to be late for her test."

I nod and then grab the black cotton towel off the rack. "Turn around," I tell Ryke, since Connor has already shifted his view.

When Ryke faces the wall, Lily stands, and I wrap the towel around her. "Get dressed and talk," I say roughly, reminding her I'm still mad.

I lead her into the bedroom and look back to Connor and Ryke. "Can you two check the bathroom for porn and toys?" I ask them. "Destroy the room if you have to."

Ryke looks a little too excited to fuck with my shit.

I follow Lily into the walk-in closet. "What don't I understand, Lil?" I ask as I kneel and push past her shoes, grabbing a large black metal case.

"It helps me. I just needed one minute. That's it . . ." Her words trail as she slowly pulls on her underwear and bra. It's hard not to look. Her frame has always been small and wiry, something I'm attracted to. But when she spins around to search for a pair of pants, I have a clear view of her bare back. Her shoulder blades jut out and her ribs are almost visible by her waist. She's been losing weight again.

"Have you been forgetting to eat?" I ask. She used to do that a lot. Sex occupied her mind more than necessary things—like bathing and eating. If I didn't force her to shower, she'd smell like sex for a whole week. It's not that she doesn't want to get fat. I think she'd prefer to be curvier. She just *literally* forgets.

She sidesteps to look at herself in the full-length mirror, and her face slowly falls. "Oh . . ." She tries to squeeze that inch of fat she was so proud she gained, but she can barely grab at the tight skin on her belly. "Shit."

She avoids my gaze as she zips up her jeans.

"It's not because I'm into self-love again, I promise," she tells me. "I've ruined everything for everyone, and it's the only thing that makes me feel better anymore. I don't have any good distractions like you. I don't have any morning runs, and I'm not about to start a company. School ends in a week, and I just need something for myself."

"If you're trying to convince me to let you masturbate, it's not working," I snap. "It's not going to happen, Lil." I stand to my feet, the black case in my hands. I bought it for her birthday last year. She used to keep some of her toys in this worn Victoria's Secret box. At the time, I thought it was a great present, now I'm ready to light it on fire.

When she finishes dressing, her eyes fall to the case in my hands. "What are you doing with that?"

"I'm throwing it away."

Her head whips back and forth, and she tries to tug the case from me in desperation. "You said we could still use them," she pleads. "Together, I mean. Not by myself. I won't ever use them by myself." It's true that I kept them, intending to use them on her when she was ready. But I don't know if she'll ever be ready, and leaving them here for a *what if* isn't worth the risk.

"They're not staying."

She tries to bring the case to her chest, but I hold it firmly in my hand and shoot her a look. "We're not five-years-old fighting over a fucking comic book," I tell her. "If this was a bottle of Maker's Mark, what would you want me to do?"

Her eyes widen at the comparison and she suddenly lets go.

"I'm sorry." It sounds more like an impulse than something sincere.

"I don't accept your apology."

Her mouth drops, and I point between us. "Me and you," I say. "We're in a fight. And if you don't start listening to me, we're going to have serious problems, Lily. I'm holding up my end. I haven't touched a drink. You have to start holding up yours." I know it's harder in a different way, but the porn and the masturbating shouldn't be her big issues. It should be the actual sex.

She stares at me for a long moment, and I wonder what she actually heard from my speech. "We're in a fight?" she asks, shock and hurt crossing her face.

I knew I shouldn't have started with that.

"Yeah, how does it feel?" It doesn't happen often.

She looks panic-stricken, and I realize that the fear of losing me . . . of losing *us* is what really motivates her. She motions to the case. "Burn it. Do what you need to do." She shoves it against my chest and tries to push me out the door. I force myself not to smile because the "tough love" is actually working. I'd rather not ruin it with a momentary grin.

"No masturbating," I tell her again.

She nods wildly. "I know. None. Not at all. Scout's honor." She holds up three fingers. I don't believe her completely, but at least she's come around from denying it.

Now I just have to bring her to the exam on time.

Forty-five

Lily Calloway

I don't have time to think about my fight with Lo, being caught by all three guys, or the fact that paparazzi sprung up like woken zombies as soon as I arrived on campus. Someone leaked my class schedule to the press, and I sprinted into the building to avoid them.

I'm going to fail the exam anyway, but Lo and Connor would never let me skip. I leave the guys in the lobby to wait, and I jog up the staircase to the second floor. My plan is to slip into the back of the auditorium before anyone can see me. I'll take the test, turn it in, and leave. How hard can that be?

I swing the door open and stop cold at the top of the auditorium-style room. All three hundred students are already nestled in their seats while TAs walk up the aisles to pass out the exams.

I'm late.

And there's no open seat anywhere in sight. Oh wait . . .

I spot one in the middle aisle of the middle row. There's not much room to squeeze past people, and I imagine disturbing everyone as I hop over thirty bodies to reach my seat. I don't want to be *that* person. Everyone always gives the late-arrival dirty looks, and since I've been on the news for the past couple of weeks, I can't imagine the looks being the normal kind of dirty. They'd be dirty with an extra pinch of malice.

My throat goes dry and my palms turn clammy. I'm about to

sprint out and make up some lame excuse to Lo, but the professor notices my lingering presence.

"Miss Calloway," he calls.

I freeze, and like a tsunami, all three hundred bodies rotate to set their inquisitive gazes on me. If this is what being an actress feels like, I want no part of it.

"Come see me down here, please." The professor motions for me.

I suck in a shallow breath and descend the carpeted stairs, trying to avoid all the eyes. Not even halfway there, some guy coughs into his hand. On the second cough, I hear "whore."

That's original.

Two more steps and someone else calls me a skank, louder this time. I glance toward the noise and I see a girl elbowing the guy in the ribs.

Five more steps and the voices start to rise as people talk to their friends.

"All right, settle down," the professor tells them.

"Go back to Penn!" a guy yells. Voices escalate and cheer in agreement.

"Better yet, go to Yale! I hear they like filth!" I don't know what that person has against Yale, but I try to keep my cool. I'm almost to the bottom of the auditorium, and I silently curse myself for walking in on the second floor.

"Shut up!" A girl's voice pitches over the talking. Huh . . . someone's on my side? "We're trying to take a test here!" Maybe not.

"Quiet!" the professor shouts, angrily now. "Everyone. The tests are out, and that means the next person who speaks gets a zero." The room hushes instantly, and I finally reach my destination.

The professor is middle-aged and always wears a nice button-down with slacks. He takes out a manila envelope from his briefcase and hands it to me. My name is scribbled across the front.

"I've spoken to your other professors," he says in a low voice so only I can hear. "We've agreed that your presence for finals week will only disturb the other students. Your exam today and your finals from all your classes are in that folder. You can turn it into my mailbox by the last day of finals."

"So they're like take-home tests?" I ask, a little confused.

"Essentially, yes. There's no reason for you to be on campus for one last week. You'll distract everyone. You've already wasted . . ." He looks at the clock. "Five minutes of their time. For some, that could cost them a letter grade."

"I'm sorry."

"It's all right. Just return the exams on time, and if you could, exit out this door." He motions to the one behind him, the one where I won't need to walk up all those stairs.

I say a quick thanks and then disappear quickly out the double doors. I peek into the envelope, all the tests nestled inside. It's generous. They could have easily just failed me. But it also reminds me how my life is changing. I can't even sit in a classroom anymore. What is next year going to be like? Will the professor give me all the tests to take home? Or maybe they're hoping I'll be expelled from Princeton before that happens.

But with my father's lawyers defending my stay here, I know I'll be back next year.

Walking down the hall, I find Lo, Connor, and Ryke sitting in the lobby where I last left them, waiting for me. They talk quietly among each other. I raise my hand to wave and call to them, but a body steps in front of me, blocking my path.

"Hey, aren't you the infamous Lily Calloway?"

He speaks loud enough that I see Lo's head perk up. His eyes hit mine and they fill with concern.

"Are you deaf?" The guy laughs.

I meet his pretty green eyes and scan his blond hair, a twenty-something guy, tall with muscular arms. He sports a black and orange Princeton tee.

"I'm Lily," I confirm. My eyes flicker past his body again. Lo is on his feet, but he hesitates about reaching my side.

Is he still angry at me?

Oh jeez, we're still in a fight, aren't we?

My heart beats crazily, and I focus my attention back on the blond. "I'm also leaving." I sidestep and he follows suit, trapping me to this spot in the hall.

I hear Lo's shoes on the tile floor, and I try to relax.

"Why would you want to do that?" Blond Guy asks. "I heard that you love going down, and I've got something here for you." He grabs my hand, and fear bobs my throat. Oh my God. I never thought this could happen in a hallway (slightly empty, albeit) during the middle of the day. Maybe he thinks I'm as wanting and easy as they say I am on the news. Maybe he believes I won't care or fight him. That has to be it.

But I'm not that girl. Sure, I may have played into his advances a year ago, but now they literally curdle my stomach. I recoil and try to untangle from his strong hold, but he grips my hand and places it right on his pants.

Whatever I feel—it doesn't last long because Lo grabs his shoulders from behind and throws his back into the wall.

I flinch, not accustomed to physical aggression from Lo, not even when he pinned Mason against my car. And he eases off the guy within a second, his eyes pulsing with something hot and black.

"This is why America invented the sexual offender registry, you sick fuck," Lo spits.

"I didn't touch her," Blond sneers, the veins in his neck bulging. "Your slutty girlfriend was all over me."

"I was not," I snap, about to charge him myself. I don't have nails, but I'm not below slapping.

Ryke grabs me, and I squirm, trying to go help Lo. "Lily, stop," Ryke says, holding me tighter.

"You want your dick to be touched so badly, fine," Lo growls, and he does something that causes me to pause, going quiet and motionless in Ryke's arms.

Lo slams the guy again, his back digging further into the wall, and he puts his hand over the guy's pants. The icky feeling I had for touching Blond vanishes. I'm not the only who did it. Though, Lo volunteered his hand.

Blond thrashes, and Lo must grip hard because his face contorts into a pained wince. "Get the fuck off me."

"What? You don't like it anymore?"

"I can sue you for harassment."

"Let's play that fucking game," Lo replies. "Let's see whose lawyers are better. I'm a goddamn Hale. My family eats shitty fucks like you for brunch. Don't you ever force yourself on a girl, ever again." Lo loosens his grip, and then he steps back from him. Blond hesitates to retaliate, but his eyes ping from Lo, to Ryke, to Connor, and he mutters a curse and retreats down the hall.

Ryke looks ready to run after him and take a swing.

Lo's chest rises, his hands clenching and unclenching. I see Jonathan in his words and actions, and I know the same comparison must infiltrate his head. Sober Lo still does mean things, and I'm not sure what the right way to protect me was—or what I could have done to help. But I do realize how much he hates even the notion of turning into Jonathan Hale. And for sacrificing a large chunk of his heart to come to my aid, I am very, *very* grateful. What he just did for me—it wasn't easy.

His eyes find me. I step forward and put my arms around him, wanting to hold him and thank him all in one swoop.

Drunk Lo wouldn't have been here.

I'd either have to give in to this guy's advances, scream for help and hope that a Ryke Meadows was around, or try to find a way to fight off a six-foot guy.

Lo kisses the top of my head, and says, "Are you sure you don't want a bodyguard? I can't always be around you, Lil."

I've contemplated it. The idea of a guy shadowing me is a little unsettling, but after this, it's definitely safer. "Only if you want me to."

"We can pick out someone who's really ugly," he offers with a small smile. It'll make him feel better, and that matters a lot to me.

I nod. "Okay."

I separate from Lo and hold up the manila folder to Connor, who has been staring at it in curiosity for the past couple of minutes. "All my exams," I explain. "The professors don't want me on campus anymore." For obvious reasons. And right now, I don't want to be here all that much either.

Being a sex addict does not give guys the right to touch me. I didn't think that would be an issue until now. Is this a problem that will persist for the rest of my life? Or something that will die when the media loses interest in me?

Only time has the answers.

Forty-six

Lily Calloway

This would go a lot faster if you'd just let me bubble in the two other scantrons while you work on that one," Sebastian tells me. He sits on the Queen Anne chair smoking his cigarette as he watches me hunched over piles of papers and scantrons. I'm basically copying the answers from Sebastian's old exams to my finals, which feels more like cheating than simply memorizing.

But I'm fairly certain that actually letting him bubble in the answers would be cheating. "I'm not a cheater." I cringe. "I'm not a *complete* cheater. Don't tempt me to your dark side."

He blows out a line of smoke. "Your angelic image was tarnished far before you ever accepted my help. You and I aren't so different, Lily. We both enjoy an unhealthy amount of co—"

I throw a pillow at him, and he catches it with his free hand, trying to protect his cigarette. Some things haven't changed after I was outed as a sex addict. Sebastian is still Sebastian. And apparently he's seen enough rich-kid debauchery that my secret was hardly anything riveting. His words.

So I called him to bring over old exams for all my finals, and he hasn't stared at me any differently than before the scandal. Which is kinda nice.

The front door bangs open.

I hurriedly shuffle the old exams into a pile. My head whips around, trying to find a good hiding place. I lift up the sofa cushion and stuff them under it.

When I meet Sebastian's gaze, he looks like he could rip out my jugular for putting his old exams with the dust bunnies and rusted pennies. Oops.

Connor's voice echoes from the kitchen. "We can keep brainstorming. We'll come up with something, Lo." They must be discussing the start-up company that Lo has to pitch to his father. He has a couple days left to choose a platform, and he enlisted Connor's expertise. They spent all morning at a meeting to throw around ideas—and when I say "meeting," I mean they sat in Starbucks.

They both saunter into the living room, Connor carrying a tray of coffees and a small pastry. "I thought you could use some test-taking boosts," he tells me. Oh, this is why I love Connor Cobalt as a tutor. I beam, but that falls suddenly at the realization that I'm (A) Lying to him. (B) Cheating. (C) Team Sebastian. (D) Accepting the treats despite all of the above.

I say thanks and scoop the whipped cream from the coffee with my finger. Sin does taste delicious.

Lo stands off to the side, busily texting on his phone. Six days have passed since our bathroom fight over my self-love, and he has yet to forgive me completely. Our fights used to revolve around our addictions—sometimes we'd just drown in them for an extended week, ignoring each other. But this is a *real*, normal fight that hurts more than I ever thought it would.

"Lo, did you come up with any good ideas for the company?" I ask. I offered to help, but every time I suggested something, he told me to focus on my health. I grab the chocolate-filled croissant on the table and tear off small pieces to eat. I dunk a portion in my coffee.

Lo acknowledges me, and his eyes lighten when he sees me eating. "The top choice is a food truck." He doesn't look enthusiastic about that idea.

I take a slurp from my coffee. "You have more time," I remind him. "It's not over until the fat lady sings . . ." I narrow my eyes. No, that's not right. "Well, in this case, the fat lady would be your father."

He smiles, and he must catch the momentary lapse of happiness toward me because his lips downturn quickly. He closes off the conversation with the shift of his body.

We're still fighting apparently.

"Where's Rose?" Sebastian asks, lighting another cigarette.

Connor stares at it, letting irritation cross his face, his chest inflating with a deep inhale. "She's taking a final, and you shouldn't be smoking in here."

"And yet . . ." Sebastian blows out a short puff. "I am."

Lo's phone rings, and he slips into the kitchen to answer his cell.

Connor steps toward Sebastian, and my evil tutor suddenly springs from his chair, both guys standing their ground with superiority. They each believe they're better than the other. I'm not accustomed to intellectual standoffs.

Sebastian appraises the cigarette in his fingers. "She hardly cares if I smoke, you know. If you did it, she'd drop you like she did her last boyfriend. She found a pack of cigarettes in his coat pocket. Next day, he was gone. Lasted one taxingly long week."

"You planted the cigarettes on him, didn't you?"

Sebastian takes a long drag and breathes the smoke right into Connor's face. "Perceptive."

Connor doesn't even flinch. "Maybe you should be."

Sebastian lets out a laugh. "You don't think I am? I know that Rose has spent almost no time with you since Calloway Couture has suffered. I know that she cried on my shoulder two nights ago, not yours. I know that she called me, not you, to help pack up her office."

She already started boxing her workplace?

"You feel threatened by me," Connor states, stepping forward so only a small space separates his body from Sebastian's. Connor has the height advantage—he usually does.

"By Connor Cobalt? A guy who is willing to sell out anyone if the benefit weighs on his side. No, I am not threatened by you. I just hate you." Sebastian gives him a long once-over. "Rose always did too. I don't know what you said that changed her mind."

"She never hated me," Connor says casually.

"She bitched about you all the time in prep school. She'd return from Model UN, and I'd have to listen to her drone on about how *Richard* made a treaty against her country's best interests. How *Richard* won the highest honor for countering terrorist actions." Model UN sounds mildly intense and slightly scary.

"For such a smart guy, you really know nothing," Connor says, his voice even-tempered. "She liked me, Sebastian. She *bitched* to you because she was attracted to *me*, a guy that riled her more than placated her, and that pissed her off." Connor steals the cigarette from his fingers. "And if you truly cared for that girl, you'd realize that every time you smoke in this house, you set off her OCD."

Sebastian's lip twitches.

"You didn't know that, did you?" Connor says. "While she cries on your shoulder about her company, yesterday she stayed the night at *my* apartment. And I spent four fucking hours calming her down because *you* put wild ideas in her head. You smoke, you mess with her things, and you return her to me restless. She paces back and forth, muttering idioms that make no sense, and I have to figure out how to put her back together. You are not a friend to her; you're a parasite."

I drop my pastry on my lap.

Sebastian is left speechless, his lips pressed tightly together.

Connor won this round. But when Rose enters the mix, I just hope he's able to win the whole battle.

After Connor snuffs out the cigarette on his empty cup, he masterfully bottles his annoyance toward Sebastian, and his eyes fall to the scattered scantrons. "You should be taking those in a quiet testing environment, preferably somewhere clean." He collects the gum wrappers and Sebastian's crinkled magazines, tossing them in a nearby trash bin.

"She's fine," Sebastian says, finding his voice again.

"What are you even doing here?" Connor asks. "If Lily's taking her finals, she doesn't need to be tutored anymore."

"I'm monitoring the exams so she doesn't cheat," he lies. I want to snort, given the fact that minutes ago he offered to bubble-in my finals for me.

"I can do that," Connor says. "Go propagate cancer somewhere else." He takes a seat next to me—right on the same cushion where I buried the tests.

I hear the *crunch* and the *crackle* of papers, muffled but still distinguishable. I close my eyes and count to five in my head. This cannot be happening.

"Lily," Connor says tensely, "am I sitting on porn?"

What?! I open one eye and meet Connor's gaze. I expect him to be calm in the normal I'm-Connor-Cobalt-and-I-don't-show-real-emotions kind of way. Instead, he wears disappointment fairly well. This is the moment where I can either out myself as a somewhat-cheater or take the hit for stashing porn. There's no contest.

I spent days without self-love or any kind of sex from Lo, trying desperately to return to good faith with him. All of that will be squandered in one moment if he thinks it's dirty mags. And I'm so sick of lying.

"It's not porn," I confess.

Connor stands and lifts up the cushion. He stares at the papers, the top exam with a random name (Jeremy Gore) and a letter grade (A-).

He shakes his head. "I knew it," he says rather calmly, adding all the pieces together so easily. Must be a smart-person trait. I bet Sherlock Holmes was a certified genius.

Sebastian rolls his eyes and takes out his phone, as if this is all very dull for him, but I imagine that Connor has him shaking internally, a few more moves away from dethroning him in Rose's life.

I gather up the tests before Connor tries to toss them out. I still have finals to take. "I can explain," I say as I straighten out the papers on my lap.

He returns the cushion to its original state, and before I can offer an explanation, the front door swings open.

"Just because the bike can reach a hundred fifty doesn't mean you should go that fucking fast. You nearly cut off a car behind you."

"You're exaggerating," Daisy says.

"He honked at you."

"Or he honked at *you*. You were riding my brake lights."

"I was ten fucking feet behind you, and next time, I'm taking you to a racetrack."

"Really?" I can hear the smile behind the word.

"Yeah, if you want to fucking kill yourself, at least you won't cause a five-car pileup while you're doing it."

When they walk into the living room, Daisy is smiling from ear to ear. Both carry motorcycle helmets under their arms, reminding me that Ryke agreed to Daisy's offer. About a week ago, he told her he would keep the black Ducati in return for teaching her how to ride *safely*, which must be a hard job with Daisy as a pupil.

"You were supposed to tutor her," Connor says to Sebastian, actual anger seething in his eyes. It's kind of terrifying.

Ryke and Daisy go quiet by the staircase, realizing they walked in on a . . . situation.

Sebastian pockets his phone in his blazer. "You and I both know that one is a lost cause. I did her a favor."

"She doesn't need another handout." He invades Sebastian's

space again. "You're a lazy, sanctimonious prick who profits off of apathetic trust fund babies. The students who need those exams are the ones who can't afford them. You *knowingly* perpetuate a repugnant cycle." He stares at him like he's shit on the bottom of his shoe. "You keep the rich kids stupid and the poor kids poor."

"What's going on?" Rose's voice ices the entire room.

No one moves. She stands near Daisy and Ryke, who must have left the front door open. No one heard her walk in.

Sebastian slips out of Connor's blockade. "I caught your boy-friend smoking that." He points to the snuffed cigarette in the coffee cup. "And then he accused me of helping Lily cheat."

Connor looks like he could kick Sebastian's ass. And that face—one of pure venom—does not come often. Or at least, I've rarely seen it since we've been friends.

Rose glances at Ryke and Daisy for verification.

"We just got here," Daisy says.

Ryke is not about to vouch for Connor either. They're not the best of friends since their personalities clash more than complement.

Rose doesn't even ask me whether or not Sebastian helped me cheat or if Connor smoked all those cigarettes. I guess she won't trust my answer anyway, even if I give her the right one.

But I have to try. "I did cheat," I tell her in a high voice.

She ignores me. So much for honesty.

My sister approaches both guys and rests her hands on her hips, looking between them. Connor stares at her with such intensity, basically speaking through his soul-bearing eyes.

Rose engages with him, not able to tear away.

Sebastian panics and places a hand on her shoulder. "Rose, he's manipulating you. It's what he does."

Rose flinches.

"Don't doubt yourself," Connor tells her. "Not for this guy, not for anyone."

Rose wavers.

"Think about it," Connor says. "You told me he's profited off of selling old tests before."

"The cigarettes—"

"You have known me for almost ten years. I have held you in my arms. I have kissed you. Have you ever smelled smoke on me before?"

Sebastian cuts in, "Rose, he convinced Brad to forfeit his Lambda Kai presidency so someone else could take the position. He can make people do things they would never do."

Connor stares down at her. "I would never manipulate you." But he doesn't deny that he's done it before, that he uses whatever power he has to get what he wants. I always knew Connor did things for his benefit, not out of the kindness of his heart, but hearing it from someone else, well, it makes it real.

Sebastian says, "He dated Hayley Jacobs just so her father would write him a recommendation to Wharton. He's with you because of your name. How many times do I have to tell you that?"

Rose's eyes narrow at Connor. "Did my father write you a recommendation?"

"He offered, yes."

"And you accepted?"

He says nothing.

"Unbelievable." Her face twists like he stomped on her heart. I rise, about to go to her side. But I hesitate as she points a finger at Connor. "You came with me to my parents' Sunday luncheons because you were trying to worm your way into my father's good graces."

"No, I came with you because you're my girlfriend," he says, stepping closer to her.

She raises her chin, which starts to quiver despite her strength. "I trusted you. And all this time—"

"I have *never* lied to you," he says. "You know more about my life than anyone else. I don't share things willingly, you know this about me. Why would I let you in?"

Rose whispers, "You're playing with my head."

"No," he says again, forcefully, so that she understands. "He is."

Sebastian's fingers dig deeper in her shoulder. "You've known me since we were kids," Sebastian says. "I have your best interest, Rose."

But her eyes stay glued to Connor.

"Rose," Connor says with such empathy, gazing at her with passion that nearly stops my heart. "You know me."

She takes a deep breath. "That's just it, Connor, I don't think I do. I don't think anyone really does."

Sebastian begins to smile, and Connor looks about ready to scream.

Rose adds, "I want you to leave."

I can't tell who she directs this to until Sebastian's smile fades completely. "Rose, didn't you hear—"

"I heard you," she says. "I hear you talk badly about Connor every time I'm with you, and while I agree he's not the most forthcoming human being when it comes to his personal life, he's still my boyfriend. I would *never* allow Lily to cheat. I *hate* that you smoke. And I'm *not* going to take your suggestion to quit Calloway Couture. I'm going to unpack my office. I'm going to fight for my company. I'm going to do whatever it takes, and I'm going to stop listening to you tell me that I *can't* beat these odds."

Go Rose. I think we're all smiling. Except for Sebastian.

He shakes his head at her. "I'll call you tomorrow when you're not being so bitchy."

"You won't," she says. "I'm blocking your number. You're not to see me or talk to me. I never want to hear from you again."

His mouth falls. "You would listen to him? Rose, I've known you longer."

"He knows me better."

Sebastian just keeps shaking his head.

Rose glances at Connor, her shoulders locked tight. "Can you please get him out of the house? I need to go . . ." Her eyes flit away, looking for her room as though it's vanished.

"Of course," he says easily. His hand falls to the small of her back, and he whispers something in her ear before kissing her deeply. She returns the affection, but there's sadness in her eyes that wasn't there before—the stress of *everything* weighing on her. And I have a feeling Sebastian has added to it every single day.

When they part, Rose turns to me. And my guards rise. Oh no. She's going to yell at me for cheating. I open my mouth, about to let out a string of sincere apologies, but her arms fling around my shoulders and she pulls me into a big, sisterly hug. One that she rarely gives, even when she's in a good mood.

"I'm sorry," she whispers in my ear. "I love you." I feel her tears on my shoulder. "I'm here if you need me now. I promise."

I don't think I deserve this. I ruined her company, but at the same time, I am overwhelmed at having my sister's support again. She's my biggest and best cheerleader.

So I hug back. I want to ask if she'll be okay with all of the Connor and Sebastian stuff, but she places a kiss on my cheek and spins toward her bedroom on the main floor.

Connor watches her carefully, and Rose meets his gaze for a single second, brushing her tears off her face. I think they can read each other's minds or something because he nods to her and she nods back and disappears.

Connor guides Sebastian toward the exit.

Sebastian's eyes flicker to the exams on my lap.

"You're not getting them back," Connor tells him.

"You know," Sebastian says, "I hope you break her heart. She deserves what's coming to her."

"So do you," Connor says, slamming the door in Sebastian's face.

When the tension begins to drain out of the living room, Ryke says, "Well, I fucking learned something today." His lips rise. "Connor has balls."

Connor takes a breath and any anxiety or anger disappears like the wind, undetectable by the average human eye. "Glad I could entertain you." His eyes flicker between the hallway Rose disappeared down and me.

He chooses me, which only puts a larger pit in my stomach. He stands in front of the couch, his hands slipping into his pockets.

"Do you really see me as an apathetic trust fund baby?" I ask, remembering some of the insults that inadvertently flew my way. I have been lazy and uncaring toward college. I should have tried harder.

"Technically you don't have a trust fund anymore," Connor tells me. His words don't lift my spirits, and I don't deserve a brightened day. I'm at fault here. "You should have told me that you were cheating when I asked."

"I can't pass without the old exams," I defend quickly.

"You can," Connor retorts. "I've tutored you, and I know that if you just studied, you could pass."

"I can't take that chance. I bombed the first two tests. I'm already behind a semester, and if I fail these classes, I'm going to be behind a whole year." I hold the tests to my chest, unwilling to let them go over Connor's moral compass. "It's not cheating. It's beating the system. Everyone does it."

"You've already beat the system by being at Princeton. By being at Penn. If you didn't have your last name, you'd be at a community college. Where you should be, Lily. How many times are you going to beat the system until it beats you to death?" His words are weighted and have more double meanings than I can process.

"You don't need an A. You're going to be fine if you graduate with a low GPA at the bottom of the class. Do yourself a favor. Toss out those tests, and I'll help you take your finals. I'll make sure you learn the material to pass. I promise."

"I have to turn them in by six o'clock today," I say. "That's not possible, Connor."

"They're take-home tests," he reminds me. "You're allowed to use your notes and your book. Just not old exams. We can make it happen."

"We can all help," Daisy exclaims with a smile. "I have the recipe for the perfect study brownies."

Ryke gives her a look.

"Not those kind of brownies."

The undertaking feels bigger than me, but I have support. "You should go talk to Rose," I tell him. I don't want to draw him away from her more than I already have.

"She'll want to be alone right now," he says. I'm not so sure about that, but he adds, "Trust me." And for some reason, I do. Maybe Sebastian is right.

Maybe Connor does have power in his words.

Forty-seven

Lily Calloway

An hour later, I've finished a political science final and moved onto Stats. A tray of warm, gooey brownies emits a sweet chocolate aroma in front of me. I'm basically eating the entire plate. Daisy flips through her motorcycle magazine, not touching a single one.

Ryke left thirty minutes ago, before the brownies were pulled out of the oven. And I suspect if he was here, he would have prodded Daisy until she at least tasted a chunk.

I should be one hundred percent focused on my test, but Lo went upstairs not too long ago. He never said a word about his phone call or my tests. He just disappeared.

I hurry through my Stats exam, unconsciously remembering some of the answers from when I previously bubbled them in with Sebastian. I finish in the next fifteen minutes, guessing on the last two. The book was helpful, but Connor's notes were better. He sat beside me and scribbled down examples that made the harder questions a lot easier.

I can't stop thinking about Lo. Upstairs. He only isolates himself when he's drinking, and since he's sober, I'm not quite sure what alone time for Loren Hale really entails. I worry all the same.

"Can I take a five-minute break?" I ask Connor by my side. "I have to go talk to Lo."

He checks his watch, calculating how long it will take me to finish in time to turn the exams in. "You have ten minutes before I'm coming to collect you. So please don't let me walk in on you and Lo fornicating."

Fornicating. I smile. It's such a fancy word for fucking. "We won't."

I dash upstairs to my bedroom, stopping at the door for a second. I hesitate to walk inside. Maybe he wants to be alone, like really alone. The thought stabs me cold, and I lower my hand from the knob. Is he slowly breaking away from me? Is that it?

My shoulders rise.

I won't let him go so easily.

I open the door and brace myself for what's to come.

Lo sits at the desk, scrolling through different websites on the computer. His back to me, I see him analyzing a business site. When I shut the door, he swivels in his chair and makes note that it's just me before he returns to his laptop.

The casual brush-off stings.

Before our fight, he would have asked me for help. He would have gushed about all of his ideas. I've been his friend in everything for years, and all of a sudden, I've become as useful as the dust on a windowsill.

"Shouldn't you be taking your finals?" he asks.

"I'm on a break," I say, sinking onto the bed.

He focuses on the computer screen.

Is he growing without me? My worst fear may be starting to come true. He's strong, committed, and sober. I'm unhealthy and struggling in my addiction. My weakness is too much for him. I'm pulling him down. I'm a weight.

And I'm losing him. Just like I lost everything else.

"Lo." I try to keep my voice steady.

He faces me this time, concern etching his brow.

I open my mouth, a pain in my heart. "Do you want to break up with me?"

"What?" he chokes out.

"It's just . . . we've never fought for so long before, and I can't tell what you're thinking anymore." My insecurities gush like a busted piñata, and I desperately wish to gather all the candy and stuff it back inside.

"Lil," he breathes, standing. He comes to me and takes my cheeks in his hands, staring down. "Don't ever ask me that again." His voice is soft but still sharp.

"I wouldn't blame you," I say, twisting his T-shirt in my hand. "I mean, I would try to stop you, but I would understand. You're strong and I'm . . ." *A mess.*

He brushes my fallen tears with his thumb. "I had rehab," he reminds me. "I had lots of help, Lil. Your addiction is much different, and there's less support there. I knew I'd be strong and you'd be struggling. It's just the way it is. I'm prepared for this. I won't leave. I won't ever fucking leave."

I'm about to go in for a hug, and he withdraws. "But that doesn't give you the right to fall into your old habits. Okay?"

"I know. I know." I fiddle with my fingers. "Are we still fighting? I mean, I get it if you still want to be in a fight. But I'm sorry. I'm really sorry I let you down." That's not completely right. I think after today, especially my conversation with Connor, I know who I'm disappointing the most. "I'm sorry I let myself down."

His lips rise just a little. "I accept that apology."

He lifts me into a hug, and I promise myself that I'll try harder. Even if everything starts slipping away again, I'll remember this moment, how long it took me to right what I had done wrong. I don't want to start that vicious cycle again. I want to break it. I want to beat my addiction for good, no matter if outside forces pull me down.

I can do it this time.

Please, let me succeed.

Forty-eight

Loren Hale

wish I could give Lily the clear steps to her recovery, the tips in rehab, all the people sharing their stories for hours on end—everything that I had, the things I sometimes take for granted. But recovery for sex addiction is just so subjective and personal. It'll never be the same. All I can do is try to be here for her as best I can, especially after the leak.

I trashed all of her toys, even the vibrator that Ryke found in the bathtub. She's nervous without them, but they're a security blanket that I'm no longer willing to let her have.

Lily groans and collapses on the bed, her hands on her belly. "I'm stuffed."

I smile. I called in three different orders of pasta and pizza from a local Italian place and practically force-fed her garlic bread. We celebrated the end of the semester. She turned her finals in this evening with only minutes to spare. She informed me what happened with Sebastian and Connor, and I'm proud of her for making the right decision.

"Too stuffed to have sex?" I ask. I lift my shirt over my head and toss it aside.

She props her body on her elbows, her eyes wide. "You—you want to have sex with me?" She asks like she's suddenly contagious. This is not the reaction I expected. I thought she'd fling her arms around me and go in for the attack, trying to touch my dick before I could.

But she remains on the bed, her legs curled up underneath her. She's already changed into her pajama shirt—which is my shirt—and I saw her slip on a pair of panties. She usually climbs into bed without them, thinking that the easy entry will entice me to fuck her. I know her games.

Tonight, I plan on having sex with her. For one, I'm horny and I'd really like to fuck my girlfriend. Second, I've finally accepted her apology. Third, she has to see her new psychiatrist tomorrow and I'm worried this guy is going to throw down some abstinence act on her.

I study her from head to toe and decide that I want to tease her a little. Giving in is just too easy. "You're right, maybe we shouldn't. You've been bad." Now in my boxer briefs, I climb onto the bed, where she lies unmoving.

"Bad good or bad bad?" she asks.

"That doesn't make any sense," I say with a smile. I reach toward the nightstand and pause. This would be the moment where I'd grab my whiskey. But in this moment, I only want one thing. And it's not booze.

I open the drawer and fumble around for a condom. As soon as Lily sees the small package, she crawls over to me and holds out both hands like she's trying to catch rain. It's beyond adorable.

"I was bad good, then," she tells me.

"You were bad bad," I refute, not giving her the condom just yet. "What did you learn this week?"

She drops her hands. "Self-love is not for me . . . even in bubbles. People at Princeton hate Yale, and my boyfriend is really sexy when he defends my honor."

"People at Princeton hate Yale?" I ask, dumbfounded.

"Yeah, I didn't get it either."

My eyes catch her ring. In the bathtub, I knew she was lying about wanting to see if the diamond could be dyed pink, but I wonder if she really does dislike it. I've only seen her stare at it with disdain.

"You know," I say, taking her left hand and rubbing my thumb over the diamond. She stiffens a little. "If you hate it, I can always get you a new one. This proposal may have been bullshit, but the engagement is real."

She retracts her hand and shakes her head. "No, it's fine. Girls would die for a ring like this."

"Just because other girls would like that ring doesn't mean you have to."

"It may not be my dream ring," she admits, "but I want to keep it." She points to my other hand, the one with the condom. "Let's get back to what's important here."

I don't give the package to her. Instead, I press my lips to hers, cupping the back of her head to bring her closer to me. She reciprocates instantly and loops her arms around my neck. My mouth melds with Lily's, our tongues brush, and I suck on her bottom lip. She deepens the kiss, her hands running up and gripping my hair. She kisses hungrily, like it's her fucking life force.

I have to break apart just to get air.

Her mouth trails my neck, and her hand moves over my boxer briefs, rubbing my cock. It feels too good to demand that she stop. My hands slide underneath her baggy shirt and find her breasts, grabbing and kneading them until I feel her gasp against my neck.

Her movements start to intensify, and she tugs at my boxer briefs, my cock springing out. *Dammit.* Swiftly, I gather her hands in mine and pull her away from my dick. It takes all my control not to let her pleasure me right away.

She stays on her knees, but they have parted considerably, and I steal a glance down at the spot between her legs. I can already see the wetness seeping through her cotton panties. When I look back up, her eyes haven't moved from mine.

"Can you teach me how to be the good kind of bad?"

Christ. *I want inside of you.*

"It's not easy," I tell her.

"Please."

She's never given over her control during sex. Not like this. And I think it's the perfect time to do something she's been waiting for.

As quickly as I can, I tug down my underwear and toss them to the floor. Still leaning against the headboard, I scoop up the condom from the sheets and tear it with my teeth. She holds out her hands again in that cute little manner. I don't have the will-power right now to let her put it on me without taking her hard and fast. So I ignore her requests and slide the condom along my shaft in two fast motions.

She doesn't say anything, but she scuttles back and lies down, waiting for me to take her, like I'm going to be on top. God, I love that I'm going to fill her with surprise.

"Nope," I say and grab her hand, sliding her back to me. I take hold of her left leg and her hip, lifting her onto my lap with ease. She straddles me and braces herself with her hands on my chest. Her eyes widen in shock.

"I'm . . . we're . . ."

I can't stop grinning.

Her head slowly drops until she's staring at my cock that's right up against her pussy, waiting (rather impatiently) to be inside. She glances back to me. "This isn't on the blacklist?"

"No, love."

She frowns. "Do you think since Dr. Banning isn't my therapist anymore that I can see that list?"

"Even if she's not your therapist, we're still going to obey that list," I tell her. I have no intention of fucking with all the progress she's made. And who knows how long her new psychiatrist will last? "So I don't want you to see it." Not yet at least.

She nods and rises on her knees, acting like she's going to put my cock inside of her. I hold on to her waist, stopping her. She looks confused, and the horny part of me is too. Why the fuck am I dragging this out?

"If you're going to be on top, we have to have rules," I tell her.

"Oh."

"You said you wanted to be good bad."

"I do." She touches my bare chest with her hands, and her eyes fall to my abs. She becomes distracted way too fucking easily.

I tilt her chin up, her eyes landing on mine again. "Don't move."

"What?"

Before I can answer her, I have lifted her by the hips and placed her gently over my cock. Her panties are still on, but I tug the fabric aside and out of my way as I lower her down. She clutches onto my neck and lets out a ragged breath that turns quickly into a moan.

"That's it," I tell her, easing her down onto me. I close my eyes for a second, basking in the tightness, finally inside of her . . . When I fill her completely, she bucks her hips, beginning to rock against me.

I seize her waist again. "Don't move."

She shudders at my words. "Then you move," she pleads.

"I'm taking my sweet fucking time," I reply, running my hand underneath her shirt, massaging her breast once more.

She lets out a long moan and presses her forehead to my shoulder, but she doesn't move her hips this time. "How are you not dying?"

I am. But I want it to last too much to give in to my impulses.

"Lo, I need to come."

"You want to come," I refute. "You don't need to do it." My lips find her ear and I suck gently on the sensitive place. Another staggered breath rumbles through her.

"That's not what it feels like."

I raise her shirt past her belly, but she refuses to disentangle from my shoulders to allow the fabric off her arms and over her head. "And I want you naked, but apparently we all don't get what we want."

She shifts a little, causing her eyes to flutter, but her arms weakly fly to the air. I pull the shirt off, and my eyes fall to her erect nipples, begging for my attention. My tongue flicks over the little buds, and she starts to gyrate against my cock. My whole body ignites, heating up with undeniable pleasure. I'm the one who groans this time, but I manage to stop her again. My hands grip decisively on her hips, causing her to still. I take the opportunity to let them slide to her ass and squeeze.

"If you move again," I tell her, "I'm going to thrust inside you twice and come and then we'll be done for the night." Her mouth forms a perfect O and she keeps shaking her head like I've announced the apocalypse. "Now be a good bad girl and stay still while I fuck you."

Her head reverses course and begins to nod up and down.

I don't mention that I can't stay still much longer either. It's all about perception, and she needs to think I could wait out eternity with my cock nestled firmly inside of her.

After I kiss her lips one last time, I grab onto her ass as tight as I can and buck my hips up. She lets out the most beautiful noise, like I've hit a thousand nerves. I do it again, pulsing my cock up and down, up and down. Fast and slow. Up and down. I thrust my cock so deep that she grabs onto me, trying to hold on. I release one of my hands from her hips to place it on her head, bringing her mouth down to mine. We kiss and fuck, and when she's on the brink, I have to slow down so she doesn't come.

She whimpers against my body, and my breathing becomes ragged as I try to make this last as long as I can. After a while, she presses her lips to my neck, not having enough energy to travel the distance to my mouth. "Please," she pleads, her voice full of sheer want. "Pleasepleaseplease." She kisses my collarbone and it's over at that.

I take her hips in my hands and begin to thrust so hard and fast in her that she starts to shriek. Her waves of pleasure crash into her and flow throw me. She grips the back of my hair, my waist, my arms, my thighs, anything to keep her upright as her orgasm pummels her.

She sinks into my body, and I pull out of her slowly. Exhaustion fills me, and I know this is the hard part. I want her to be satiated; I want one long, rough lay to be enough. One day, I know we'll get there. But today is not that day.

She is already sliding off my body and kneeling beside my waist. I glance at the clock and gauge how much time we have left, and then I feel her take my dick into her palms.

With one hand, I gather her hair out of her face, and she sinks her mouth around my cock. My breathing evens out as I watch her tongue lap at the head and lick all the way down the shaft. It's hot as hell. I close my eyes and relax against her movements. She touches my cock with the perfect amount of force, knowing all the places to suck. And it doesn't take long before I'm rock hard again. Her movements become faster and more determined. I even hold her head steady when she wraps her lips around my long shaft. Her eyes flit up to mine in a doe-eyed way . . . and she has my entire cock in her mouth. This, right here, is what turns me on the most.

She begins to move her mouth back and forth again, and I have to pull her off. "But I want you to come in my mouth," she says.

For fuck's sake. She does not make this easy.

"Well, I want to come in your pussy," I retort. "I see we have a predicament. Should we flip for it?"

"No!"

I grin. "I didn't think so." I roll her onto her back and my hand slides between her legs, feeling just how soaked she is. I know she's on the pill, so I don't bother grabbing another condom. I want to fill her with my cum, to leave myself inside of her all week.

I hover over her body, my eyes on hers. She looks at me like I'm the only man in the world, like she could stay here in this bed forever. We have ten more minutes and that's it, but I don't think she's counting. If her new psychiatrist forces her to be abstinent and this is the last time we can fuck, I'm going to make it worth it. I'm going to make her remember every movement and detail.

I'm going to make this one unforgettable.

Forty-nine

Loren Hale

A lot can happen in one month.

Lily miraculously passed her finals and all her classes, which means she'll attend Princeton next year as a senior. Only one semester behind. Connor's emergency tutoring probably had a hand in her success.

The summer has turned fiercer, and now at the end of June, we're all silently praying for rain.

The weather is the only thing I can predict anymore. I thought four weeks would have been enough to dissuade the media and return us to our semi-normal lives. The press may be slightly less ravenous, but cars still sit outside the gates of the house, snapping pictures whenever we leave.

Tuesdays and Thursdays are the worst.

We sit in a corner office of a New York City high-rise, and Dr. Oliver Evans gives me one of his patented you're-not-really-supposed-to-be-here scowls. I didn't trust Lily to see a new *male* therapist for her sex addiction, so naturally I tagged along for her first meeting.

Oliver's theories about sex addiction are a one-eighty from Allison's, and our initial encounter didn't go so well. I almost hit the guy and walked right on out. But Lily's adamant about appeasing her parents and making things right with her family. She wanted to return to these weekly appointments, and the only way I'll sleep at night is if I accompany her.

So Oliver stares at me like I'm getting on his last psychiatric nerve. He's forty-something with dark brown hair and rectangular spectacles that make him look more mousy than smart.

"It's been four weeks," I remind him. "I thought we'd be friends by now, Oliver."

He senses my sarcasm and scribbles something in his notebook. This isn't couples therapy. It's just supposed to be for Lily, but he often starts writing whenever I start speaking. He thinks it pisses me off, but I just hope he gets a hand cramp.

"Lily, how are you doing abstaining from sex? A month is a milestone for a sex addict. You should be proud."

She folds her hands in her lap. "It's been good."

It *was* good. For the first couple of weeks, I actually believed we could make a no-sex rule work. But by the third week, she was skittish as hell. She wouldn't let me sleep beside her, and she flinched whenever someone touched her—not just me. What was once abstaining from sex turned into abstaining from touch. I sensed her withdrawing from me and everyone around her. She wouldn't leave the house, wouldn't do normal things. So I cut the cord on that experiment, and it wasn't because I was horny too.

I knew I was losing my best friend.

I voiced my concerns to Oliver when she first withdrew from my hand. I was just trying to lace her fingers with mine, and she shrunk into herself like I was a monster under her bed. He told me it was natural. That she was returning to the norm. I don't know what kind of *norm* this guy lives in, but regular people don't flinch when they hold hands. It's not like I was asking her to rub one out for me.

So I made a deal with Lily. She wants to appease her parents, fine. But we're not listening to this asshole's advice.

"It's normal for a deviant like yourself to miss sex."

He calls her a deviant a lot. It aggravates me, and I'll spend the next twenty minutes after this meeting telling her all the reasons why she's not one.

"I do miss it," Lily lies. "I miss the way it makes me feel." She felt it pretty damn well last night. She came so hard that she ended up in a fit of laughter afterward. We tried the abstinence bit. It didn't work, and we have no more *what ifs*. We're finally finding our groove in intimacy, and the only thing standing in our way is this guy.

"We can't have you missing it, Lily," he tells her. "The more you dwell on your deviant fantasies, the more you revert back to your deviant ways. You're just a whore now, but if you let this cycle continue, you could become something worse. A pedophile. A sex offender."

Lily's head whips in my direction, and she clutches my hand, silently begging me not to lash out. This isn't the first time he's basically called her a future pedophile.

"Give me a minute while I gather the tools." He stands and rummages around his office closet.

Shit.

This is why I don't want her to stay here. I must wear a pleading look because she says, "I'm fine. We can't leave."

"We can actually," I refute. "There's the door. Fuck the trust fund."

"It's not about the trust fund." *I know.*

She's trying to fix all the damage she created. She's even rebuilding a relationship with her father. We still don't attend those Sunday luncheons, but he calls her after they end to catch up.

Her mother is a different story.

Lily squeezes my hand, and I stare at the way her fingers intertwine with mine. Last week, we wouldn't have been able to do this. Last week, she would have burst into tears before I touched her.

"Just trust me. It's like a game," she says.

I narrow my eyes. "A game in which you get shocked for fun?" I mock gasp. "Are you into the S&M part of BDSM and didn't tell me?"

She punches my arm, and I grab onto her wrist, pulling her in for a kiss. She's going to need it.

Fifty

Lily Calloway

What did I say about kissing and touching during our sessions?" Dr. Evans says angrily.

I try to subdue my smile as I break away from Lo. "Sorry." I don't feel that apologetic. I'm only here for my parents. I don't believe in Dr. Evan's methods anymore, and I try my best not to take his words to heart.

But the armor that I'm building still has a few chinks.

Like right now. Dr. Evans holds a small electrical box, and I have the sudden urge to vomit all over his ugly carpet. He sticks two electrodes to the inside of my wrist and then passes me the box. I set it on my lap and rotate the knob to the lowest shock level.

"I think you can go higher than that today."

"She doesn't want to," Lo interjects.

"Make no mistake, Loren, this is my office. I can have you escorted out if I feel like you're hindering my patient's treatment."

"It's fine," I say quickly and turn the dial a couple notches. Too bad I don't have the remote. That device rests in Dr. Evans sweaty palm, the commander of this torture.

"I'll let you choose what you want to try today. Fantasies or porn."

"Porn." Having to relay my fantasies out loud is incredibly embarrassing, and he shocks me more when I start describing positions and body parts.

"Actually, how about we do both." He reaches into his desk, pulls out a magazine, and slides it to me. I set the mag on the armrest between Lo and me, and then I flip it open, already knowing the drill. Nude women don't make me aroused, but the photographs with the couples do. As soon as I glance at a picture—*Buzzzzz!*—the shock ripples through my wrist and up my arm.

I let out a short breath and clench my hand. Lo rubs my back, and another shock jostles my wrist. My hand twitches.

"What the hell?!" Lo shouts.

Dr. Evans ignores Lo for the moment. "Look at the pictures, Lily, and describe a fantasy you might have if you were staring at these on your own."

I instinctively glance at Lo, considering he would be in my fantasy, which is the wrong reaction. The shock pulses through my hand again, and I try to keep my arm still so Lo can't tell. But he's breathing heavily beside me, forcing himself in the seat and not at Dr. Evans's throat.

"Loren, can you please move to the other chair." Dr. Evans points to a cushiony one in the *corner*, as far away from me as possible.

Lo opens his mouth, and I have to cut him off. Last time he told Dr. Evans to suck his cock, and I'm not sure that's going to blow over well a second time. "He's fine. I don't even see him," I say quickly, returning my focus to the pictures.

Buzzzz! I flinch. What did I do?

I'm starting to think Dr. Evans just likes to press that little button.

"Find a picture that's particularly arousing for you."

I flip through the magazine, bypassing all the large jugs and vaginas but having no luck. They really don't make these for women. "Anything?"

"The internet just has a better selection," I admit, still flipping aimlessly.

"Use this, then." He holds out an electronic tablet. I haven't been on the internet since Lo banned surfing the web, and the lack of temptation has been nice. My days are easier without it.

I swap the magazine for the tablet and log on to Tumblr. This feels different than browsing through the magazine. Maybe because this has been a staple in my routine. I haven't looked at mags since high school.

Having Dr. Evans watch me do this is a little personal.

"Find a photograph and describe your fantasy."

I don't want to, but I remind myself that my parents have been dealing with more difficult stuff than this. *Suck it up, Lily.*

I easily land on one that causes me to shift in my chair. A sting pinches my wrist. *Fuck.* I cringe, and Lo cranes his neck to look at the tablet.

"Talk," Dr. Evans urges.

It's a gif of a girl without any pants (or underwear) and a fully clothed guy. We can only see the lower half of the couple, but the guy runs his hand back and forth between her legs. "My fantasy?" I ask, wanting to avoid this portion.

"Yes, what do you visualize when you look at the photo."

"Lo," I say, "doing this to me, and then maybe he'd actually put his fingers . . . in . . ." *Buzz! Buzzz! Buzzzz!* "Motherfucker," I curse under my breath and close my eyes tight.

"Take it easy, Oliver," Lo sneers.

"Find another, Lily."

I scroll through the tablet and land on a photograph of a girl's oiled ass, but large male hands massage her butt and even edge closer and closer to her clit. Holy shit. *Buzz!*

The shock doesn't dissuade me from picturing Lo massaging me this way. Maybe he'll get some ideas from this session. Maybe it's worth the pain.

But as Dr. Evans shocks me again, all my thoughts morph into shame. I guess I shouldn't want to like this. Dr. Evans boosts my fears when he says, "You're trying not to be deviant anymore. This is bad." He shocks me one more time and I wince. "Understand that we're trying to relate these images to a negative stimuli. You should reach the point where these images don't arouse you anymore. We're going to shock the whore out of you, one way or the other."

I give Lo another look, but his lip has curled into disgust and he grips the armrest with white knuckles.

The clock ticks languidly.

We have one more hour.

Fifty-one

Lily Calloway

My favorite part of therapy is the ride home. Even though I feel like I'm a million leagues below the sea, Lo never stops talking. He brings me back to the surface.

I press my forehead to the fogged window, rain pelting the glass. After four weeks in a drought, the downpour almost feels like a dream. He flicks on the windshield wipers and navigates the road.

"Next session I'm going to call him a whore," Lo tells me. "Give him a taste of his own fucked-up medicine." His eyes keep flitting to me in concern.

"You're going to flip us off the road," I say.

"You're being quiet." He merges onto the highway.

"I'm just thinking."

"About Dr. Oliver Evans's lack of pornographic magazines for females? What the fuck was he doing giving you a guy mag?"

Though this was furthest from my mind, I will gladly take the distraction bait. I smile and rotate fully in my seat to face Lo. "You remember in tenth grade when you used to buy me magazines and rip out all the pages with only girl parts?"

He laughs. "It wasn't all selfless. I thought the more you masturbated, the less you'd have sex with actual guys."

"Huh . . ." I suppose that makes sense. "Did you know that I used to dump out your bottles of Everclear?" I admit with a grin. The liquor was so strong that he scared me whenever he plucked a bottle from the cabinet. I guess I was too afraid to dissolve our system to actually tell him this, so I did the next best thing.

"I always thought I just didn't remember drinking them."

It feels nice to know that we had each other's backs, even if it seemed like we could care less. "I never told you," I say softly, "but I was always worried about your health. Your liver . . ." We don't usually talk about the risks, at least we never have before. But somehow, banding together to take on evil Dr. Shock Therapy has made us closer in a different way.

He lets out a long breath. "I know you were, Lil. And it's one of the reasons I can't drink again."

I frown. "What do you mean?"

"We have to take all these kinds of medical tests in rehab, and the doctors basically told me that if I continued down the path I was on, I'd do serious, irreparable damage to my liver."

My eyes suddenly start to burn, silent tears building. "Why didn't you tell me before?"

"Because I knew you'd be upset and probably blame yourself," he says, "and it's not your fault." He glances at me and then back at the road. "Lil, please don't cry. It's really not your fault, and I'm fine. Nothing's wrong with me."

"But it could be." I wipe my eyes and shake my head. "And how can this not be my fault, Lo? I enabled you all our lives. I should have—"

"What?" he says roughly. "What could you have done? Tell me to stop? I wouldn't have. Physically taken the bottles away? I would have hated you. Tattled to my father? He wouldn't give a shit. The only person who could have stopped me was me."

"I could have done *something*." I can't sit here and act like I'm not to blame at all. I supplied him with booze sometimes. I facilitated his addiction.

"You did do something. You were there for me when no one else was." He drives down another street and turns on the lights as the sun descends. "And, Lil . . ." His eyes meet mine for a brief moment. "If you're going to blame yourself for enabling me, then I have to take fault for enabling you."

"It's not the same. Your addiction can kill you."

"And those men you slept with couldn't have beat the shit out of you? You couldn't have contracted an STD or HIV? I let you take those risks and you let me take mine." He turns a sharp left and I brace myself against the door. "How about we call it even? And then we make a pact to never do it again."

"Okay," I say. "Can we shake on it?"

His lips rise mischievously. "We can do better than that."

Is he thinking what I'm thinking? "Like . . ."

He laughs. "Well, I saw you staring rather hard at that massage picture."

Ohhhhh. *Yes.* No. Wait. "We shouldn't."

His brows furrow into a hard line, but he keeps his gaze on the road as the rain falls heavier. "Why not? And you may want to choose your answer carefully. If it begins or ends with the name Oliver Evans, I'm going to eject my seat."

"It's deviant."

Lo lets out a long groan. "Please, for the love of fucking God, never say that word again."

"Well, it is."

"The only thing deviant is what that psychiatrist is putting you through. You shouldn't be shocked for being aroused by those photographs. *I* get semi-hard looking at them."

I frown. "You do?"

"Yes!" he says, half laughing. "Any human would, Lil. Even if I thought aversion therapy was ethical, which I don't, I'd only recommend it to people who stare at those photos with violent thoughts. Like rape or child molestation. You're not a pedophile. The fact that he treats you like one kills me."

I watch the rain scatter my window as I think this through. It's not weird to be aroused by them, but it's wrong to *compulsively* abuse porn. That sounds right.

"Hey," Lo says, wanting my attention again. I turn to him, and he gives me a hard look, his eyes flickering between the road and me. "If his therapy methods are fucking with your head, then you're going to stop."

"I'm fine, honest. Talking to you helps."

He grabs my hand and kisses my palm.

"So we went to our respective press conferences, finished publicly apologizing," I list off. "I'm seeing my new psychiatrist. All we have left is the wedding, and after that I'll receive my trust fund. My parents should forgive me fully, and everything will turn back to normal—or as normal as we can be." Once a week, my father actually calls me to catch up. He even told me he was proud that I was seeing this psychiatrist. After everything that I did to his company—the backlash that he's been through—for him to tell me that he's proud was enough to cause happy tears. I can't screw with that.

My mother will take more finesse to win over, and I know she won't be completely content until the marriage. I can't afford to stumble anymore.

"What if they don't?" Lo says softly.

"What?"

"Have you ever thought that maybe, even after you do all of this, that your mother may still not forgive you?"

I shake my head, not willing to believe she could be that cruel. "She has to."

But the way Lo stares at the road, like he sees a colder future than the warmth I've planned, makes me worry.

Fifty-two

Loren Hale

Some days are harder than others. There are days where I don't even think about alcohol, and then days where my brain circumnavigates around drinking and nothing else.

Today all I can think about is my mother. My real mother. *Emily Moore.* After my father gave me her address, I often imagine her house, what she looks like, her life without me.

What I do know for certain is that she's a substitute teacher in Maine. Married. Two kids. When I was little, I rehearsed the same confrontation in my head. I'd stand on the stoop of my birth mother's house. I'd ask her why she didn't want me, why she never called or left a note. But in my mind, I was thinking of Sara Hale—not this Emily Moore.

The name has changed, but my questions haven't. I just have to figure out when to go and who to take with me. Maybe Ryke or Lily, but neither know I've been plotting the date to travel to Maine. Ryke will disapprove, thinking I've embedded myself further into my father's world. So I'm leaning toward a trip with Lily.

But I can't meet Emily today, even if I want to.

Ryke wants to teach me how to rock climb. Not in a gym. Like on a real fucking mountain. I had to ask whether we were going to use ropes and a harness—considering the guy free climbs (he's stupid enough to scale a mountain with nothing but his hands, legs, and some chalk). We're planning on climbing the normal, sane way. He can do the whole Spider-Man routine when I'm not watching.

I can't leave until I finish filtering the morning mail with Rose.

The kitchen table overflows with letters, manila envelopes, and small packages.

Paparazzi have sold photos of Lily buying tampons in the grocery store. It's ridiculous. And her "fan" mail accumulates with each new headline on the cover of a gossip magazine. Most letters are from old men who think she'll reply or meet them somewhere for sex. That's what's been happening lately. People are grabby as hell. I thought that the guy in the hallway of Princeton was just a fluke, but a lot of men feel as though Lily wants all sex, even from them, just because of her addiction. And they make a go of trying to get it from her.

It's like she has a twenty-four-seven *Open* sign plastered to her body now. And there's no way for her to spin it around to "closed," which I know she wants to. Thank God she has a bodyguard.

I rip open a couple letters and nearly vomit at a picture of some dude's balls.

"Shred this one twice," I tell Rose, throwing the photo into her pile. The shredder rumbles by her feet as she feeds the machine more and more mail.

She glances at the photograph, flips it over, and lets out a snort. "*I'll be thinking of you while you touch yourself,*" she reads. "Your sentiments are not shared, Mr. Gordon."

"This guy is living at the state penitentiary. That makes me feel fantastic." I toss her another letter and then slice open the packages with a knife.

I really wish we didn't have to go through this mail at all. I'd much rather burn it without even opening, but some people actually send money. Sometimes as a joke, other times I think they honestly believe Lily will fuck them for cash. Rose, Lily, and I agreed to collect the money and donate it to a women's shelter in the city. At least someone profits off this.

So Rose and I spend all morning ripping and tearing and shredding. Lily would join us, but Rose and I specifically try to censor her from Mr. Gordon's balls and company. One day, Lily accidentally opened a letter with photographs attached, and her eyes grew wide in horror, as though the person was one step away from breaking into our house to rape her. I've thought about that possibility too, which is why I installed a better security system.

Lil doesn't admit it, but Rose and I see that she's afraid to leave the house. She rarely goes out, and when she does, it's usually after a great deal of pleading.

Lily has accepted my mail-sifting routine with Rose, also calling it our "bonding time." I haven't been Rose's number-one fan, not even after the media-palooza went down. But what was once a frost-bitten relationship has surprisingly begun to thaw.

"Since I have to go to business meetings now," I tell her, "I'm going to need some everyday kind of suits. You still have those black ones from your menswear line, right?"

She goes still and the shredder stops growling. "You don't have to help me, Loren. I don't need your charity." In one month, Rose almost lost every single investor she had for Calloway Couture. Only *one* has stayed on board out of sheer loyalty.

I roll my eyes. "It's not charity. I need suits. Now that you fired a certain someone, yours are no longer plaid and ugly." I can't say Sebastian's name unless I want to be assaulted with rage.

"He did have horrible taste," she says, lips pursed. As soon as Rose ripped the guy from her life, he snapped a picture of himself for Rich Kids of Instagram and called her a cunt-bag. If you even utter his name, she looks ready to lunge for the ball-cutting shears.

Rose assesses my current wardrobe. A black V-neck and faded Diesel jeans. "You go to your office looking like that," she reminds me. "Why would you need suits?"

"I have weekly meetings with my father. If I show up in this, I'll never hear the end of it."

Running my own company terrifies me. I don't want to pour my heart and soul into it and then have the entire thing destroyed. What Rose is going through—it fucking sucks. Maybe that's why I've preferred apathy all of these years. You can't be hurt when you have nothing to lose.

She mulls over my proposition and then begins to stuff the shredder again. It rumbles to life. "Fine, but you have to pay full price."

I laugh. "No family discounts? I'm going to be your brother-in-law."

"Unwillingly," she says with cold eyes. Jesus Christ. I'm never going to live *that* down.

I blame Connor.

He somehow coerced me into revealing my true feelings about this wedding. I admitted to not wanting to marry Lily, not like this at least. I want to do it on our own terms. And somehow Rose has warped that into *I don't want to marry her at all*. If I could, I'd be engaged for five more years. She'd be my fiancée and we'd get hitched when we're both healthy and in love. But that's not a future that will come true, so I stop trying to imagine it.

I smother that conversation by slitting open a small package. I made the mistake yesterday of reaching blindly into a box. I never, *ever* want to touch another man's cum again. Rose couldn't stop laughing while I soaked my hands in disinfectant for thirty minutes.

I dump the contents onto the plastic-lined table. A neon hot pink dick stares back at me. Without touching it, I slide the dildo into a trash bag.

The next box has what looks like an expensive vibrator, brand-new, wrapped in its original packaging. I leave it on the table as I read the card.

And then an excited squeal resounds from the staircase. Lily sprints down the stairs, her glee-filled eyes pinned to the vibrator.

I grab her around the waist before she can grab *it*. She points to the package. "That's new!"

"I'm aware," I say. "You still can't have it."

She cranes her neck. "It's a Zell500. That's a luxury brand. You can't just toss it in the trash." Her eyes go big. "That's sacrilege."

I'm tempted to read her the card: *A beautiful toy for your beautiful pussy, my lovely Lily.* It's fucking creepy, and I know it will deter her. But I don't want to scare her either. That's what we're trying to avoid with all of this.

"It's a vibrator, Lily," Rose snaps, "not the Holy Grail."

I give Rose a smile. "So you don't want it, then?"

She glares like she's ready to put *me* in the shredder.

I stifle a larger grin and turn to Lily. "Sorry, love. It's going in the trash."

She surrenders rather easily. I unhook my arms from her and slide the vibrator into the garbage with the others.

The front door opens, and Ryke saunters into the kitchen, carrying two large vases, white lilies poking his face. As soon as Lily spots the flowers, she slips behind my back and clutches onto my shirt—like whoever sent the floral arrangements are about to jump from the vase and grow life-sized.

"These were by the gate," Ryke says. "I would have left them, but the paparazzi were trying to get photographs of the cards." I hold open the trash bag, and Rose suddenly has a fit.

"They'll break!" she yells at me. "And then the glass will tear the bag, slice someone, and blood will be everywhere. I can't clean blood out of the hardwood."

I narrow my eyes. "Just so we have this clear, *I* rank above the floor."

"It's Brazilian cherry," she says like that makes all the difference. She turns to Ryke. "Throw the vases in the recycling bins in the garage."

He tips the vases upside down, only the flowers and cards falling into my trash bag. Lily still hasn't disentangled from my shirt. I gather her hands and intertwine her fingers with mine. "Hey, what's wrong?" I ask.

Her eyes fix dazedly to the trash bag, and I'm not sure where she's truly gone. But she's not in a fantasy. She's somewhere sadder and darker.

Very softly, she says, "I don't want lilies at the wedding."

She's never referred to it as *my* or *our* wedding. It's always *the* wedding. Marriage is supposed to be this happily ever after, but for her, it feels like a means to an end.

"You don't have to think about that," Rose tells her. "It's not for another year. We're not even going to plan it anytime soon."

Ryke nods to me. "You ready to go?"

"Yeah, I just need to change out of my jeans."

"You can change in the car," he tells me. "I have shorts and stuff in there." He checks his watch. "I just want to beat a storm that's supposed to roll in."

Right, because we're going to be outside. Climbing a mountain. *Just don't kill me, God. That would be so fucking cruel to kill me now.*

Before I leave, I kiss Lily lightly. "What are you doing today?" I ask, worried that she'll spend the afternoon and night bingeing old cartoons, isolated in the living room. She claims it's a normal bout of summer laziness, but I know her well.

She can't be afraid of the world forever.

"I was thinking about going to your office. Maybe get some work done," she says. My lungs fill with relief. I love that I have chosen a business she can take pleasure in, something that can be both of ours one day. I want her to graduate college first, accomplish what I couldn't.

"Call Garth," I tell her.

She crinkles her nose. "He smells like old cheese."

I grin. I chose the perfect bodyguard. "Don't leave this house without him."

"Don't fall off a giant rock."

"I'll return him to you alive," Ryke tells her.

"You better." Lily holds a nonthreatening finger at him.

He smiles coyly, like he plans on fucking with the ropes or the harness to scare the shit out of me, just to retaliate for the mankini prank in Cancun. I'm a little nervous, but after climbing in the gym with him, the mountain shouldn't be too difficult, even if he gives me extra slack. I can handle the challenge.

Fifty-three

Loren Hale

We don't even make it out of New Jersey before my phone buzzes in the middle console. The word *Dad* flashing in big bold letters.

"Don't answer that," Ryke says.

I'm driving. And I disobey his orders, answering the phone and keeping one hand on the wheel. I feel Ryke's hot glare without taking my eyes off the road.

"Loren." My father's voice sounds through the receiver. "I need you to stop by the house sometime today." His tone is pretty casual, so I figure the topic centers on my new company. It's barely on its feet, but he loves to add his opinion.

"I'm heading out of town, so I won't be anywhere near Philly."

"Then readjust your schedule."

"It's not that easy—"

"I'm not asking."

Ryke shakes his head repeatedly beside me, probably watching my eyes begin to darken the longer I talk to our dad. "You should have rejected the deal for your trust fund," he says under his breath.

I pull the speaker away from my mouth to talk to Ryke. "I heard you the hundredth time you said it."

"You're his bitch," Ryke rephrases, as if that'll make me understand.

I grit my teeth, the highway signs zipping overhead. I need to get off the next exit if I want to see my dad.

I press the phone back to my ear. "What is it about?" I ask him. "The leak."

I nearly jerk the car into the other lane, a Trailblazer next to us.

"Lo!" Ryke yells, clutching the door. He snaps on his seat belt.

Shit. "Sorry." I start switching lanes, properly this time, heading toward the exit.

"Wait, where are you going?" Ryke asks angrily. He knows I'm heading to Philly. He just doesn't know why.

I put the phone on speaker, realizing that Ryke will throw a tantrum unless he hears the truth from my father. I set the cell on my lap. "You know who the leak is?" I ask aloud, my heart thrumming. After a month without the knowledge, I was resigned with the fact that it just didn't matter. Mostly because I didn't have the energy to hunt down Mason or Aaron *and* care for Lily. I chose the right option, to be there for my best friend. But I want the information that has eluded us for so long. And the resentful, dark, and bitter part of me wants this fucker's head on a spike.

"Yeah," he says. "I found the leak."

"How?"

"The tabloid who first reported the news finally broke and gave us their source. It took five million to loosen their lips and uncover this bullshit." He doesn't add *you owe me every penny.* Even so, I feel like I do.

"Who is it?" I ask, my hands clutching the steering wheel so tightly.

He doesn't say anything.

"Dad?!" I shout. A car honks, and I realize I swerved into his lane and cut off a pickup truck.

"Keep your eyes on the fucking road," Ryke chastises. "Or pull over and I'll drive." No, he'll take us the other direction. And right now, I'm too wired to go climb a mountain.

"Is Ryke with you?" my dad asks roughly.

"We're on our way," I tell him, ignoring how Ryke is searing a death glare into the phone.

"No, we fucking aren't," Ryke refutes.

"You both should come," he tells us. "This is important, and I don't want to discuss it over the phone." He hangs up.

I flick on my blinker and drive along a side street, off the highway.

"What the fuck are you doing?" Ryke asks.

"He knows who the leak is," I say like he's an idiot. "What the fuck are *you* doing? We've spent months trying to track down this asshole."

Ryke stares at the road with a hard gaze. "Maybe you should drop me off somewhere."

I frown. "What? Where?" What's wrong with him?

"Like anywhere but there."

And then I realize that Ryke hasn't come into contact with my father since the Christmas Charity Gala. Before rehab. Before *everything*.

A brutal silence strings though the car. And then I say softly, "Are you scared of him?"

"I can't stand to look at his face."

"What did he personally do to you?" I ask.

"I hated him because my mother did," Ryke says briefly, but I can tell his mind is reeling, so I'm not surprised when he divulges more. ". . . when I was older, I tried to look at him differently, but she painted a portrait of a monster. So when I stare at his face, that's all I fucking see."

His words sink in, and I don't have anything to say. I can't change the way he pictures Jonathan Hale. That damage is too deep-seated.

"I tried to forget about him," Ryke says, staring out the window. "I tried to act like I just didn't have a dad. And then . . ." He shakes his head.

"What?" I prod.

". . . and then I met you. And all that hate just came back ten times stronger than before."

I hesitate before I ask. I fear his answer. "Why?" This is where he'll say I'm just like my father. I'm the monster of the story. The thing to be hated.

"You defend him," Ryke tells me. "He says some pretty fucking horrible things right to your face, and you just stand there and take it or you walk away. And then the next day, you'll talk about Jonathan like he's a fucking savior." I can't feel that great burst of relief when he doesn't compare me to him. I just feel like shit.

I grit my teeth. "What am I supposed to do? Punch him? I wasn't into the whole *let me beat the hell out of my father* tragedy growing up. Sorry."

"You're right," Ryke says, surprising me. "You were stuck in that house, with that fucking asshole. But right now, you have the option to leave him. And you're going back."

"He's not all bad."

"And there you go, sticking up for him again."

"He's *my* father."

"He's *our* father," Ryke retorts.

I hit the wheel with my hand, nervous and pissed and so fueled right now. "I can't cut him out of my life!" Not because of the money. Not because of the trust fund or the information I need from him. I can't leave Jonathan Hale because he's my family. He's my dad, and before Ryke and Lily, he's all I fucking had.

"Pull over for a second."

"I'm not turning around."

"Just pull over."

I drive into a gas station and park the car by the pump. I face Ryke, and my chest rises at the empathy in his eyes. He's about to drop a bomb on me, but he knows I can take it.

"No one is going to tell you this," Ryke says. "Everyone says it behind your back, but you're going to hear it from me, right now."

I stare at him for a long moment, already hearing his words before he says them. I think I know. I've always known.

"Our dad abuses you," Ryke says, his eyes reddening. "He's verbally abusive, and he's fucked with your head."

I let this sink in, but I'm so numb to the answer. I just nod. "Yeah, I know."

Ryke nods a few times too, watching me, trying to gauge my mental state. And maybe he's reliving the fact that he was the older brother, the one who was handed the better deal of two really shitty ones, not having to be raised by him, not having to endure the onslaught of *fucking grow up! I didn't raise you to be such an idiot! Why are you crying? Stop. Fucking. Crying.*

"Don't guilt yourself over this," I tell Ryke. I feel nothing. I should be red in the eyes like him, but I just can't be. "I know what I'm doing."

"Yeah," Ryke says, nodding again, but he's more upset than before. "The fact that you believe you can have a real relationship with him fucking terrifies me, Lo. That's what kills me. And that's why I don't want to go there and watch him try to emotionally manipulate you."

I break his gaze and stare at the wheel. "I'm not asking you to come with me." My voice is edged but considerably low. "I can drop you off at your house."

We sit in uncomfortable silence again. For maybe five minutes, both of us just thinking.

And then Ryke says, "If I go, you think he'll lay off you?"

"Is that even a question?"

Ryke nods. "All right. Let's go."

"Are you sure?" He would do that? He'd go stomach a whole hour or two with our father just so the verbal assaults are redirected his way?

"Yeah. I'm sure."

I don't know what I'm feeling. My lungs seem to lift from my chest, and I know what words I want to say. I know what words I can't.

Thank you.

In this moment, I truly feel like I have a brother. One that's probably too good for me.

Fifty-four

Y ou don't drink?" My father is hung up on this one fact about Ryke. Overhead fans circulate cool air on the patio, and I sit in between Ryke and my dad like someone about to referee an arm wrestle.

"Not since high school," Ryke says. "I overdid it." He doesn't mention how he crashed his car into a mailbox.

"And that's why you've deluded Loren into thinking he's an alcoholic—because *you* couldn't handle your liquor?"

The muscles in Ryke's jaw twitch. "Get to the fucking point, Jonathan. Who's the leak?"

My dad leans back in the iron chair, cupping his glass of scotch. "I'll get to the *fucking* point when I feel like it. Maybe I want to have lunch with my two sons first." He presses a button on his phone. "Carter, make three burgers for us."

"Any preferences, Mr. Hale?"

"The usual."

"They'll be right out." The line clicks.

"I'm not your son," Ryke says, even though he does, on occasion, call Jonathan his father when he's trying to make a point. Like in the car. "My mother took full custody of me, in case you forgot."

"How old are you?" my dad asks mockingly. "Oh wait, you're

twenty-two. In the eyes of the American judicial system, you're an adult. And as an adult, you're not your mother's property like that Ferrari she bought with my money in her goddamn driveway."

Ryke rubs his jaw in agitation and looks around the patio like he's trying to find some excuse to leave, but then his gaze drifts to me and he stops searching for that escape.

We can't go until we find out who the leaker is. And if that means eating a burger with the devil, then so be it.

My father sets his scotch down and focuses on me. "Have you met your mother yet?"

Shit. I can feel Ryke's confusion and livid heat permeate in the air. "Not yet, I've actually been waiting for Lily to . . . adjust."

"You're going to meet your mother?" Ryke asks, accusation lacing the words.

My father doesn't cut in, which means he's curious about our relationship, wondering how close we've become these past months.

"Yeah," I say.

Ryke shakes his head. "How long have you had her name? How'd you find her?" And then realization floods his face, looking between our dad and me. "You two have been speaking this whole time . . ." But his hate is redirected at Jonathan. "Can't you leave him alone for one minute?"

"He wanted to know who his mother was. It's not your place or mine to make that decision for him." He sips his scotch casually, incensing Ryke more.

"I don't care about that. I care that you used that information to draw him back in. I care that you push him to drink."

"Ryke . . ." I start and then stop, not wanting to defend my father. Not now. "I was going to tell you that I started talking to him."

"When? When I find you in the hospital bleeding from your stomach because you drank?"

My father groans. "You're not still taking that ridiculous pill."

Ryke turns on him. "It's not a fucking joke."

"It is," my dad says. "You're making him soft."

"Yeah, you made sure he was fucking sharp, didn't you?"

"Stop, both of you," I say coldly. "I don't want to talk about alcohol or Emily."

"Fine," my father says and stands to replenish his glass. "What do you do, Ryke? Or are you like your mother, gobbling up all my money on furniture and clothes?"

"How about we leave my mother, the woman you fucking cheated on, out of the conversation as well."

"Forgive me if I don't like the bitch," he says. "I always wanted you two to meet, and because *I* wanted it, she could barely tolerate the idea. And here you are, closer than ever. It's as if it was always meant to be." He grins, as if he set fate into motion.

"It wasn't your doing," Ryke refutes. "I didn't meet Lo because of you. I met him because I wanted to."

My father rolls his eyes dramatically. "I can't ever win with you. Ever since you asked me some silly goddamn question and you didn't like the answer."

"I was *fifteen*," Ryke sneers. "I just found out I had a brother. I felt lied to and cheated on. I needed your compassion and you fucking spit in my face. But I guess I should have known better."

"You didn't need compassion." My father grimaces at the word. "You needed the truth, and I gave it to you. It's not my fault you were too weak to handle it."

"What are you guys talking about?" I ask, hesitating. Maybe I shouldn't know. But I hate being in the dark.

My father is quick to answer. "Ryke asked me a simple question that day. Would you like to tell him, Ryke?"

"Fuck you," Ryke sneers.

"I suppose not." He takes a small sip from his drink, smacking his lips before he continues. "He asked me if I could take back the day that I fucked your mother—take back having *you*—would I?"

My throat goes dry, not expecting that. I think I know his answer. Because even in his hatred, his bigotry and vileness—there is one fact that my father has never let me question.

He loves me.

And it's a fucked-up love. Ryke is right. It does mess with my head. And it's something I have so much trouble walking away from. Sometimes I don't want to. Other times, it's all I dream about.

My father's eyes hold this unbridled clarity, unwavering from mine, the haziness of his drink gone to honesty. "I told Ryke that I would do it all over again. I have zero regrets, in this lifetime or the next."

Zero regrets.

That's what I pick out from that. *Zero regrets.* Not even when he grabbed me by the neck, not when he called me a shitty fuck at ten years old. Not when he made me feel like I was never good enough to be his son. *Zero regrets.*

Right.

No one says anything more at first. Ryke is probably worried that I resent him. He wished I wasn't alive. But truth is, I kind of did too. Until I looked at Lily. Until I talked to her. I don't think I could have survived this life without that girl.

I redirect the conversation to Hale Co., which my father only likes to discuss in small quantities. The company took a minor hit in comparison to Fizzle, but he's still working on launching a new baby product. Something about cribs. It's ironic that the world's worst dad has a fortune from baby things, but since it was my grandfather's business first, it makes the irony less valid. Unless he was an alcoholic asshole too.

The burgers arrive when he says, "This marriage helps Fizzle, but do you know what would really benefit Hale Co.?"

Ryke freezes, the lettuce falling out of his bun.

I must be slower because I don't get it. "What?"

My father cuts through his burger with a knife, juices oozing out. His eyes find mine. "It's a baby merchandize company. Babies would help." I can't breathe. "Little Hale babies in little Hale onesies. It would be great goddamn marketing." He takes a bite of his burger. "You can't beat that."

"No," I say instantly. My blood feels like it's on fire. I have been coerced into marrying Lily. I'm not going to have children because my father tells me to. There has to be a line somewhere.

"You didn't even think about it."

"I said no. Not now. Not in a fucking year. Not ever."

My father sets down his silverware and wipes his mouth with a napkin. "Is this a new development?"

"No."

"Is something wrong?" He frowns. "Are you sterile?"

"For fuck's sake," I snap. I didn't think I'd have to discuss this with him. "I don't want kids. It's not because I can't have them. I don't want them." *I don't want them to turn out like you. Or me.*

Ryke stays quiet, but I can tell he's processing. The only person I told was Lily. That's the only one who mattered.

"You'll change your mind," my father says like he knows me so well. He picks up his knife again. "And it's okay if it's not anytime soon. Hale Co. can wait."

We finish eating, and after all the tense conversation, it's hard to remember why we were here in the first place. One of the servers clears the last dish, and I ask the question. "Who's the leak?"

"That, I can't tell you," he says.

"You've got to be shitting me," Ryke growls, saying exactly what I'm thinking.

My father ignores Ryke. "The good news is that I have it under control, and it's being handled quietly. If I tell you two, I'm sure you'll cause a fucking mess that I won't be able to clean."

I don't agree with him. I can't. "I need to know," I refute. "This isn't some guy who did me wrong or fucked me over in a small way."

"You won't change my mind, Loren."

"Why'd you tell me to come here, then?!" I shout, blindsided by all of this. We sat here for *nothing*.

"To have lunch with you and to tell you that you need to drop this. Let it go."

I spring up from the table like my soles are on fire. "Let it go?!"

My father glowers. "Loren, you're overacting."

"Lo," Ryke says, rising and resting a hand on my shoulder.

"Overreacting?" I let out a manic laugh. "I have a girlfriend at home who's scared to walk out of the fucking house without getting assaulted. And I'm overacting? It took her a month to stop tossing and turning at night." I grip the chair. "She has men mailing her goddamn plastic penises from prison and alleged sex tapes being rumored every day. This bastard toyed with her for weeks, texting her vile things before he finally leaked it. And you have his fucking name!"

My father is on his feet. "And what the hell are you going to do? Yell? Shout? Stomp your shoes and make noise?" His eyes grow dark. "There is nothing you can do that I haven't already done. It's over. Let. It. Go . . . please." His voice has softened considerably, and I pale.

Please. He doesn't use that word, and I know what I have to do. I have to trust him.

But I don't know who he's protecting—me or himself.

Fifty-five

Lily Calloway

Garth must have been ex-CIA or a stunt driver on some Hollywood lot before becoming a personal bodyguard. He lost the paparazzi tailing us within two minutes. It usually takes me a solid hour driving in aimless circles, and I get so bored that I make stops at The Donut Man for jelly-filled pastries. Now that I think about it, maybe the donuts are the reason it takes me so long.

Lo has tried to conceal the location of his office from the press. For now, it's the one place void of cameras peeping through windows or gates. Being here makes me feel normal again.

I kick my feet on his desk and lean back in the nice leather chair. Garth is broad-shouldered, his peppery hair receding and his forehead oily. He sits on the couch, currently transfixed by his mini-tablet. We don't talk much other than to discuss where I want to go, which is fine with me. Talking can be overrated.

Lo's office has more personality than our bedroom. Posters of his favorite science fiction and superhero movies line the walls: *Battlestar Gallactica*, *Star Wars*, *X-Men* (of course), *Spider-Man* (the Andrew Garfield version), and *Kick-Ass*.

We ate up a whole day just stocking the bookshelves with all his comics, organizing them by issue. When he told his father he wanted to start a comics publishing company, he probably expected Jonathan to laugh in his face, tell him to grow up, and find a serious job. But no, his dad signed a check and wanted a formal business plan the next day.

I thumb through one of the manuscripts out of the large pile. Lo has to read original comics (not all good) and choose which ones he wants to publish for Halway Comics. He lets me read them if he's on the fence, but when I graduate from Princeton, I won't be helping him with this side of the business.

I focus on the comic in hand. The art is surrealistic with a satirical edge. Some of the people even have dog heads. And some of the humans are drawn with animal feet. Lo can find the meaning behind most comics, but my brain just sees a dog-man with a big butt.

The comics I gravitate toward are more realistic and classical, like ones where the superheroes can spring from the page and fit in our world. Lo will try anything and everything, even panels that contain black dots and no words. I do love sexy superheroes, but those are hard to find in indie comics publishing. The most I've seen are sexy-clad characters that look like they'll murder me in my dreams.

I sift through his pile and find a more realistic comic. Not superheroes, but it's a noir strip with a detective as the lead. I flip through the pages to look at the pretty art.

Ahhh! I throw the manuscript on the floor and cover my eyes with my hands.

There is nudity in that comic book! And I've sworn off porn.

"Everything okay, Lily?" Garth asks.

"Yeah," I croak. "I'm just gonna . . . go downstairs." I bypass the dirty comic book on the ground and slip out of the room. I take the winding staircase down to the main level.

The first floor.

My dream.

I enter the store from the back (employees only) entrance and walk into the dimly lit space. Red linoleum booths hug the walls and windows, plastic wrap covering their cushions. The appliances and furniture are all hidden behind smocks, and I can still smell the fresh coat of warm gray paint on the walls. Red and gray and a bit of blue. I picked the color scheme, even after Lo warned me that the palette fit Captain America. We've been anti-Cap since he threw Wolverine out of an airborne plane.

I still love it.

Rows of low shelves create aisles and resemble a video store, but they're going to be filled with comic books when the shipments arrive. The front area is sectioned with a small kitchenette for pastries and coffee. Not everything is here in the store yet. And it'll be months before the place is ready to be opened for the public.

Lo pitched Superheroes & Scones to his father as a marketing strategy for Halway Comics. But I know the idea has nothing to do with his company. What he did was buy me something of my own, something I could look forward to after college. He found me happiness, and I think it's worth more than any silly engagement ring.

A store that sells coffee, scones, and comic books.

It's perfect.

And for once, we're doing something good with our inheritance rather than wasting it away. For two people unwilling to let anyone in, sharing this intimate part of our lives—the nostalgic happiness of comics—has to mean something.

While we're under construction, I can hide out in one of the plastic-wrapped booths with a comic, like my own secret getaway.

Someone knocks on the door, and I jump out of my skin. I can't see the figure since the glass is shrouded in *Coming Soon* posters. It doesn't even say what's coming, and the building looks equally as closed and deserted with more ads all over the brick. For all anyone knows, this could be a future porn shop. Oh jeez. Now I can't stop thinking about *porn*.

The rapping on the glass continues, and I take a tentative step toward the noise. The figure is shadowy and indistinguishable. But the shape looks tall enough to be a guy.

What if it's the press? Or worse.

A stalker who stalked me here.

The knocking is louder and more persistent. I end up scurrying underneath the nearest booth before my heart abandons my chest. Maybe he didn't see me. Maybe he'll just go away.

If it's someone I know, they'd call me, right? I pat my pockets for my phone. Oh no. I left my cell on Lo's desk, along with Garth. Well Garth is not *on* Lo's desk (at least I hope not), but he's definitely upstairs, consumed with his mini-tablet.

Bang. Bang. Bang. Those knocks sound mean.

I scuttle further underneath the table, curling my knees to my chest. I imagine the glass shattering, the man barging his way through. Should I scream for Garth or just pretend not to be here?

Garth makes the decision for me. His hefty boots pound their way across the store, and the lock clicks, the door jangles, and the stalker is met with my intimidating bodyguard. That should deter him.

"Where's Lily? I've been trying to call her." The voice is calm, smooth, familiar, and so very, *very* unthreatening.

"I'm right here!" I crawl out from under the booth and dust the cobwebs off my kneecaps. Connor raises his eyebrows as if he knows exactly what I was doing under there.

Garth must be confused because he (truly) says, "What were you doing under there?"

"I thought I saw a . . . rat," I say quickly, "so I was inspecting the area to lay some traps later." Before they can foil my lie, I turn to Connor. "What brings you to S&S?" I really should not try to shorten the name, because every time I say it, I immediately think of S&M. My mind has dangerous side roads.

"Lo wants me to look over a contract. He said he left it in his office." He gazes at me with a little more concern than I appreciate from Connor Cobalt. I like his self-satisfaction much better.

"Okay, I'll bring you back there." I add to Garth, "Can you stay here? Watch the door?" I try to smother the worry in my voice, but I fear I'm not doing a good job.

"Of course."

In Lo's office, I flick on the lights, and Connor targets the file folder on the desk. I find my dinky flip phone and scroll through all the missed calls from Connor.

"So who did you think I was?" Connor asks as he opens the file and sinks into the leather chair.

"What?"

"This is a new building. I don't think rats have moved in yet. So obviously you were hiding from whoever you thought was at the door." He's too astute for his own good, and I'm sure he already knows the answer to his own question.

I pick up a Black Widow action figure on Lo's bookshelf. "I wish I was Rose," I say softly.

"Why is that?" *She wouldn't be so scared.*

"She'd handle this better than me. She doesn't even have a bodyguard." I want that kind of confidence, but I just don't think it's something a twenty-year-old can learn. I'm too late.

"There's a difference between courage and pride. Believe me, I'd sleep better at night knowing she had a bodyguard."

"She is alone a lot," I say. How can she not be brave? She's willing to face the swarming paparazzi and media-hungry press by herself every day.

"Yes, but that girl would rather carry her own Taser than let someone else defend her, all to prove a point. So when she meets an adversary twice her size and in a much larger quantity, she's going to realize that some battles are best fought with a sidekick."

"Oh," I say, finally understanding, thanks to his superhero

analogy. My sister is not a team player. She'd rather do things on her own.

"While my talents are immeasurable, I don't have the power to save her from halfway across the city," Connor says. "And our relationship is a bit different from yours."

"That's an understatement, I think."

He smiles. "Yes, it is." He closes the folder. "What I mean to say is that I'm trying not to be afraid for her. Since we were teenagers, she has always looked to me for reassurance, even if she won't admit it. I'm her . . . rock." He stares off as he finds the right words. "The unwavering thing. Confident, poised, unrelenting, and annoyingly persuasive. If she sees that I'm frightened, she'll gloat on the outside, as though I lost a round of chess, but internally she'll begin to question herself. And I don't particularly like when Rose loses her confidence and becomes less self-assured. She's more vulnerable, and it breaks my heart."

This is brand-new honesty for Connor Cobalt, no insults hidden beneath the words. It's just . . . the truth, from the soul. I kind of like it.

"Do you love her?" I ask, returning the action figure and taking a seat on the couch.

He flips the folder back open and reads the contract in his brisk, superhuman manner, turning the page faster than I can read a magazine on a toilet. "Love is irrelative to some." He dodges my question with a strange answer. As he concentrates on the contract, he begins closing the door on his brief openness.

I squint at him as I realize something else. "How come you don't say *wicked* anymore?"

He briefly tears his eyes from the papers. "What are you talking about?"

"You used to say *wicked smart* and *wicked cool*. It was my favorite thing about you." His lingo has changed since I first met him. Not completely, though. I mean, when we run into someone he knows, he'll sometimes throw out a "hey, bro."

His lips rise. "I usually dumb down around the intellectually deficient so I don't come off like a complete prick." I think he just called me stupid. "But I see you as a true friend, so I've backed off some of the pretenses. Most people wouldn't be able to stand all of me."

"Can Rose?" I ask, still trying to process everything he's saying.

His lips just lift higher. I suddenly come to the conclusion that I won't ever know what Connor Cobalt really sounds like in his head—what words he finds abhorrent, what he thinks of certain situations, his *real* honest reactions that aren't half insults and half something a little nicer. Maybe Rose already knows him. Or maybe she's just as clueless as the rest of us.

I stick to a safe subject. "So next semester, you'll be at Wharton and Rose will be in New York." They both graduated from college in May (along with Ryke), and we threw a small celebration for all of them a couple weeks ago.

Connor's dream came true—an acceptance to Penn's prestigious Wharton School of Business for his MBA. Rose always scoffed at grad school. She thinks it's just a piece of paper to brag over, at least for someone who's an heir to a fortune. So she'll spend her time at the Calloway Couture office in New York City, commuting from Princeton, New Jersey.

"That's the plan," Connor says.

I'm worried for them, and I know neither Rose nor Connor would appreciate my concern. But long-distance relationships are difficult, and I can see all the drives back and forth not being worth the trouble—especially if Rose continues to struggle with her intimacy issues. She conquered sleeping in the same bed as Connor during Cancun, but she has yet to make the leap to sex.

I want her to find love and the fireworks, but nothing I do or say will change her problems. I'm just her little sister, and a broken one in her eyes.

Connor's gaze falls to the floor where a comic book is splayed— the page opened to a pair of giant naked boobs and an erect penis. "Lily."

"I wasn't looking at it!" I defend. "I mean, I was, but then I wasn't." I grimace. How can speaking be this hard? I take a deep breath and realign my thoughts. "I was flipping through it, and then when I came upon the . . ." I frown. ". . . genitals. It burned my eyes and magically flung from my hands."

"I'll forgive you for the hyperboles if you're telling the truth."

"I am! Cross my heart." I start drawing crosses over my heart with my finger, but then I get confused. "Am I supposed to draw Jesus crosses or X's?"

"Sometimes I wonder if we speak the same language."

"X's," I say with a nod, ignoring his slight. "Definitely X's."

He returns to the contract, and I sidle to the window, peeking through the blinds to check for paparazzi or sketchy men lurking on the side street.

I don't know how to vanquish this fear. I have an overwhelming desire to hide in the bathroom and masturbate my anxiety away. But I want to feel like I did in Cancun. Safe and not so crazy compulsive. I yearn for that stasis again.

My new therapist doesn't seem equipped to help me, and I can just imagine his methods to combat this fear, a monster-sized shock machine in hand. So I refuse to share my anxieties with him.

But I won't drown in self-love either. I'm going to try something new, and just wade in my unease until I figure out how to handle the close scrutiny and media properly. Until I figure out how to breathe again.

Fifty-six

Loren Hale

I feel like a creep.

Sitting in my rental car for an hour and staring at the same four-story brick house. The lawn has newly mowed lines, a sign poking from the grass: *McAdams Middle Honor Student*.

Maine carries a breeze that beckons people outdoors, but I'm still rooted to the seat, my joints frozen solid. My biggest fear is staying in this damn sedan, coming this far and not mustering the courage to walk up the driveway.

I can smash a bottle of liquor on another guy's door, but I can't put one foot in front of the other to say hi to a woman. There's irony somewhere in that. And maybe if I wasn't scared out of my fucking mind, I'd laugh.

I rub my neck that gathers with nervous heat. I should have brought Ryke and Lily like I originally planned. When I told Lily that I was looking into meeting my mother, she was nothing but supportive. They both wanted to come.

But I ended up only buying one plane ticket.

I have to do this on my own.

No one has entered or exited the house. From the outside, it resembles a normal middle-class family home. It's what I could have had.

Normal.

I let out a long breath and run my hands through my hair. *Just go. Just get it over with, you fucking bastard.*

Before I can process what I'm doing, I climb from the car and reach the mailbox. I breathe like I'm in the middle of a five-mile jog. Inhale. Exhale. One . . . two . . . three. But I'm not sprinting. I'm not running. I'm barely walking.

My worn sneakers land on the front stoop. My legs weigh me down. My shoes, however ugly, are filled with lead.

I raise my fist to the door, falter, and drop my hand to my side. *Come on. Do it.* I've replayed conversations in my head, thinking about this moment for years. *Come on, Loren. Grow the fuck up.*

Inhale. Exhale.

One . . . two . . .

I ring the doorbell.

The door opens. And my mind goes blank.

A woman stares at me with an identical stunned and stupefied expression. I never called her, never warned her about this meeting. I was too scared that she'd shut me down. I just wanted to see her face, hear her voice, all at the same time.

She's young, not even forty. I search her features: slender nose, thin lips, and shiny brown hair. I suddenly realize I'm looking for *me* in her.

"I'm—"

"I know who you are." Her voice is velvet, the kind you can close your eyes and fall asleep to. I bet she reads her kids bedtime stories. The thought knots my stomach. "I've seen you on the news."

I wait for her to invite me in, but she grips the knob like she's seconds from swinging the door in my face.

"What are you doing here?" she asks.

I'm not sure what reaction I expected. My dad—he told me that she didn't want me. I thought, maybe, he was lying. I still grasp to that futile hope that she cared for me like a mother would a son.

Inhale. "I just wanted to talk." My voice sounds coarse compared to hers. Like an animal to an angel. It fucking sucks. And I can't stop staring at her, like she's moments from being ripped from my memory.

"There's nothing to talk about." Her eyes carry apologies even if her words don't.

"Right," I say and nod to myself. I could walk away. I could leave it at that. I've seen her. What else do I need? What the fuck am I searching for? "You're my mom." I want to take back the words as soon as I say them.

She cringes, the door shrinking closed, but she stays beside it, wedged between the frame. And she stares at me like I'm a mistake, a black mark on her resume that she's been trying to scrub clean. She doesn't say it, but I can see the phrase all over her face. *You're not my son, not really.*

She didn't raise me. I was a bad part of her life that she's been trying to forget.

She clears her throat, uncomfortable. "Did Jonathan tell you anything?"

"Not much."

"Well . . . what do you want to know?"

The open-ended question takes me aback for a second. What do I want to know? *Everything.* I want all the answers that have been kept from me. "What happened?"

"I was a teenager . . ." She glances over her shoulder for a minute and then says, "I was young and was easily drawn to a guy like Jonathan. We slept together once. That's it. And I was careless, and that's why you're here."

Something nasty sits on the tip of my tongue, but I swallow down the more spiteful retort. I sweat through my shirt, so fucking hot. I wipe my brow and say, "So that's what I am to you, then?"

Her eyes flit past my body. A neighbor across the street stares hard from his mailbox, and I wonder if he's trying to place me—to figure out where he recognizes me from.

"You can invite me in," I offer.

She shakes her head and clears her throat again. "No. It's best if you stay outside."

"Right." That's all I can say without yelling, without screaming everything that weighs on my chest. *Why didn't you come back for me? Why didn't you fucking care? I'm your goddamn son!* I spent years without a mother, without that maternal figure. The most I had were the people who paraded in and out of my house in the mornings. Makeup-smeared, half-dressed women who had no words of wisdom for me, no answers to my problems, no sweet, nurturing voice to ease me to sleep.

"You have to understand . . ." Her eyes fall to the ground. "I didn't want you."

"Yeah, I got that," I say sharply. My father was right. I shouldn't have sought her out.

"I was in high school," she says. "I was just a girl, and I planned to go to college, to have boyfriends and a life. You were going to take all of that from me."

You were going to take all of that from me. The words ring in the pit of my ears.

I stare at the bright sky, just staring, just looking for something that will never reveal itself to me.

What the hell am I doing here? Not just here, at this house. I feel like I was born to destroy people's lives. I did it before I even came into the world. And I did it after. *You were going to take all of that from me.*

"Out of respect for Jonathan, I told him that I was going to an abortion clinic."

I shut my eyes, and a hot tear slides down my cheek. I wipe it. Exhale. "I wish you went through with it," I suddenly say. Because then I wouldn't have to bear this pain. My face wouldn't twist this way. Lily wouldn't have spent her childhood in my broken house. Her mother would have loved her as much as she did her sisters. Ryke would have grown up with two parents instead of one. My existence ruined so many people, so many things. Life would have been easier without me.

"What?" Her velvety voice spikes.

"You heard me," I say, no longer nice. "I wish you would have killed me."

She pales. "You don't mean that."

"Why wouldn't I?"

She touches her lips for a moment, just staring at me. "Because . . . your father, he gave you everything."

You have everything, Loren. Don't be such an ungrateful little shit, Loren.

"Yeah." I nod. "He gave me everything." Before she can speak, I ask, "So what stopped you? Your parents? Some religious belief? Cold feet?"

"Jonathan stopped me," she says. "He was furious with the idea of losing his child. We came to an agreement. I would have you, and then you would be his entirely. I would get the life I planned, and you'd grow up in luxury, something I wouldn't have been able to give you on my own. I thought you would be happy."

"Yeah, I'm still working on the happiness part."

I wait for the flash of regret to fill her eyes, but it never comes. I'm the spoiled rotten heir, the one who drinks until he's wasted. The one who went to rehab like it was some publicity stunt. And I have a sex addict girlfriend.

Emily quiets as a school bus rolls to the curb. The doors open and middle school kids dart out. A girl with my light brown hair and my nose adjusts her backpack, walking toward the house.

Emily forces a smile for her daughter. "Hi, honey, can you go inside, please?"

Her daughter squints at me, fixing her large round glasses on her nose. "Aren't you Loren Hale?"

I hate that a middle school girl knows me. My face is all over the tabloids. Yesterday, they dissected a photograph of me leaving a restaurant hand in hand with Lily.

And then it hits me fully.

She's my half sister.

"Yeah, that's me."

"And you're at my house . . . ? Do you know my mom?"

Emily waits impatiently for her daughter, about to interject, but I do her a favor and shut down her inquiry.

"Not really," I say. "She's a friend of my father's."

"Mom," she whispers. "You know famous people?"

Emily shrugs, her shoulders stiff.

And then my eyes catch a pin on the strap of the girl's jean backpack. *Mutant & Proud*. What are the odds? "You like *X-Men?*"

"The cartoons," she says. "*X-Men: Evolution.*"

"My girlfriend likes those too."

"You mean your fiancée? I just read in *Celebrity Crush* that you're getting married." She rocks on her feet and pushes her glasses further up her nose as they slide down. "Is it true?"

"Yep, it's true."

Her eyes brighten like she'll have something good to tell her friends tomorrow at lunch.

Emily widens the door so her daughter can pass. "Willow, inside please."

Willow examines me with an inquisitive gaze before she submits to her mother's pleas. And then she slips indoors and out of sight.

"You named your daughter after a Buffy character?" *Maybe we like the same things*, I stupidly think. Probably because Willow strangely does.

She frowns. "What?"

"The televisions show, *Buffy the Vampire Slayer?*" She's still confused. "Never mind."

"What do you want, Loren?" she finally asks. "What did you think would happen by coming here?" Her voice lowers and the door begins to close so I can't see past her body and into her house. I can't see the life that I never would've had. "You're twenty-one. You're an adult."

"You're not my mother. I think I got it," I say roughly. I *hate* that I don't hate her. Not even a little bit. I take a step back, my eyes flitting over the house, over something that I don't want to destroy. I ruin everything I touch.

And I'm not going to mess up her life. Even if mine is all fucked up. Right as I'm about to leave this all behind, something else catches my eye in the window.

A girl. A child. No older than two or three. She peers through the glass, clutching a stuffed dinosaur. I see me. Growing up and being lied to. Never knowing about my brother and finding the answers in the most jarring, horrific way. The secrets. The betrayal.

I face Emily again. She seems at peace with her decision and her life, but she's repeating the same mistake as my father. As Sara Hale. She doesn't see it now, but the lies she weaves will eat at her family from the inside out.

"You should know," I say, "that even though I'm not your son, I'm still their brother."

Her lips press in a line.

But I keep speaking. "And maybe you don't see it like that, but take it from someone who's been in their situation before—*they* will." I think of Ryke. "I'm not saying that you have to tell them about me now or anytime soon, but they'll find out eventually. If not from the press, then from some stranger, and they should hear it from you."

"I'll keep that in mind," she says shortly. "Anything else?"

Fuck you. I can't say it, though. I don't really feel it. More like, *Fuck me. For being so stupid. For thinking you'd care.*

I shake my head, everything draining from me like I've been slit open on the sidewalk. I take another couple steps off the stoop, glance up at the three-story brick house. Middle-class family. Happy. Normal.

I turn around and never look back.

Fifty-seven

Lily Calloway

With Lo in Maine, he wanted me to skip my therapy session with Dr. Evans today, but the therapist called me and said that if I skip, he'd contact my parents and tell them how poor my progress has been. So I sit alone in Dr. Evans's office, constantly checking my phone. Lo said he would call after he sees Emily. If their meeting doesn't go well, I'm worried that he may choose to escape with alcohol. I really wanted to go, but at his request, I've stayed here.

Dr. Evans applies the electrodes to my wrist and hands me the small black box with all the wires poking out. He nestles behind his desk in his seat, wearing a smug look. He loves the fact that Lo isn't here to interrupt the session.

"So are we doing magazines again?" I fidget in my seat, a little nervous to be doing this with only Dr. Evans in the room. When Lo's here, it feels less weird.

"I think we should move on to another compulsion today."

I try to wrack my brain. What else could I conquer with aversion therapy besides fantasies and porn?

His eyes drop to my thighs. "It would have been easier if you wore a dress or skirt, but I think you can manage."

My heart bangs against my rib cage. Maybe I heard him wrong.

"I want you to masturbate. You'll be shocked until your brain responds to the negative stimuli."

Oh my God.

My head moves on its own accord, shaking fiercely from side to side. "No," I blurt out. "No way." I am not masturbating in front of him!

"Lily, your parents hired me specifically," he explains. "This is what works. You need to condition your mind to recognize masturbation as a bad impulse."

My parents are my weakness. I have vocalized that I'd do *anything* to fix what I've done. But how far am I willing to go?

"Is there anything else I can do today?" I ask.

He mulls this over, fingers by his temple in thought. "I suppose we can try something else," he says, to my relief.

Dr. Evans stands and walks to the front of his desk and leans his butt on the edge, the remote still in one hand. The other falls to his zipper. *Oh fuck.* This is not the *something else* that I had in mind!

"What are you doing?" I croak, frozen in my chair.

"Whores like you are obsessed with male genitalia. You're going to look at it, touch it, suck it, and I'll shock you until you're nice and normal."

"No."

Rose found my *perfect* therapist, Dr. Banning, after meeting with horrible ones. And I wonder if she had to put up with situations like *this* for me, just so I would avoid it. I know she did. I know because I remember the look Connor and her shared when they were discussing therapists they visited together.

Dr. Evans is already tugging down his silver zipper, and his dick emerges from his khaki pants. My hands shoot to my eyes as the familiar *buzzzz* pulses in my skin.

I'm not looking. I'm not looking. I'm not here. Not really.

The room quiets, and I think maybe I've won.

And then I feel it. On my leg.

I jump up like my entire body has been electrocuted this time. The shock box falls to the floor, ripping out the wires that connect to the electrodes on my arm. I stumble back, my eyes bugging. Dr. Evans closes the distance between us, right in front of me. I refuse to drop my gaze to his dangling penis.

"Get away from me," I sneer. I'm not about to fall to my knees with my tongue lagging out of my mouth. I'm not the same girl who'd fuck everything away for a quick high. I'm stronger. Even without Lo. I know that now.

Dr. Evans shoos my threats, and he grabs my wrists. His mouth finds my ear. "You will sit down and comply, or I'll tell your parents just how much of a whore you really are."

Tell them, is my first thought. I won't sacrifice my own pride, my own dignity, for them. Nothing in the world is worth the shame that I will feel from this. Nothing.

I stare right back, and all my hate and resentment toward everyone who has vilified me as a slut or whore rumbles up in two words. "Fuck you."

His grip tightens, and I realize how small I am compared to him, compared to any man. I might as well be a bag of bones. I take a deep breath and scream, "GARTH!"

Dr. Evans presses a hand over my mouth and his other hand starts descending to my shorts. "If you won't do it yourself, I'll have to do it for you."

I fight back and struggle against his hold, trying to bite and kick, but he ends up pinning me back into the seat. His hand rests in between my legs, pressing the spot over my pants. I can't stop screaming against his palm.

The door whooshes open, and before he can do anything else, my bodyguard bounds over and throws him back against his desk. I shake like a trembling leaf, but I'm on my feet and in one piece. Garth jostles Dr. Evans like a stuffed doll. He looks ready to annihilate the man, so I'm surprised when he releases his grip. "You'll be hearing from Greg Calloway's lawyers. I'd advise you to pack up your office today."

Garth turns to me and gives me a sympathetic, almost apologetic, look. I'm just glad he was here. Lo was right about the bodyguard.

He ushers me out of the room, and I glance back for one last image of my evil therapist. My heart does not slow down just yet. I think . . . I think I'm in shock a little bit. I can't close my eyes or blink.

Dr. Evans slumps down to the ground and stares dazedly at the wires from the shock box.

"Are you okay?" Garth asks in the lobby.

"I think so." I'm trying to parse through my emotions. I feel less like a wilted flower, but mostly, I just can't stop breathing so quickly. I rub my wrist. Yep, I'm in shock.

"Back home?" he wonders.

"Can we make a stop first?"

He nods and we drive a few blocks over to another high-rise. My hands still shake, but they also feel a little disconnected from the rest of my body. When we arrive at the office, I knock on the door, my breathing on a slow descent.

The door swings open, revealing a woman with a black bob and a warm smile. I haven't seen her in almost two months. I don't realize how much I missed her until her arms are around my shoulders, and mine are around hers. Tears prick my eyes.

"Oh, Lily," she says, "we have lots to talk about."

Yes, we do. I know what good guidance looks like now, and I'll never let it go.

I wipe my eyes, about to tell her that I want to reinstate our sessions. But something else tumbles from my mouth. "Do you think I can call you Allison?"

"I'd like that very much."

Fifty-eight

Loren Hale

The plane lands in New York. I don't go home. I end up at a parking lot of a local bar. Cold. Alone. Stuck with my own thoughts. It's a dangerous game.

I grip the steering wheel, pain cutting through me like sharp knives. I can't stop seeing Emily's contorted face, one full of unease—uncomfortable, wishing I would just go the hell away. I lost my mother again, but that's a stupid thought. I can't lose something that I never had.

I pinch my eyes and scream, my throat burning. I need to run. I need to push these feelings away. I hear my father in the back of my head. I hear Emily. I hear the press, the media. *You have everything, Loren. Why the fuck are you crying? Look around, what could you possibly be sad about?*

Nothing. I'm not allowed to be upset, to feel anything but gratitude. I am privileged. I am rich. My eyes skim the bar, the *Open* sign flashing in neon blue. I am a rebellious new adult, needing attention. Right? That's what this is. Alcohol will draw every eye to me, make people pity me. Make them feel sorry.

That's not it, I think. Alcohol will drown my warring thoughts. Alcohol will shut out every voice in my head.

It will also fuck everything else up.

I don't know what to do. I'm going out of my goddamn mind. I slam my palm against the steering wheel, another scream knotted in my throat, and the tears I stifled suddenly stream down my face. I couldn't say no to my father, I couldn't stop the leak, and my mother never really wanted me—not even now. I always fail. Always.

My hands tremble as I slip out my cell and dial a number quickly. I just want to hear her voice. I press my forehead against the wheel, no more energy to even keep my head upright.

"Where are you?" Lily asks with worry. "You were supposed to call hours ago. Your flight landed, right?"

"Yeah, I'm on my way home," I lie.

"Are you still in New York? We can meet up for dinner," she offers, probably not buying my lie.

"Why do you love me, Lil?"

"Lo, really, where are you?" Concern spikes her voice.

"Just answer me." I let out a long breath. "*Please*. Why do you love me?" I grip the phone harder, tears clouding my vision.

"When we were eleven, we were at your house, reading comics," she says, and for some reason, I know exactly which memory she's trying to draw for me. We were on my bed, surrounded by several open and splayed *X-Men* comics, and we would read the same one at the same time. She'd wait patiently for me to hurry up, her eyes skimming the panels quickly while I soaked in each line, each bleed of color. "Do you remember?" she asks after a long pause.

"Yeah," I say, my voice shaking.

"We both knew you were kind of like Hellion. You make the wrong choices, even when you know where the right ones lie."

I nod to myself, tears spilling. I try to breathe a full breath, but the pain chokes me.

"But that day, you said you aspired to be Cyclops. Scott Summers was strong. He took care of everyone in the face of crisis. He was a man that people wanted by their side." Her voice shakes too, like she's near tears. "Lo," she says, "you've made it. You're my Scott Summers, and without you, I wouldn't be here."

I close my eyes and let that sink in. She doesn't have to say, *I love you because . . .* The sentiment is attached to each and every word. She loves me because she believes I'm strong. She loves me because she's a part of me.

She loves me because I've become a better man through all of this.

"Lo," she continues. "Whatever Emily said, I need you to know that I'm not going anywhere. I'll always be here when you come home. There will always be an *us*."

"A Lo and Lily," I breathe.

"Or Lily and Lo."

I smile. "Thank you."

She pauses. "Do I have to say the rest?"

"No, but you can if you want."

"Don't fucking drink, Loren Hale," she says sternly, but it comes off more cute than rigid. It works all the same.

"I love you, Lil." I straighten up and wipe my eyes with the back of my arm.

"Are you coming home, then?"

"I have to make a stop first."

She sucks in a worried breath. "Lo."

"Trust me," I say.

"I love you too," she tells me.

I turn on the ignition and let those words carry me.

Fifty-nine

Loren Hale

don't remember the office being this cold or dark, but I walk in with purpose. I'm no longer sorry or sad. I'm fueled by something else, something darker and stronger, that begins to eat at my core. It's a demon that my father carries, the one where anger turns into vile words. The one where we stop being pathetic and we start being mean. I thought being sober would change me. Make this part of me vanish. But I realize it's not only alcohol that powered my hate. It's programmed inside of me from years and years of being raised by someone like him.

"You're finally back," Brian says, lounging behind the desk with this nonchalance that has always dug under my skin. "Did you get tired of ignoring my calls?"

"You were nothing if not persistent," I snap dryly, slumping down into the chair. I met Brian in rehab, and we discussed my life in grave detail. He was supposed to be my outpatient therapist, and I guess I kind of fucked that up when I stopped going to our sessions. Even more so when I stopped answering his calls.

"So why are you here, Lo?" He leans even further back in his chair.

"How do you not fucking hate me?" I ask in confusion.

"I assume you had a valid reason for skipping the session," Brian says calmly, "and if not, then that's on you."

"I'm not talking about skipping sessions," I snap. "How can you sit there and listen to my problems and not roll your eyes every two seconds?"

"Why would I do that?" He doesn't flinch, doesn't look confused or upset. Brian is a blank slate that bounces my words right back at me. All this time, I thought he stared at me like I was this royal douchebag—that I was some loser he had to stomach. But I know I was projecting. I wanted him to hate me. I was begging for it because I'm not worthy of anyone's compassion.

"I have more money than you will ever have in your lifetime," I tell him. "You have to sit there and listen to me *bitch* about stupid shit for hours on end, and then I return home to my nice house with my nice car."

"You think I should hate you because you have money and because I have to listen to your problems? Is that why you stopped coming?"

"No, I stopped coming because I couldn't bear to stare at your ugly face any longer."

He actually smiles at that. It's genuine, which makes me feel like a bigger dick. He sets his pen on his desk and sits up. "I know you, Lo," he reminds me. "We've talked for months, so I know that no one, especially your father, has ever told you this."

"If this is your fortune cookie wisdom, you can save it."

"Having money doesn't make you an unfeeling automaton. You're human. You can still have problems. The difference is that you have the ability to fix them. You just have to want to. Not everyone can receive the same help you can or afford the rehab facility you went to." My stomach curdles at the truth. "But that doesn't mean your recovery can't be difficult. It doesn't mean that what people say on TV or in the tabloids doesn't hurt as much. You still bleed like the rest of us. You can cry. You can be upset. That right has not been taken from you."

I stare dazedly at the ground.

"And, Lo," he continues. "I usually don't offer my personal opinion to my patients, but I'm going to make an exception with you."

"How kind."

He doesn't smile this time. "Underneath this rough, I-hate-myself-and-everyone-around-me exterior is a good guy. And I think that you have the ability to accomplish great things if you just start forgiving yourself."

"For what?"

"I think you know what."

"Well, you're so keen on giving personal opinions, why don't you tell me," I snap.

He doesn't. Instead he grabs his pen, leans back in his chair, and clicks a couple times. "Sometimes the person we think we'll become is the person we already are, and the person we truly become is the person we least expect." He clicks his pen again and points it at me. "There's your fortune cookie wisdom."

I think he's telling me that I have a chance. That the life I imagined—where I become the self-loathing man behind a desk, where I become my father—doesn't have to be the one meant for me. I want to take the leap while my mind is clear, while I can see an alternative future that doesn't look as grim. I want Lily. A house. The white picket fence kind of happiness. I didn't ever think I deserved that, but maybe, one day, I can become the kind of person who does.

I shift in my seat, but I don't break his gaze. "I went to see my mother. My real mother," I tell him.

His head tilts, but his face has gone blank again. This time, I don't feel like punching him for his lack of reaction. I just talk.

It pours out of me like I've carved open my stomach. Every word makes me lighter and freer.

I don't stop.

Sixty

Lily Calloway

The next morning, Lo and I head to his office. He shares all the details about his mother, and he lets me hug him whenever I reach out. While I can't physically relate to a parent abandoning me, I understand what it feels like to want your mother to love you and not to receive the same affection in return.

He sinks into his leather chair, and I hesitate to bring up what happened with Dr. Evans so soon after his emotional reconnection with Emily. It's why I didn't mention it on the phone last night. Last thing I wanted was to instill guilt and have him break his sobriety. (He admitted to sitting in the parking lot of a bar—I knew it.)

I skim the comic books on his shelf while he works on a couple contracts. A guy who runs another indie publishing company has been giving Lo advice, so every week Lo grows more confident about the job. He even talks about hiring a partner to help with all the areas he's weak in. And that idea, of asking someone for help, doesn't make him balk in the least.

I'm supposed to be unpacking boxes downstairs at Superheroes & Scones, so my lingering presence must catch Lo's attention. "You okay, Lil?"

I pull a *She-Hulk* comic off the shelf and focus on the cover while I speak. "I actually decided to go back to Allison for therapy. And my father is okay with it. He says it won't break the deal." He also told me that he'll be filing a lawsuit against Dr. Evans. Hopefully, I helped some other girl that could have been harassed.

"Fuck," he curses. "I forgot to ask you about your last session with . . ." He trails off, and I meet his eyes, which have grown as big as saucers.

"I'm glad I went," I tell him. "I would have never fired him otherwise."

"What the fuck did he do?"

I hug the comic to my chest like a pillow, letting it give me some sort of strength. "He wanted me to masturbate while he shocked me," I say very quickly.

Lo grips the table, his eyes turning into pure fury.

"But I said no! And then he didn't like that so he unzipped his pants."

Lo jumps to his feet. I drop the comic and rush to stop him from leaving the room.

My hands press to his chest. "I said no, Lo," I say proudly. "I screamed it, and then I screamed for Garth. Everything worked out fine."

"Everything is not *fine*," Lo tells me, hurt caressing his amber eyes. "Fine would be you never having to deal with that sick fuck."

"It's over," I say. "My father is handling it. I don't want to keep dwelling on every bad thing that happens to us. I want to move on. Don't you?" I'm ready to start the newest chapter of our lives. One where we're not assaulted by our vices. One where we're happy.

His shoulders slacken and his hands rise to my cheeks. "Are you okay?" he asks, searching my eyes for the truth.

"I feel strong," I say. "I know that's probably weird."

He shakes his head and his eyes seem to say *no, not at all.*

"There's something else," I start. Worry shrouds his face. "Not like that. It's a good thing, I think." I take a deep breath and his hands fall to mine. "I've decided that I don't want to see the blacklist of what I can't do . . . sexually, I mean." I grimace. *Really, Lily?*

Wrinkles crease his forehead. "Why?"

"I realized that it doesn't matter what I can't do with you," I say. "We're together . . . for real this time. No piece of paper or list can tell me what I'm missing. I have everything I could want."

I can't even blink before his lips are on mine, before his arms have pulled me to his body. I am cloaked in Loren Hale. He brushes his hand against the back of my neck before ending the kiss, but he doesn't retract fully. I'm still very much in his arms.

And then he lifts me up with two hands firmly planted on my ass. My legs swoop around his waist instantly. Obviously my limbs are processing what's happening faster than my brain.

His eyes melt into mine as he slowly carries me backward and sets me down on his desk. My heart beats like a drum at this—a fantasy I've imagined since I was in high school. Desks. Sex over them. Sex on them. Sex near them. Of course I can make furniture into something stimulating.

Is this really happening or is it all in my dirty mind?

The corners of his lips rise at my confusion and anticipation. His amusement only riles my cravings, but I try to push them back, not wanting to turn into a compulsive monster.

His hands run along my thighs, my legs still tight around his waist. "How many times have you pictured this?"

"On this specific desk?"

He grins and kisses me again. I deepen it and hold on to the back of his hair, gripping tightly. He groans a little as he pulls away, and then he tugs off my shorts with ease. I'm about to sweep my legs back around his waist, but I stop myself. Shockingly, I even stop him, planting two firm hands on his pecs. Oh, those are nice.

"Lil?"

Right, focus. I meet his perplexed gaze. "I'm not stupid," I say.

His frown morphs into hurt. "I never said you were."

I shake my head. This is all coming out wrong. "What I mean is," I start again, "after all those times you denied me sex on the beach, in the car, basically anywhere but our bedroom and bathroom, I've figured out that public sex has to be on that blacklist."

He takes a step back, and the distance hurts more than I thought. I reach out and grab his hand for some sort of connection. He lets me hold on tight. "You said it doesn't matter what's on it," Lo reminds me.

"It doesn't," I say. "It doesn't, I promise. I just don't want to break it."

My words appease him enough to walk back to me, to slip his hand from mine so he can place both on my cheeks. "I won't let you break any of those rules. That's my promise to you."

"But—"

"It's *my* office," he says with a humored smile. "It's my *private* place."

Ohhhhh. *YES!* I bite my bottom lip to try to hide my grin.

"So you're all smiles now?" he asks. "You know what I think about smiles?"

I shake my head, still smiling as his hands make their descent. His fingers teasingly slide just beneath the hem of my panties.

His lips brush my ears. "They're not nearly as sexy as this." He slips his fingers inside of me and presses against a tender spot. My face instantly contorts into one of sheer pleasure, my mouth opening and my eyes fluttering. A noise escapes my throat.

He looks all too pleased. "Who's smiling now, love?"

Definitely you. I grab onto his shoulder as he replaces his fingers with his hard cock. I have the urge to rock against him, but I make myself stay still as can be. I want to show him that I have control. That I'm trying.

He thrusts in and out, and I clutch onto his back, his arms, anything to hold myself together. His hand grazes my neck, and he leans forward for a kiss, but I have trouble just staying still. Moving my lips seems like a difficult feat. He doesn't seem to care. He presses his mouth against mine and urges it open. When I don't respond, he goes to sucking my bottom lip. Noises bubble up from my throat, noises that I wasn't even sure I could make.

Now he's smiling.

He pumps faster and harder, and I lose my grip, almost falling backward on the desk. He catches me and then slowly sets me flat against a few loose papers.

"Eyes on me, love," he orders in a husky breath. I realize I'm staring at his cock. I look up to meet his gaze. It's heady, intense, and fills me fuller than any other body part. I don't break it.

Not now. Not ever.

Sixty-one

Lily Calloway

"Oh my God! I found your porn!" I walk out of Ryke's closest with a shoebox. I can only imagine it holds incriminating evidence, verifying that I'm not the only porn-lover of our friends. My glee is all too apparent.

Lo and Ryke glance up from the floor, spread out with bubble wrap and boxes. We're packing up some things from his old room at his mother's house. He's moving from his flat in Philly to a new apartment—same city, just a place with more guest bedrooms and less paparazzi lurking outside.

Instead of buying all new things for the extra space, he's trying to consolidate what he has here. Ryke planned the packing party during Sara Hale's book club, so she's not home. Lo doesn't really want to meet her face-to-face, considering he's the result of her failed marriage.

"Open it," Ryke tells me, motioning toward the shoebox in my hands.

I flip the top and my spirits pop. Baseball cards. Hundreds of them. One of the guys looks kind of hunky . . . maybe . . .

I hold up a card with the hot young player. "You totally jerked off to this."

Lo grins, even as he struggles wrapping an odd-shaped lamp.

Ryke gives me a look. "*You* would," he refutes. "And maybe I would too if I was attracted to men. But no, I traded those with kids from grade school, I didn't jizz on them." He turns to Lo. "Does she do this to you?"

"What?" he asks in amusement. "Try to find my porn?"

I freeze, eyes wide. "You have porn?" Oh my God, there may be porn at our house. Right now. I gasp. "Where?"

"At my dad's place," he explains. "From my teenage years." Oh. That makes sense. He wouldn't keep porn around me—even if I've done really well these past few weeks.

"So I'm the only one you like to embarrass?" Ryke asks me.

"You can't get embarrassed," I remind him, "and you told me to be comfortable talking about sex, so it's your fault." It's true I've opened up around Ryke, and I think we can even call each other friends now.

"Fucking fantastic." He grabs a roll of tape and tries to roll it over a box, but the dispenser shrieks in revolt. He grumbles a few curse words and throws it on the ground. "Lily, can you go find me another roll of tape? There should be one in the kitchen cabinet."

"I'm on it." I exit the bedroom and journey through the large house that has more unnecessary bedrooms than necessary ones. I find the kitchen and start opening as many cabinets as I can, avoiding the dishware and pots. A few drawers later, I find the miscellaneous area. I squat and discover tape behind a tub of bulbs.

Success.

I spin around, about to head back to Ryke's room, but something stops me. Something situated on the tea cart by the breakfast table. A small box is wedged in an overflowing basket of mail.

It's brown, like any normal package, but this one is different. My heart lurches to my throat. Swallowing a lump, I approach the box, confirming my suspicion. Tiny X's are typed all across the packaging.

My hands shake as I set the tape on the cart and inspect the label.

From: Kinkyme.net

It's the same site that sent me the dildo, but I assumed the leak just mailed the package directly to my parents' house. Wait. That's not right. A note accompanied the sex toy, so the leak had to mail the box to their house first, place the message inside, and *then* send it to me.

This is Ryke's house. We never come here. He knows this. He knows more about us than almost anyone. We let him in.

Lo was right from the beginning, wasn't he?

Tears well. Ryke made this elaborate plot, infiltrating our lives, just to cause Lo more pain—to ruin his life because he destroyed his just by simply existing.

Why is it that the people you come to love are the ones that seem to hurt you the most?

I continue reading the box.

To: William Crane

A fake name to cover his tracks. I grip the box, hating everything and then nothing at all. A horrible pain shreds my chest. Lo won't just be hurt by the news. He'll be devastated. How can he handle another disappointment, another betrayal? Even imagining his reaction brings a flood of tears, dripping down my cheeks.

I have a sudden urge to rip open the box and see what's inside. Before I search for a knife, the patter of shoes echoes, the sound growing toward me. And then the noise silences by the doorway— the *kitchen* doorway.

Sara Hale sets her purse and her book club's hardback on the counter. Her golden-brown hair complements her flower sundress. As soon as she makes eye contact with me, her glowing face tightens. And then her gaze drops to the box in my hands.

"What are you doing here?" she asks, not peeling from the box. "What is that?" Her lip spasms. "You need to leave right now."

Each time she speaks, I can barely register the words. They zip right into my ear and out the other.

"Did you not hear me?" Her eyes sear with hate. I don't know where it's coming from. I don't know what I did to her. "Get out of my house!"

"Mom, what the hell?" Ryke rushes down the stairs and into the kitchen, Lo right behind him. I'm too stunned to do much of anything.

"You brought her here!" Sara shrieks, and then her eyes ping to Lo, who hurries to my side. "And *him?*"

Lo touches my shoulder, and he glances at the box in my hands. "Lo," I say softly. I don't know anything anymore. I'm so confused.

Ryke follows my gaze, and before Lo or I can do a thing, his brown eyes light with fire. He faces his mother. "What the fuck did you do?" His voice is hollow and cold.

"Get them out, Ryke," she retorts, pointing toward the front door.

"What the fuck did you do?!" he screams, his hands on his head. His chest rises and falls.

"Sweetie, let's talk about this later." She reaches out to touch his arm, but Ryke jerks back, throwing his hands in the air.

"What the fuck is going on?" he says. "What the fuck did you do?" He shakes his head repeatedly, and it's then that I know for certain who the real leak is.

Ryke had nothing to do with the scandal. Lo's brother is just as innocent as the rest of us.

"I don't want to talk in front of them," Sara says.

"Did you tell the press that Lily's a sex addict?" Ryke asks, his eyes reddening as he suppresses more volatile emotions. He's about to explode.

I've always wanted to see Ryke Meadows flinch, but not from something like this.

"Ryke—"

"Did you fucking tell them?!" he yells, clutching the granite counter.

"Yes," she suddenly says, touching her chest as though a weight has been lifted. All this time, we assumed that the blackmailer was a man. Yet, here *she* stands.

Lo is rigid beside me, and if the perpetrator was anyone else, he'd most likely be sending the person to hell with his words. I think we're both more concerned for Ryke in this moment.

The painful silence stretches. Ryke stands still, unmoving, and his tears gather and threaten to fall.

"Ryke, honey," Sara says, "you have to understand that Jonathan—"

"Stop," Ryke says, his voice breaking. "I get why you did it. You ruined a girl's life because you wanted to be free of him. You wanted people to know that you were cheated on. You couldn't say a word about his infidelity because of the divorce contract. But if the media found out inadvertently, you'd still keep Jonathan's money and everyone would know about Loren's real mother. Tell me I'm wrong."

She doesn't say a thing.

Ryke shakes his head again, his voice shaking even more. "So you *tormented* Lily to hurt Loren, to retaliate against Jonathan fucking Hale, to stick it to his son, and I guess you strung Lily along for a while because Jonathan was squirming. You liked that. You took pleasure in his stress. And then when you leaked the news to the press, your book club friends and everyone else realized that you were cheated on. Right? You weren't the gold digger after all. That's great, Mom. Congratulations. You succeeded."

"Ryke—"

"You know what else you did?" He blinks and tears fall. "You lost your only son." He goes to turn around, and Sara grabs his arm.

"Wait, honey—"

Ryke untangles from her hold but stops and faces her again. "What? What could you possibly say that could justify terrorizing a girl for *months*?"

"You were never supposed to meet him," she says under her breath, her cheeks slick with her own tears. She points at Lo. "He's not your family."

"He's my brother!" Ryke yells. "He would never hurt me the way you just have." He takes a ragged breath, tugs at his shirt, and holds back a scream. "You don't get what you did, Mom. Do you even know what you did to *me?* Do you fucking understand?"

Sara's chin quivers as she cries. "Please, stop. Don't go." She touches his arm.

"You've made me choose between you and Dad my whole fucking life. You can't stop me from having a relationship with Lo. You can't make that decision for me."

"I'm your mom."

"And you lied to me!" Ryke shouts, pain enveloping his face. "You ruined someone's life for a fucking feud, and you were willing to sacrifice *me* doing it."

"No," she says, shaking her head. "If I thought you'd react like this, I would have never—"

"I don't believe you," he says flatly. "If you knew me at all, you'd realize that I'd hate you for what you've done. I can forgive you for a lot of things. But this . . ." He lets out a weak laugh like he's stuck inside a nightmare. "What the fuck, Mom?" He takes a deep breath. "I'm gone in an hour. I have a few more boxes."

She can't stop crying. Sara hugs the counter, expecting Ryke to come into her arms, to comfort her and say everything's okay.

But he can barely look at her without his breath shortening.

"Just answer me one thing," Ryke says. "How did you find out that she was a sex addict? I never told you that." He didn't? I thought maybe that's how she learned.

Sara sniffs and gestures to his pocket. "Your cell . . . your texts . . ."

Oh God.

Ryke pinches his eyes.

She read his texts. I'm sure there are many mentioning my addiction, or hinting at it. Ryke always asked how therapy went. He was the first person to tell Lo and me that aversion therapy is sadistic and to stop seeing Dr. Evans. And before that, he most likely texted back and forth with Lo about my progress with Allison.

Lo kisses my hand a couple times, and he wipes my tears with his thumb. I let go of his palm because I think we both know that I'm not the one crumbling right now. I don't even need to nudge Lo. He's beside his brother within the second.

"So you found their numbers from my cell?" Ryke asks, trying to suppress more tears, his eyes bloodshot.

"I just . . ." She cries into her hand.

"You what?" Ryke says. "You wanted me to stop hanging out with Lo? You wanted Jonathan's son to suffer because Lo took me from you? That's . . . fucked up, Mom. That's real fucked up."

"Please . . . it sounds worse than it is."

"I assure you, it's that bad." Ryke tries to take a deep breath, but he can't quite let it out. "Well, you got what you wanted. I hope you're happy with that." Ryke turns to Lo. "Can you help me finish my room? And then we can get out of here."

"Sure."

We leave his mother bawling in the corner of the kitchen. I almost feel bad. Almost. But when I see Ryke, that pity for her transforms into hate again. Because she hurt her son more than she could hurt me. This was personal, and even though she was going after Jonathan, she hit Ryke directly in the heart.

The door closes, and Ryke just shatters completely.

He squats in the middle of the room, his hands on his head, not able to take a full breath. "What the fuck?" he keeps repeating. "What the fuck?" He laughs painfully into a broken sob.

Lo bends beside him and sets a hand on his back. "Hey, you're all right. It's okay."

Ryke covers his face in his hands and he screams, all the pent-up rage coming. He suddenly shoots to his feet, his reddened eyes pinging around the room, crazed and tear-streaked. He finds a baseball bat.

"Whoa, whoa," Lo says, prying the weapon from Ryke's hand.

"I need to hit something," Ryke says, restless.

"Just sit down."

"I can't!" Ryke screams. "My mother fucking ruined your life! None of this would have happened if it weren't for—"

And then Lo pulls him to his chest, for a hug. Ryke hesitates for a second, and I wonder if he's going to release his aggression on Lo by punching him. Instead, he fists the back of Lo's shirt, and they stay like that, with Ryke choking, with his body vibrating in agony and guilt, and Lo clutching tightly, not letting go.

"It's not your fault," Lo says, holding on to his older brother.

Many months ago, the roles were reversed. Lo would have never been strong enough to be a support for someone else, especially someone that hardly ever breaks down.

I wipe a few silent tears. I know the kind of remorse that puts deep pain on your chest, the kind that feels as weighted as Atlas bearing the world. It's soul-crushing.

"Listen to me," Lo breathes in his ear. "Meeting you was the best thing that's ever happened to us. I'm sober and Lily's in recovery. None of that would have been possible if it wasn't for you." He shakes Ryke, and a tear slips out of Lo's eye. "You are the fucking reason I'm with the girl I love; you're my *brother*, so don't you ever feel guilty for what's happened now. That's not on you." He holds up Ryke's face to look him in the eyes. "Hey, you hear me?"

Ryke nods over and over, trying to believe the words. After a long pause, Ryke says in a strained voice, "Our parents spent so much time hating each other that they didn't even fucking realize what they were doing to us." He shakes his head in a daze.

Lo squeezes his shoulder.

I stay quiet, not wanting to disturb them, but I'm thankful that, through all of this, they both have each other. Sara and Jonathan have unconsciously drawn their sons together.

Ryke stares at the boxes. "I'm never coming back here."

"Are you sure?" Lo asks.

"Yeah." Ryke nods. He pats Lo's back. "Yeah, I'm sure." And through the silence, I hear the words that pass between them.

You're my family.

I think we can finally move on.

Sixty-two

Loren Hale

My father didn't tell me that Sara Hale was the leak to protect himself. Or me.

He was protecting Ryke.

While the news has devastated Ryke, I am freed by it. I can stop being so rooted in hate. Now I can try to be a better man than my father. I can breathe.

My fist raps a black door. No one stands beside me. No one's here for me to lean on. I am alone with my own resolve, and maybe months ago, that wouldn't have been enough.

The door flies open and almost swings right back in my face. I brace the frame with a hand. "Hear me out," I tell him.

Aaron Wells lets out an exasperated sigh, but he surrenders to my plea. "What do you want, Loren? I thought we already had this talk four months ago?" It's been that long?

"This is a different talk."

His eyes darken and he crosses his arms over his chest. "You're not coming inside this time, and just so you know, Julie isn't home. So don't try screaming for her either."

"I don't want to talk to Julie."

"Then what do you want?" *What do I want?* Why do people always ask me that?

"You met me at a really bad time in my life, and you were just being nice by inviting me to your party."

"And then you broke every wine bottle in my parents' cellar. Yeah, I remember," he says. "Is this your way of apologizing? Is this like step seven in AA or something? Do you have to go around and ask for forgiveness from everyone you screwed over?"

I shake my head. "It's nothing like that. I'm not asking you to forgive me, and I can't forgive you for what you did to Lily." I want to, but maybe that type of strength is beyond me.

His jaw locks, and I sense that he's about to slam the door in my face. "But," I say quickly, "one of us should have been the bigger person and stopped it before it got out of hand."

"You mean before you and your father made sure I wouldn't get accepted into an Ivy League," he growls. "Thanks for that."

"Look, you don't have to be my friend or anything. You can hate me all you want, but I came here to tell you that I'm sorry." The words are hard to produce, and I don't feel exactly better by saying them. I'm not searching for that relief. I just know that this is right. And this is what I have to do. "I'm done," I say. "Whatever shit we had in the past, it's the past for me. You want to carry it around, fine. Regardless, I want you to have these." I remove two white envelopes from my back pocket.

His eyes scan over them with curiosity and then he snorts. "Are you buying my forgiveness with tickets to Wrigley Field?"

"You told me that you couldn't get a job and compete with Ivy grads," I say. "That should help start your career. Greg Calloway and my father wrote references for you. I know there's lots of bad energy with the companies, but Fizzle and Hale Co. are still world-renowned. It still means something."

Aaron stares at the letters and shakes his head. "I don't want your fucking charity, especially if you're only doing this to make yourself feel better."

"I'm doing it because it's right," I say with irritation. "Burn it if you want. And I promise, you won't ever have to see me again."

I turn around and descend the stone steps. Lily waits in the car for me, tapping her hands to the dashboard and singing aloud to whatever song blares through the speakers. I immediately smile.

"Loren!"

I look back. Aaron's face has softened into something less hateful. Almost like the first time I met him, when he was just that nice lacrosse kid inviting me to his party. "I'm sorry too," he says.

Hearing the words are almost as hard as saying them. I see him terrorizing Lily for months, cornering her in the halls. I realize how difficult it must have been to listen to me say the same thing. My throat closes up before I can speak. So I just nod.

I set my sights on Lily again.

She is my past, my present, my future. So when I open the door and slide into the driver's seat, I'm not surprised that it feels like I'm returning home.

Sixty-three

Loren Hale

My nerves rocket the closer we reach our house in Princeton. I can't stop fidgeting, and Lily keeps giving me weird looks. I spout off some story about a new client for Halway Comics.

Our apartment feels abandoned when we walk inside.

"Rose!" Lily calls out. She doesn't know that Rose is staying over at Connor's tonight, that I have specifically vacated this place for us.

"She must be working late," I say.

"She works too much." Lily heads to the kitchen. "Maybe we should cook her dinner . . ." She thinks about this, probably remembering she can't cook. "Or order her dinner and bring it to her office? She'd like that."

She would. If she was at her office.

"I'm sure Connor already had dinner delivered to her," I say, hooking my fingers in her belt loops.

"True. He's been spending more time with her lately, hasn't he? I think he's worried another Sebastian will Jedi mind-trick her."

I'm surprised she's not focusing on the fact that I'm tugging her into my chest. It's becoming easier and easier to touch Lily without her jumping my bones like a wild animal. The horny, insane part of me will probably miss her crazy sex drive. But the part of me that loves her, the one that I choose to listen to, is so fucking proud of this girl.

"How about we call it a night?" I say and slip my hand down the back of her jeans.

She gasps a little and grabs onto my T-shirt. "Is that code for what position we'll be taking?" she asks with a delighted smile.

"I don't speak in code. You'll know exactly what I want." I squeeze her ass. "Me. You. Bedroom. Now." My teeth catch her earlobe lightly, and her breath deepens. And then I press feather-light kisses on her neck. At the fourth one, she squirms with laughter.

"Okay! Okay! Okay!" She throws her hands up in surrender. "Do not tickle me with your kisses! That's a dirty game."

I can't stop grinning.

She spins on her heels, and I follow her close up the stairs. She stops a couple times to check that I'm right behind her. The third time, I give her a look. "Do you think I'm going to disappear, love?"

"Maybe," she says softly and then scampers the rest of the way.

She presses her back against the door, blocking our entry. I try to remain calm, but I know what's behind those doors. And she unknowingly prolongs this process.

"I think I'm going to get fat off scones," she tells me, relishing this fact.

"You're supposed to sell the scones, not eat them."

"Who made those rules?"

"Capitalists."

She crinkles her nose. "I like my way better."

I nod to the door. "You going in?"

"I'm trying something new," she tells me. "Restraint."

Jesus Christ. She has to choose *tonight* for her personal achievement? "Should we discuss donuts next?" I say jokingly.

She looks like she's taking this into serious consideration, and

I give in. I reach past her waist and turn the knob, opening the door behind her back.

Her eyes go big, and she *still* doesn't turn around. "Are you testing me?"

I put my hands on her shoulders and walk her backward, leading her slowly into our room. Step by step. Her eyes fix on mine until she looks down, obviously feeling something soft under her bare feet.

"What . . ."

Red petals decorate the bedroom floor, while burning candles flicker on the dresser and nightstand. It's simple and perfect. I drop to my knee.

Her hands press to her lips, and I see that gaudy ring on her hand glinting back at me. It represents coercion and deception, all the wrong reasons for a marriage that should be filled with love.

We have lived through lies for too long. I'm ready for this to be honest, not another sham. I'm so ready for her to take it off.

Her eyes have already welled with tears and I haven't even spoken yet.

I pull out a small box from my pocket. Colorful and wrapped in comic book strips.

All my nerves seep out of me. I am filled with something else, something warm and pure that makes me never want to leave this moment.

"Lily Calloway, will you marry me? For real this time?"

I open the box, and a ruby cut into a heart sparkles back at her. Diamonds circle it.

"Yes!" She jumps a little, tears seeping out of the corners of her eyes. I rise to my feet, and with one kiss, I have her planted firmly back on Earth. She tangles her fingers in my hair and lets *me* deepen the kiss.

When I part from her, she begins yanking at her gaudy ring.

She gets wild-eyed. "Lo, it's not coming off," she panics. "It's not coming off!"

"Calm down," I coax. I test it out, but it's tight around her swollen finger. Maybe she is gaining some weight. I kiss her temple and take her hand in mine, leading her to the bathroom. We spend a couple of minutes soaking her finger in soap before the ring comes loose and clinks on the counter.

What if my ring doesn't fit her?

She reaches for the box, and I grab it from her. "Let me," I say.

She holds out her hand. The ring slides effortlessly, the leftover soap on her finger probably helping. She appraises the ruby and the band for a long moment. "I love it, Lo." Her eyes twinkle as they meet mine. "I love you more."

After all we've been through. Years and years of mistakes, it feels like a dream to be here in this moment.

Right now.

Sober.

Alive.

With her.

I pull her to me, and I lean in for a kiss. Her hand instinctively rises and slides across the back of my shoulders. When we break apart, I rest my forehead against hers. Our breaths mingle, and I say, "I have another proposal. Or . . . more like a confession."

"Is it bad?" she whispers.

"Terrible."

She doesn't pull away from our closeness and her eyes flit to my lips. "I can handle it."

"I don't know about that."

Her lips twitch as she recognizes the tone of my voice. Oh, how I do love teasing her.

I nudge my nose with hers before my lips find her ear. I nip it softly before I say, "I confess, that I'd very much like to make love to you." My heart flips at the last words. We never say *make love*. We fuck. We screw. We bang. Making love is for the softhearted without tar-coated pasts. Lily claims she doesn't deserve to make love, but I'm determined to change her attitude.

"Is it different than fucking?" she asks me with wide eyes.

"Very much so."

Frown lines crease her forehead. "How?"

"I'll show you."

Her eyes brighten with possibilities, but she doesn't insist, doesn't ask or compel me for more. *She waits for me.*

Just as I asked.

ACKNOWLEDGMENTS

Self-doubt is a writer's biggest foe, and without the support and encouragement from family, friends, and especially our readers, we wouldn't have mustered the courage to continue, let alone begin to defeat our greatest adversary.

We lay down our hearts for all the readers who have spread the word about the series, who have shared the book with another person, who have simply said a few kind words to us. Your support is more than just appreciated. We'll remember it each time we begin a new chapter and face a new enemy.

For taking a chance on Lily and Lo and believing that they deserve a happily ever after, you are the superheroes of this tale. It takes a brave reader to stand beside Lily and Lo and commit to seeing their journey through. You have stuck with this couple through some of their lowest points and hardest battles, and for that, we thank you.

Connor and Rose's First Date

This was a complete and utter mistake. What was I thinking agreeing to go on a date with *him*? He's a pompous arrogant ass who changes around everyone he meets. The worst kind of chameleon. Though . . . his blue eyes aren't that revolting. They are a nice shade. *Ugh*. No, I am not complimenting him before he even arrives.

I must remember *why* I agreed to this date.

Front-row seats.

The Tempest.

I'm sure he's using me for his personal gain. Maybe it's to worm his way into my family's good graces for Fizzle. He already charmed my sister Lily, who practically waved pom-poms when he asked me out. She's supposed to be loyal to *me*, not to that conceited asshole, and Connor better realize she'd never betray me. Lily might be . . . unreliable . . . distant, at times, but she's still my greatest ally.

He won't win her over and steal her from me. *Just like Loren did*. I huff out the tension that keeps straining my collarbones and shoulders. I am *better* than these ugly nerves.

And I've been around Connor too much at Bowl Championships and Model UN to be fooled by the smile and charisma. There's always a motive—and I doubt, very much, that this date has pure intentions.

It doesn't matter, though.

Tonight, I am using him as much as he's using me.

I want to see the play, and he has amazing seats. I'll endure him for Shakespeare.

It's settled.

I strut out the door and down the front porch steps in my four-inch heels and a black Chanel dress. My hair is half down, half up with a silver clip, and I made sure to wear my *fuck you* lipstick. The dark shade of burgundy looks like it'd stain if you kissed me.

And if Connor thinks there will be *any* kissing tonight, he can take those dreams and ignite them in an incinerator—where they'll remain for eternity.

I check my phone as my heels hit pavement, my parents' Villanova mansion looming behind me: *6:58 p.m.* The driveway is grand and imposing like it could greet royals in the eighteenth century, and yet, it's empty. Desolate.

He's supposed to be here at seven.

I wasn't about to let him inside my parents' place. Watching him schmooze my mother and father would make me fucking vomit. And they'd hang on every word like he's spitting gold.

No, thank you.

It's hard enough knowing he's seemingly perfect for me on paper. I can already see my mother frothing at the mouth at the idea of Calloway and Cobalt *babies*. Just kissing him is completely off the table. I'd rather chop his cock off than let him be so victorious as to enter me that . . . intimately.

My face is on fire.

I take another tight breath.

"You're just going to a play, Rose," I mutter hotly to myself. There is no reason to be this unnerved.

If I were at Princeton right now, it'd be better. On my own turf. But I'm in Philadelphia, and I have to make do. I'm ready for this battle or whatever game he'll be playing tonight.

I tap my heel, the *clink, clink, clink* music to his demise. I smile a little, and I check my phone again.

Seven p.m.

My lips flatline. I swear to all that is unholy, if he stands me up on purpose, I will *murder* him. Slowly. Painfully. If he thinks Lily will ever let him tutor her again after he makes a fool out of me . . .

I'm about to go inside and call this off. I'm not letting this happen. I'll cut him before he slices through me. Whirling on my heels toward the mansion, I brandish my phone and scroll through my most recent calls . . .

I hear tires on pavement and see the glare of bright headlights. Gradually, I spin back around. *He didn't stand me up.* My lungs inflate with a strange feeling.

And he's not late.

He's right on time.

Am I glad he's here? I wish I wasn't, but I know I am. *It's better than being made a fool of.* Another emotion barrels through me, one that makes each breath a little sharper. Nerves have returned, but I refuse to be nervous.

The vehicle approaches, and he's not in a *car*. My eyes narrow. Of course, he's in a limo.

I snort.

I'd think he were trying to impress me if my sister didn't blurt out how Connor Cobalt rides around in a limo like an everyday thing.

My stomach twists in a knot when the limo slows and parks in front of the mansion. The long side faces me as though my carriage has arrived.

This was a colossal mistake, Rose.

I exhale a breath through my nose. *Do not be nervous.* Yet, it's still assaulting me. Nerves. Ugly things. I've had less anxiety facing a room full of people at the Model UN final.

"This is just a play," I mutter under my breath.

Technically, it's a date. I'm not an idiot, and I understand there are assumptions that first dates lead to hand-holding, kissing, and sometimes even sex. Connor might be assuming those things. That he'll climb out of his limo and be able to seduce me into his bed.

He can fuck right off with that.

I'm a virgin.

At twenty-two. I plan to be one until I'm ready to have sex, and that won't be tonight. I'm barely ready for his lips to touch mine.

I can count on my hand the number of times I've been kissed. Hugging feels like being smothered with bees and holding someone's hand makes my skin crawl. I haven't found someone to prove me otherwise.

I'm not ashamed by my inexperience, but it makes dating more difficult. The older I get, the more the assumptions pile sky-high. Guys already think that I've swept the bases. Dry humped. Blow jobs. Fingering. Sex.

Usually, I'm up front.

"I'm a virgin," has come from my lips so much, it might as well be tattooed to my fucking forehead. But I've realized, for some time, that there is one person I don't want to know this information. One person that I'm terrified will use it against me.

That person is currently exiting the limo.

I slip my phone back in my purse and watch Connor hold the door open for me. I will begrudgingly give him credit for his style. A tailored suit in black that might be Brioni. It fits his six-four height and build to perfection. His wavy brown hair is artfully styled, as usual. But his blue eyes seem to light up and his smile curves as he sees me.

"Rose."

"Richard." I adjust my purse on my elbow. "I see you brought your limo. Couldn't splurge for a horse-drawn carriage?"

His lips lift higher. "I thought you'd find that a bit obtuse, seeing as how it'd take four times longer to get where we're going."

"You know what they say." I take a step forward. "Chivalry is fucking dead." My heel breaks. "Fuck . . ." I stumble, and he catches my arm before my knees hit the pavement.

"I have you." His words are a husky note that sends shock waves down my skin.

"The only thing you have is my arm," I tell him, face burning. I try not to let on that his voice is doing a number on me.

"And that's what I meant," he refutes. His blue eyes flit to mine in challenge. "What did you think I meant by it, Rose?"

I refuse to blush, but my traitorous face has already heated. "Just don't drop me." I grab onto his arm as much as he's grabbing onto mine. With my free hand, I take off my good heel and then I remove the broken one.

Standing on the tips of my toes, my stomach roils while I'm barefoot on the disgusting pavement, and I do my best to focus anywhere else.

Him.

He's a worse sight, isn't he?

As soon as I'm stable on steady ground, I back away from Connor. Yes, on my tiptoes. The space puts air between us, but the tension still feels thick. I try not to look at my feet, but I can feel the dirty ground on my bare toes.

Hair stands at the back of my neck, a sudden wave of anxiety infiltrating.

His eyes flit to the house behind the gate and then to his watch. "You have time to grab another pair."

"No," I say without hesitation, thinking about him talking to my parents. "It seems the universe has spoken. We're not supposed to go on this date."

He grimaces. "The universe." He stares at my broken heel. "You're going to give up because of a shoe? I've never taken you for a quitter."

I bristle. "I'm not *quitting*," I say. "I'm merely listening to higher powers that have come to smite this date down. It's not supposed to happen, Richard."

"This is fixable, Rose." His eyes flood mine. "I can fix it. If you'd give me the chance."

I don't accept help from others easily, and from him . . . it seems like the biggest of mountains to climb.

He steps back to the limo, hand on the top of the opened door. "Rose Calloway, the only one who's ever made Model UN and Quiz Bowl noteworthy, worthwhile, stimulating—"

"Is that how you feel about your losses and demise?" I cut in.

He grins, as though he's never lost before. "Would you please accompany me to *The Tempest*, where we have front-row seats?"

He's dangling it like a carrot. *Front-row seats.*

And God, it's working. Ugh.

If this date goes poorly, I'm blaming my love of Shakespeare.

Quickly, I walk across the dirty pavement and slide into the limo. He follows me and shuts the door behind him. He goes to tell his driver something, and I do a horrible thing and glance at the bottom of my feet.

"Rose."

I look up.

Connor's holding out a water bottle and paper towels. Do I seem that big of a diva that I can't withstand some dirt on my feet? Or does he know about my OCD?

I'm scared of the answer.

So I don't ask.

I just take the paper towels and water from him—glad that he didn't demand to wash my feet himself. Maybe Lily is right. Maybe he's not that bad.

I feel myself softening and it terrifies me, so I reinforce every barrier. Every ounce of armor. I pour a little water onto the towel and then scrub my feet.

Connor doesn't say anything, but I'm keenly aware of his gaze.

"Stop staring," I tell him.

"What else do you want me to look at?" he asks. "You're my date."

My eyes, full of fire, pin to him. Barriers and armor attached; I start drawing my canons. "I'm the girl you're taking out so that you can tell your friends you went on a date with Rose Calloway, right? Or are you just trying to add my family to your roster of connections? Is that it?"

He tips his head. "Why do you always think I have ill intent?"

"Because I don't know you, Connor," I tell him. "No one really does. You change around people to get what you want, and if you wanted *me*, you'd put on some front—"

"This isn't a front," he says, cutting me off. "I'm as real with you as I can be."

Those words leave me cold.

He's said them before. *I'm as real with you as I can be.* When I was eighteen. He was my student ambassador the day I was taking a tour of Penn's campus and interviewing for their honor's program. Before I chose Princeton.

"Nothing has changed," I tell him.

"Everything has changed," he refutes.

"How?"

"You're giving me a chance." His blue eyes dive deeper into me, and I want to believe him and the authenticity I think I see. Or am I just hoping?

My throat swells. All fiery retorts smothered, I return to washing off my feet. When I finish, the limo rolls to a stop at a curb. I glance out the window and see the fancy boutique store.

"Wait here," he tells me.

"You're not picking out a pair of shoes for me. Your style is horrendous."

He laughs like he knows it's a lie.

It is.

Seconds later, the door opens again, and he holds out a pair of blue flip-flops. Again, I'm not an idiot. I understand what this means. "Thank you." I take them from him and slide them on my feet so that I can enter the store without touching the ground.

"I told you I can fix things." We walk side by side to the store, and I sense his hand nearing mine. My pulse quickens.

The air between our fingers is electric, and though he does not touch me, a shock wave is still running through my veins.

Oxygen is richer and heady, and I wonder if most good dates are supposed to be this way. Intoxicating and miserably dizzying in these short, drawn-out seconds.

He holds open the glass door for me.

"You like that, don't you?" I wonder, more curious. "Having people indebted to you?"

He opens his mouth and then shuts it like he's rethinking. Maybe his first instinct is to lie. In the doorway, he tells me, "Yes, I like it. But not with you. I don't want you to feel like you owe me anything. Because you don't."

"Good," I say tightly. "Because we're not fucking. And I'm definitely not kissing you tonight." I walk past him, muscles tight, posture strict. A store attendant is already waiting for me with a *literal* silver tray of heels. He must have told them what I needed.

"Hello, Miss Calloway," she says brightly. "Hartford Loft is pleased to help you with any of your needs. Mr. Cobalt said you'd like a pair of heels."

"Did he pick them out?" I ask.

"No, I pulled these just for you."

I smile, trying to make it less icy. *Fail.* Surely. "I'll take these. Thank you." I point to the last pair that have simple black bows on the back. I tell her my size, and she rushes to grab them.

Maybe he also told her we're on a time crunch.

Connor leans against a pillar, near a mannequin.

"Oh look," I say. "You found your twin."

He doesn't even glance toward it. "I didn't expect a kiss tonight," he says, bringing up what I thought was a conversation I walked away from. "I want you to know that. I'm just glad to enjoy your company."

I stiffen. "Now I know you're lying."

He tries not to smile. "Why can't you believe that I actually like spending time with you, Rose?"

I stare unblinking at him. "You once told me that I leave a trail of bodies with my glares. That people are afraid to approach me. I didn't deny it. I know it's true. But why would you want to spend time with a person like that?"

"Because I'm interested in you," he says. "Because I *like* you."

The store attendant returns with the boxed shoes and pales. "Um . . . sorry to interrupt."

Perfect timing. I grab the box, about to head to the register.

"Oh, no, they've been paid for, Miss Calloway."

I frown and look to Connor. I didn't see him give her his card. "I have an account here," he says. "They have a tailor."

Oh.

"I have money," I tell him coldly. "I can buy my own shoes." I glance at the box, realizing that the gesture is . . . sweet. That maybe . . . maybe I liked it. "Thank you," I mutter under my breath.

He smiles a softer smile that doesn't make me want to claw his face.

And then we return to the limo. I slip my cleanish feet into the new heels, and we head to the theater. True to his word, they are amazing seats. I place my hands in my lap, avoiding the armrest.

What if he isn't using you?

That thought pricks my head the longer the play goes on. It's hard to concentrate on Prospero and Ariel when I'm sitting next to Connor. But I try my best as if I'll be quizzed at the end of the play. I don't give him the satisfaction of glancing over, but it's difficult when his presence commands the air around him.

"'Hell is empty and all the devils are here,'" Ariel says.

I cave.

I look at Connor.

He's staring ahead, transfixed by the play. And then he glances to me and his lips go to my ear to whisper, "'What's past is prologue.'" It's another line from the play that doesn't come until act two.

His eyes flit to mine, a headiness drawing around us. Swirling. I'm swept up in him, and maybe he's using me. Maybe he's not. Maybe he's being real.

I want to believe he is.

Belief is the first step, I realize. Belief that he might like me. Belief that I might even like him. Belief that if he touches me, the world won't implode, and that I also might like it.

I relax my arm on the armrest between us and look back to the play. Gently, I feel his fingers slide against mine. I don't recoil.

I smile. These new dizzying feelings well up inside me.

Connor holds my hand.

And I let him.

When the curtains close at the end, we stay in our seats for longer than we should, discussing *The Tempest* and Shakespeare's greatest works. The rabbit hole of literature finds us in an argument over Faulkner of all fucking things, but I find myself smiling more than I have in weeks.

An usher tells us politely that we need to leave.

I hadn't realized we were the last ones in the theater. By the surprise on Connor's face, neither had he. Time must've slipped past us. They're already sweeping popcorn off the aisles.

Earlier tonight, I'd been dreading this part of the date—the part where the play is over—but now I just wish it could've lasted a little longer.

Connor gives the usher a courteous smile. It looks fake to me, and I think he's about to pay the usher off to leave us alone here. I don't wait to see.

"Let's go." I stand up fast and collect my purse.

"Thank you," Connor says graciously to the usher, and my date leads us outside, where the limo is already waiting. He holds the door open for me again. His burgeoning grin is back to being a heinous sight, and I hate that I don't want to leave it.

Once we're seated side by side in the limo, Connor asks me, "Where to?"

I could extend the date, but I'm afraid to give him that much. I've already given him more than I ever thought I would. "Home. *My* home, or rather, where my parents live—and no, you are not invited inside."

Most men would balk at my bluntness.

Connor just grins. "To the Calloways' residence." He tells the driver our destination.

"Right away, sir."

Once we're on the road, Connor pops open a champagne bottle. We drink a little and continue discussing literature. Though the air feels different. The dizziness is wearing off.

It's coming to an end.

His hand lies on mine on the seat, and my pulse hitches when he threads our fingers. I won't admit aloud that it feels good. His hand. The warmth of his skin. It's reassuring, calming, and possibly that's just the power of Connor Cobalt—to make people feel at ease.

I like it. I suppose because I need it.

Maybe I even want it too.

I don't like when it's gone, when we've arrived and we're stepping out of the limo together and he's walking me to the front door.

I stand here. In my new heels and with these new memories and uncorked feelings. And I look up at the most confident, egotistical man I've ever known, and the only thing I breathe is, "You can't kiss me."

He only smiles. "I know." His brows rise as he looks beyond me. Lights have turned on in the mansion.

"You can't come inside," I say even faster.

"I know." His blue eyes stay on me. "But can I see you again?"

"Of course you'll see me; you're tutoring my sister. We'll run into each other—"

"That's not what I mean, Rose." His voice is quiet, level, and so opposite from mine. I can't deny the attraction tugging me toward him. "You know that's not what I mean."

He wants to continue dating me.

The knowledge surges a deeper feeling inside my lungs. I could say *no*, but I'd be lying to myself if I said I wanted this to end here.

Even though I'm afraid to take this further, to see where this could possibly go, I'd disappointment myself if I didn't meet Connor's challenge.

"I'm not a quitter," I remind him with heat, and I lift my chin. "You can take me out again."

His eyes are alight. "We'll both enjoy it."

I try not to smile. "Is that a promise or a bet?" Before he can reply, I sense my mother nearing the window. God, if she peeks out and *spies* on me like I'm a teenager and not a grown fucking woman, I will lose it. "You have to go. Now."

He takes my hand in his, and I take in a breath that won't release. He studies my jutted-out collarbones. "May I?" he whispers, his lips nearing my knuckles as he lifts my hand.

No.

Yes.

"Quickly," I murmur so softly I barely hear my own voice.

If he's quick, my mind slows the moment to infinite seconds as Connor presses his pink lips against the softness of my hand. It is gentle. Almost too gentle. But the gleam in his eyes rouses me, as though he's imagining taking me rougher and more deeply.

I try to collect myself when I pull my hand back. "Thank you for the awful evening. I loathed every moment."

"So much so that you want to do it again," he volleys, walking backward down the porch steps. I hope he trips. When he doesn't, it's disturbingly attractive.

"It must be the champagne," I call out an obvious lie.

"Or you like me."

"Be careful getting into your limo, your head might not fit inside anymore."

He laughs, already backed up against the limo. He waits to open the door and looks me over with fondness. "You look beautiful tonight." It feels like the first moment and not the last.

The dizzying newness stays with me as I breathe, "*À la prochaine*, Richard." *Until next time.*

"*Bonne soirée*, Rose."

I suppose it is the beginning of something. Not the end of everything.

BONUS PLAYLIST

Songs

"We Are Stars" by The Pierces

"I'm Gonna Wait" by The Temper Trap

"My Silver Lining" by First Aid Kit

"Set Me Free (Feel My Pain)" by Charli XCX

"Burn" by The Pretty Reckless

"Yamaha" by Delta Spirit

"Hard Time" by Seinabo Sey

"Whispered Words (Pretty Lies)" by Dan Auerbach

"Another Story" by The Head and the Heart

"Getting Even" by White Lies

"Skin & Bones" by David J. Roch

"The Cold" by Exitmusic

"Byegone" by Volcano Choir

BONUS: TEXT MESSAGE THREADS

Spring Break

THE ARRIVAL
3:12 P.M.

> **ROSE**: Toothpaste, toothbrushes, hairbrushes, shampoo, conditioner, sunscreen, aloe, a first-aid kit, razors, shaving cream, face wash, lotion, floss, scissors, deodorant, t-shirts (for pajamas)

> **ROSE**: Does anyone need any other essentials?

> **LO**: Scissors? Are essential because . . . ?

> **ROSE**: In case I need to stab you, Loren. To everyone else in the group chat who is taking this seriously, do you need something?

LILY: Do they have underwear?

CONNOR: It's a gift shop, not a department store.

LILY: . . . is that a no? 🫤

ROSE: There aren't any underwear options.

LO: Really, what the hell do you need scissors for?

ROSE: To cut the tags off the shirts I'm buying for pajamas.

RYKE: I have a fucking knife.

ROSE: Better to stab your brother with.

LO: Great. This trip is already the death of me.

LILY: NO ONE IS DYING.

LO: Only my patience, love 😛

ROSE: I'd say "get a room" but it looks like we're all sharing one indefinitely.

LO: I'm rethinking everything. This might not be that bad.

ROSE: What?

ROSE: Seriously?

LO: Yep. We might be in your hell more than mine, Rose.

LILY: Let's all get alone. Please.

LILY: *along (ughhh)

CONNOR: We'll all be fine. The room situation isn't catastrophic to anyone. Most especially to Rose.

RYKE: Why is Melissa not in this fucking group chat?

LILY: Do you want the somewhat-girlfriend to be added?

RYKE: It'd be fucking nice.

ROSE: Add her. See if she needs anything.

LILY: Added.

ROSE: Do you need anything from the gift shop, Melissa?

MELISSA: Shampoo without sulfates. Also, I like triple-blade razors only. And a nail clipper, but nothing store-brand because junky ones always give me hangnails. Thanks.

CONNOR: We'll see what we can do.

LILY: Wait, you can get her fancy shampoo but there isn't any underwear?!

ROSE: Richard is just pretending to be nice. We can't accommodate specific requests. Trust me, I've searched these aisles four times already for name-brands.

CONNOR: They have essentials only.

LILY: I trust in you two!

MELISSA: How long will you be? I want to go to the pool first, but I'd really like that nail clipper.

ROSE: We shouldn't be that long.

MELISSA: Great.

LO: Great.

1:45 A.M.

UNKNOWN: Have fun sucking cock in Cancun.

THE DAY OF EXPLORING
11:12 A.M.

LILY: Connor or Rose, Lo and I have VERY important question.

LILY: What is the proper term for a turtle's nose?

LILY: I said muzzle or snout. Lo thinks it's just called a nose.

ROSE: It's not a muzzle.

LILY: A snout, then??? I've looked up the anatomy of a turtle online, and it's not helpful. There are too many conflicting reports, and I need correct answers only.

LO: What Lily said. Correct answers only.

ROSE: Are you asking what their nostrils are called?

LILY: Is this a trick question?

CONNOR: She's wondering if you're confused about how they breathe or about their facial anatomy.

LILY: Do they not breathe out of their nose and mouth??? 😨

LO: Jesus, you two were supposed to make this *less* confusing.

CONNOR: Let me simplify. The holes above their mouth are called nares. Turtles respire through the nares and cloaca.

LO: What's a cloaca?

ROSE: Look it up.

LILY: OMG THEY BREATHE THROUGH THEIR BUTTHOLES?

LO: Thanks for the mental image

ROSE: You asked, Loren.

LILY: So wait, I guess Lo and I were both wrong about their noses.

CONNOR: Actually, no. There are multiple species of turtles, and there is one called a Fly River turtle.

ROSE: Also known as a pig-nosed turtle.

CONNOR: It has a snout.

LILY: Ah-ha! I was right! I knew it! 😬

LO: I never doubted you for a second, love

LILY: 🙈

THE DINNER
5:33 P.M.

CONNOR: Where is everyone? Rose and I have been waiting in the lobby for ten minutes.

DAISY: Sry, just got out of the shower! I was the last one in it. Be down in a sec.

ROSE: You're excused, Daisy. The rest of you, however, have zero excuses.

LILY: Lo & I are waiting on Daisy in the room. We didn't want to leave her.

LO: Yeah, we don't abandon people, Rose.

ROSE: Go fuck a cactus, Loren.

LO: Someone woke up on the wrong side of the bed. Maybe you should switch sides with Connor.

ROSE: Maybe you should shut up before I rip your tongue out.

LO: So scary. I'm petrified.

CONNOR: Is Ryke still joining us?

LO: Yeah, last I checked.

LILY: Ryke & Melissa were headed to the lobby. They're not there yet?

ROSE: No.

LO: They're probably fucking in the elevator.

DAISY: Oooh, the hotness of it all 😊

ROSE: Gross. No. That's disgusting. Those things are filthy.

RYKE: For fuck's sake, I'm in this thread too.

LILY: So you aren't having sex in an elevator and texting us at the same time? Or did you already have elevator sex? Omg, are we catching you before the act?

DAISY: I'd also like these details 😋

MELISSA: Get a life. Or better yet, get a boyfriend of your own and stop wishing you had mine.

DAISY: Sry. I was just joking. Honestly.

ROSE: Just everyone come downstairs so we can talk about this in person. This is getting ridiculous, and we're going to be late for the dinner reservation.

DAISY: I'm almost done. Be there in a sec with Lily & Lo.

RYKE: Yeah, we're coming too.

LILY: . . . but did you already come?

LILY: nvm, you don't have answer that! Sorry! I know not my business!! Okay, goodbye. See you soon.

THE LAST MORNING

4:03 A.M.

LILY: I can't sleep. U awake yet?

LO: We're right next to each other, love. You can whisper to me in bed.

LILY: I don't want them to hear us and to accidentally wake them up.

LILY: Did I wake you up by texting?

LO: No, I've been up. Couldn't really sleep.

LILY: Me either. My ears kept ringing from the club last night.

LO: Can't believe I don't have a hangover. Strange.

LILY: Good strange?

LO: I guess. Maybe. Yeah.

LILY: All of last night feels like a blur. Did it really happen?

LO: Your sisters getting drunk on absinthe? If you told me that'd happen at the start of a trip, I'd call you a liar.

LILY: I am good at that

LILY: Lying

LO: We both are, love

LO: You think Daisy's okay?

LILY: I hope so. She said she is.

LILY: I'm glad Ryke was there.

LO: I hate that I'm glad he was too. Stop yawning. You're making me yawn, Lil.

LILY: You did it first!

LO: Did not 😊

LILY: I love you

LO: I love you so much more, it hurts

LILY: We must love each other the same then, because I know what that feels like. To love someone so much, it hurts

LO: I want to kiss you

LILY: You can kiss me

LO: Just one kiss, love

LILY: Just one, Lo

Rose Calloway

You know the stories where the strong, brawny man struts into a room with his head high, his chest puffed, and his stocky shoulders pulled back—he's the king of the jungle, the big man on campus, the one who quivers girls' knees. He carries an air of unwarranted superiority for the pure fact that he has a dick, and he knows it. He expects the girl to go tongue-tied and agree to his every demand.

Well, I am living that story right now.

The man settles into a seat at the head of the conference table (instead of the chair nearest me) and just stares in my direction.

Maybe he thinks I'm going to be that stupefied girl. That I will cower beneath his deep gray eyes and his combed dishwater blond hair. He's twenty-eight, stained with Hollywood elitism and self-righteousness. When I first talked to him, he name-dropped actors and producers and directors, waiting for me to go slack-jawed and dopey. "I know so-and-so. I did a project with what's-his-face."

My boyfriend had to grab the phone out of my hand before I cursed at the Hollywood exec for irritating the shit out of me.

He finally speaks. "Do you have the contracts?" His chair screeches as he leans back.

I pull out the stack of papers from my handbag.

"Bring them here." He motions to me with two fingers.

"You could have sat beside me," I retort, standing on two chunky heels with brass buttons, military-inspired and part of the new Calloway Couture collection.

"But I didn't," he says easily. "Come here."

My heels clink across the hardwood, and I make the perilous catwalk up to Scott Van Wright.

He props one ankle on his thigh, his finger to his cheek as he unabashedly peruses my body. From my slender legs, to the hem of my black pleated dress with sheer quarter-sleeves, and to the high collar that frames my stiff neck. He traces my dark-glossed lips, my rose-blushed cheeks, and bypasses right over my pissed-off eyes, spending an extra moment fixated on my chest.

I stop by his legs and throw the contracts on the table in front of him. They slide off the polished surface and land on his lap. One stapled stack even slips to the floor. I smile wide since he has to bend down awkwardly to reach them.

"Pick that up," he tells me.

My smile fades. "It's underneath the desk."

He cocks his head, giving me *another* long once-over. "And *you* dropped it."

He cannot be serious. I cross my arms, not responding to his request. He just sits there, waiting for me to comply.

This is a test.

I'm used to them. Sometimes I even dole them out myself, but this one is going to lead me nowhere good.

If I bend down, he'll establish this strange power over me. He'll be able to command me in the same way that Connor Cobalt can force people to do his bidding with simple words.

It's a manipulator's gift.

I'm not even close to possessing it. I think I wear my emotions too much to have that type of influence over other people.

"Grab it," he says, his gaze halting on my breasts again.

I remind myself why I need Scott and why I want the swarm of cameras to document my every move. I inhale. Okay. *You have to do it, Rose. Whatever it takes.* I cringe and drop to my knees. In a dress. This is a job for a personal assistant, not a client.

I hear him click his pen as I scoop up the papers. I'm not wearing a low-cut top where I'll flash him. I don't have huge breasts to really ogle either. The most he can do is slap my ass and try to peek up my dress, the hem perilously rising on my thighs.

When I stand back up and smack the papers to the table, his lips curve upward.

Scott Van Wright (asshole), 1—Rose Calloway (pathetic), 0.

I sit in the nearest chair while Scott stuffs the contracts in his briefcase.

My boyfriend urged me to bring his lawyer to the meeting, but I didn't want Scott to think that I couldn't handle the situation myself. I won't have a lawyer while the cameras follow me, and I'd rather take command now.

Not that I'm doing a terrific job.

If I ordered Scott to do anything, he'd laugh at me. But I attended a few law courses before I graduated from Princeton. I know my rights.

"Just so we have this clear, you work for me," I remind him. "I hired you to produce the show."

"That's cute. But after you signed that contract, you've officially become *my* employee. You're the equivalent of an actress, Rose."

No. "I can fire you. You can't fire me. That doesn't make me your employee, Scott. That makes me your boss."

I expect him to withdraw from this losing battle, but he shakes his head like I'm wrong. I know I'm right . . . Right? "My production company has sole ownership over *anything* the Calloway sisters film on network television. If you fire me, you need just cause and you can't jump to another producer. I'm your only shot at having a reality show, Rose."

I remember that clause, but I never thought it would be an issue. I figured I'd be around Scott maybe twice during the whole filming process. But these were his first words when he walked into the conference room: "We're going to be seeing a lot of each other." Lovely.

My eyes grow hot. I have to concede on this one. He won. Somehow. I hate it.

"So, now that we have that clear," he says, sitting up and edging closer to me. His knees almost knock into mine. I go utterly rigid. "There are a few details we need to go over in case you misread them in the contract."

"I don't misread things."

"Well, *evidently* you weren't using a portion of your brain or else you would have realized that you work for me now. And we wouldn't have wasted . . ." He checks his watch. ". . . five minutes of my time." He flashes me a sardonic smile like I'm a little girl.

"I'm not an idiot," I retort. "I graduated at the top of my class with highest honors—"

"I don't care about your fucking degree," he says sharply. "You're in the real world now, Rose Calloway. No university is going to teach you how to navigate this industry."

Doubt surfaces. I don't know much about reality television, but I've been immersed in the media long enough to know it can help someone as much as it can destroy them.

And I need that help.

I understand exactly why the network would take an interest in the daughters of Fizzle. My father's brand has beat Pepsi for the past two years in sales, and he's working to make Fizzle the soda of choice among Southern states. We should be as anonymous as the face behind Coca-Cola, but ever since my family was thrust into the public eye, we've been under intense scrutiny, and it's all because of my younger sister's scandal.

My brand should have exploded from all the media and press, but the name Calloway Couture has been linked with Lily's dirty secrets. And what once was a thriving fashion line in H&M has become destitute in boxes and boxes, piled in my New York office.

I need *good* exposure, the kind that will have women desiring a one-of-a-kind coat, a unique pair of a boots, an affordable but chic handbag. And Scott Van Wright is offering me a prime-time reality show that will tempt viewers to purchase my pieces.

So that's why I'm agreeing to this.

I want to save my dream.

Scott says, "There will be cameras in your living room and kitchen at all times, even after the three-person crew leaves. You'll only have privacy in your bedrooms and bathrooms."

"I remember this."

"Good." Scott clicks his pen. "Then maybe you'll remember that each week, I expect to have interviews with the cast, which includes you, your three sisters—"

"Not three," I say. "Only Lily and Daisy agreed to the show." My eldest sister, Poppy, wouldn't sign the contract because she didn't want her daughter to be filmed. My little niece has already endured enough paparazzi since Lily's scandal.

"Fine, she would have been a boring addition anyway."

I glower.

"I'm just being honest."

"I'm used to blunt honesty," I tell him. "I just find yours crass."

He eyes me in a new way, as though my words carried a plume of toxic pheromones. I don't understand. I am so mean. I am *glaring* like I want to rip off his penis, and yet, he's *attracted*. There is something seriously wrong with him.

And maybe my boyfriend.

And really, any guy who'd like to be with me. I'm not even sure *I* want to be with me.

"As I was saying . . ." His knee brushes mine.

I roll backward, and he only grins more. This is not a cat-and-mouse game like he believes. I am not a mouse. And he's not a cat. Or vice versa. I am the fucking shark, and he's a lame human in my ocean.

And my boyfriend, he's the same species as me.

"Continue," I snap.

"I'll be interviewing you, your two sisters, Lily's boyfriend, and his brother." *6 people + 6 months + 3 cameramen + 1 reality show = infinite drama.* I've done the math.

Scott will be conducting the interviews, though . . . I internally gag. "You're forgetting my boyfriend," I say. "He's a part of the show too."

"Oh right."

"Don't act like you forgot, Scott. You just said you were practicing honesty, and now, well, you're a bit of a liar."

He ignores my slight. "Every episode will be aired one week after we've filmed. The premiere will be in February, but we're filming ASAP. Like I mentioned over the phone, we're trying to make this show as real-time as possible. It's been six months since it was publicized that your sister is a sex addict. We need to capitalize off that buzz as quickly as we can."

"You and every other person with a camera," I say. There's always at least two chubby males stationed outside my gated house with lenses pointed at us. Lily jokes that they're probably hanging around waiting for her to give them blow jobs. I would be more amused if I didn't see the mail that perverts send her, most accompanied with pictures of their hairy genitals—it's a sick fan club. I sift through her letters before I hand them to her now.

"And lastly," Scott says, "you have no control over how you're edited. That's my call."

I have about as much power over the reality show as I do paparazzi's snap-quick photos.

I can try to act like a non-bitchy, non-argumentative angel on film, and Lily can try to be a virginal saint. But at the end of the day, the cameras will catch *us*. Flaws and all. And there's no forcing something different. That was the stipulation that all my friends and sisters agreed to.

To do the show, we're not pretending to be someone else.

And I would never ask that of them.

We're rolling the dice on this one. People may hate us. They already call Lily a whore on gossip blogs. But in the small chance that people grow to love us—my company may be saved. I just need good publicity so that a retailer has a reason to stock my clothing line again.

And maybe Fizzle won't be so bruised by Lily's impropriety too. Maybe my father's soda company will rise in stock price rather than fall.

That's the hope.

"Are you okay with this?" Scott questions.

"I don't know why you ask. I signed the contract. I have to be okay with it or else you'll take me to court."

He lets out a short laugh and scans my body for the third time. "I can't imagine your boyfriend knows what to do with you."

"Because you've never met him."

"I've spoken to him. He sounds malleable." He taps his pen. "If I told him to drop on his knees and suck my cock, I think he would."

My nostrils flare. I am fuming. "You think that." I stand. "And when he stabs you in the fucking front, I'll be the one smiling by his side."

Scott *grins* at this. "Challenge accepted."

Stupid intellectual pricks.

Funny thing is, I'm dating one.

So while I'm stuck in this moronic cockfight, I know I'm partially to blame.

I knew I should have lowered my standards—dated a guy who

rides around on his skateboard with his shirt inside out. I grimace. Just kidding. I'll take my suit-and-tie boyfriend. I'll take the high IQ and the rapid-fire banter. I just hope Scott's eagerness to unsettle him won't disrupt the reality show.

But if I know anything, it's this:

My boyfriend loves winning.

And he hates to lose even more.

Krista and Becca Ritchie are *New York Times* and *USA Today* bestselling authors and identical twins—one a science nerd, the other a comic book geek—but with their shared passion for writing, they combined their mental powers as kids and have never stopped telling stories. They love superheroes, flawed characters, and soul mate love.

CONNECT ONLINE

KBRitchie.com
KBMRitchie

Ready to find
your next great read?

Let us help.

Visit prh.com/nextread